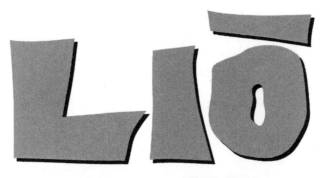

# THERE'S A MONSTER IN MY SOCKS

**Other *Liō* books by Mark Tatulli**

***Liō: Happiness Is a Squishy Cephalopod***
***Silent But Deadly***
***Liō's Astonishing Tales***
***There's Corpses Everywhere***
***Reheated Liō***
***Zombies Need Love Too***

# LIO

## THERE'S A MONSTER IN MY SOCKS

by MARK TATULLI

Andrews McMeel
Publishing, LLC

Kansas City • Sydney • London

Andrews McMeel Publishing, LLC
an Andrews McMeel Universal company
1130 Walnut Street, Kansas City, Missouri 64106

www.andrewsmcmeel.com


12 13 14 15 16 RR2 10 9 8 7 6 5 4 3 2 1

ISBN: 978-1-4494-2304-9

Library of Congress Control Number: 2012938488

ATTENTION: SCHOOLS AND BUSINESSES

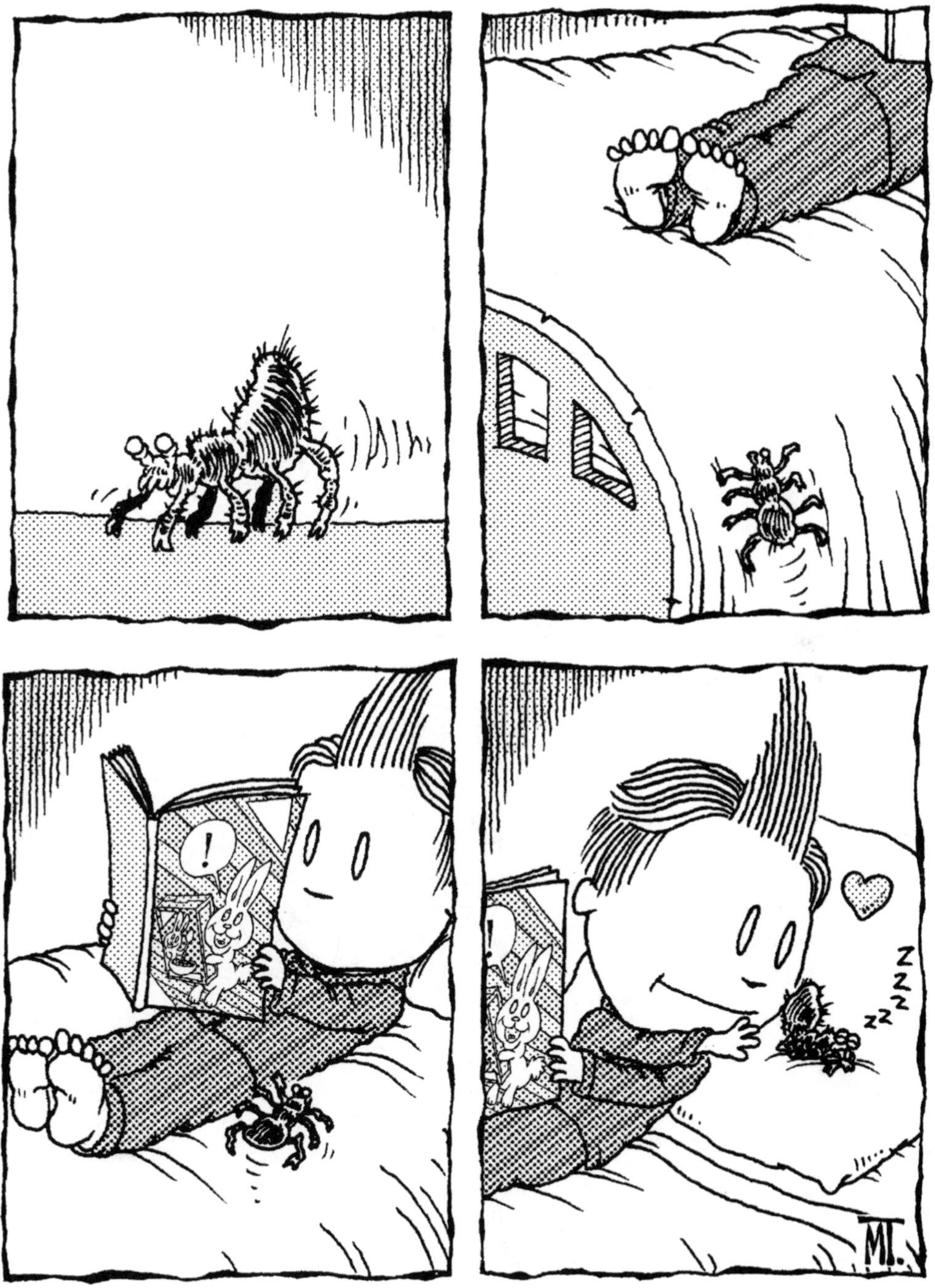
!
Z Z Z
z z
MT.

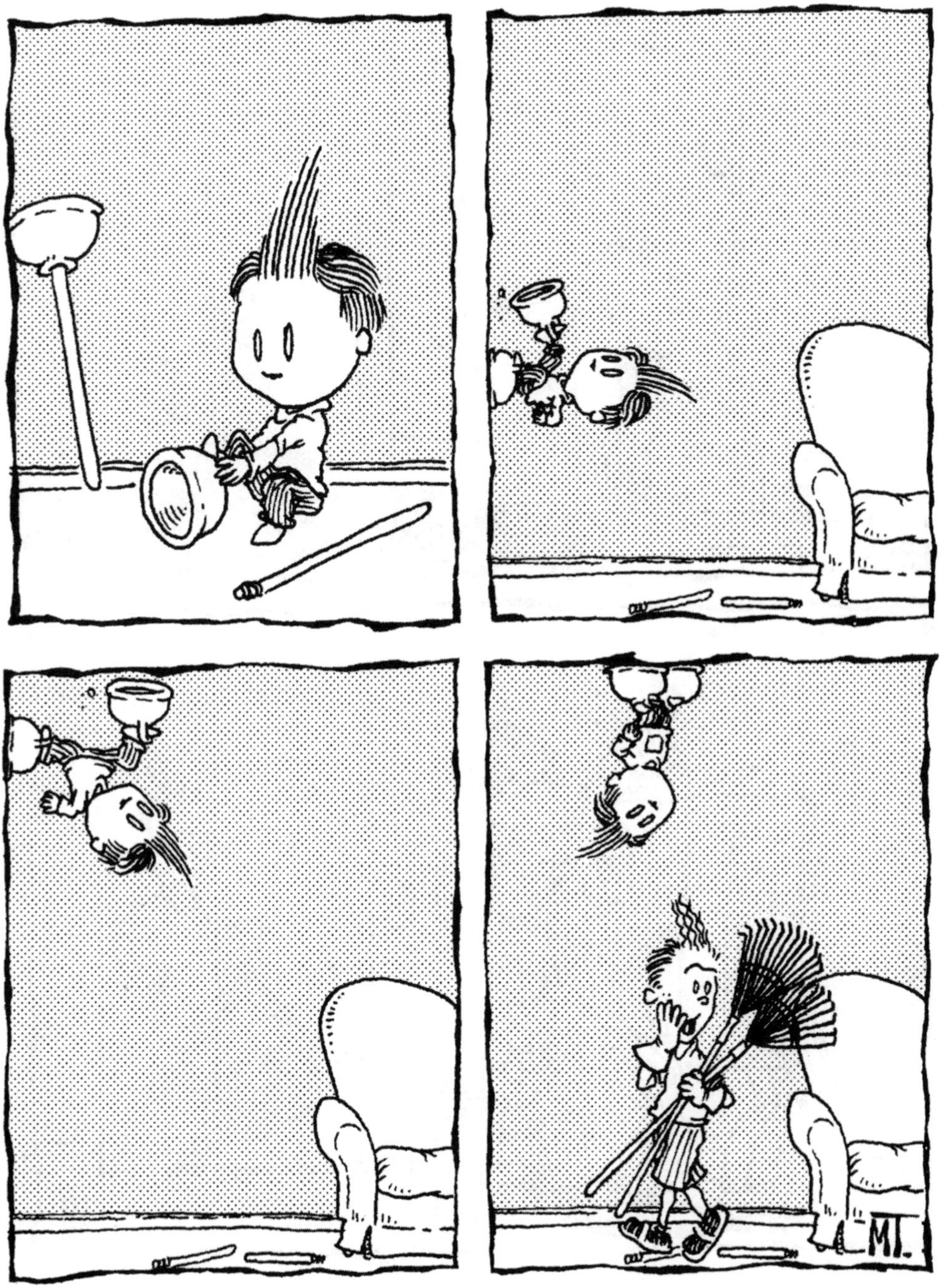
MT.

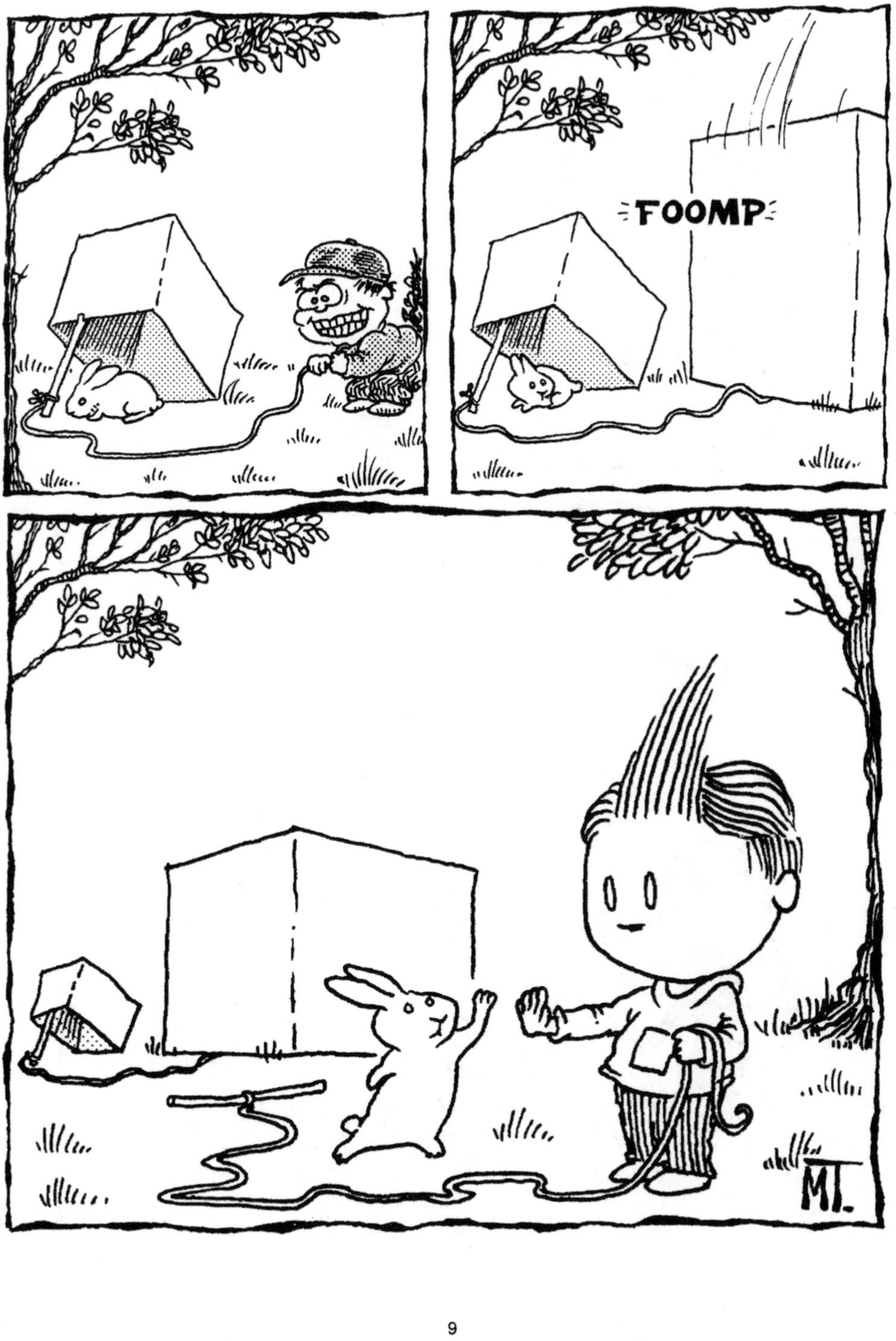
FOOMP
MT.

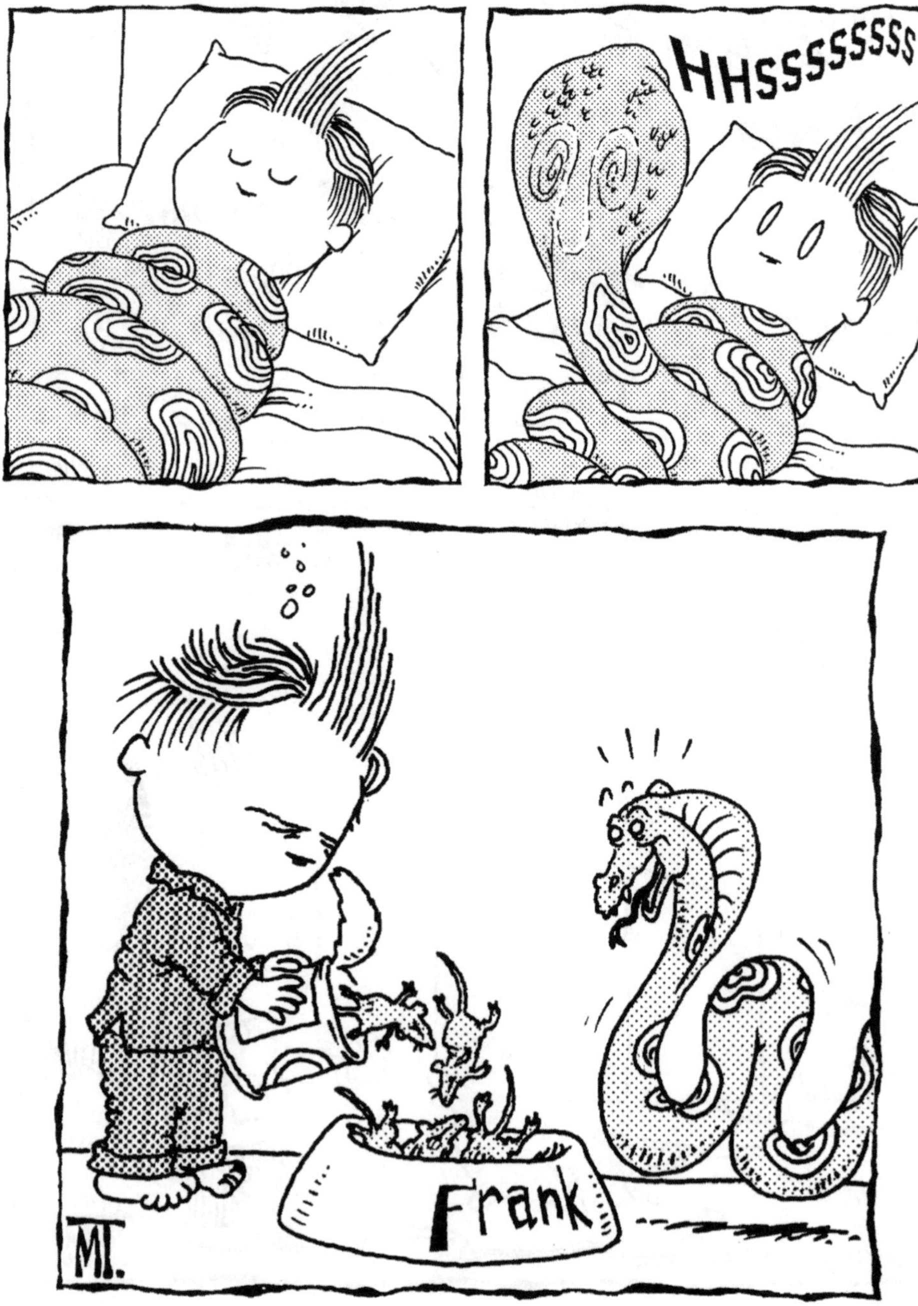
HHSSSSSSSS
Frank
MI.

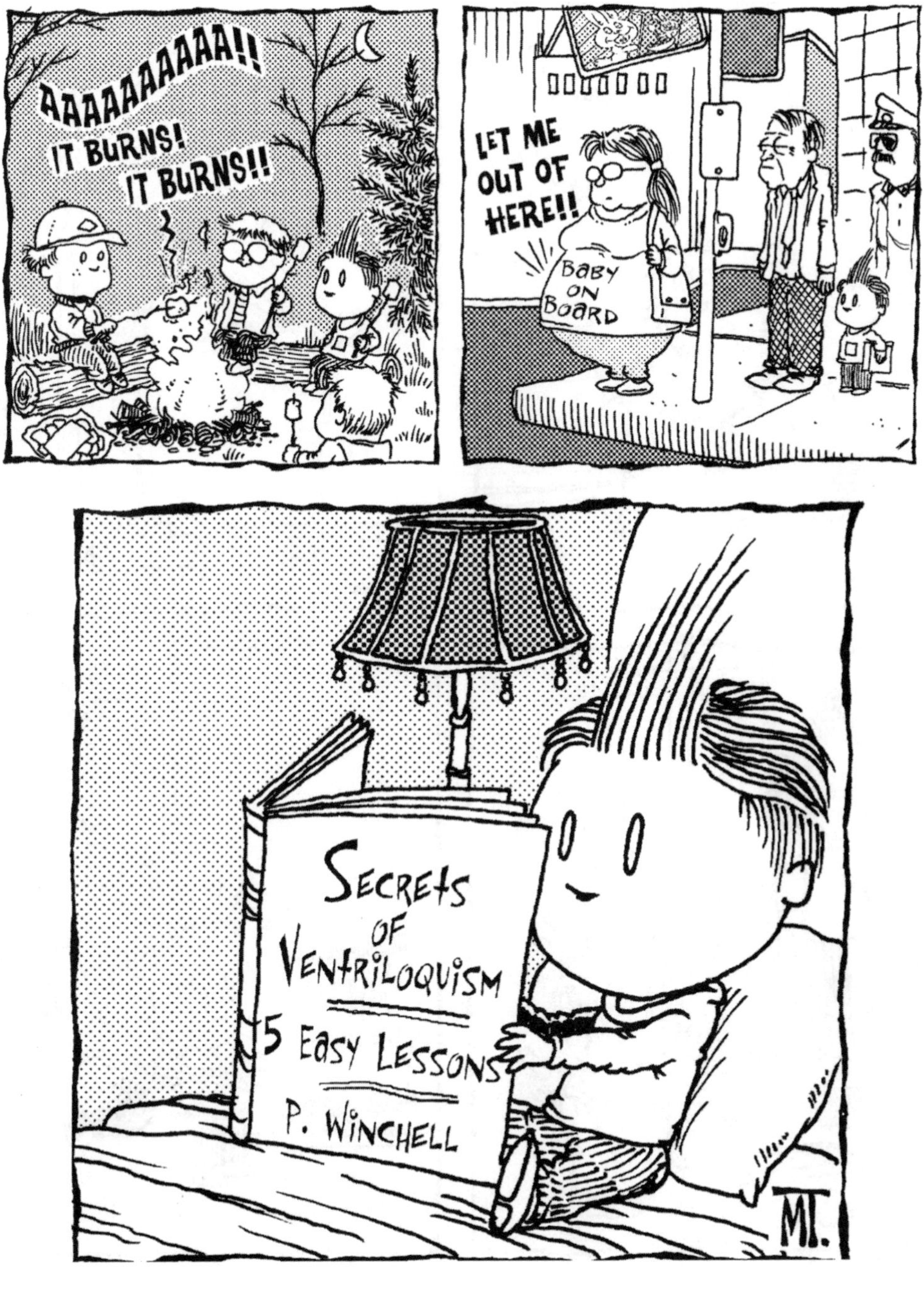
AAAAAAAAAA!!
IT BURNS! IT BURNS!!
LET ME OUT OF HERE!!
BABY ON BOARD
SECRETS OF VENTRILOQUISM
5 EASY LESSONS
P. WINCHELL
MI.

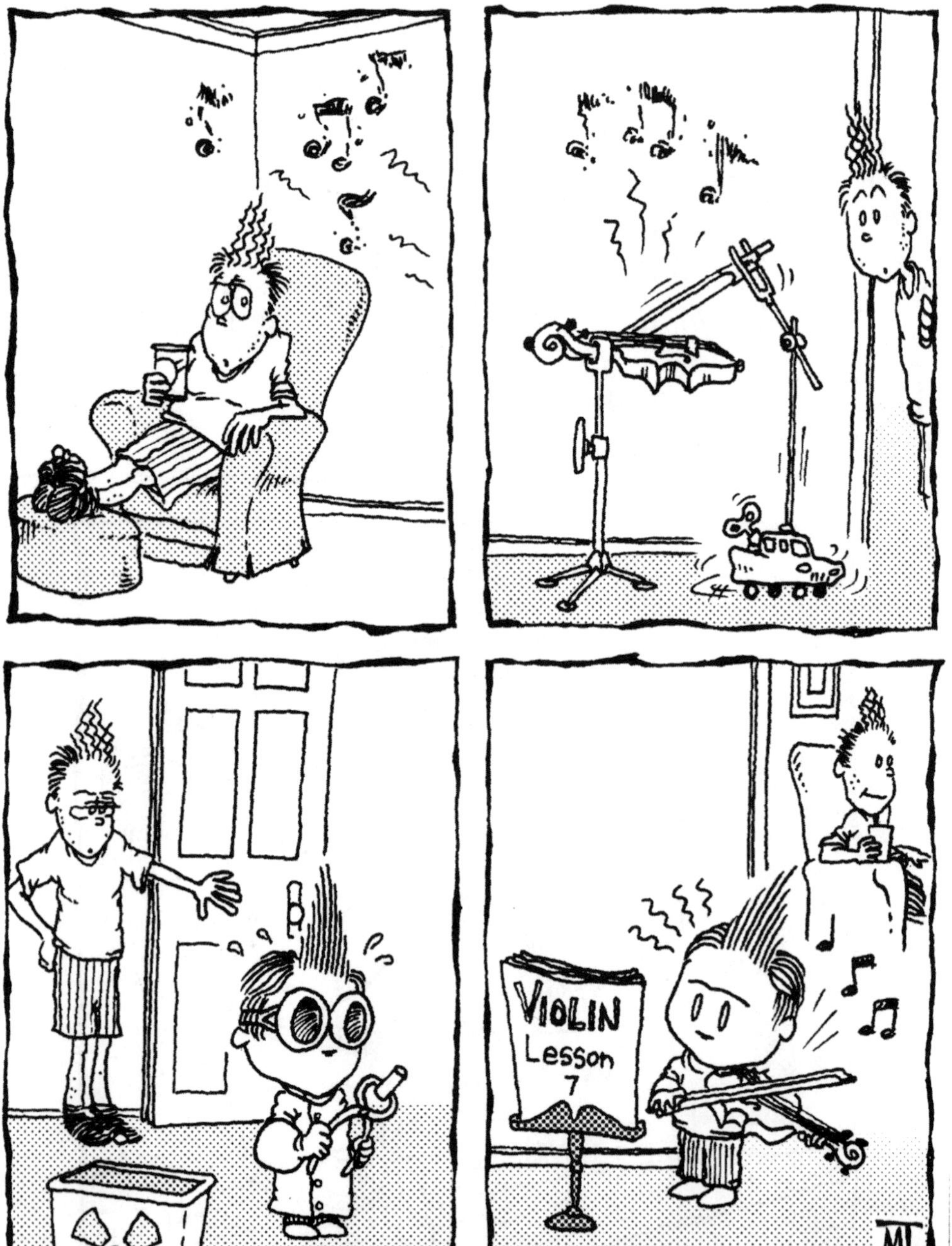
VIOLIN
Lesson
7
MT.

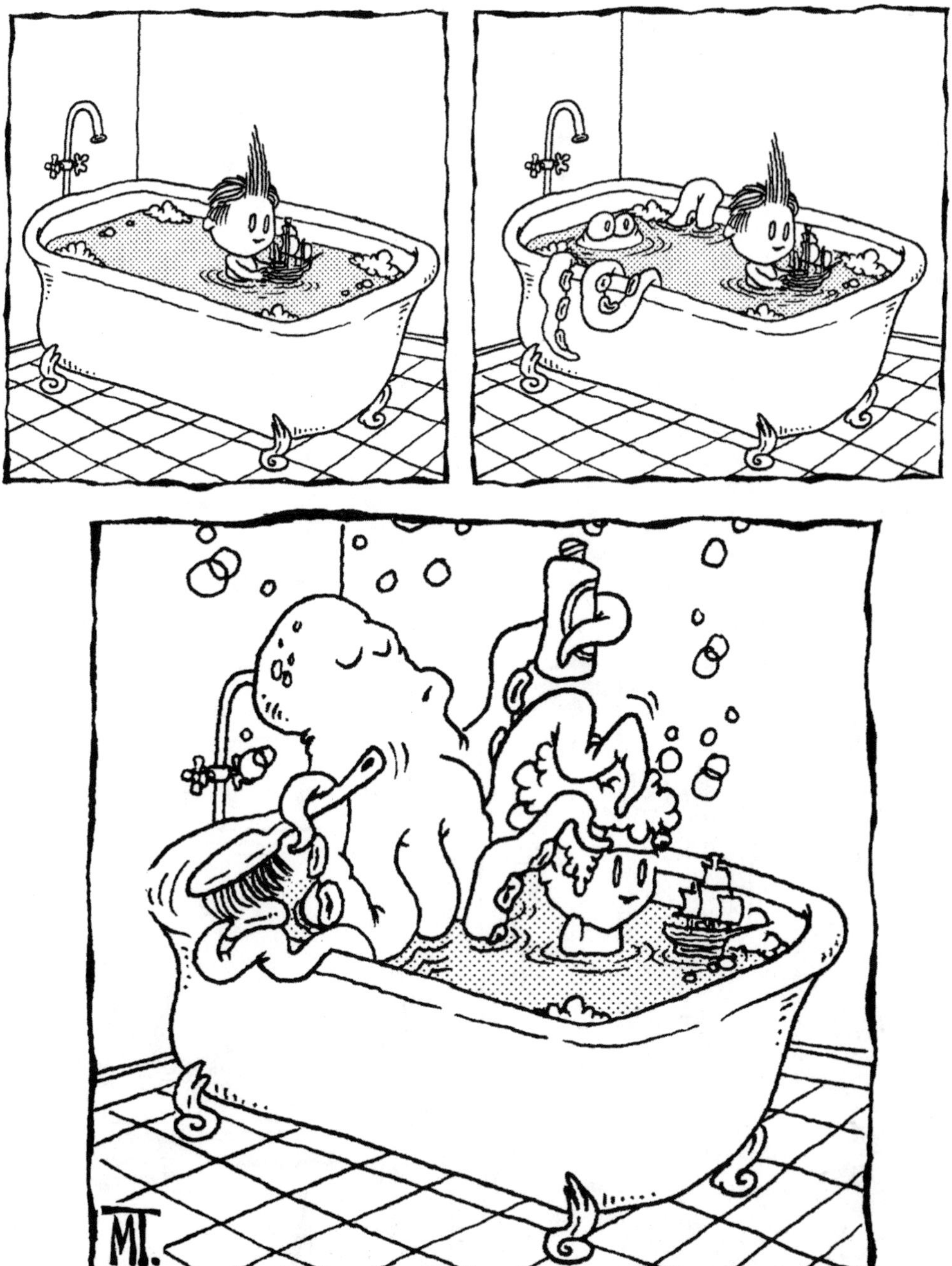

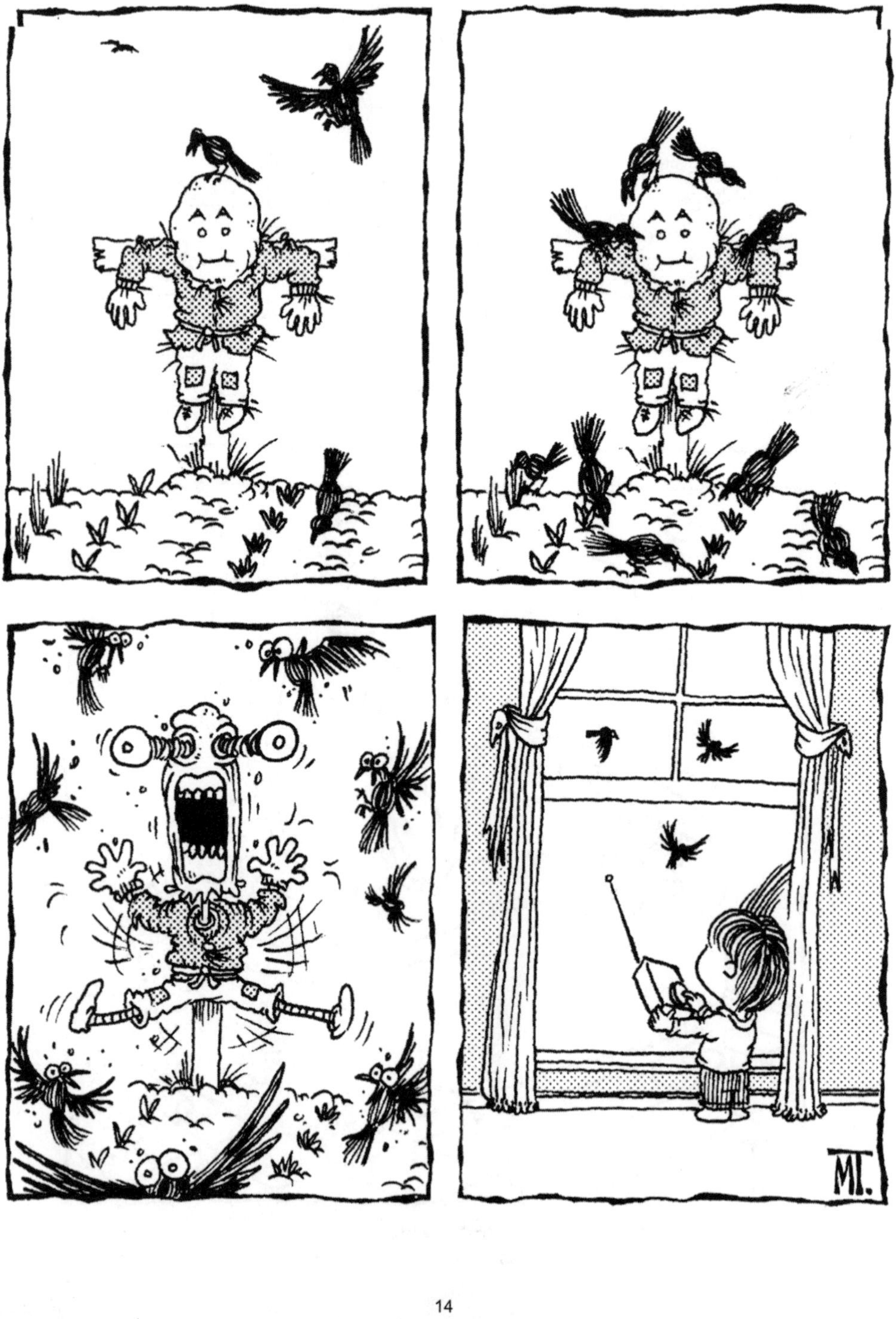
MT.

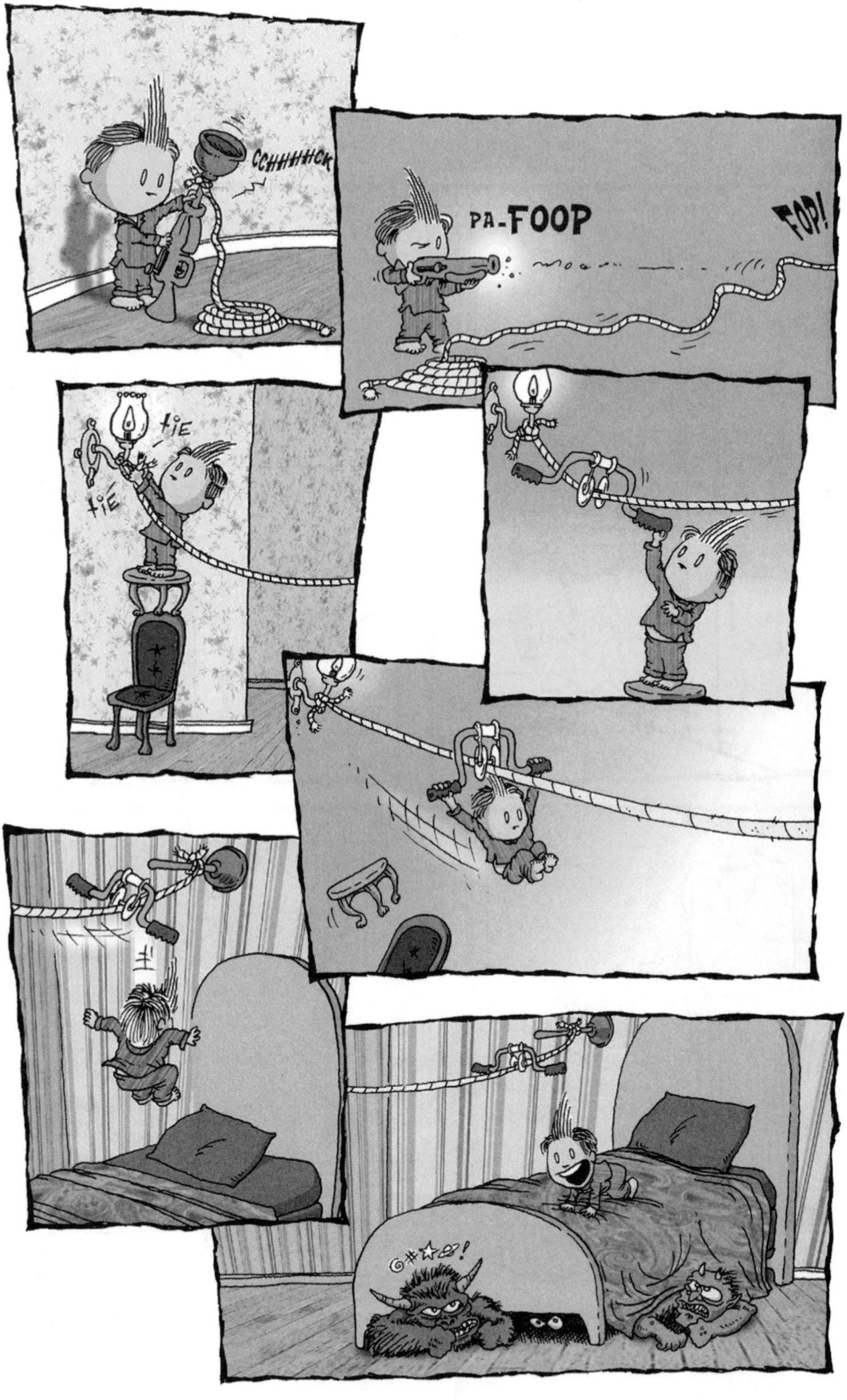

CCHHHHHCK
PA-FOOP
FOP!
tie
tie

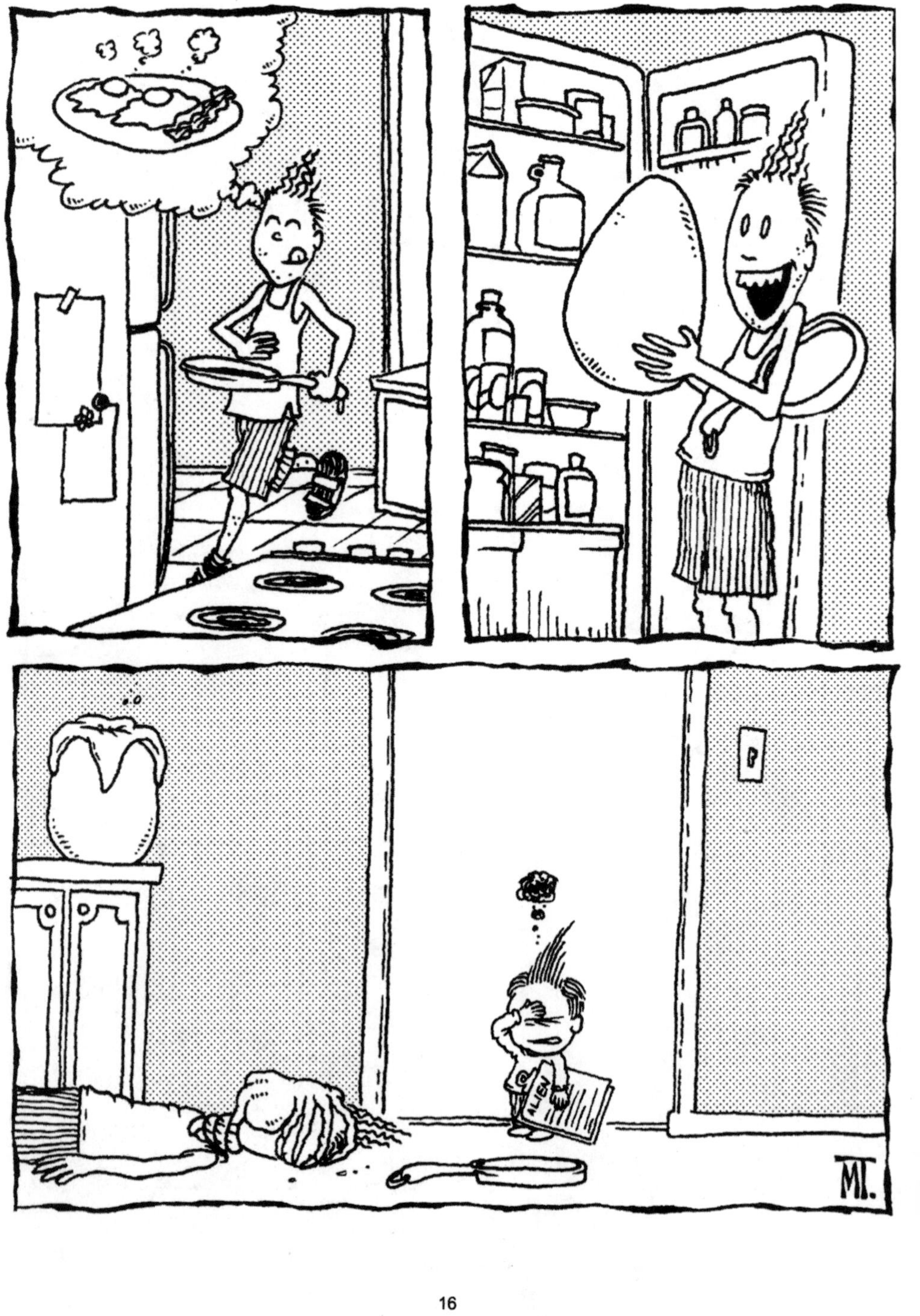
ALIEN

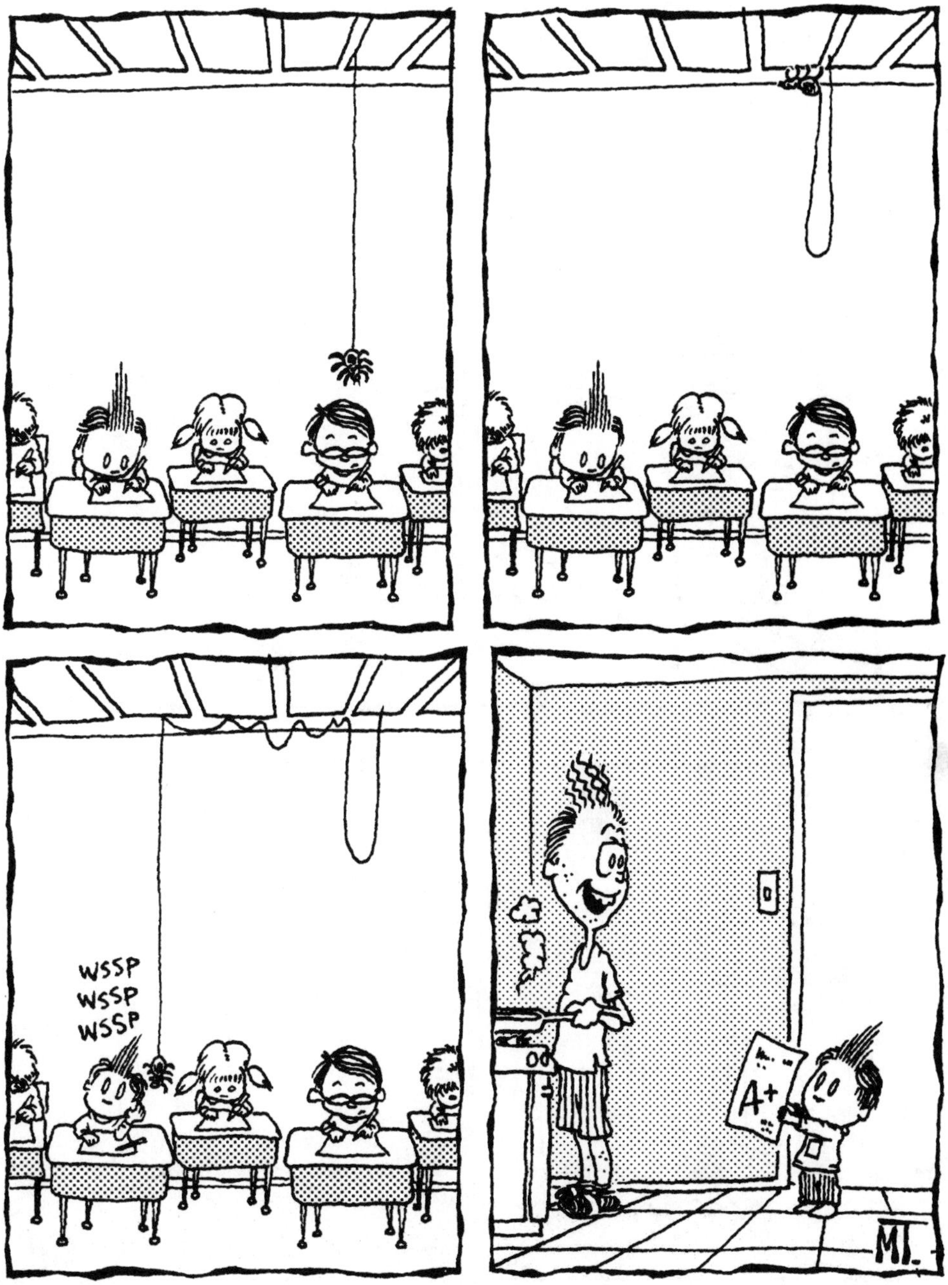
WSSP
WSSP
WSSP
A+
MT

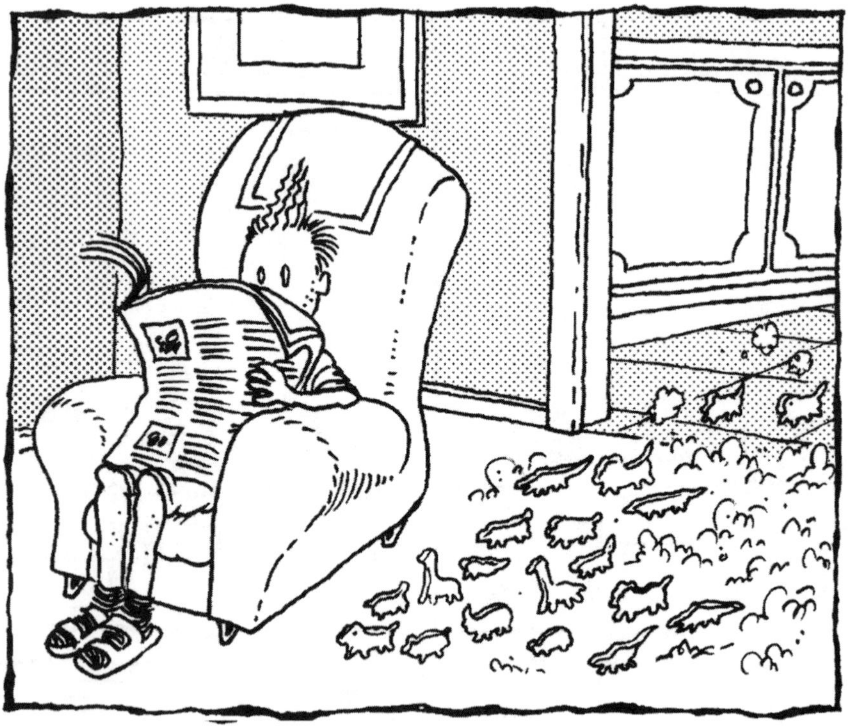

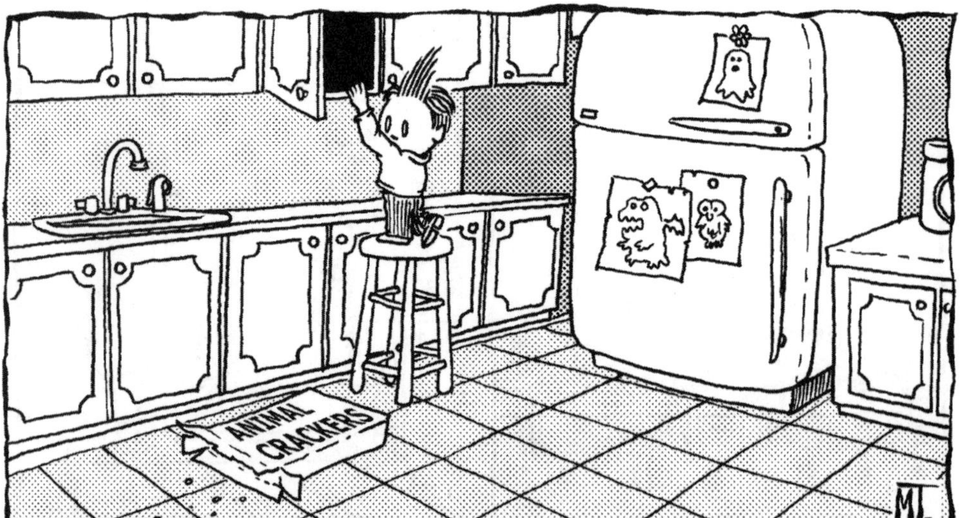
ANIMAL CRACKERS
MT.

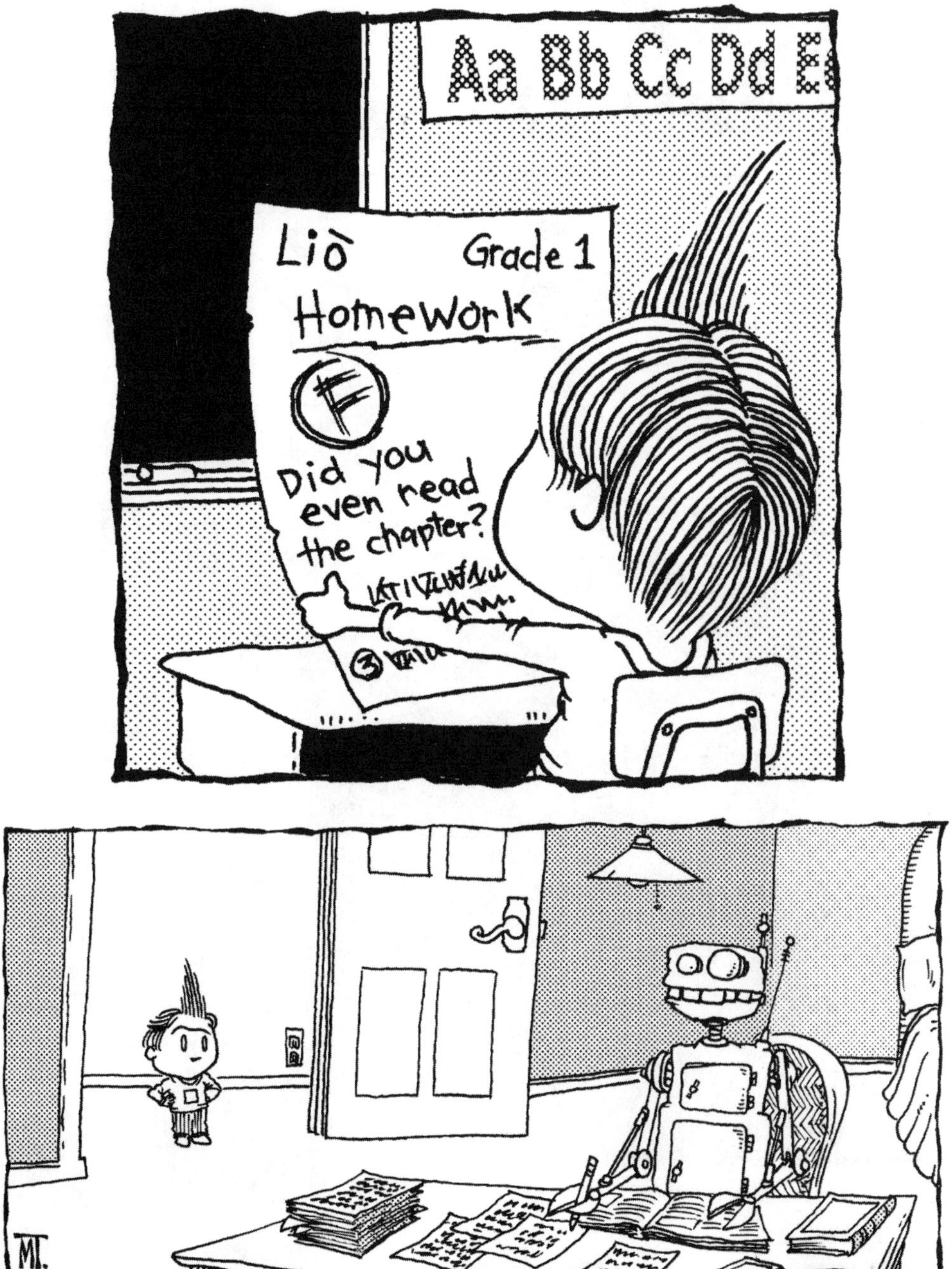
Aa Bb Cc Dd
Liò
Grade 1
Homework
F
Did you even read the chapter?
MT.

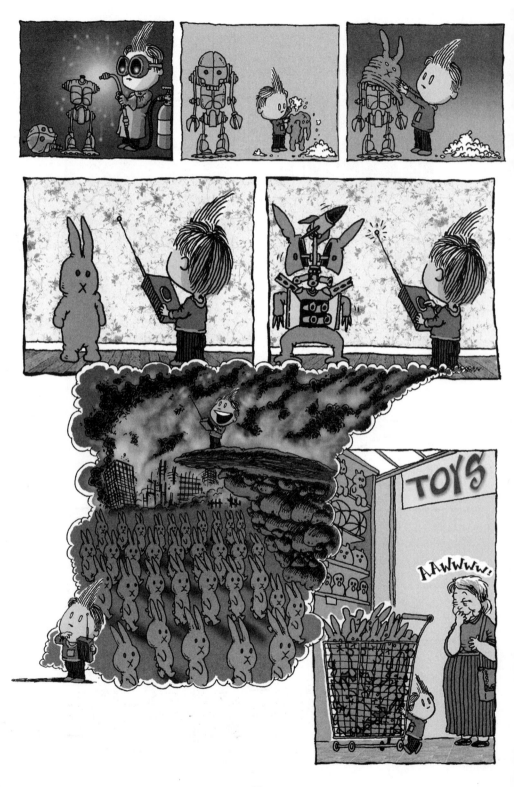

AAWWWW!

TOYS

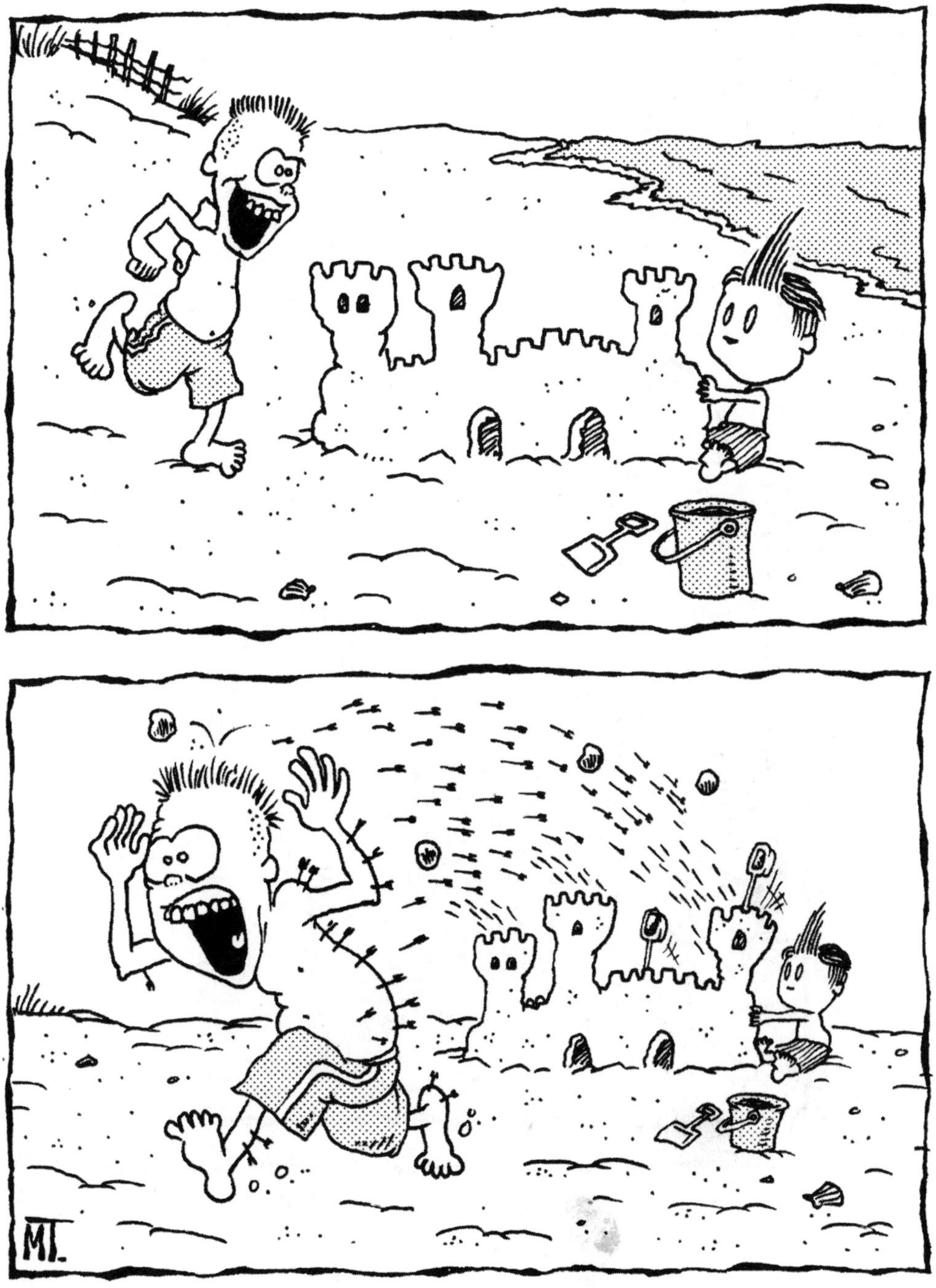

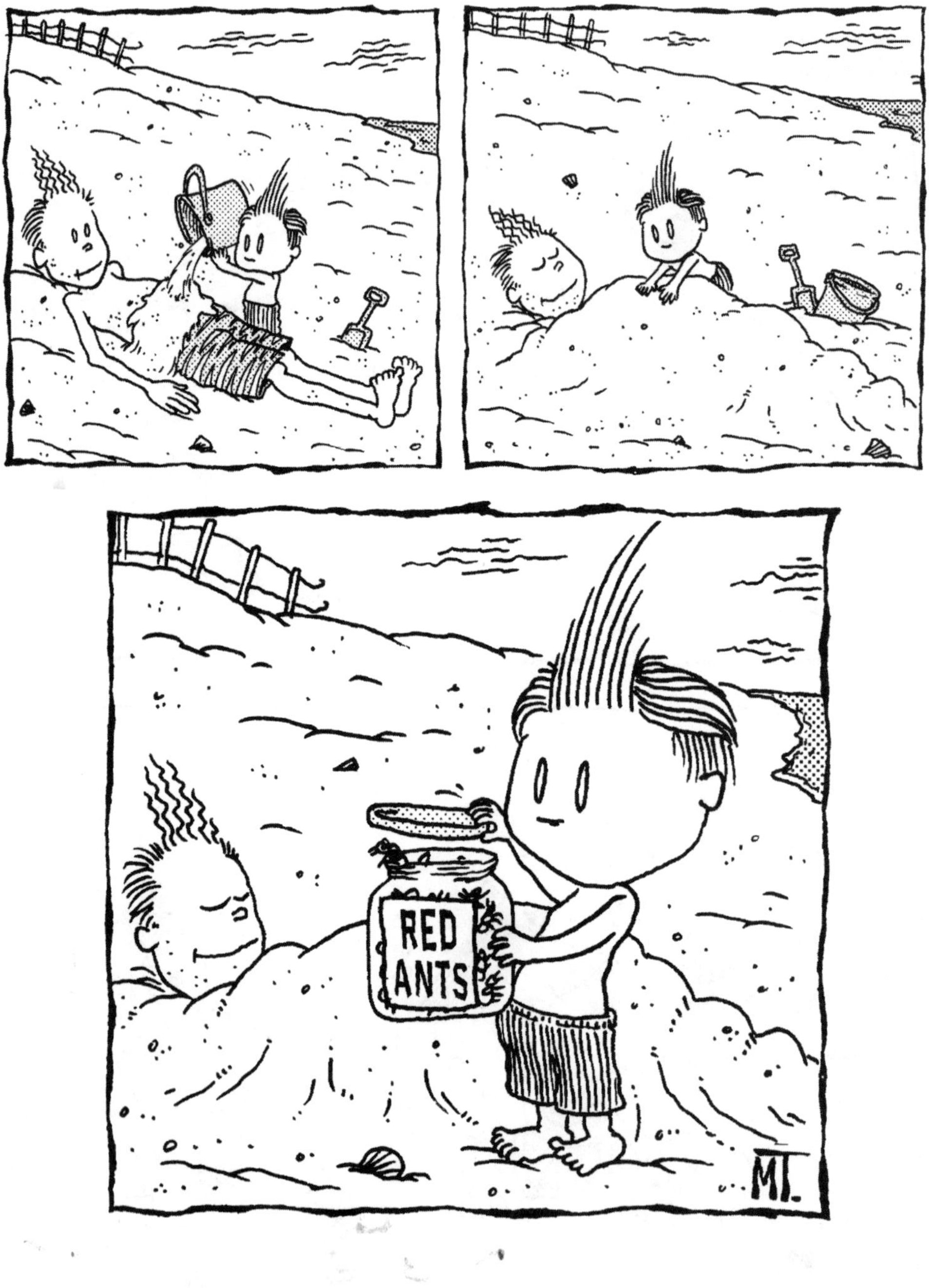
RED
ANTS
MI

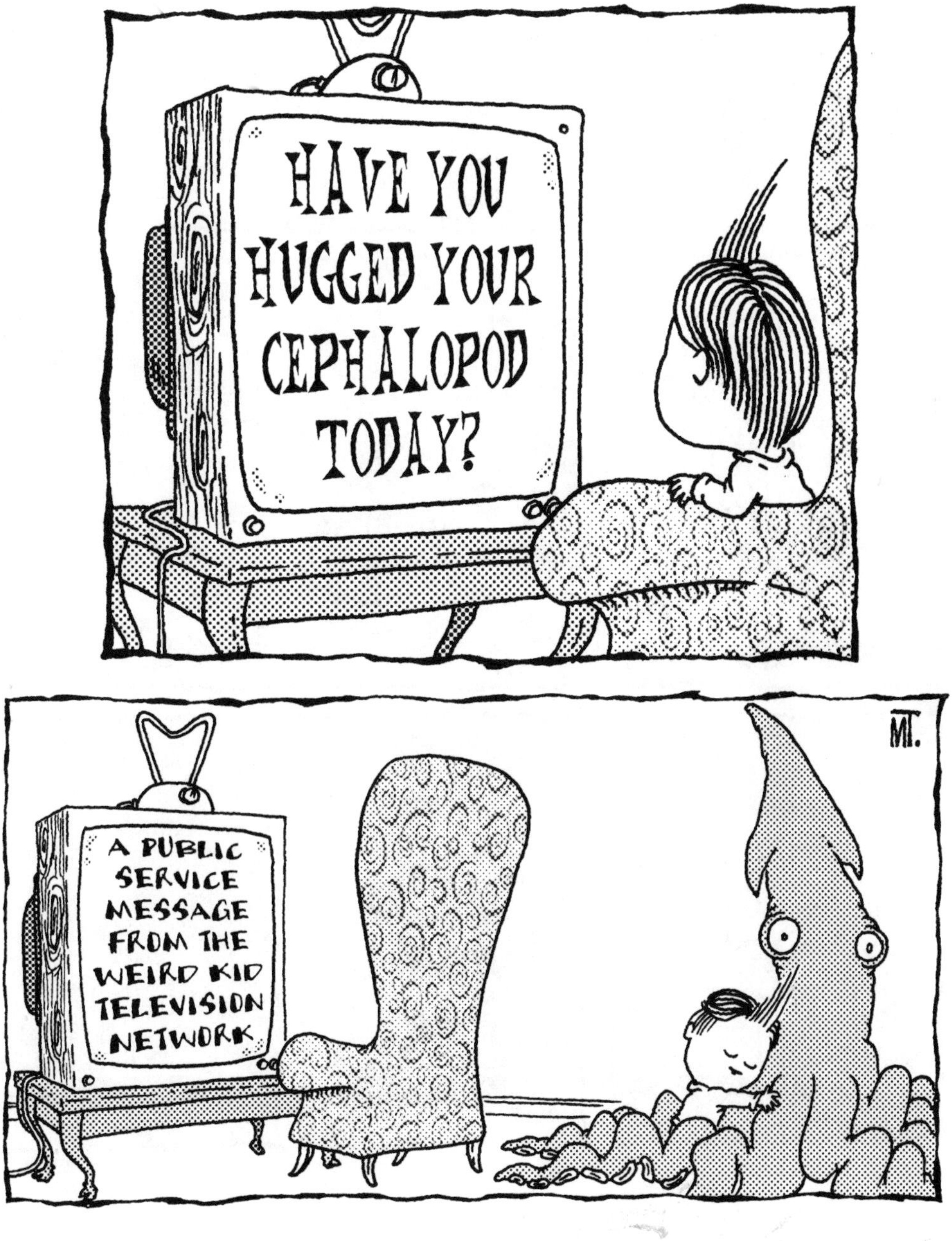
HAVE YOU HUGGED YOUR CEPHALOPOD TODAY?
MT.
A PUBLIC SERVICE MESSAGE FROM THE WEIRD KID TELEVISION NETWORK

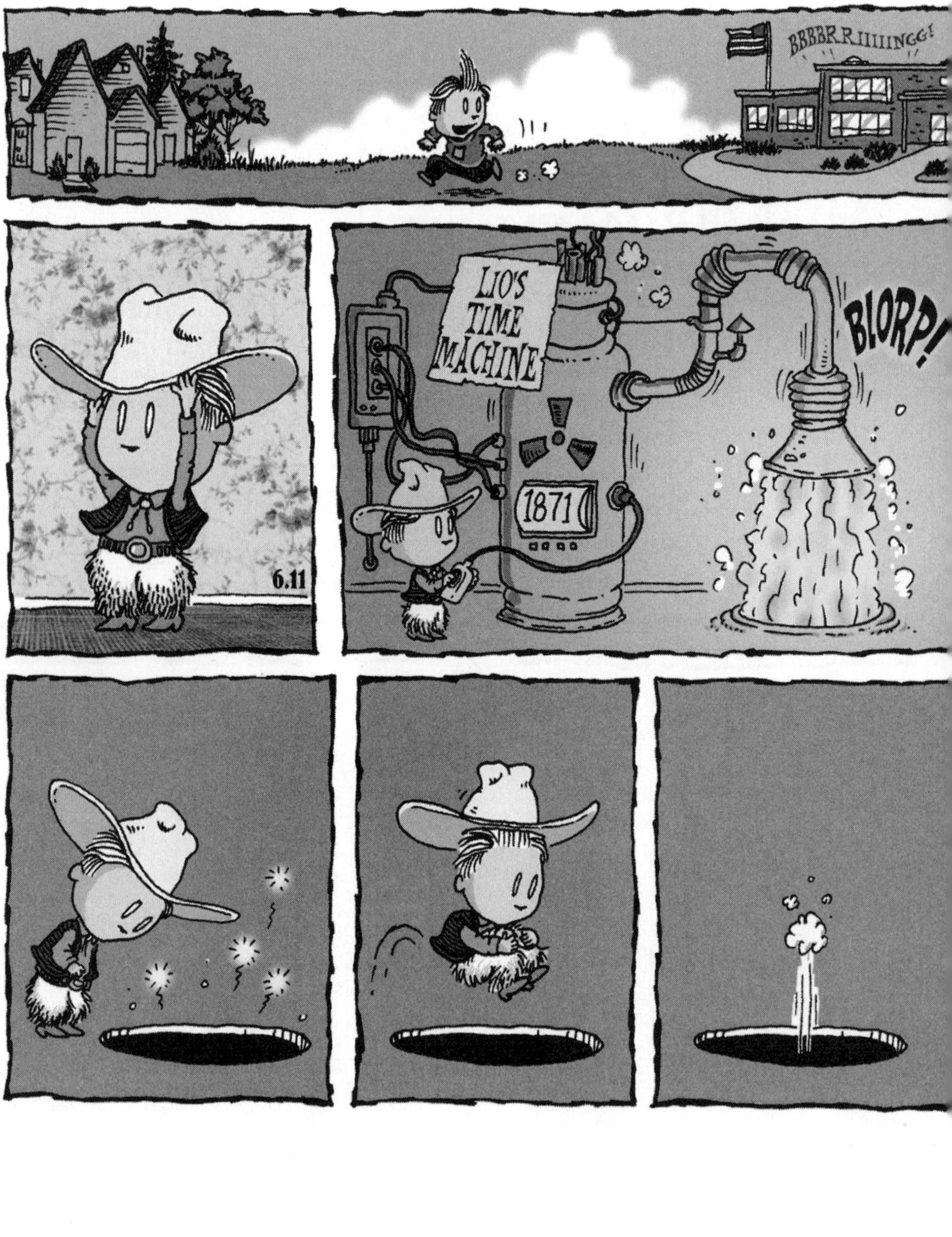
BBBBR RIIIIINGG!
6.11
LIO'S TIME MACHINE
1871
BLORP!

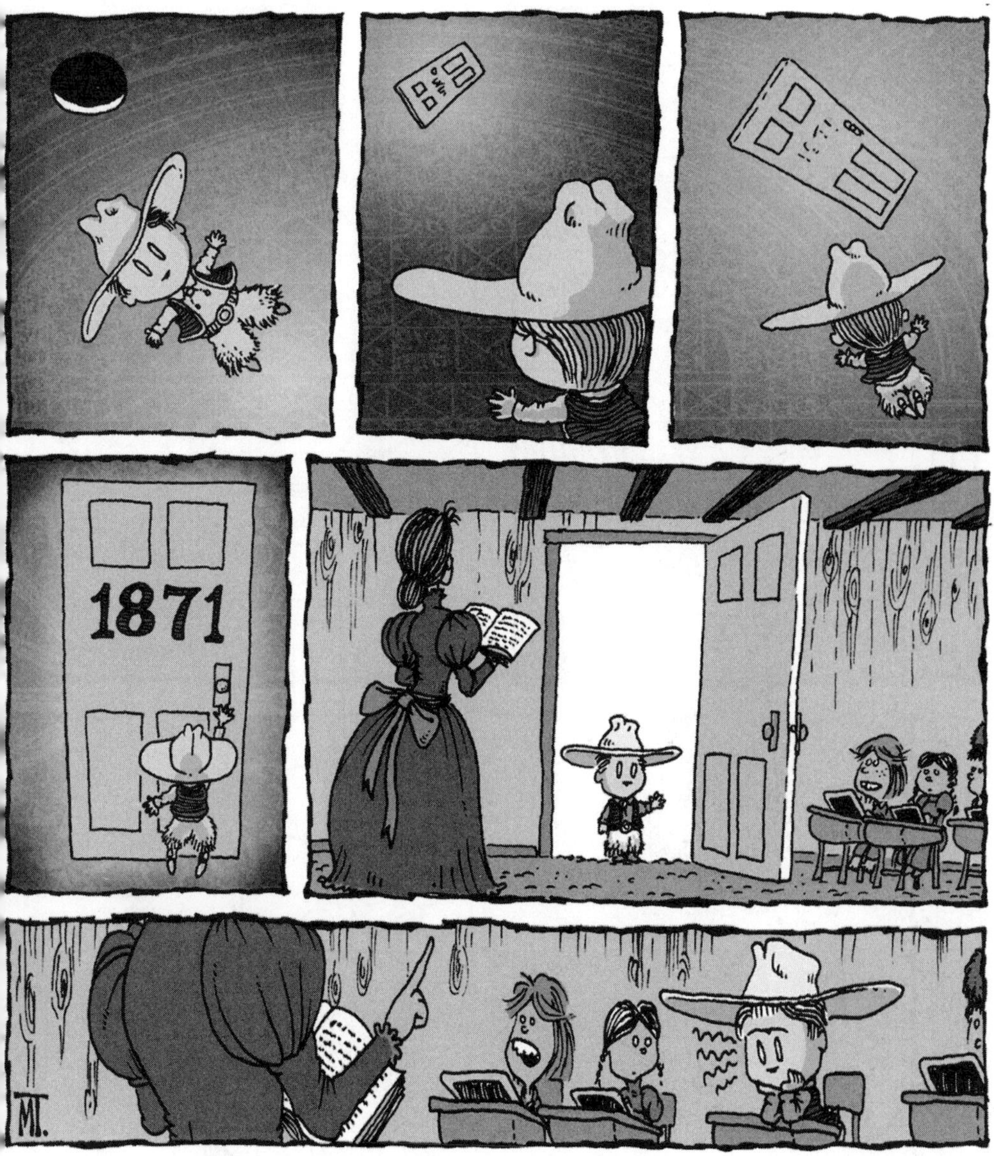

1871
MT.

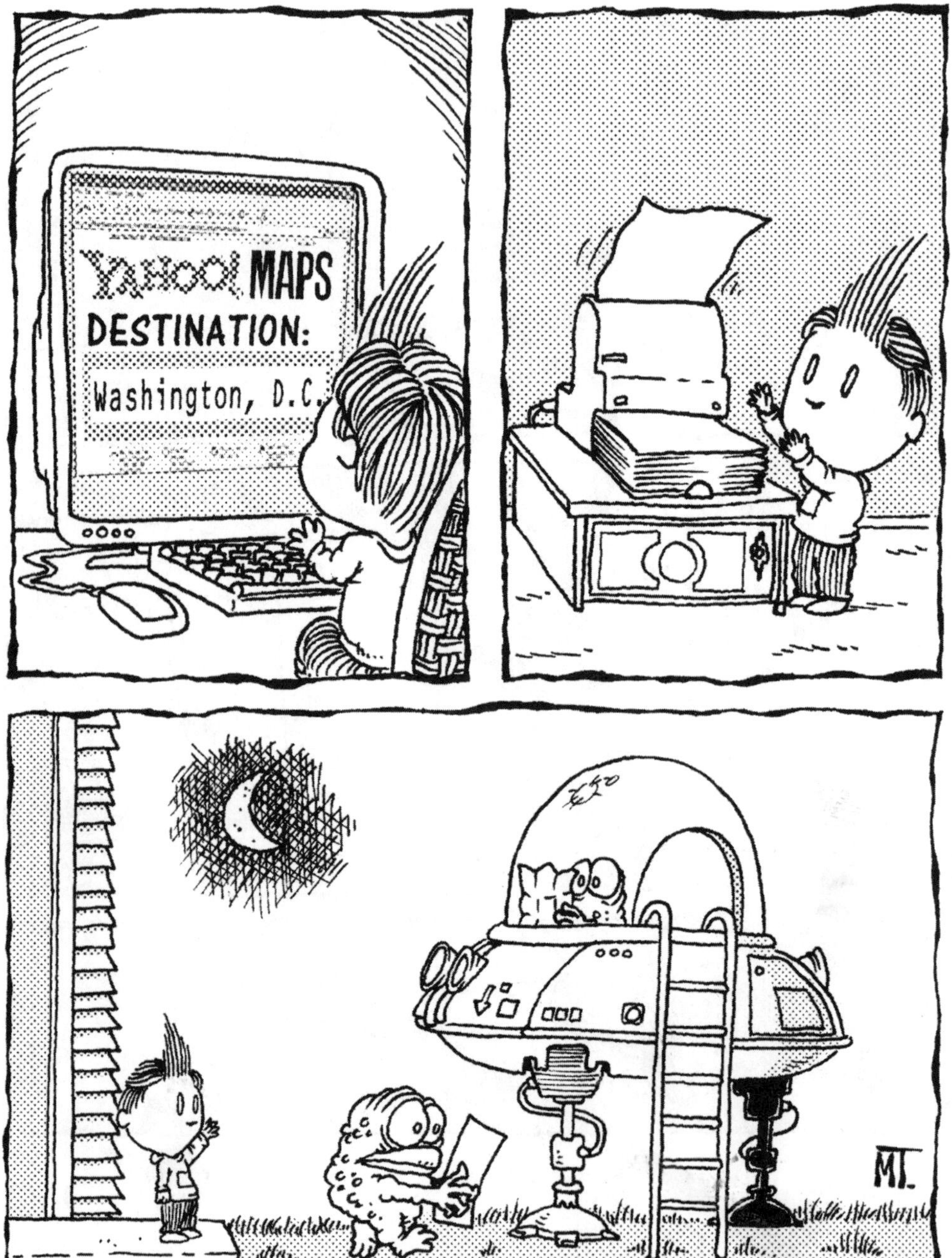
YAHOO! MAPS
DESTINATION:
Washington, D.C.
MT

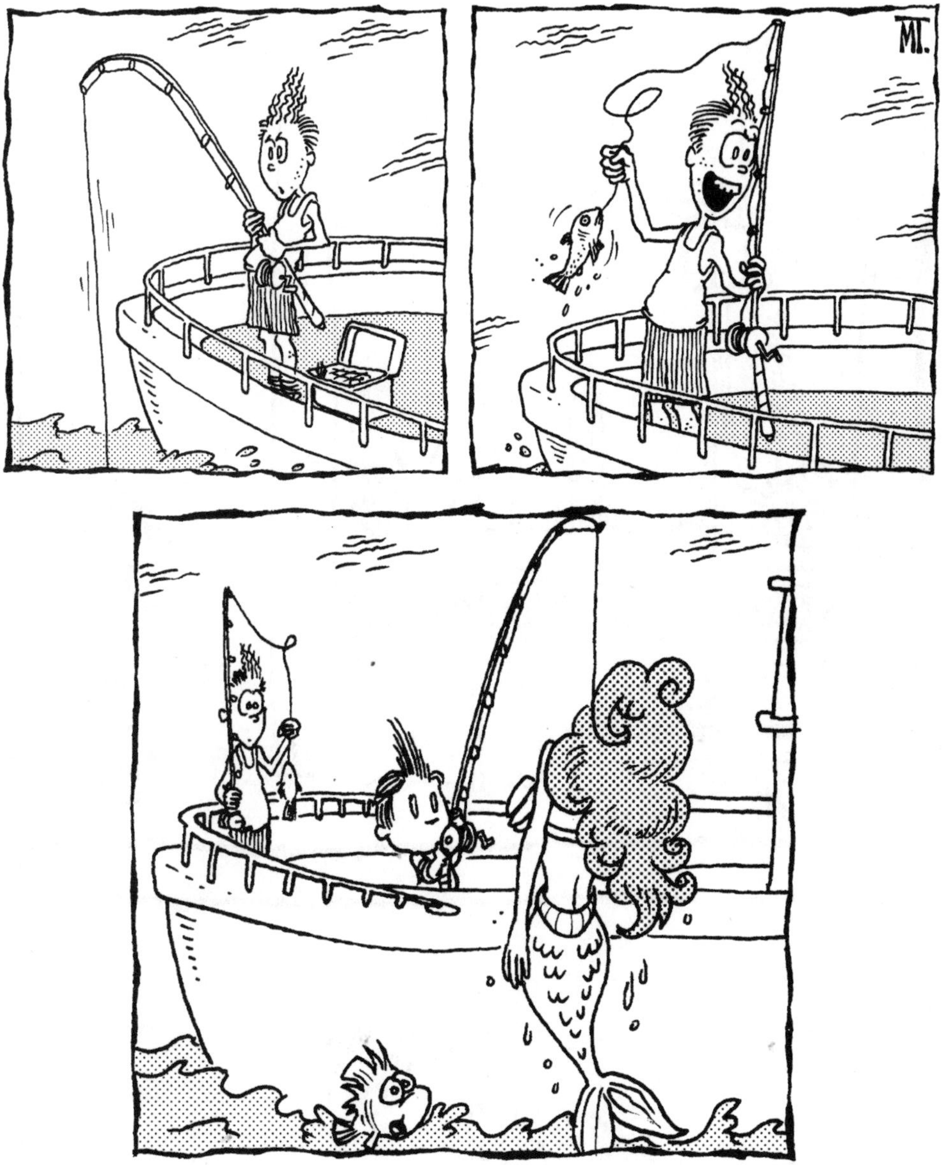
MT.

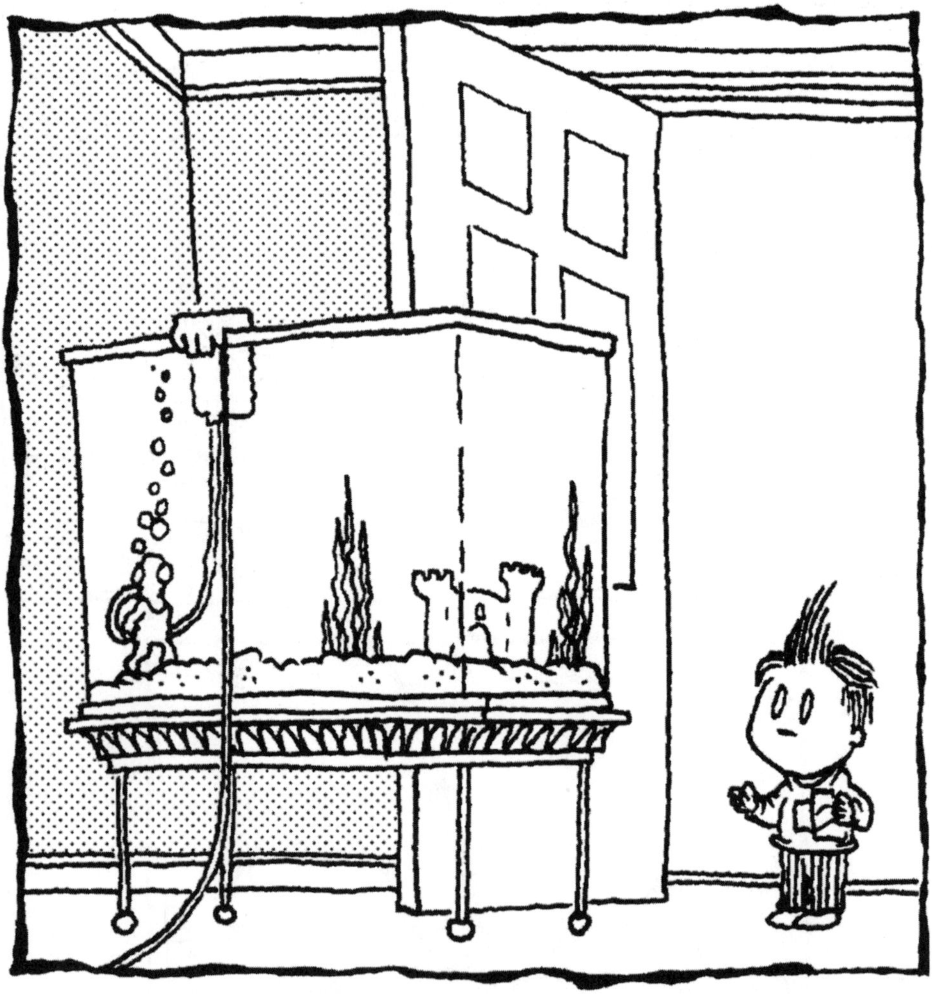

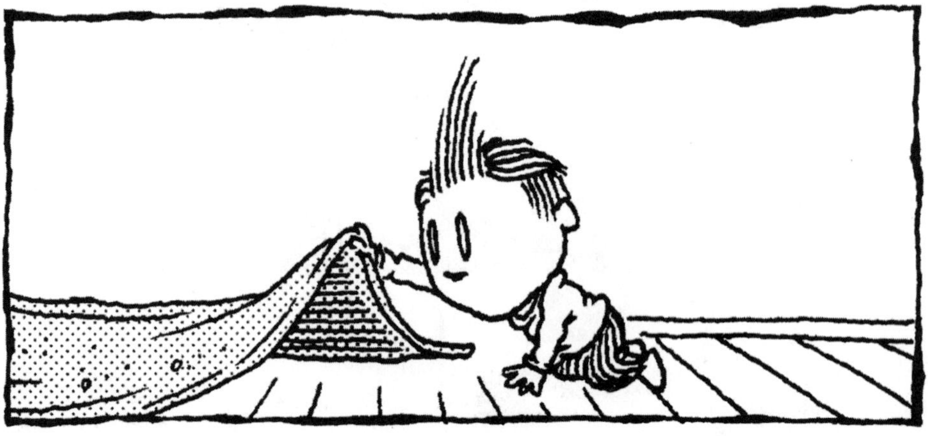

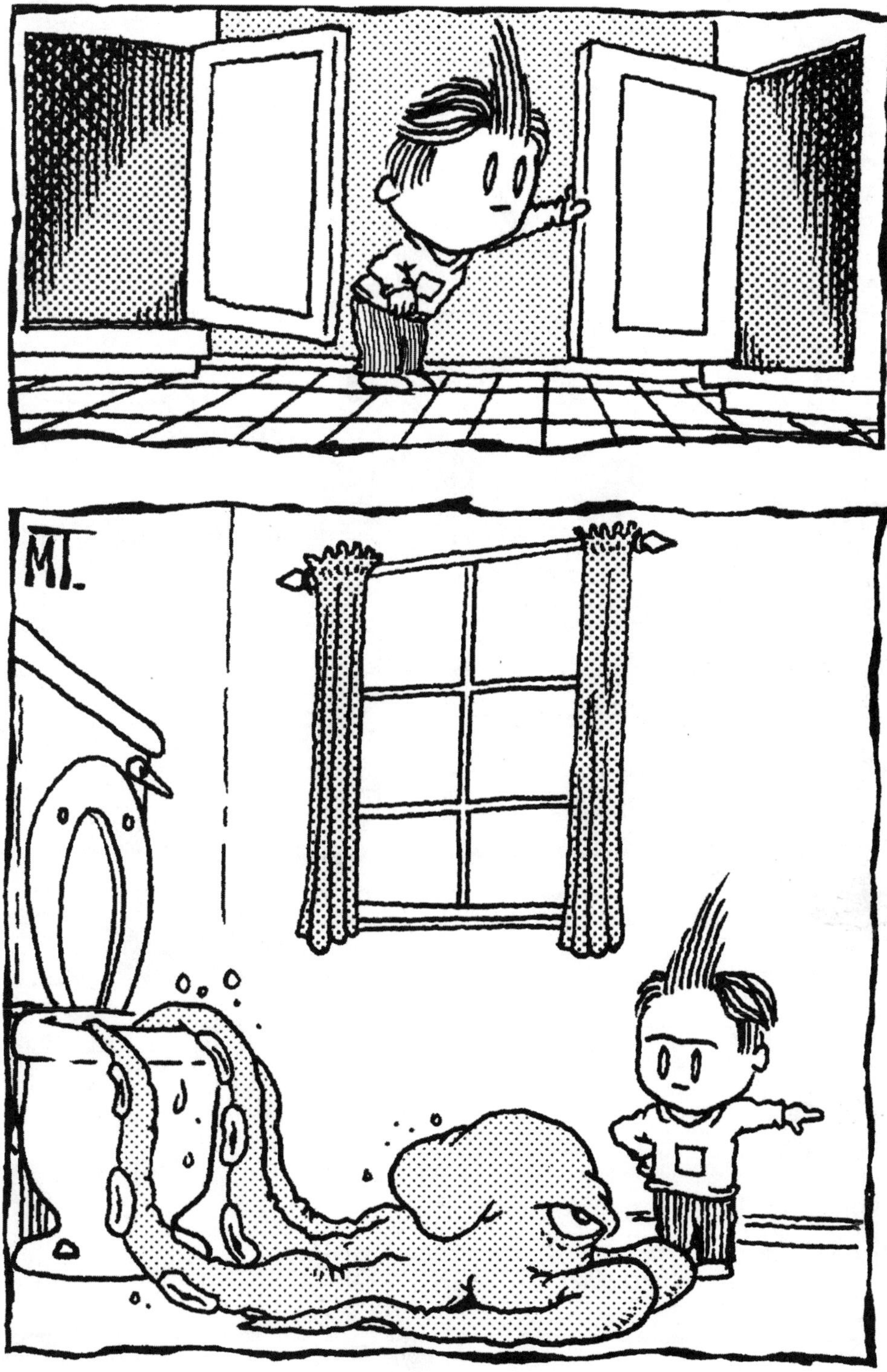

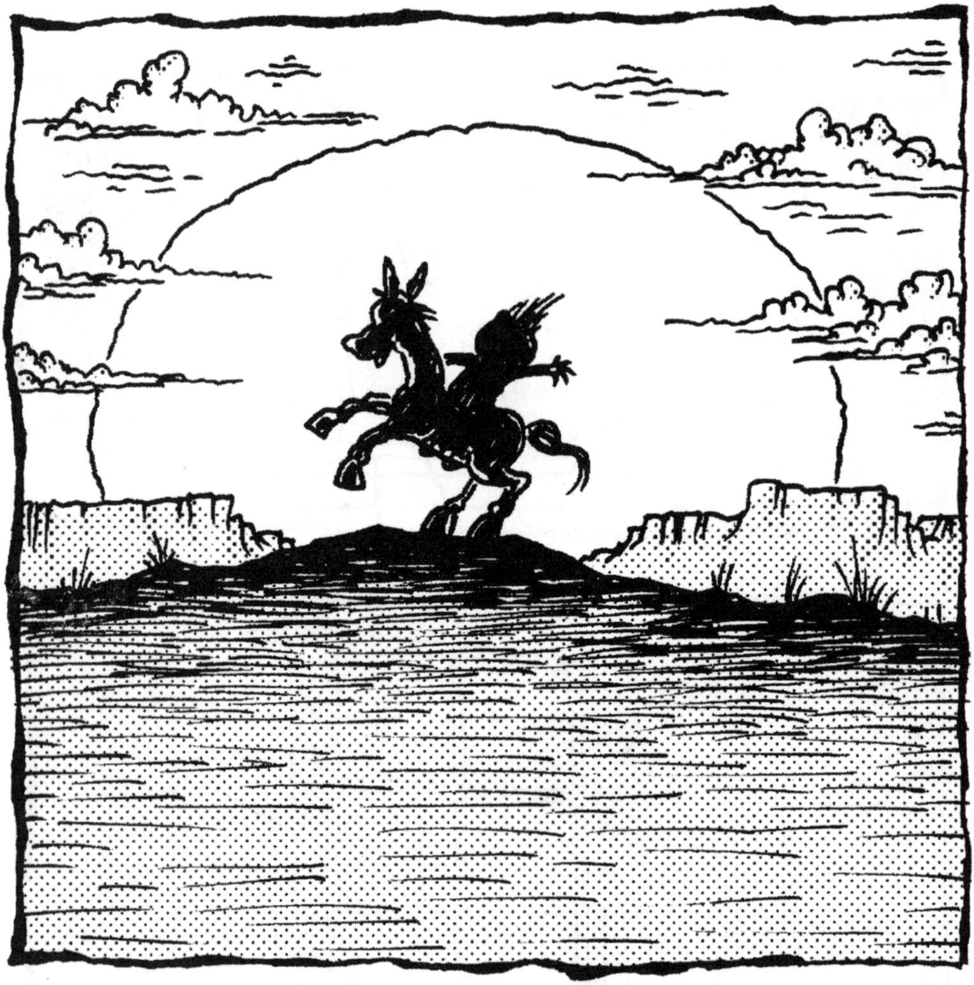

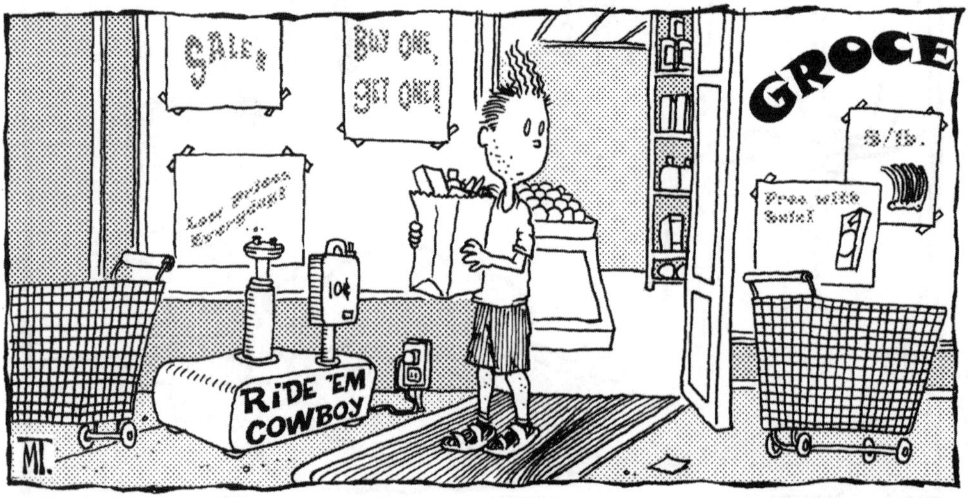
SALE!
BUY ONE, GET ONE!
GROCE
$/lb.
10¢
RIDE 'EM COWBOY

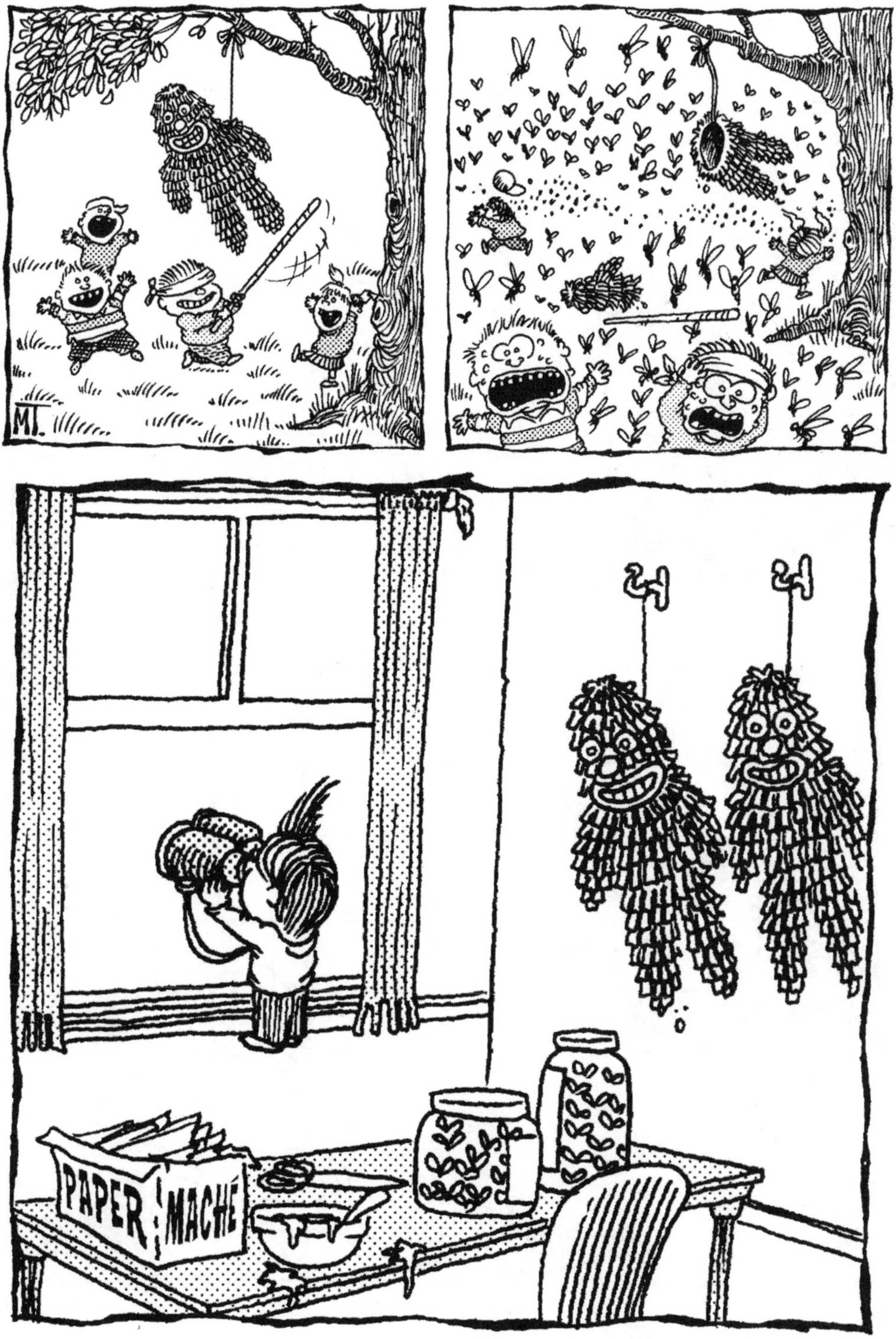
PAPER MACHÉ

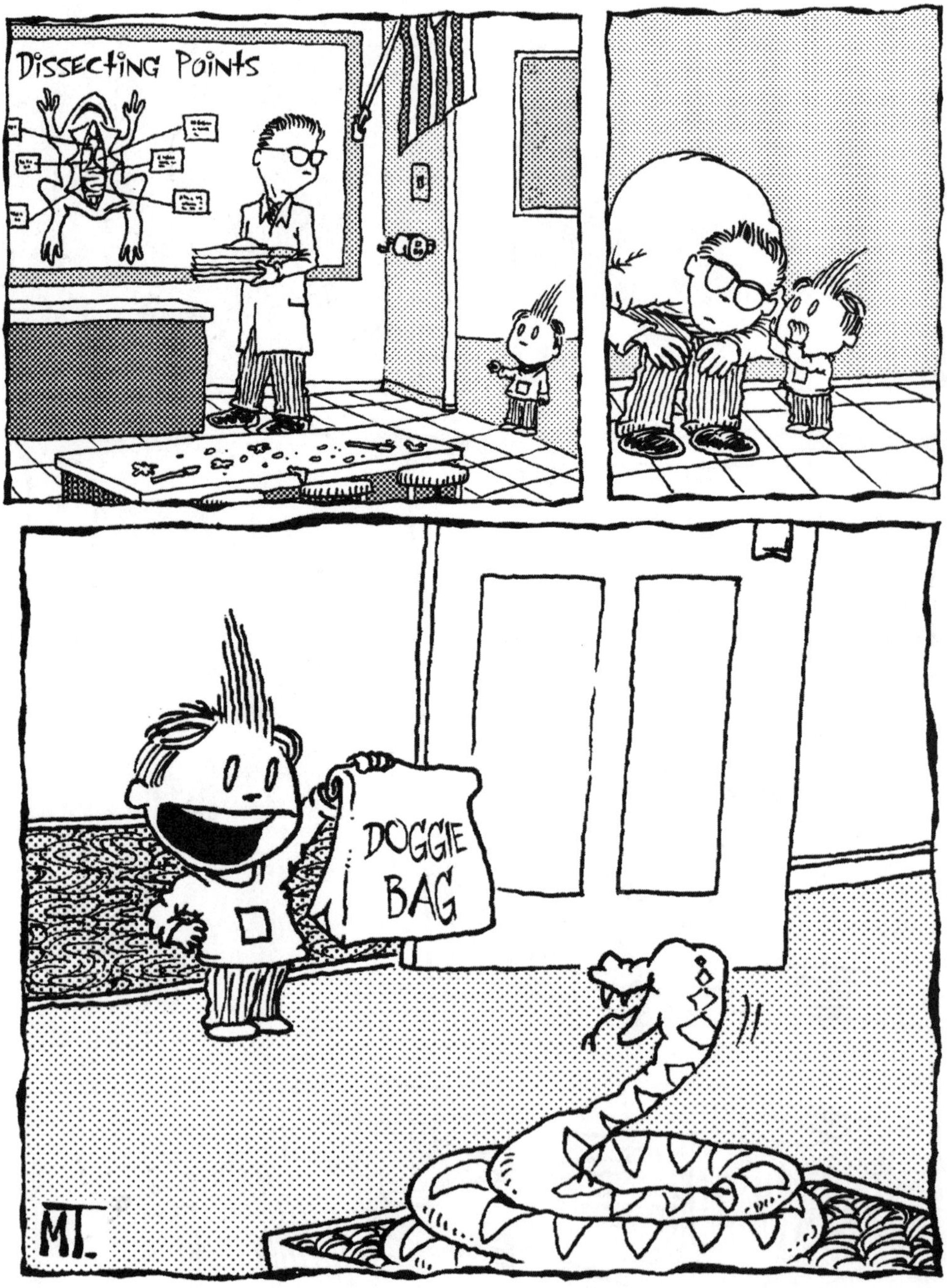
Dissecting Points
DOGGIE BAG
MT.

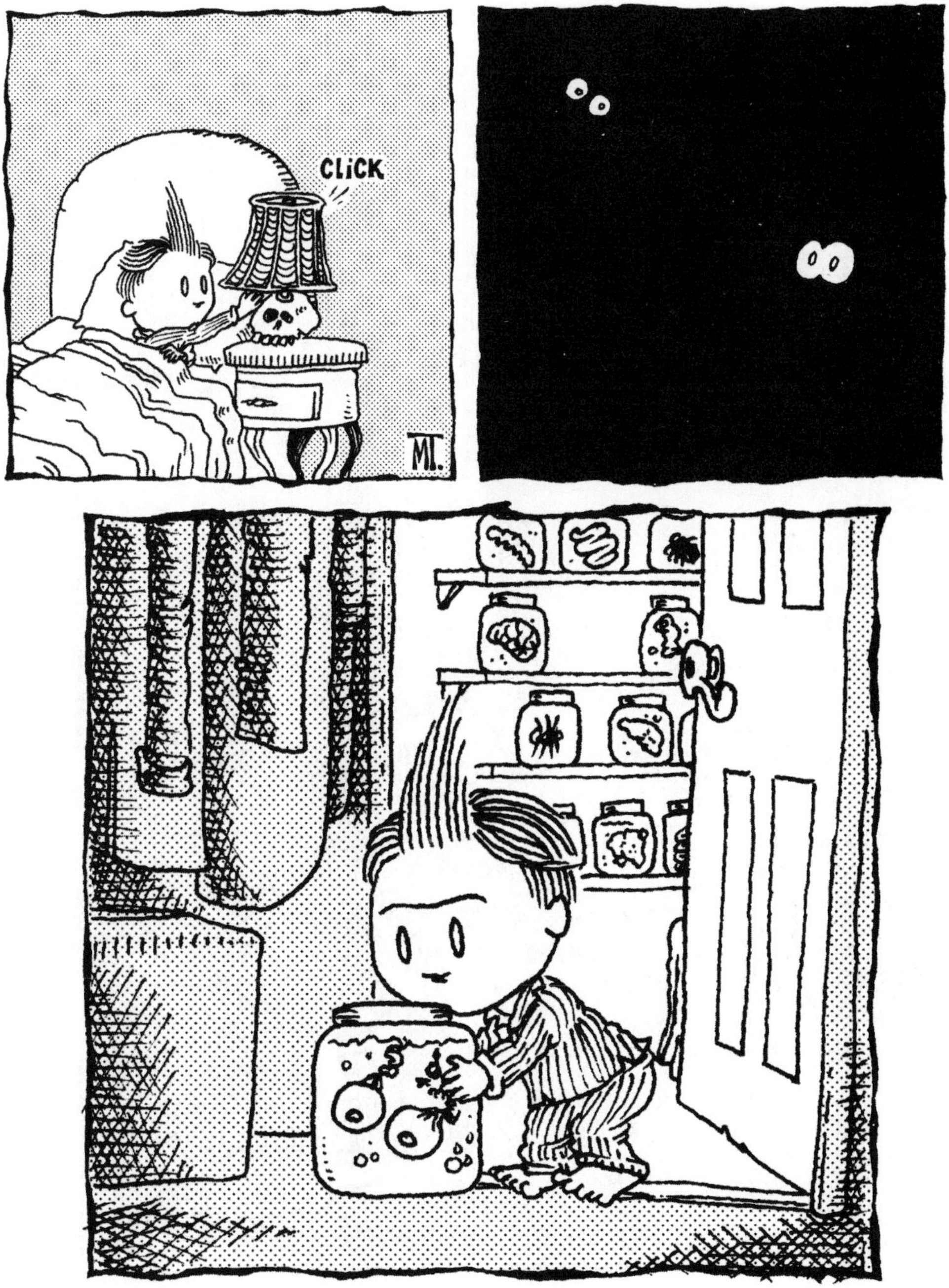
CLICK

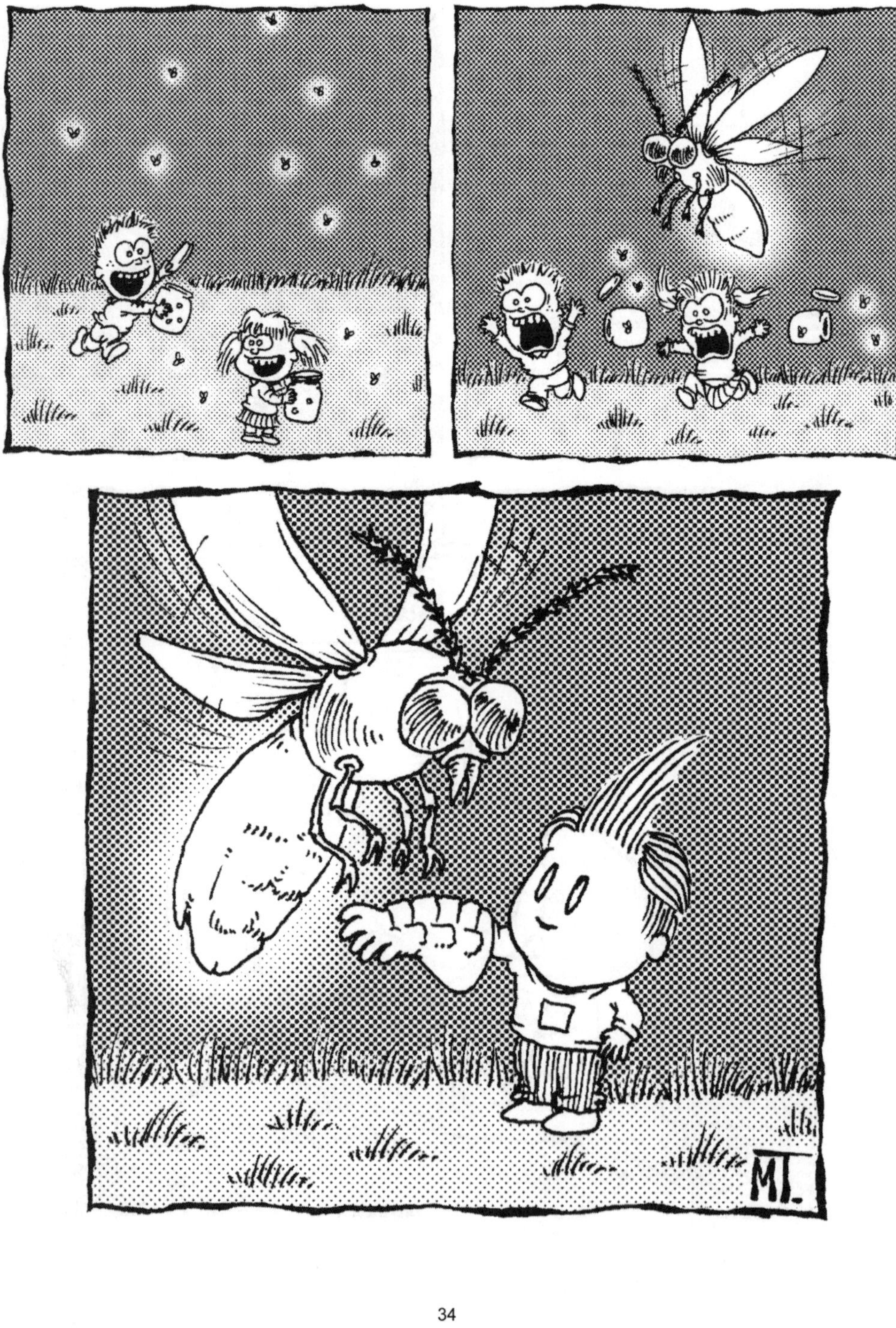
MT.

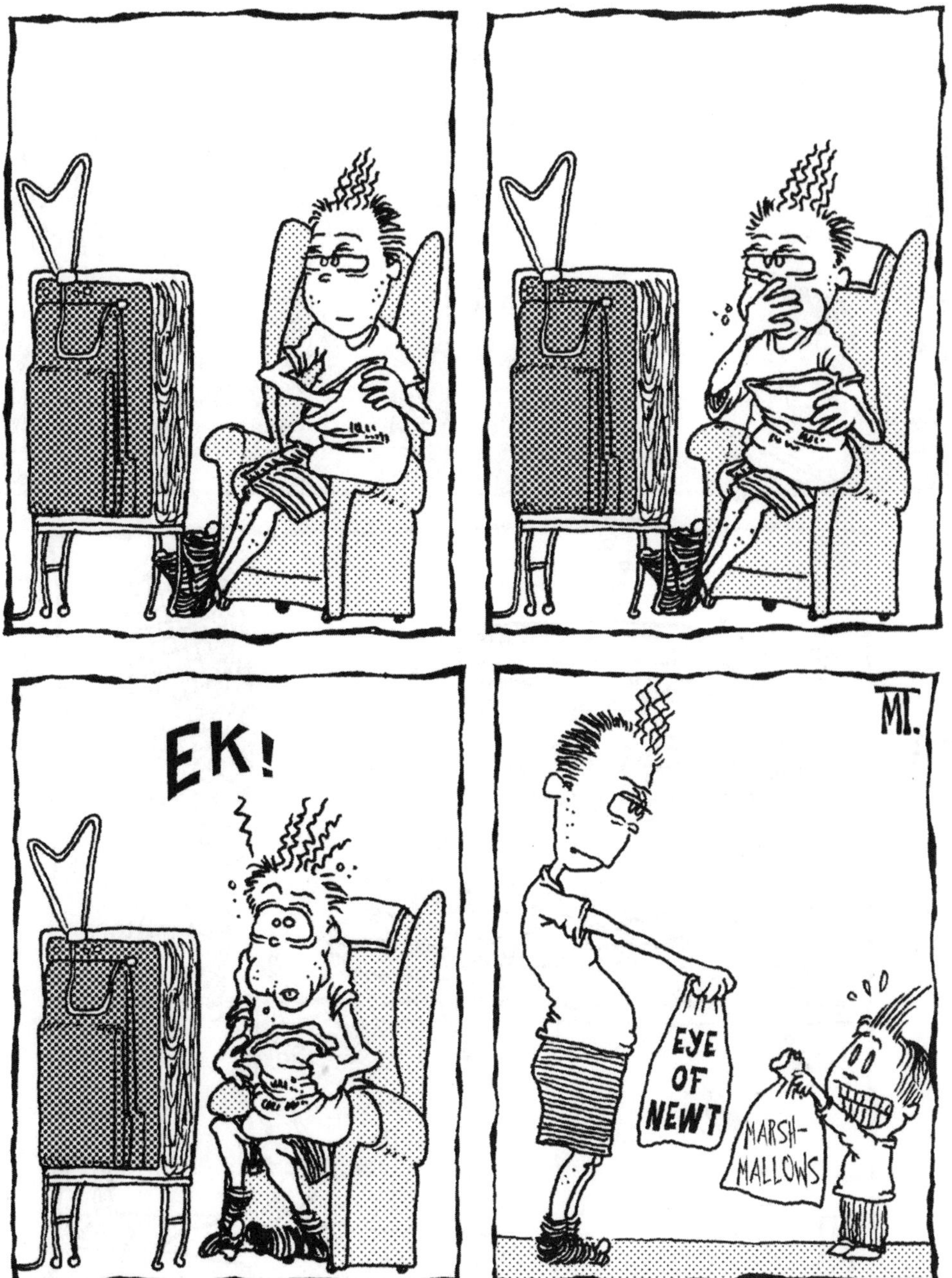
EK!
MT.
EYE OF NEWT
MARSH-
MALLOWS

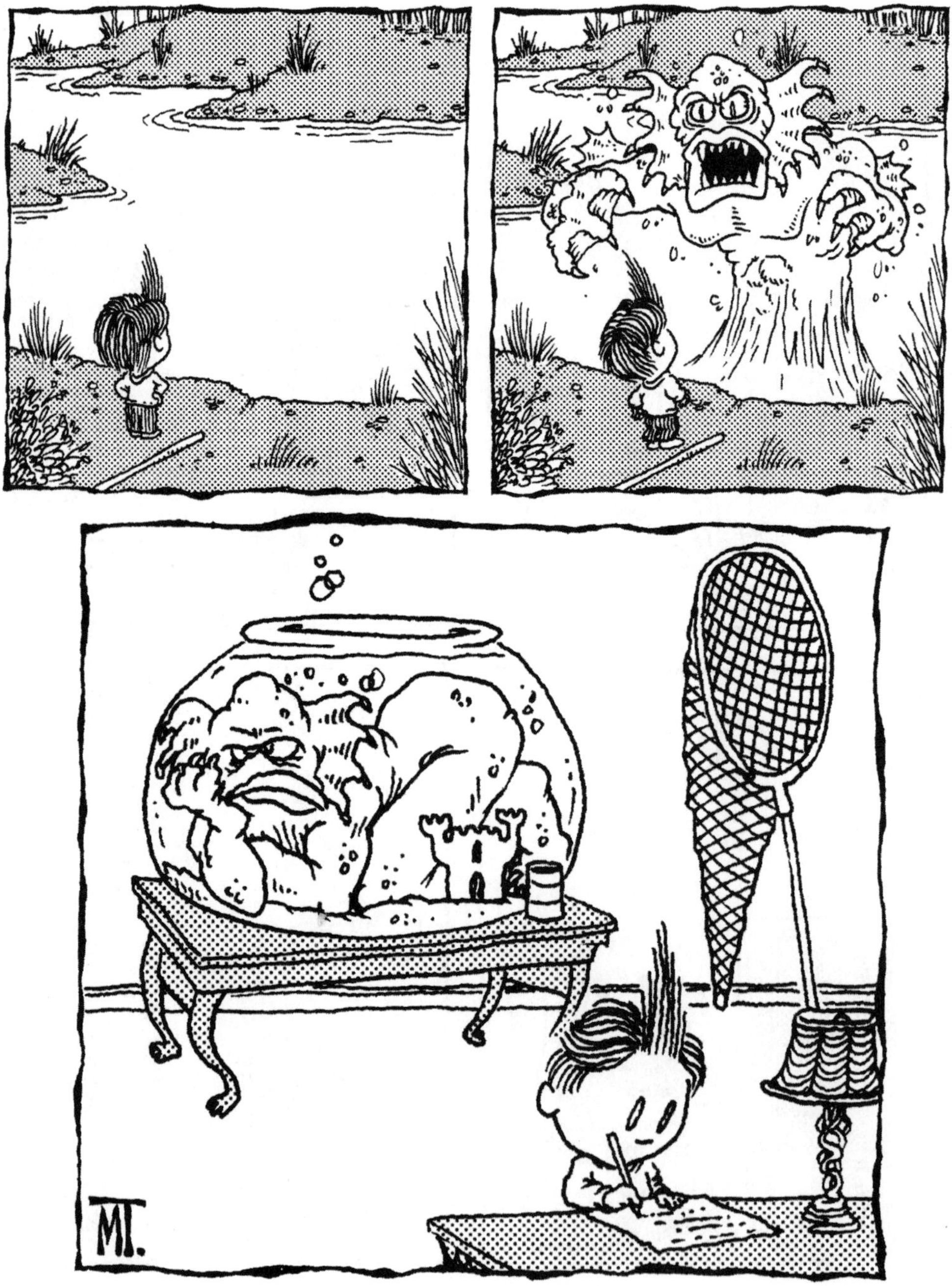
MT.

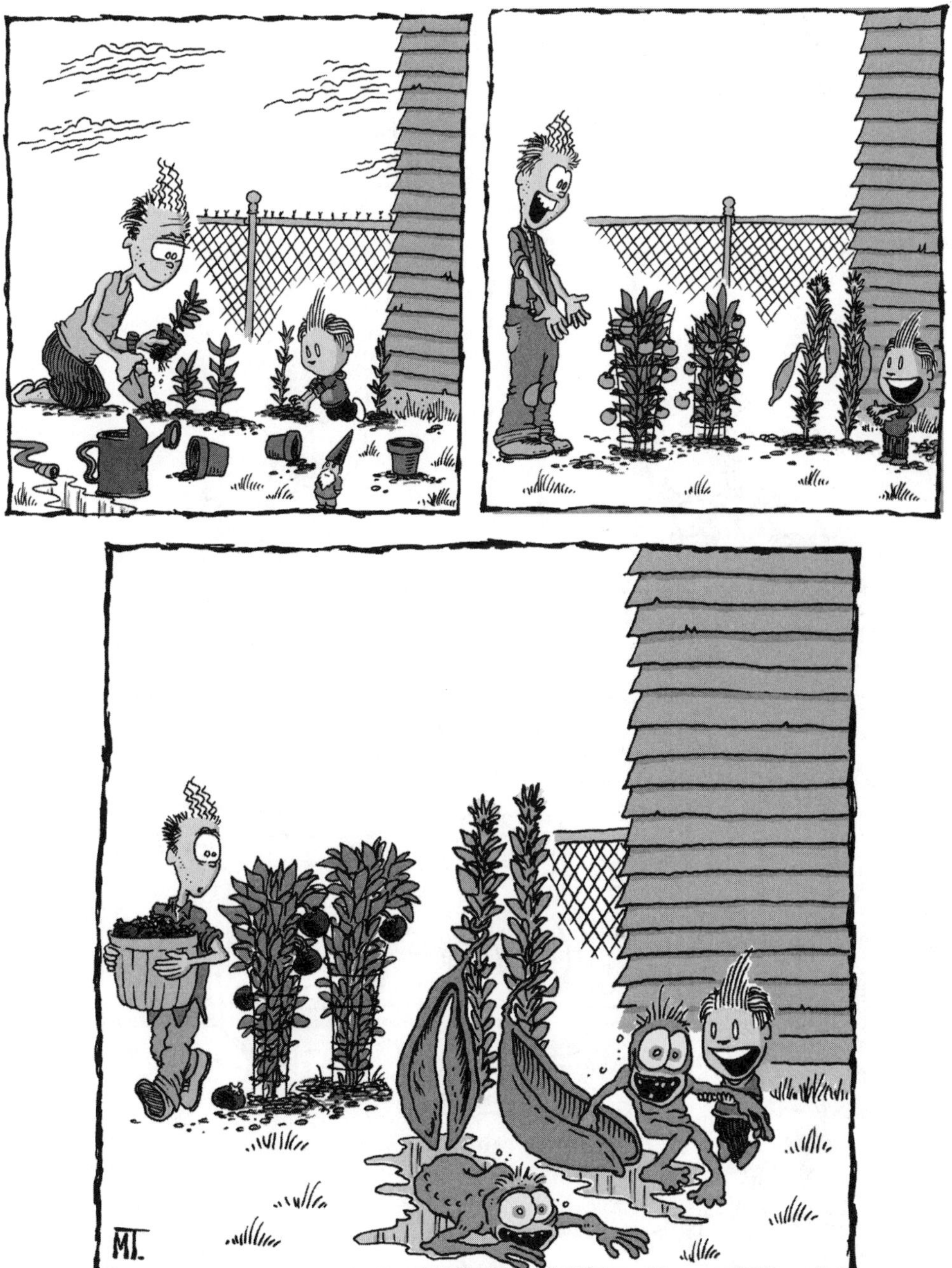
MT.

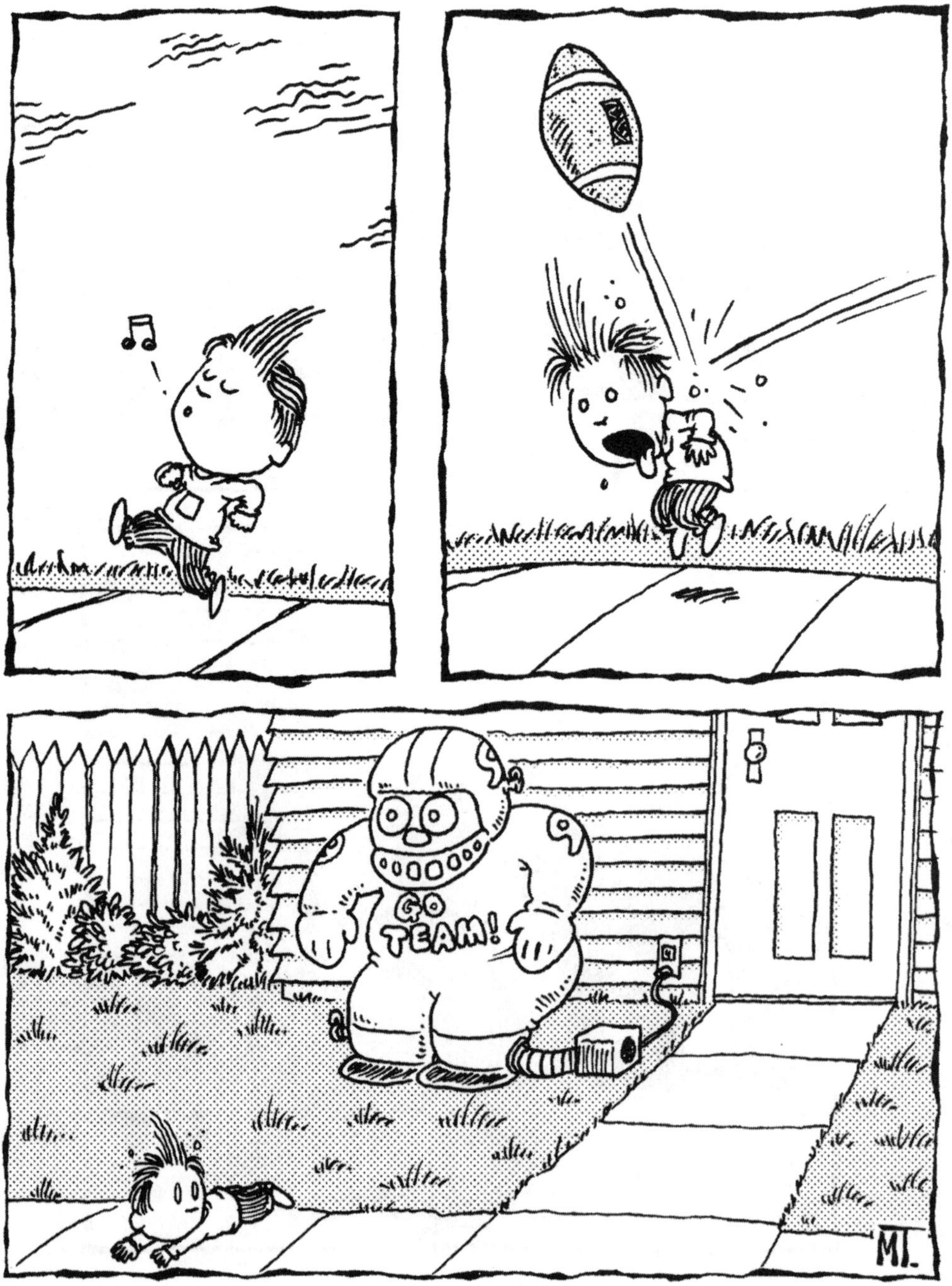
GO
TEAM!
MI

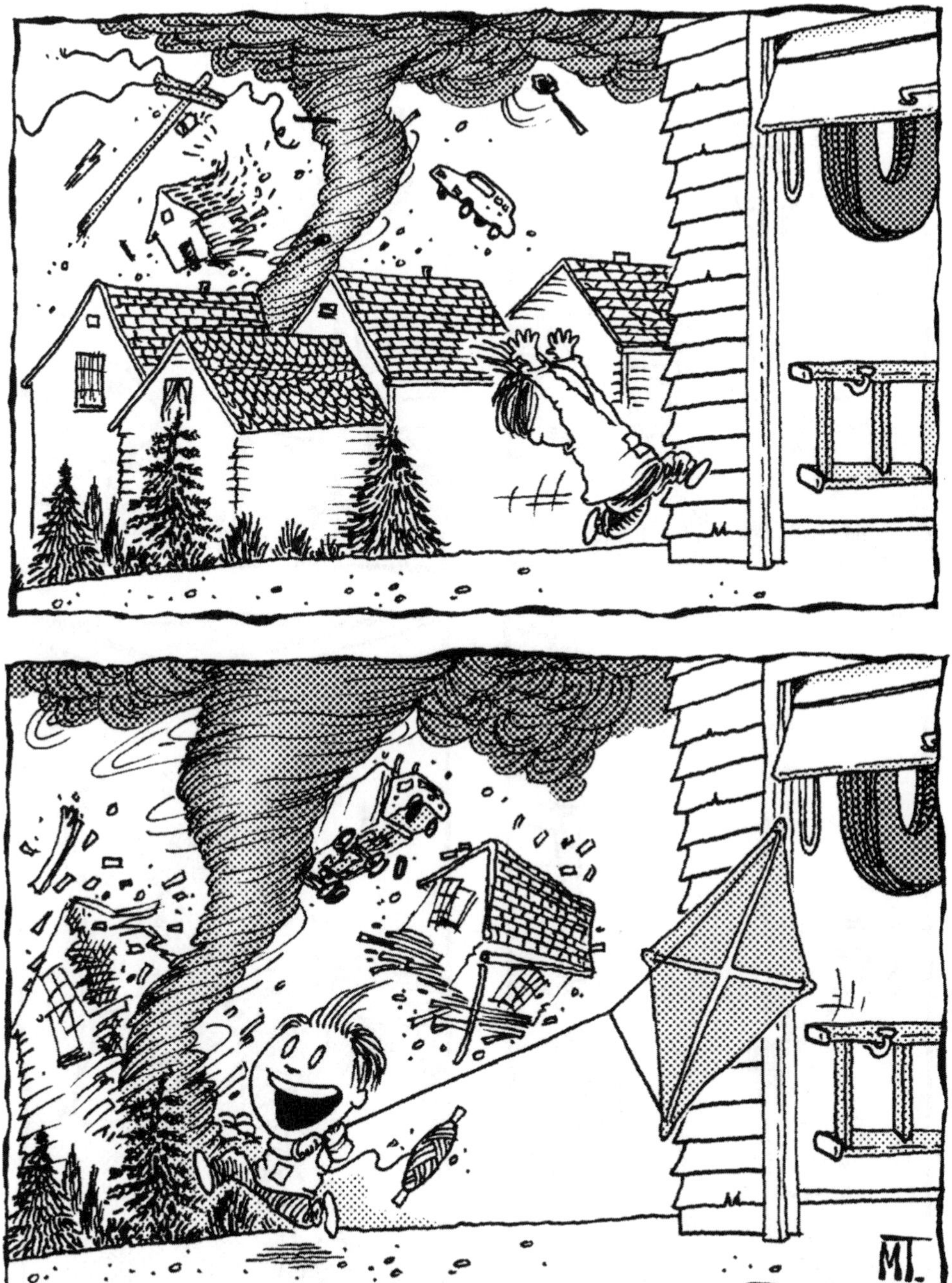
MT.

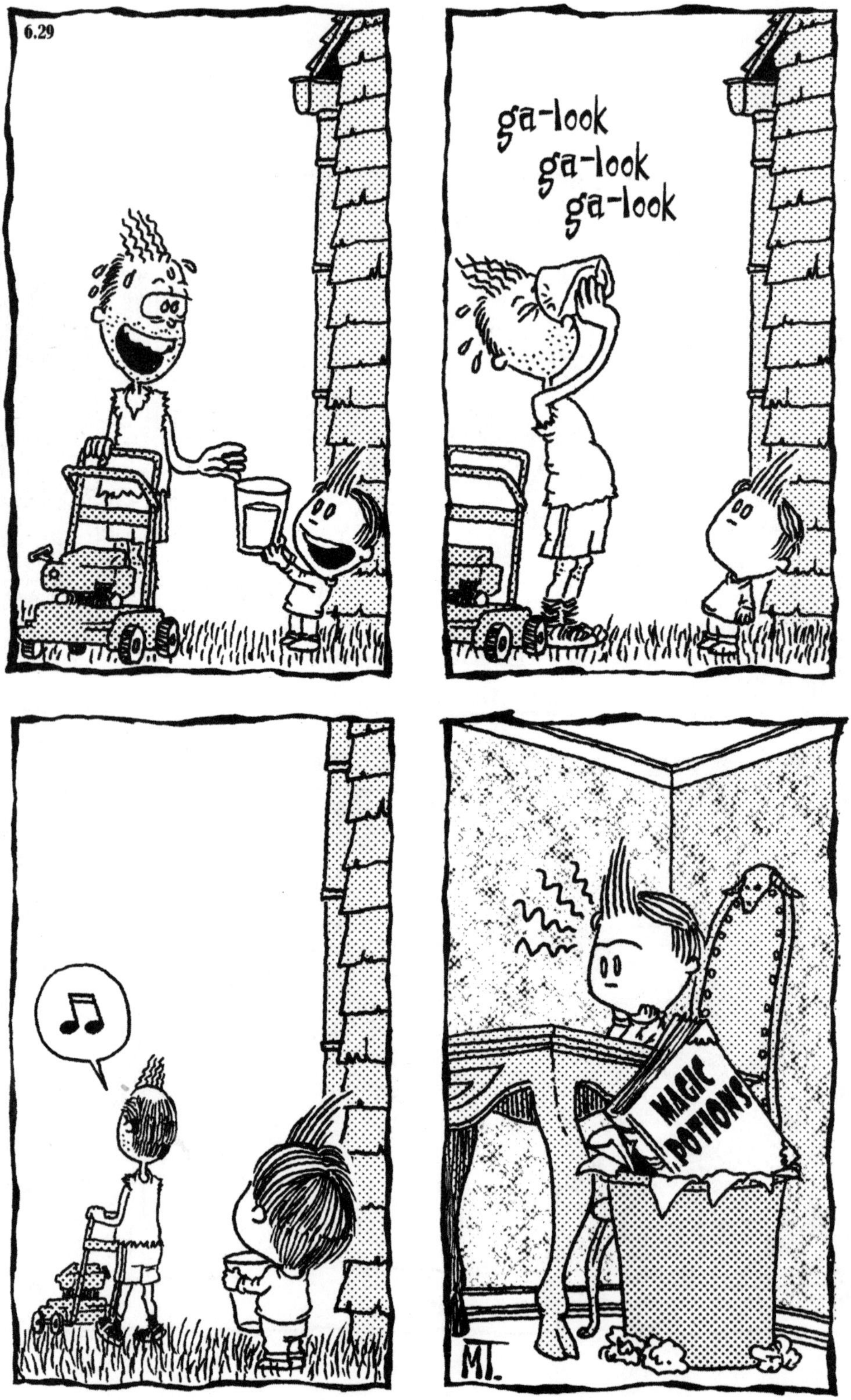
6.29
ga-look
ga-look
ga-look
♫
MAGIC POTIONS
MI.

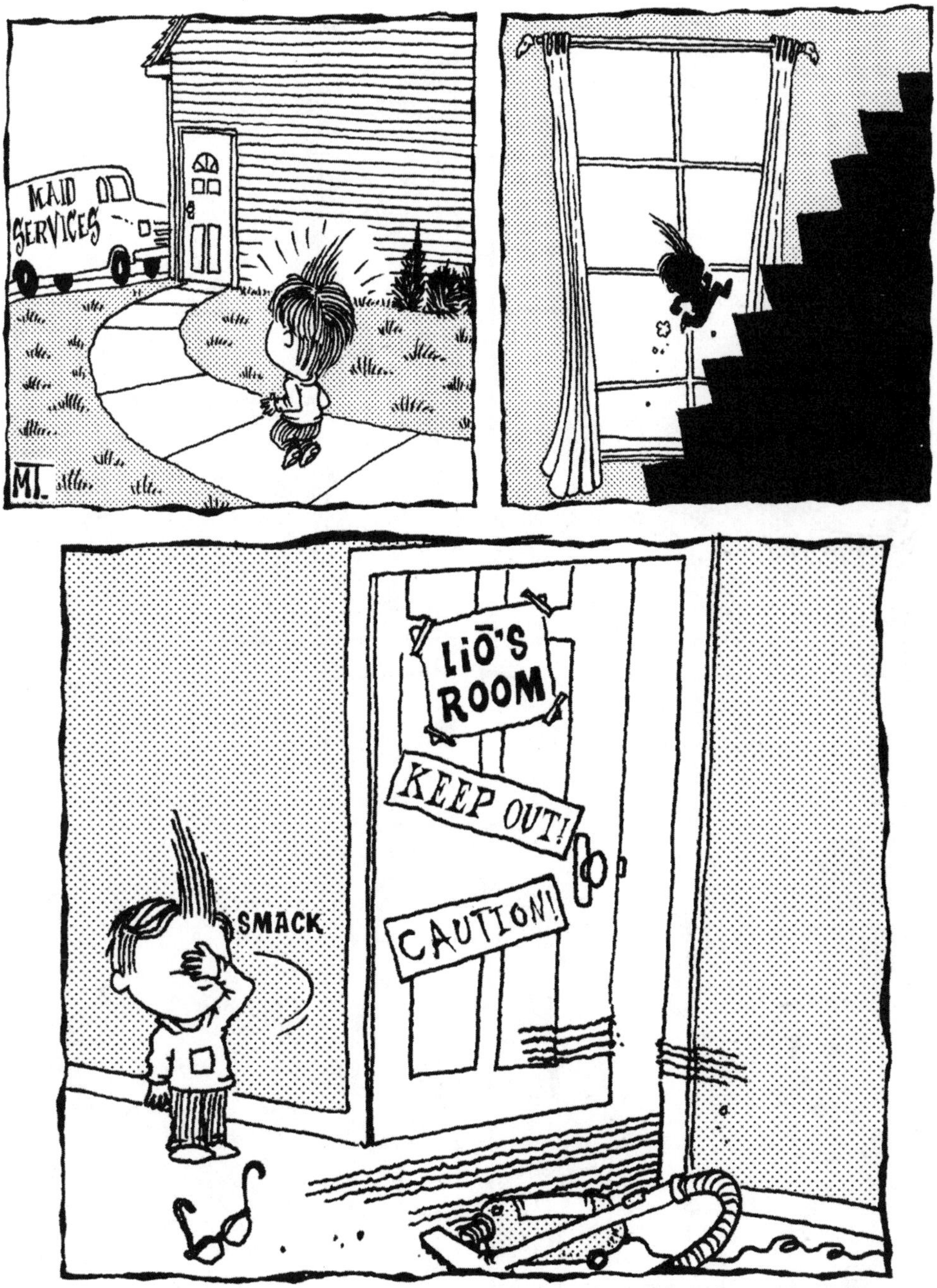
MAID SERVICES
MT
LIŌ'S ROOM
KEEP OUT!
CAUTION!
SMACK

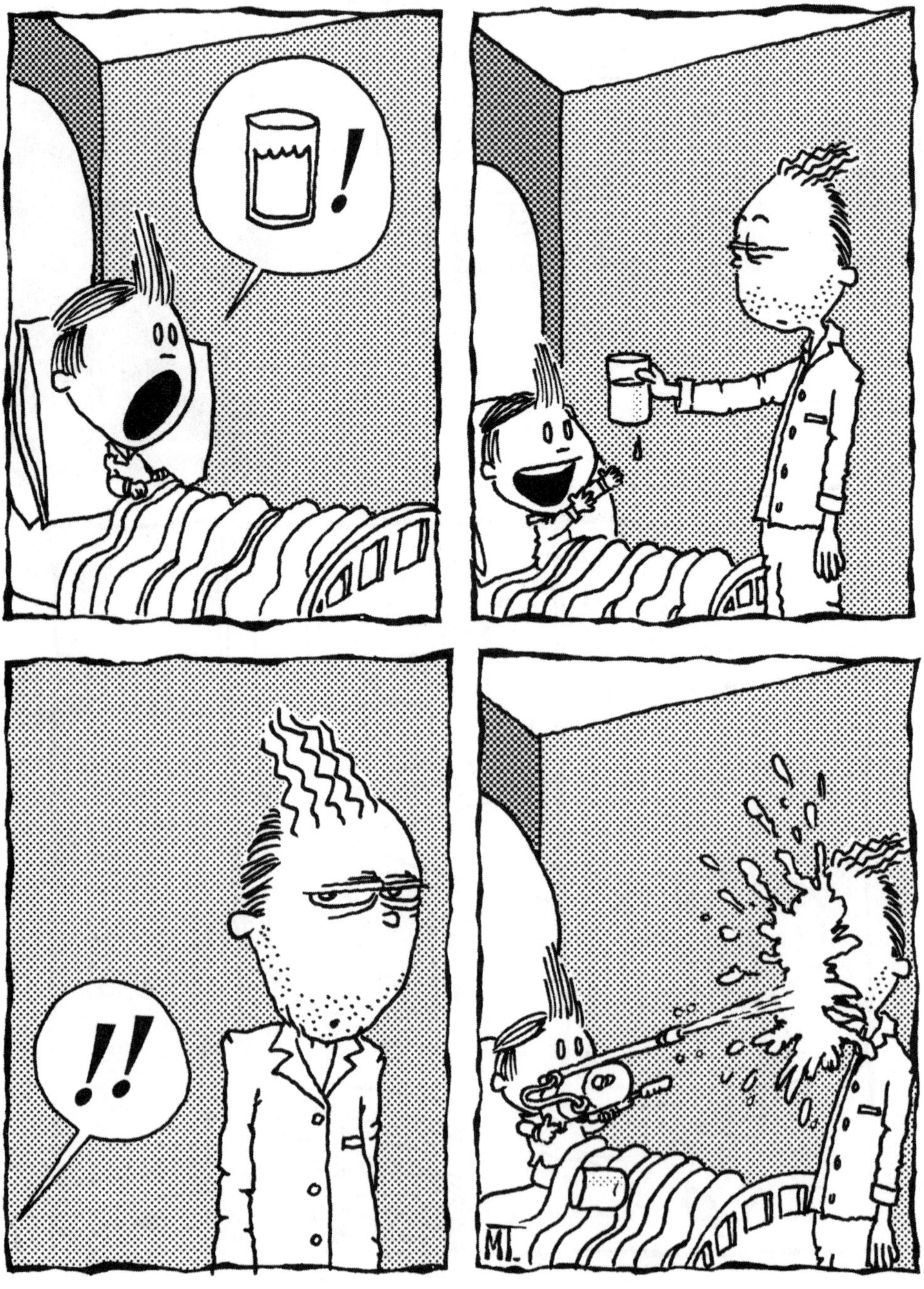
!
!!
ML

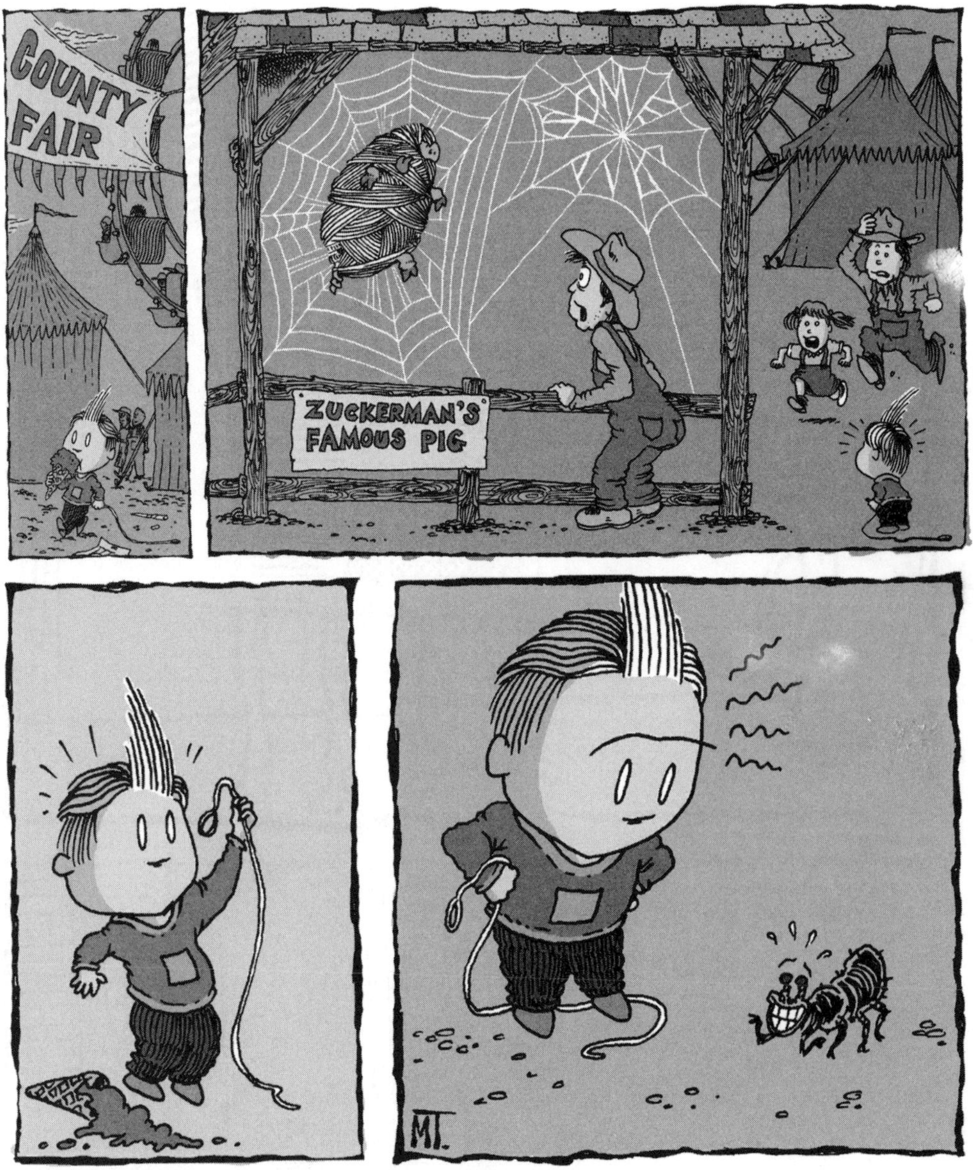
COUNTY FAIR
ZUCKERMAN'S FAMOUS PIG
MT.

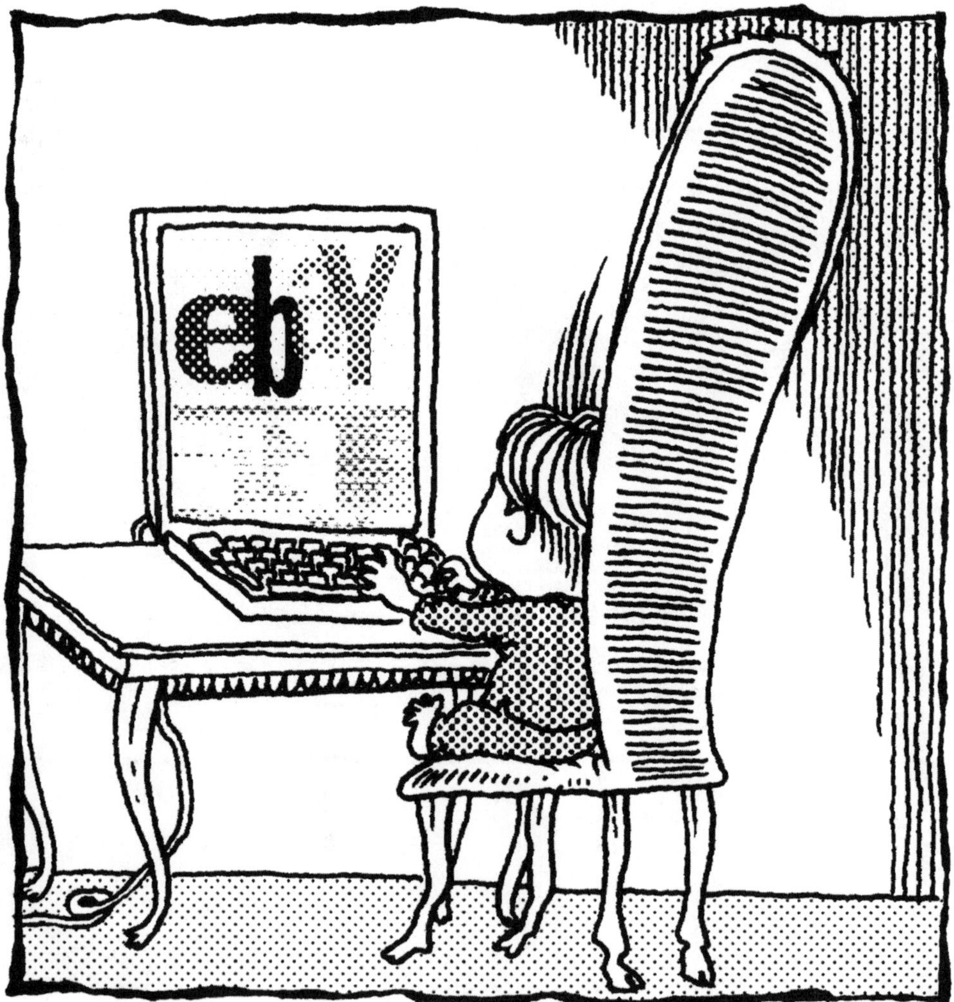


ebY


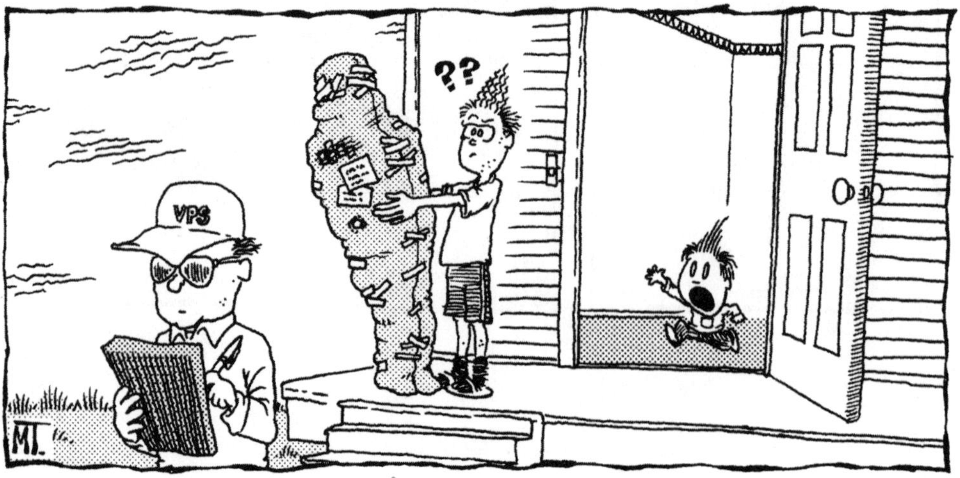


??
VPS
ML

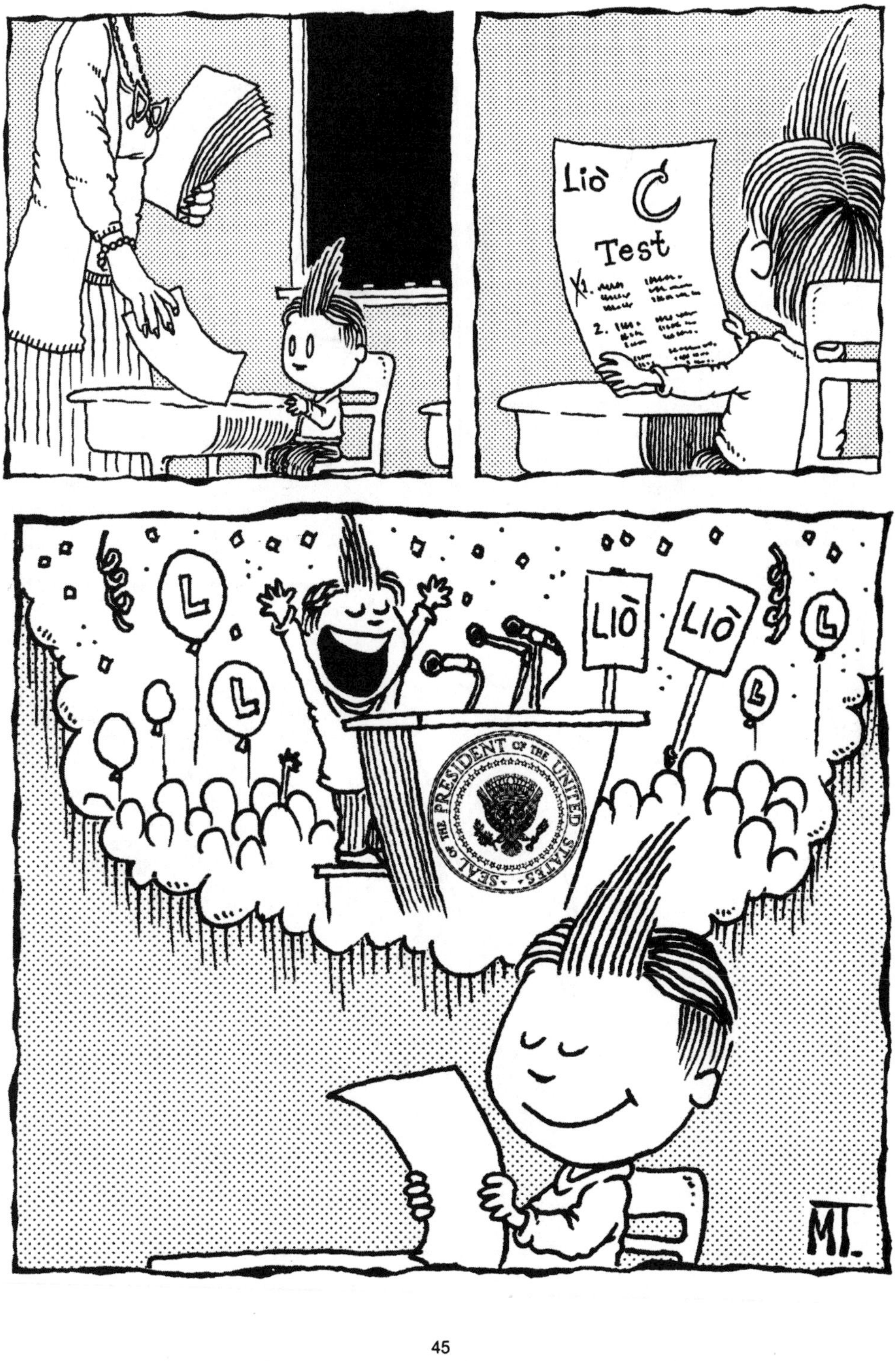
Liò
C
Test
1.
2.
LIÒ
LIÒ
SEAL OF THE PRESIDENT OF THE UNITED STATES
MT

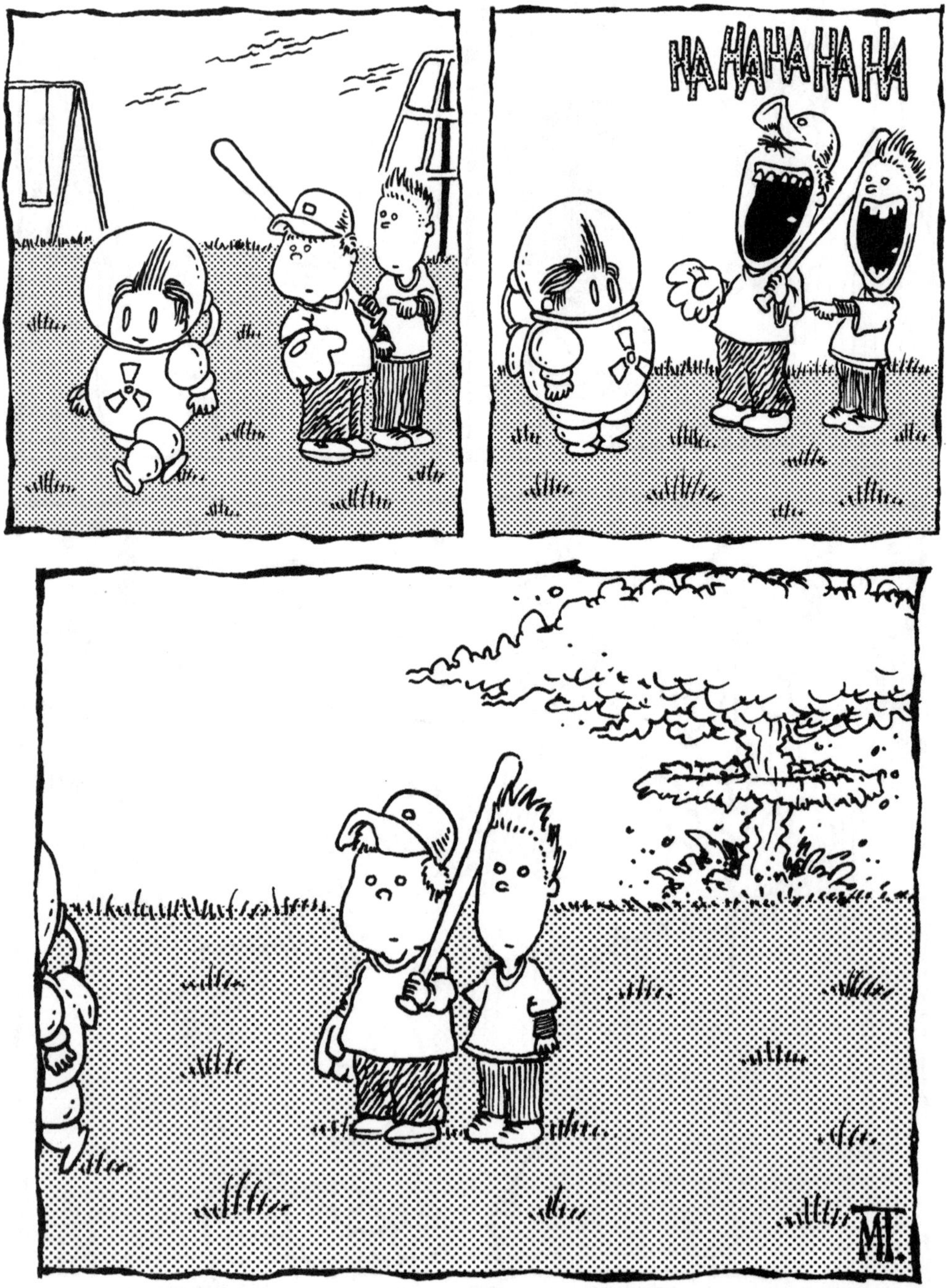
HA HA HA HA HA HA HA
MT.

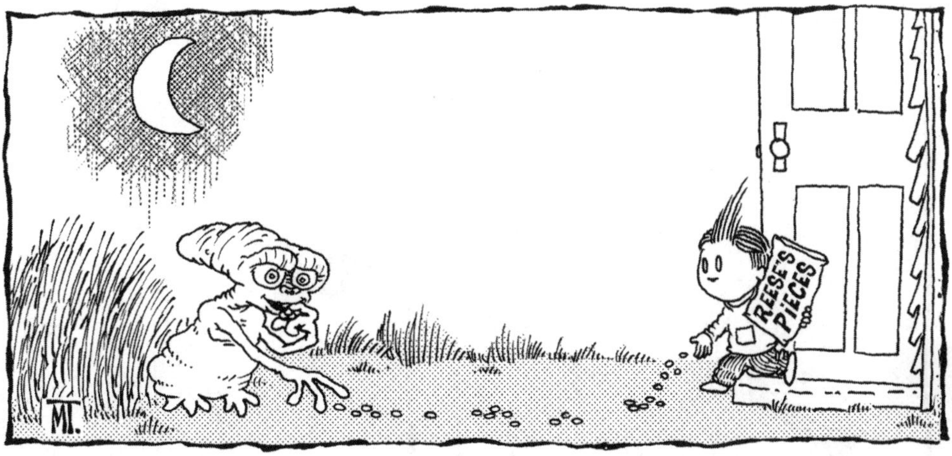
REESE'S PIECES
MI.

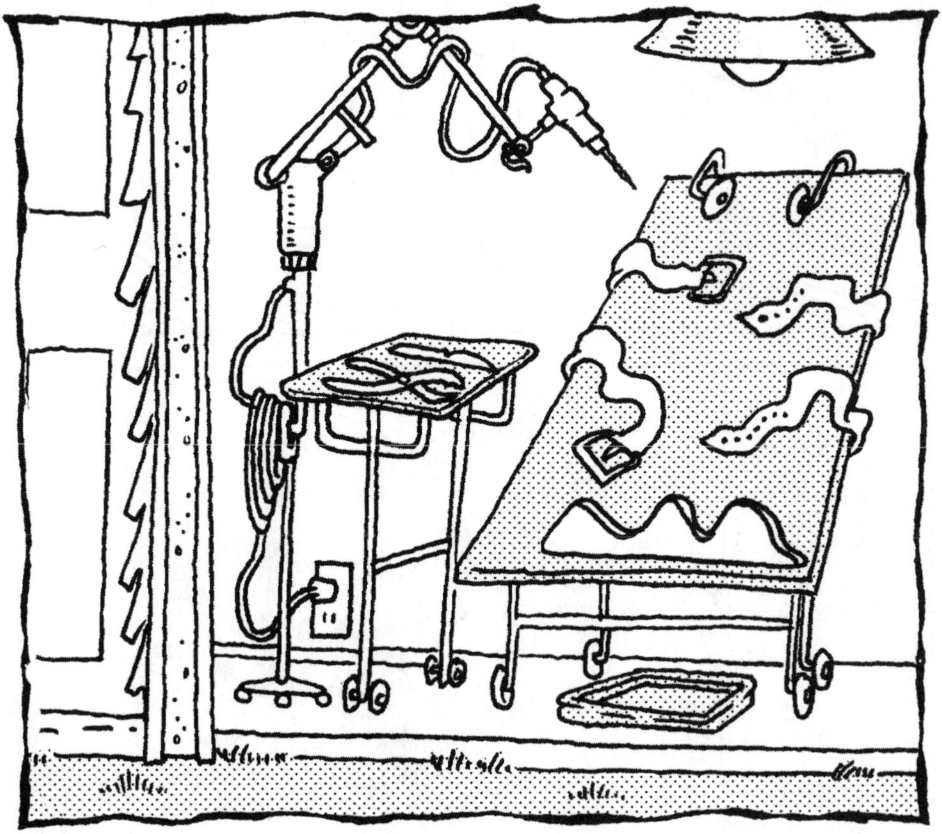

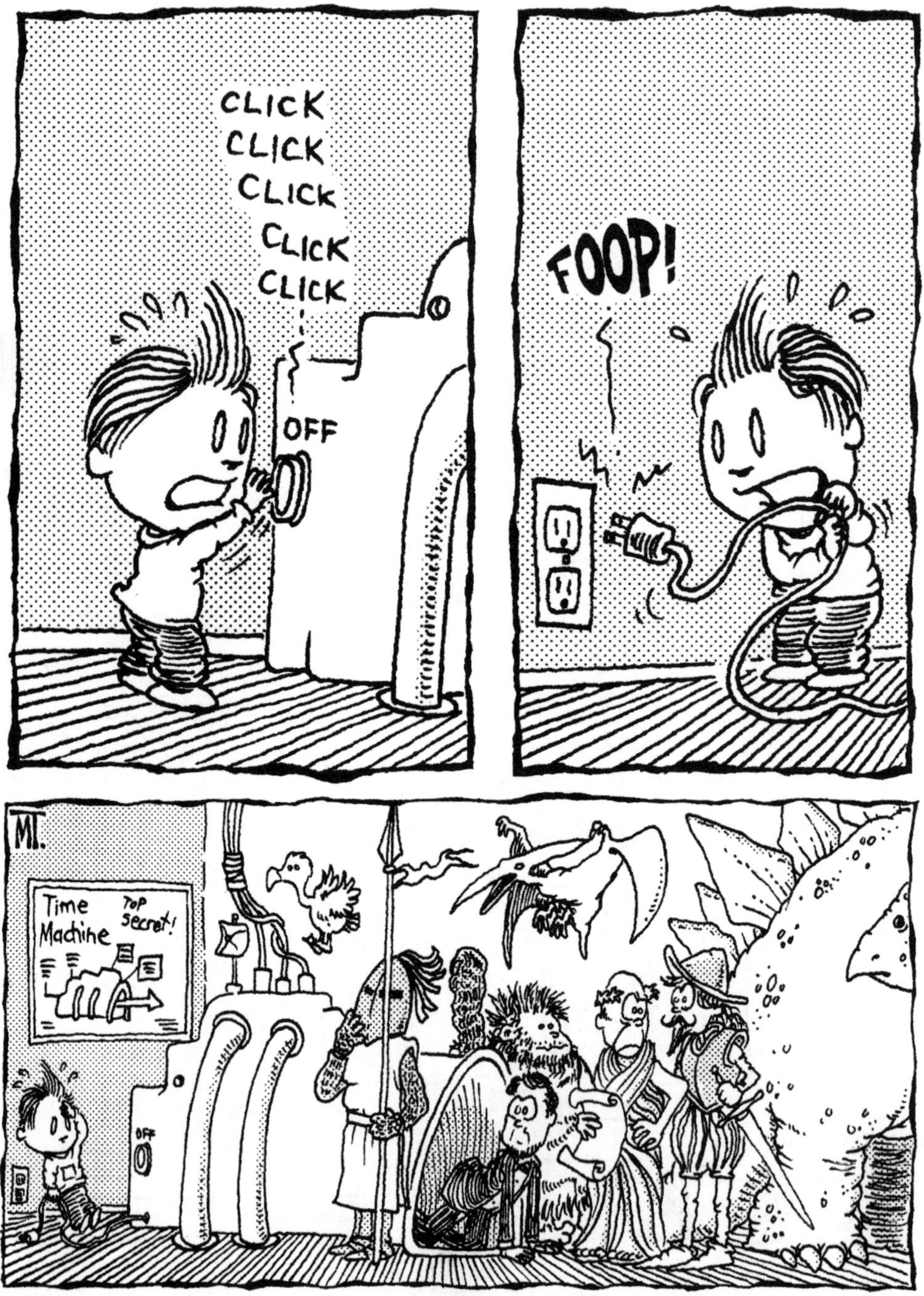
CLICK
CLICK
CLICK
CLICK
CLICK
OFF
FOOP!
Time Machine
TOP secret!
OFF

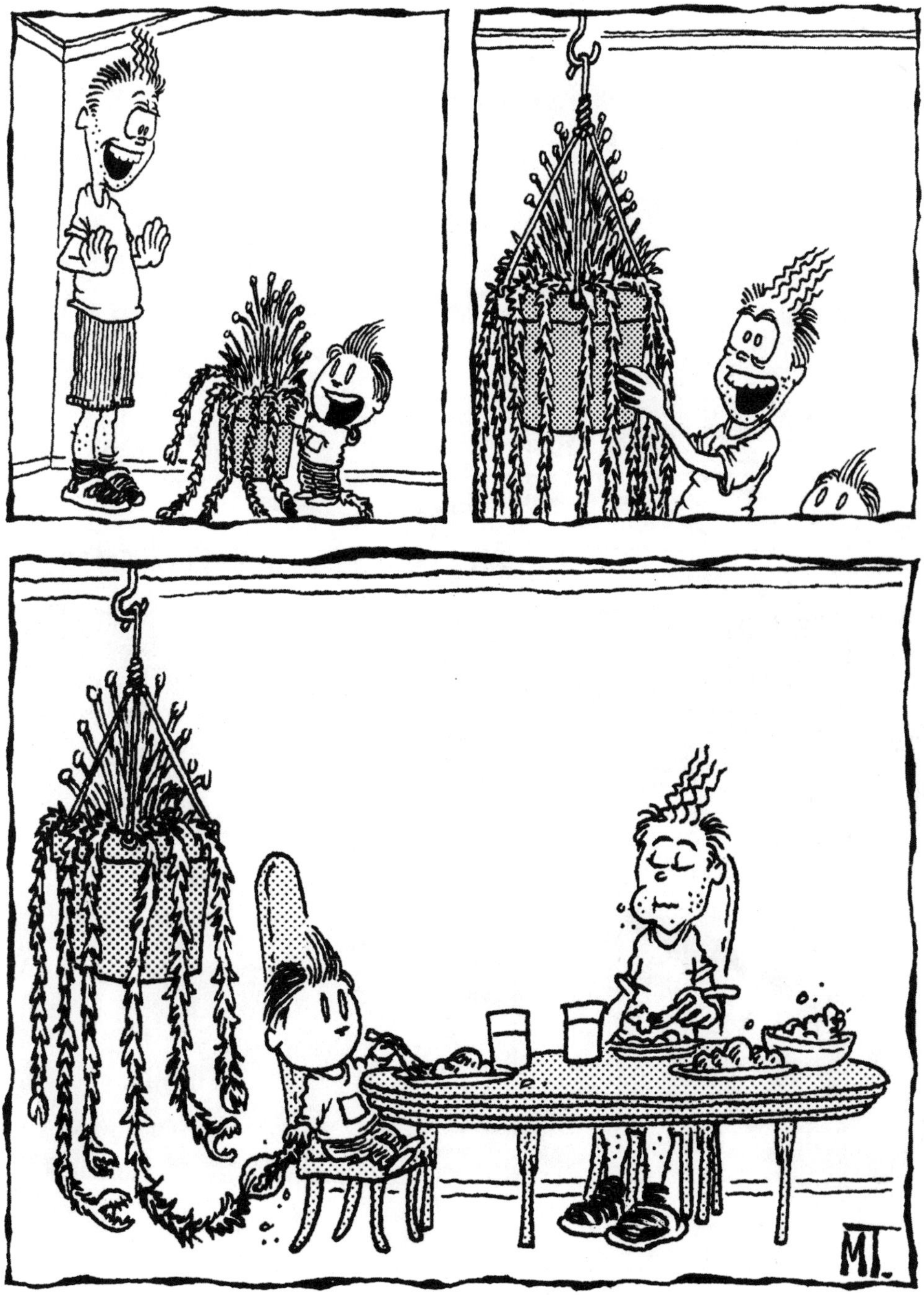
MT.

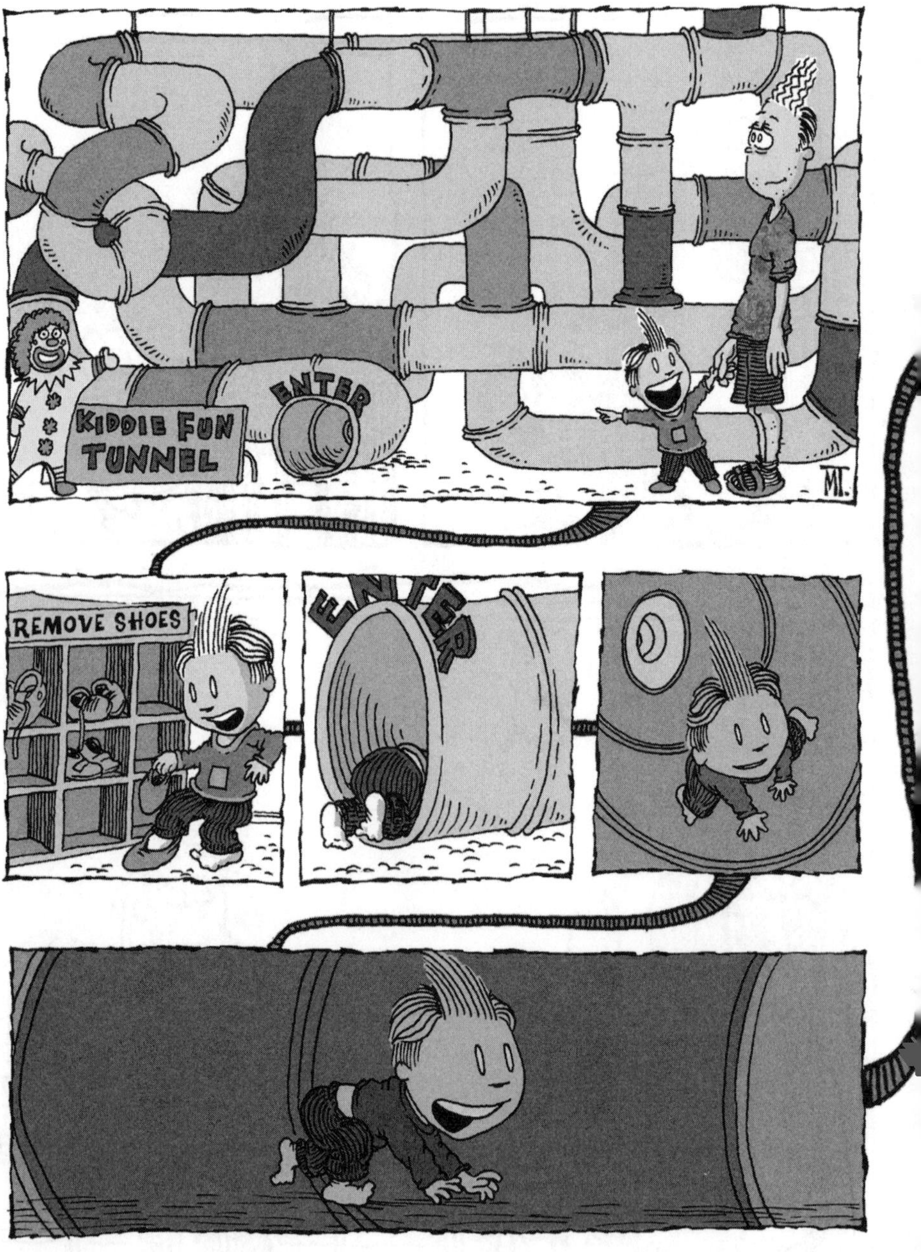
ENTER
KIDDIE FUN TUNNEL
REMOVE SHOES
ENTER

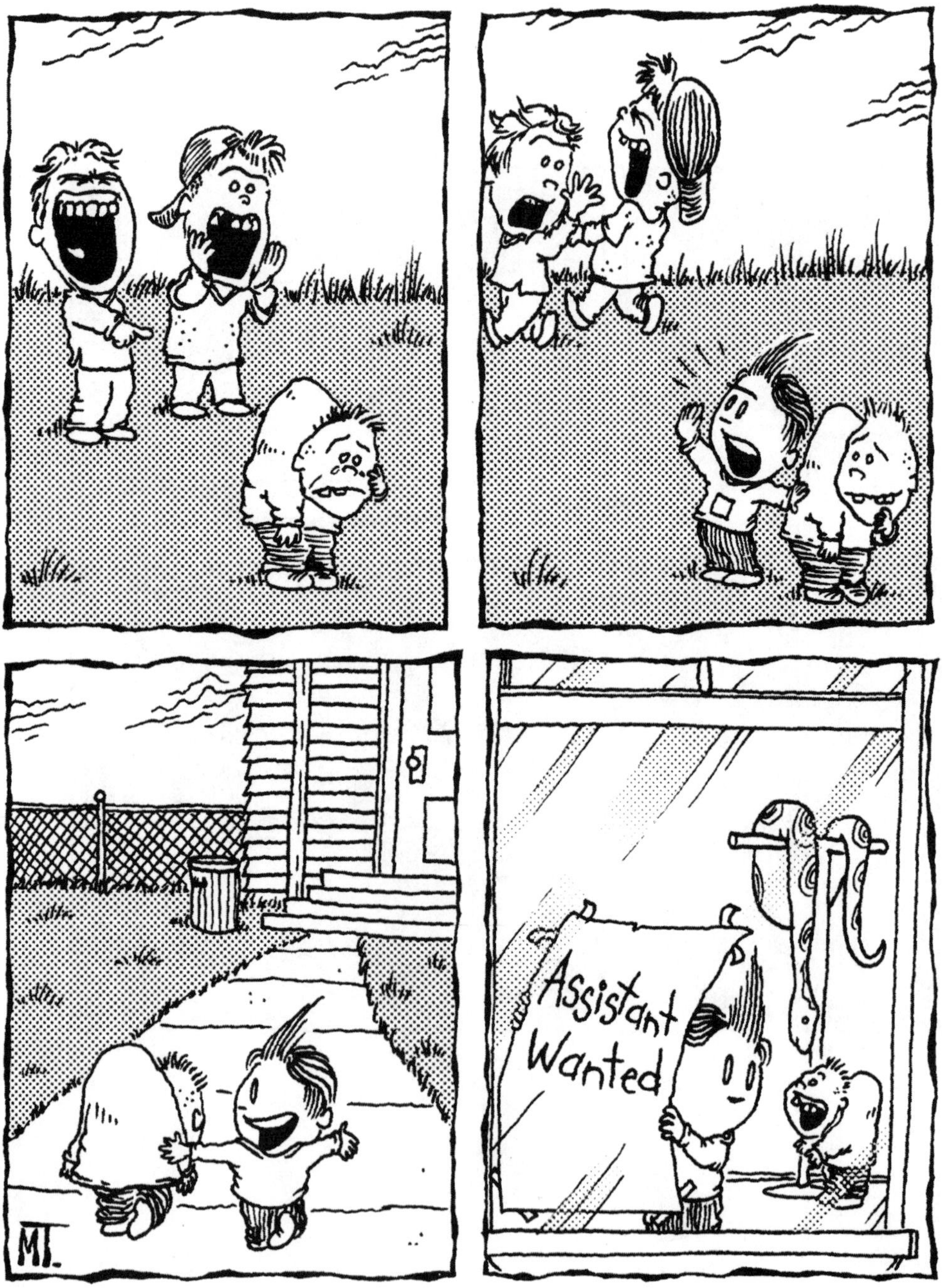
MT
Assistant
Wanted

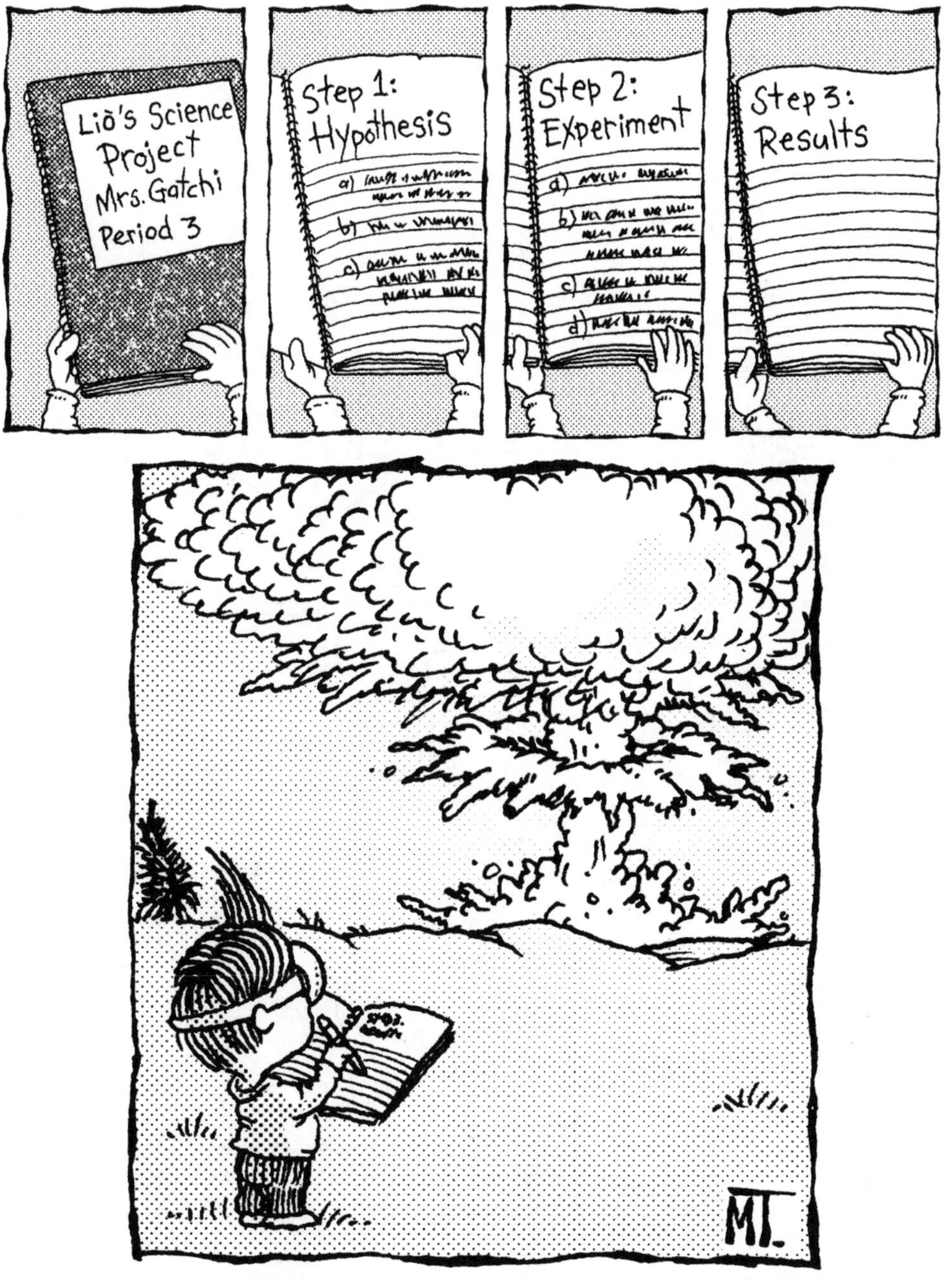

Lio's Science Project
Mrs. Gatchi
Period 3
Step 1:
Hypothesis
Step 2:
Experiment
Step 3:
Results
MT

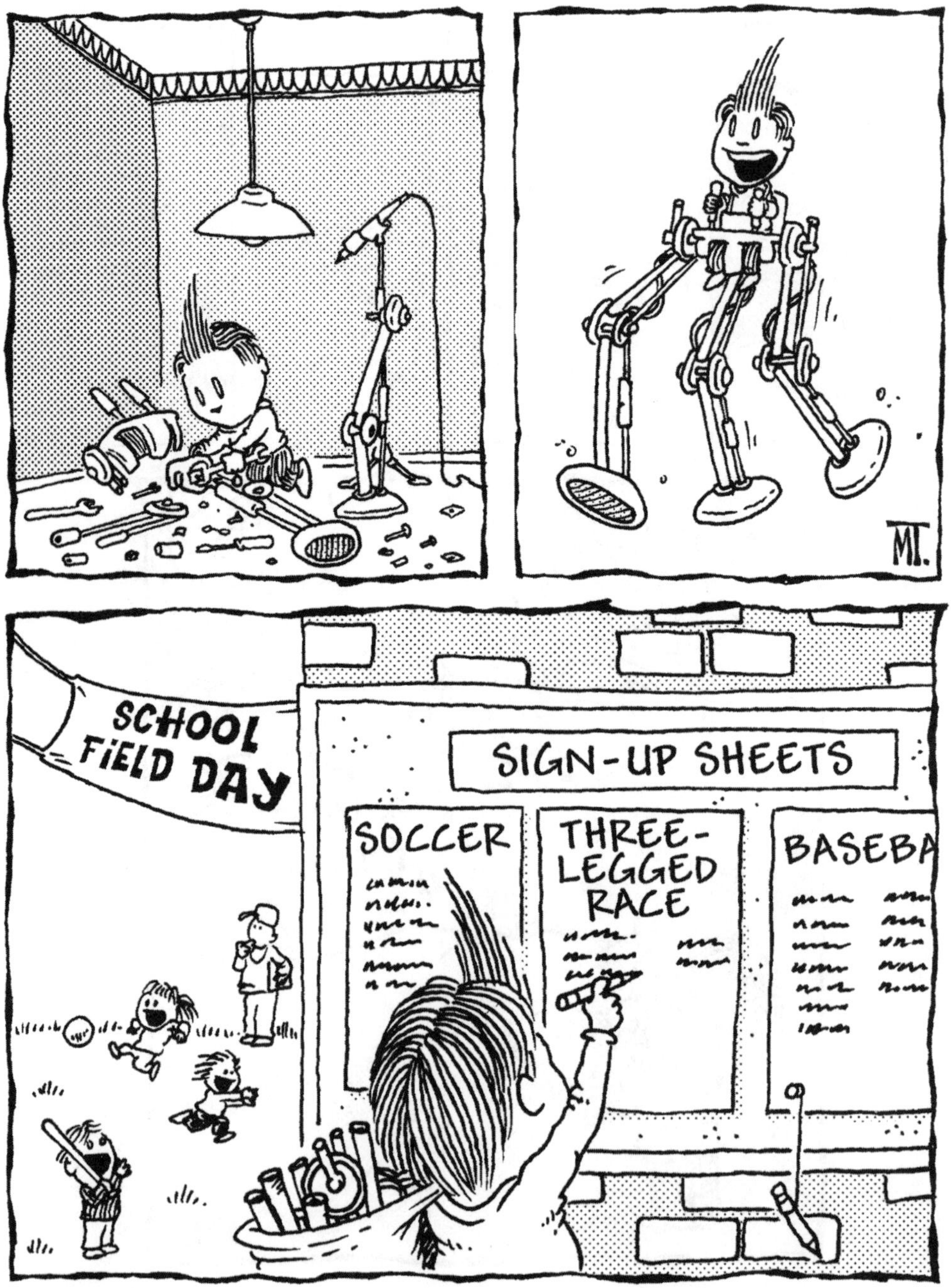
MT.
SCHOOL FIELD DAY
SIGN-UP SHEETS
SOCCER
THREE-LEGGED RACE
BASEBA

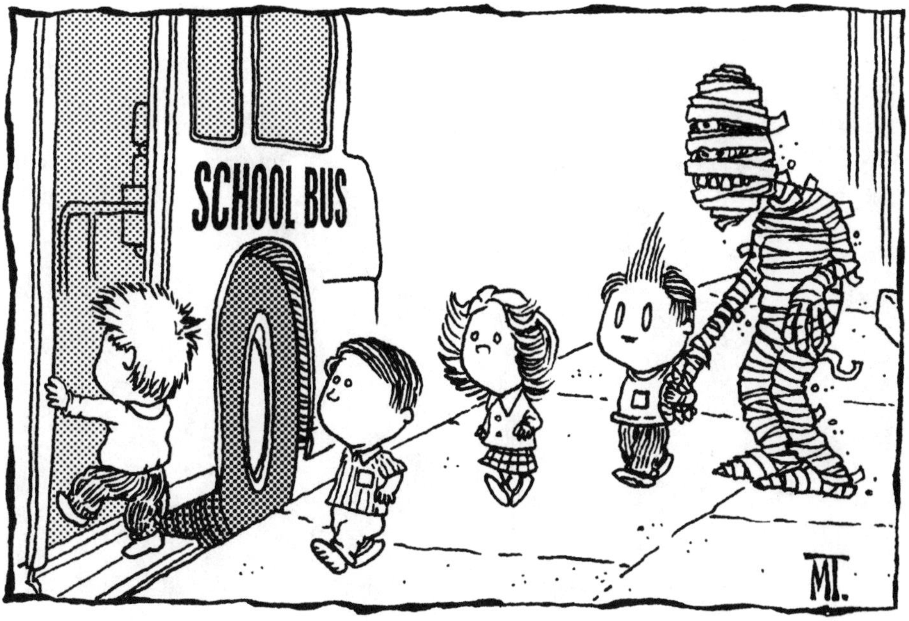
SCHOOL BUS
MT.

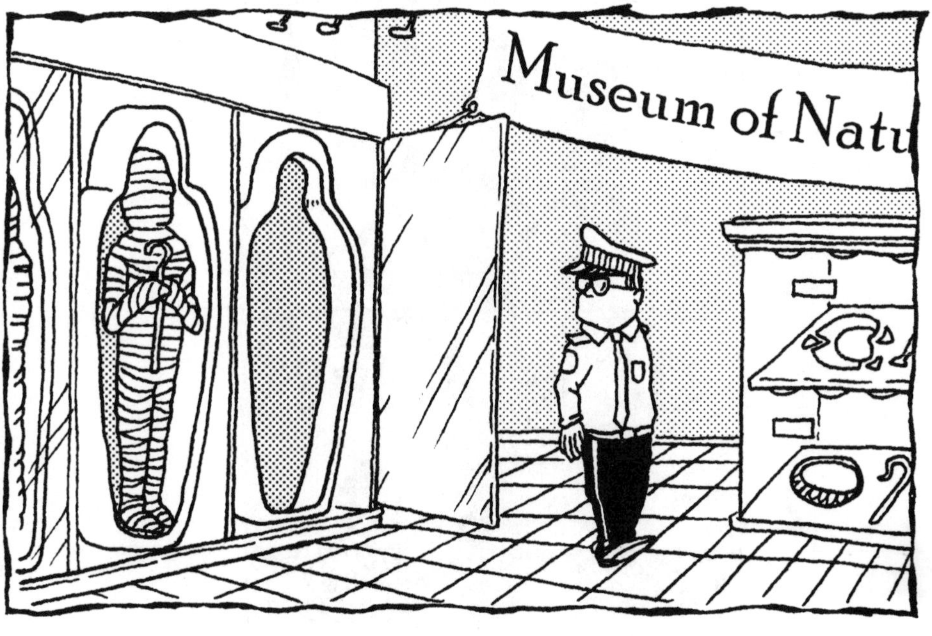
Museum of Natu

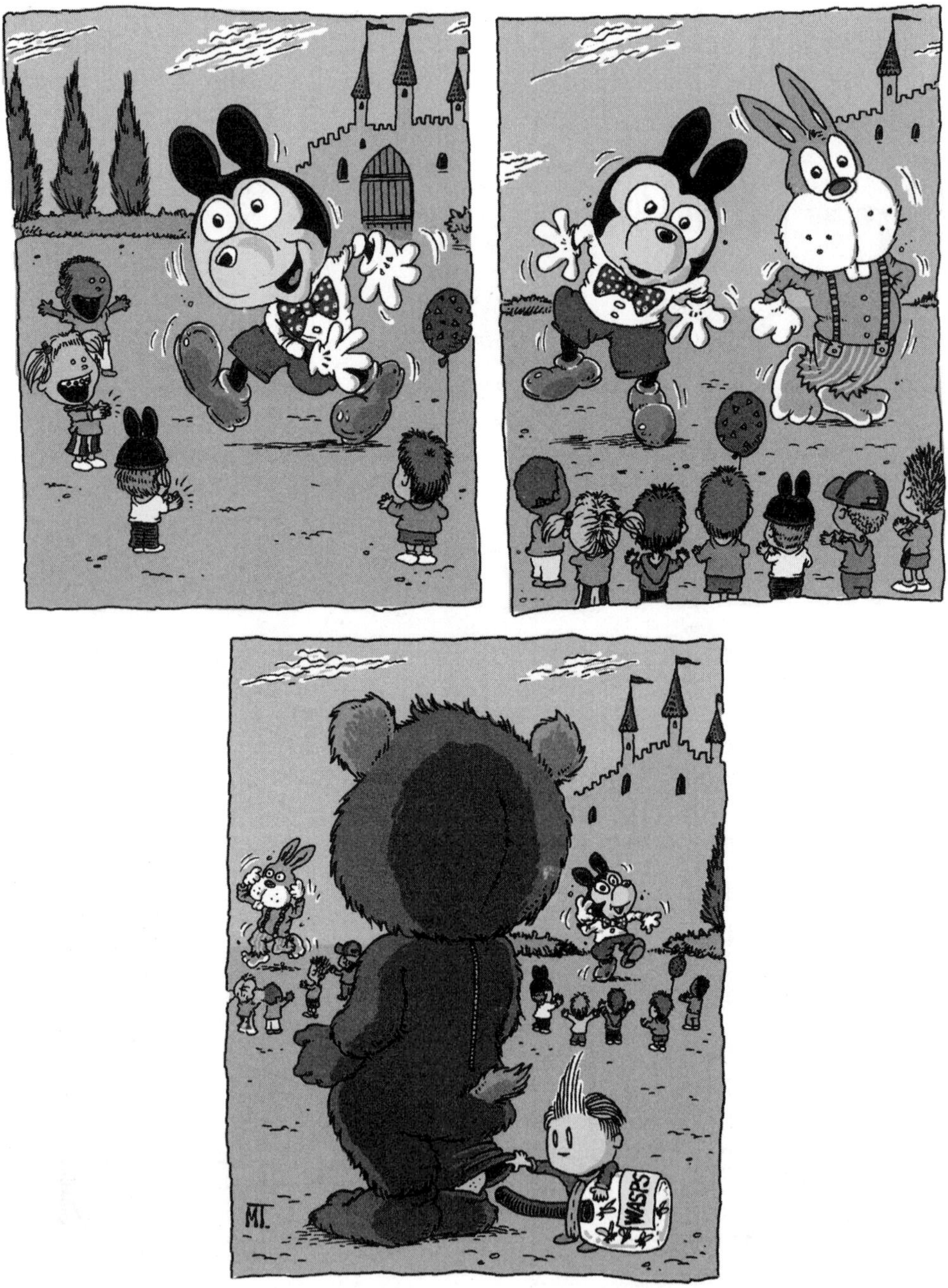
MT.
WASPS

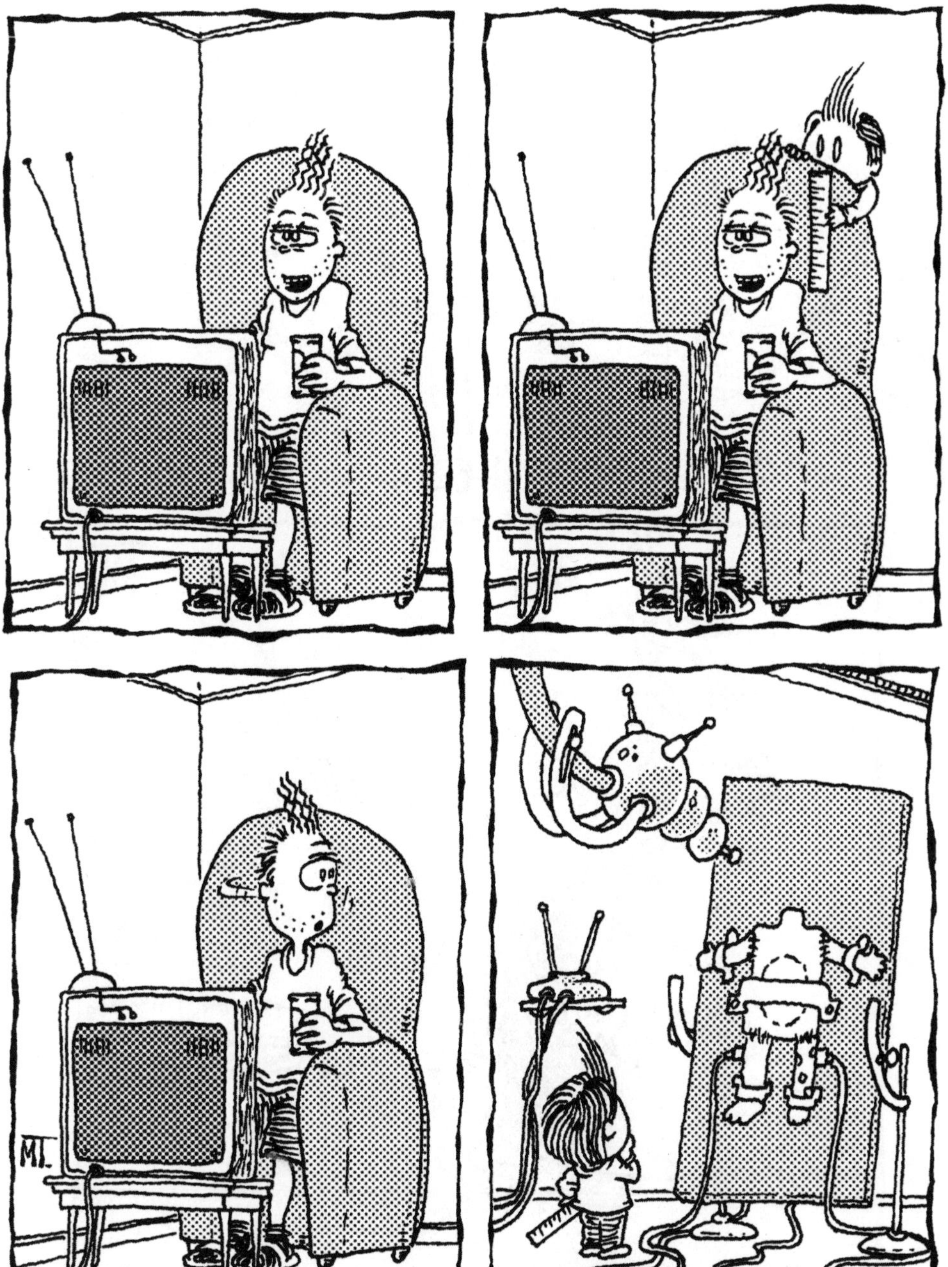

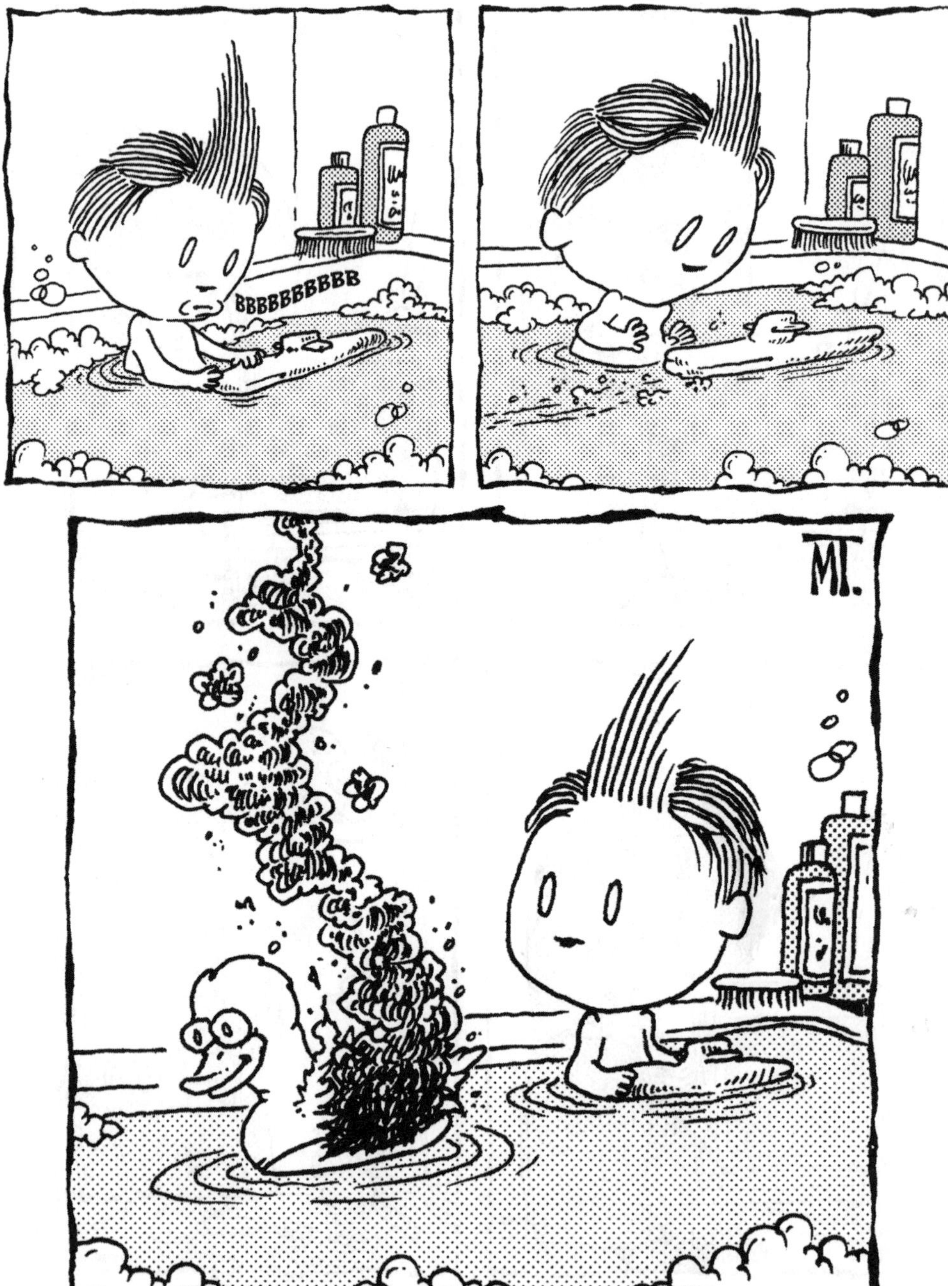
BBBBBBBBBB
MT.

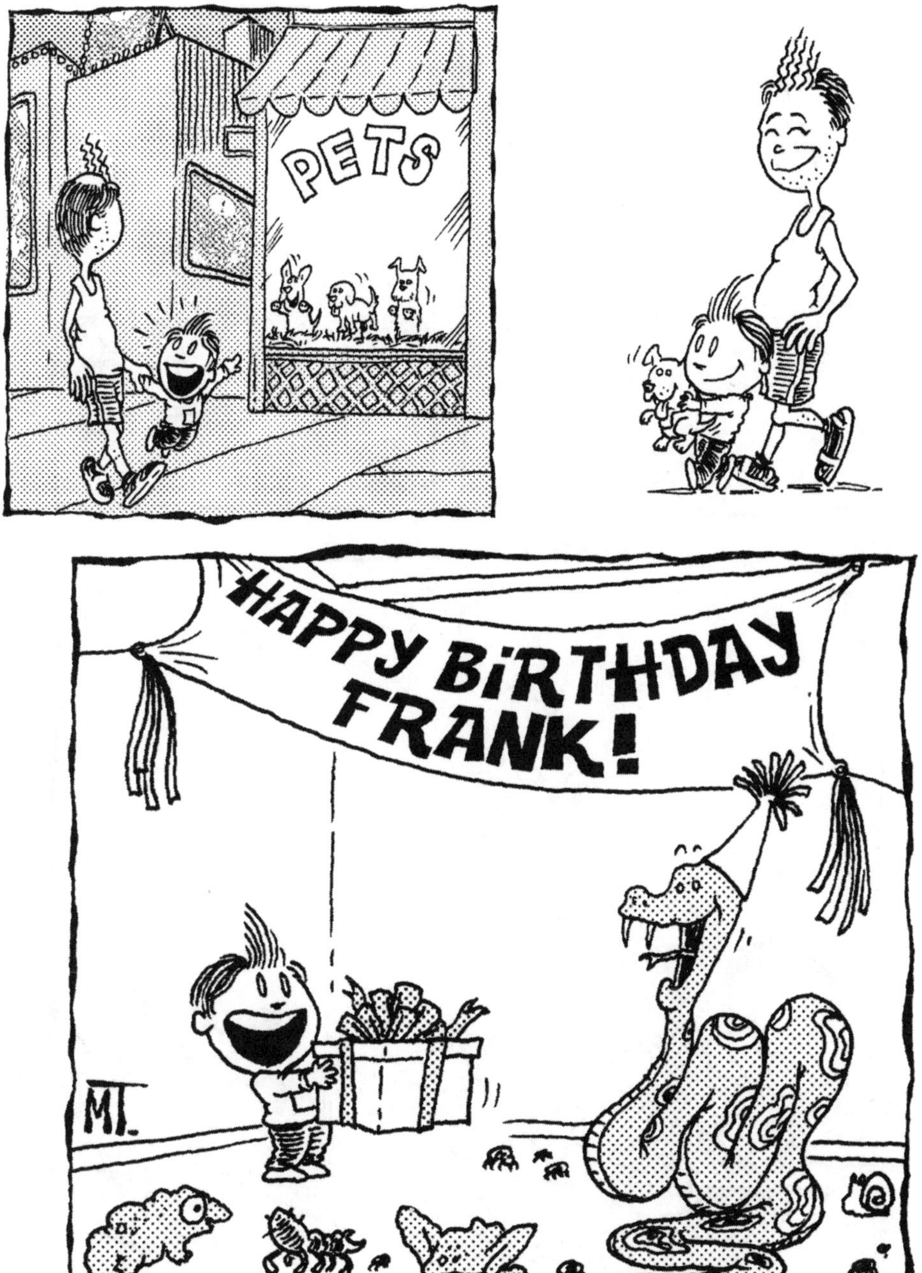
PETS
HAPPY BIRTHDAY FRANK!
MT.

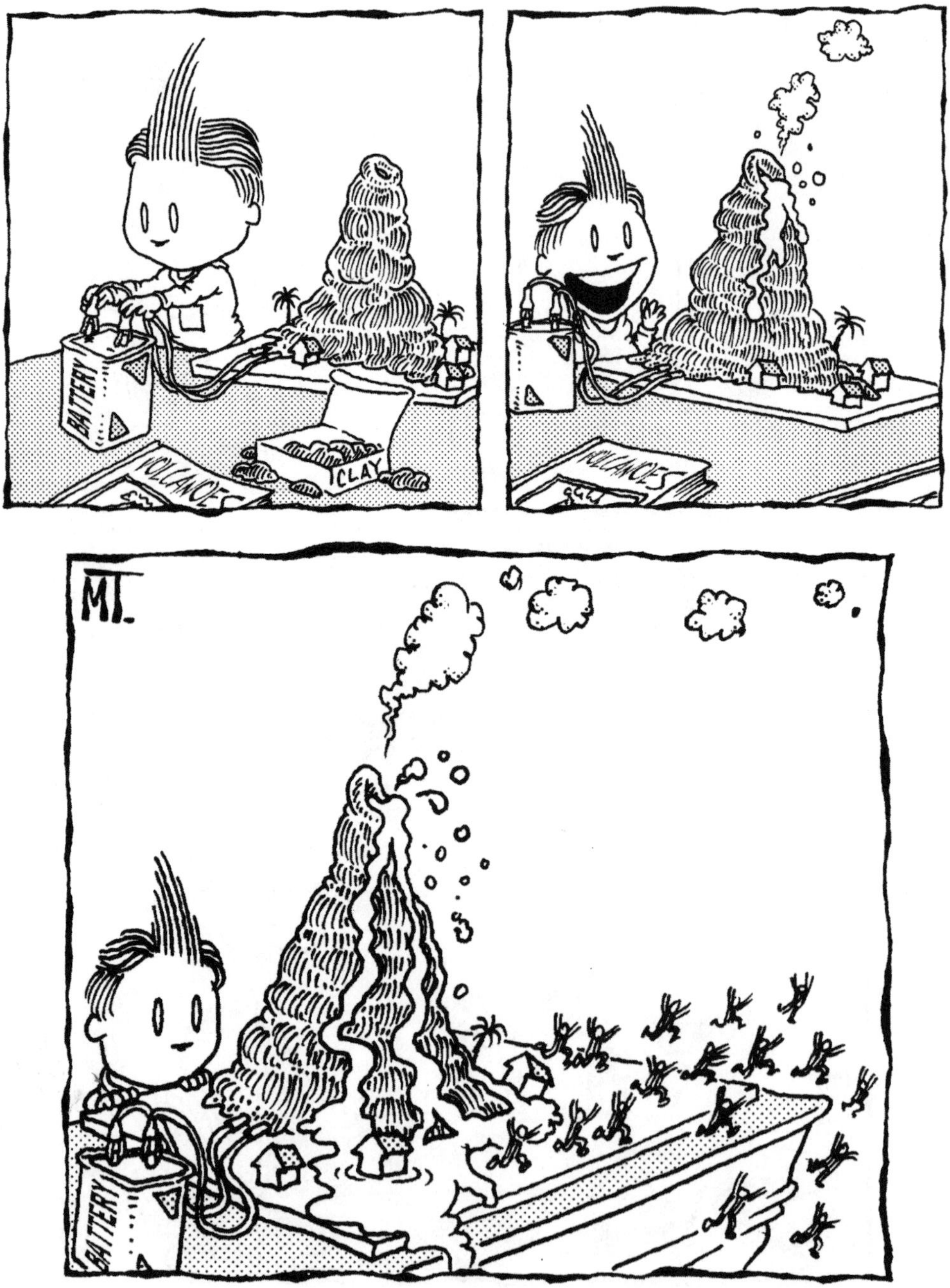
BATTERY
VOLCANOES
CLAY
VOLCANOES
MT.
BATTERY

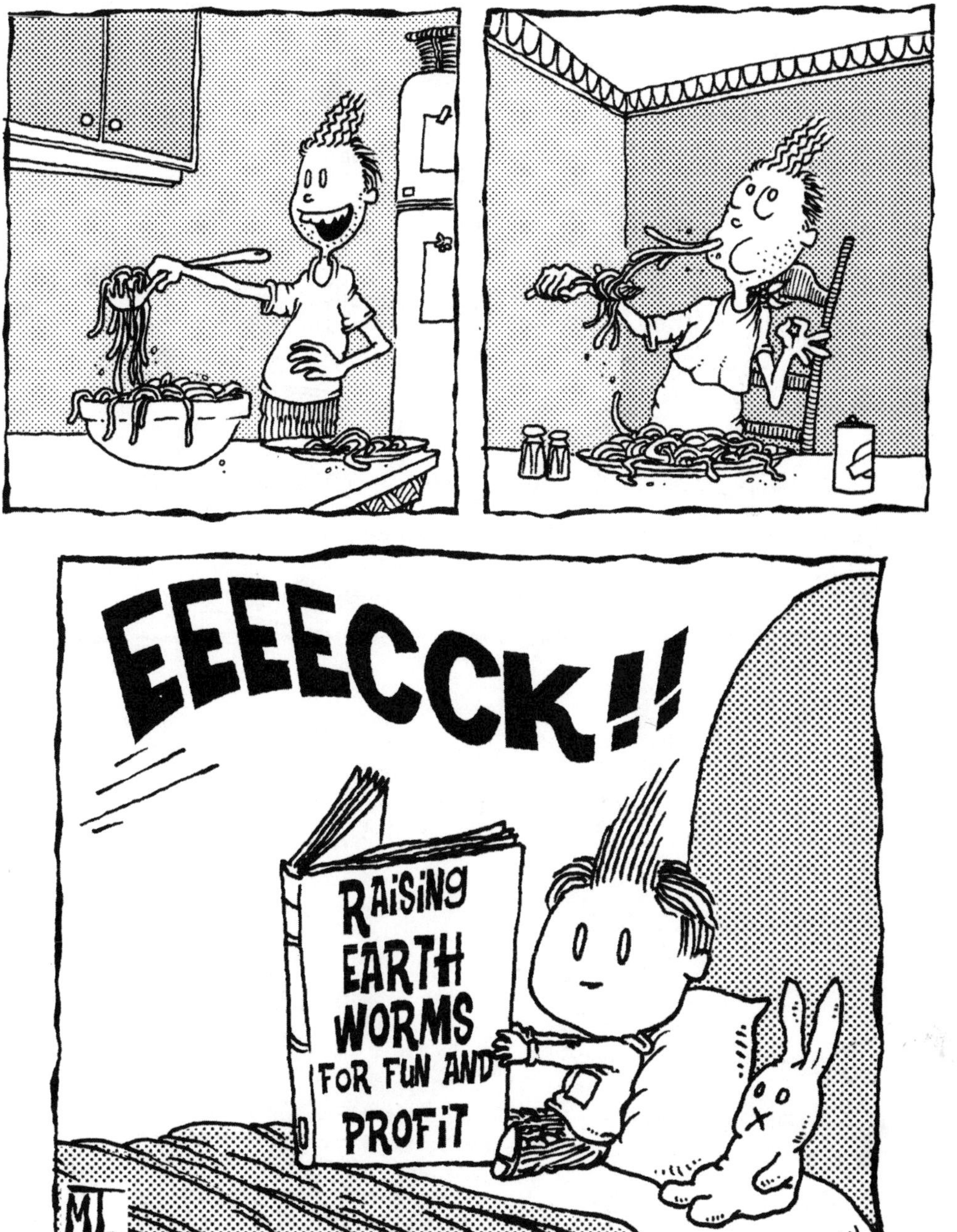
EEEECCK!!
RAISING EARTH WORMS FOR FUN AND PROFIT
MT

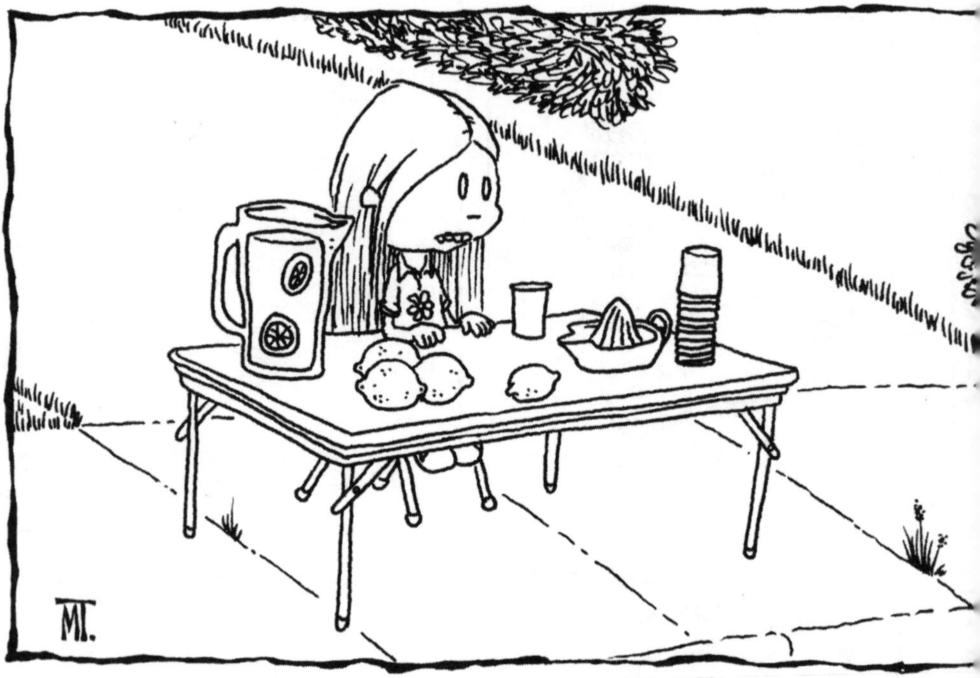
MT.

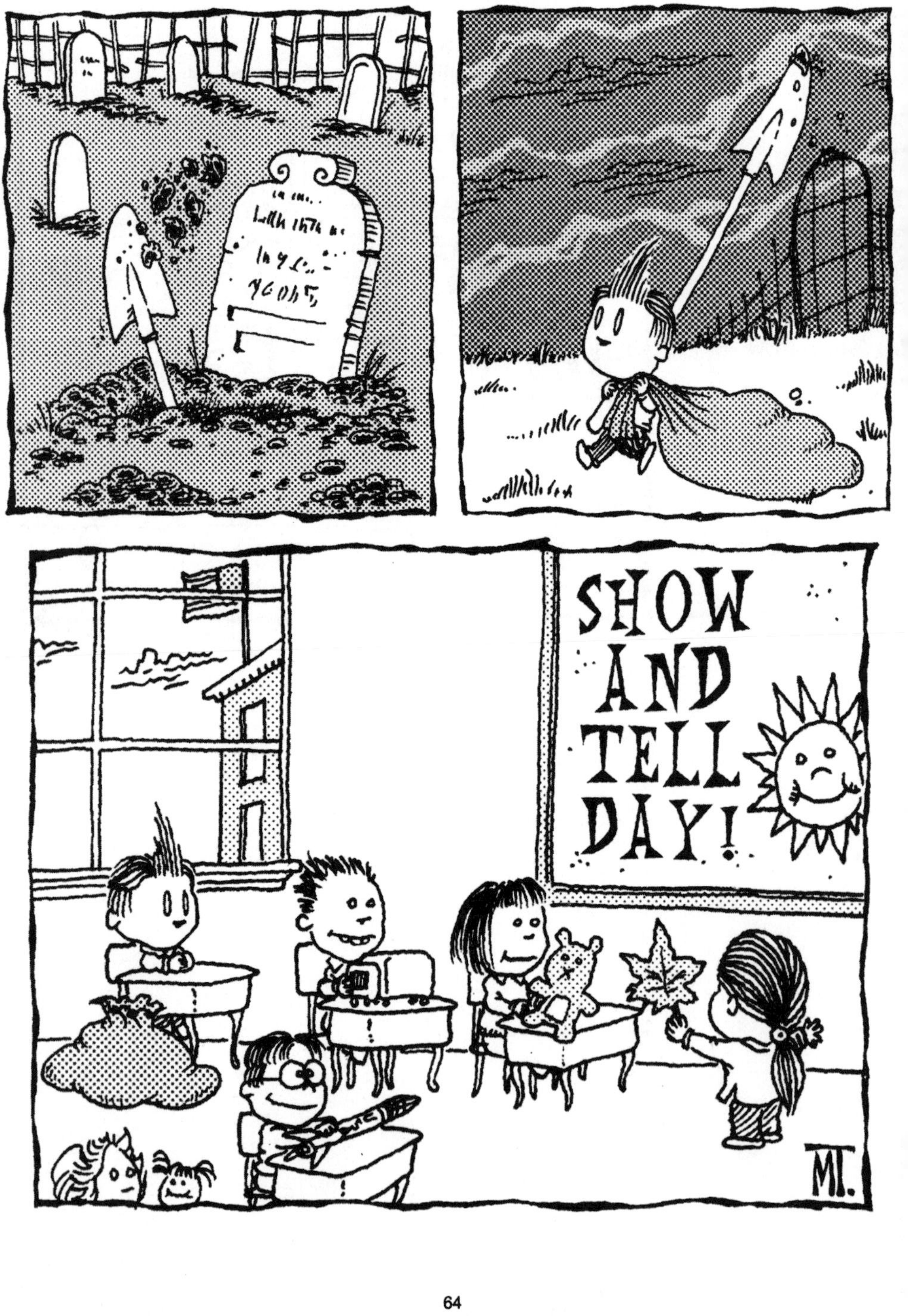
SHOW AND TELL DAY!
MT.

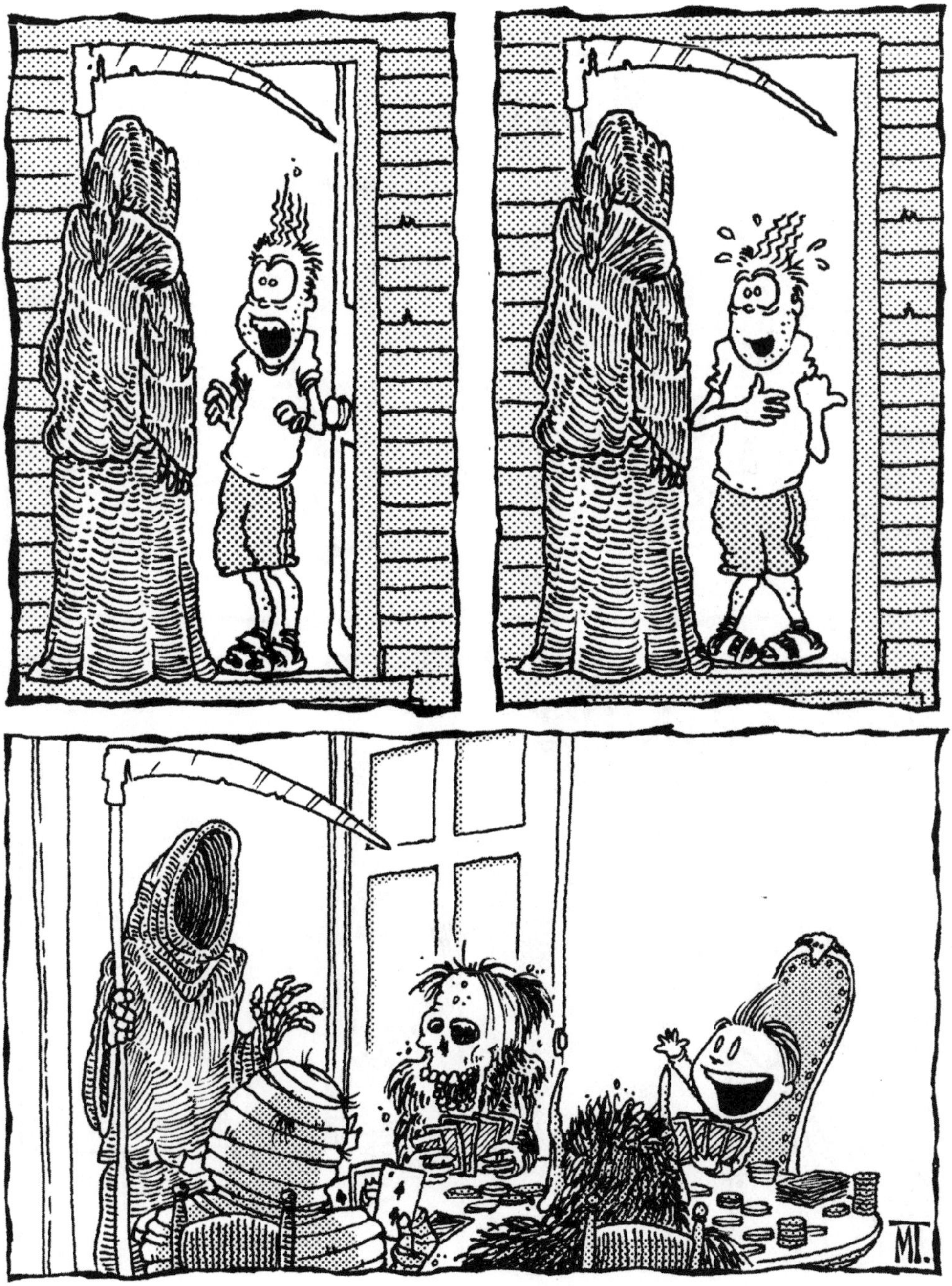

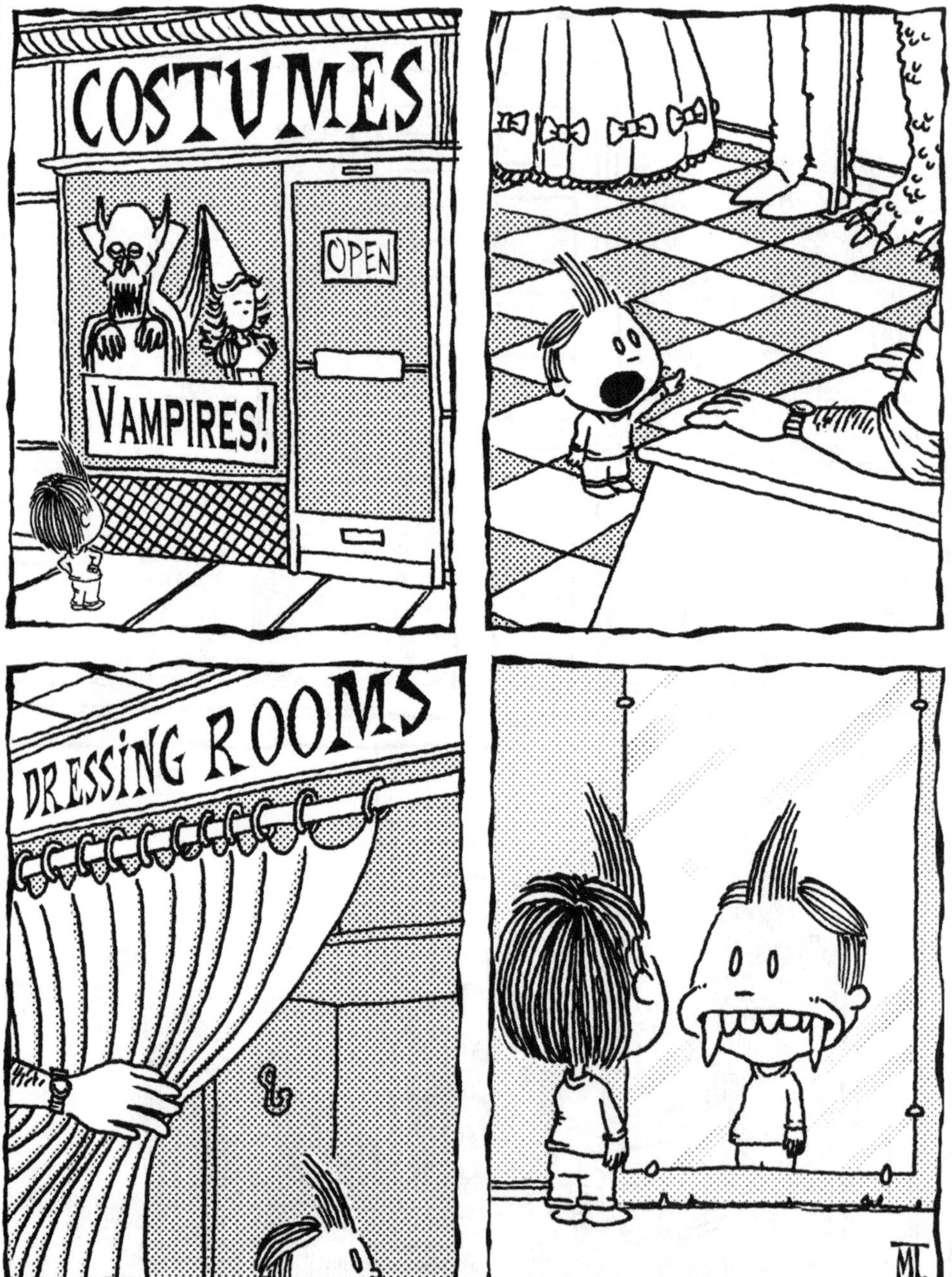
COSTUMES
OPEN
VAMPIRES!
DRESSING ROOMS
MT.

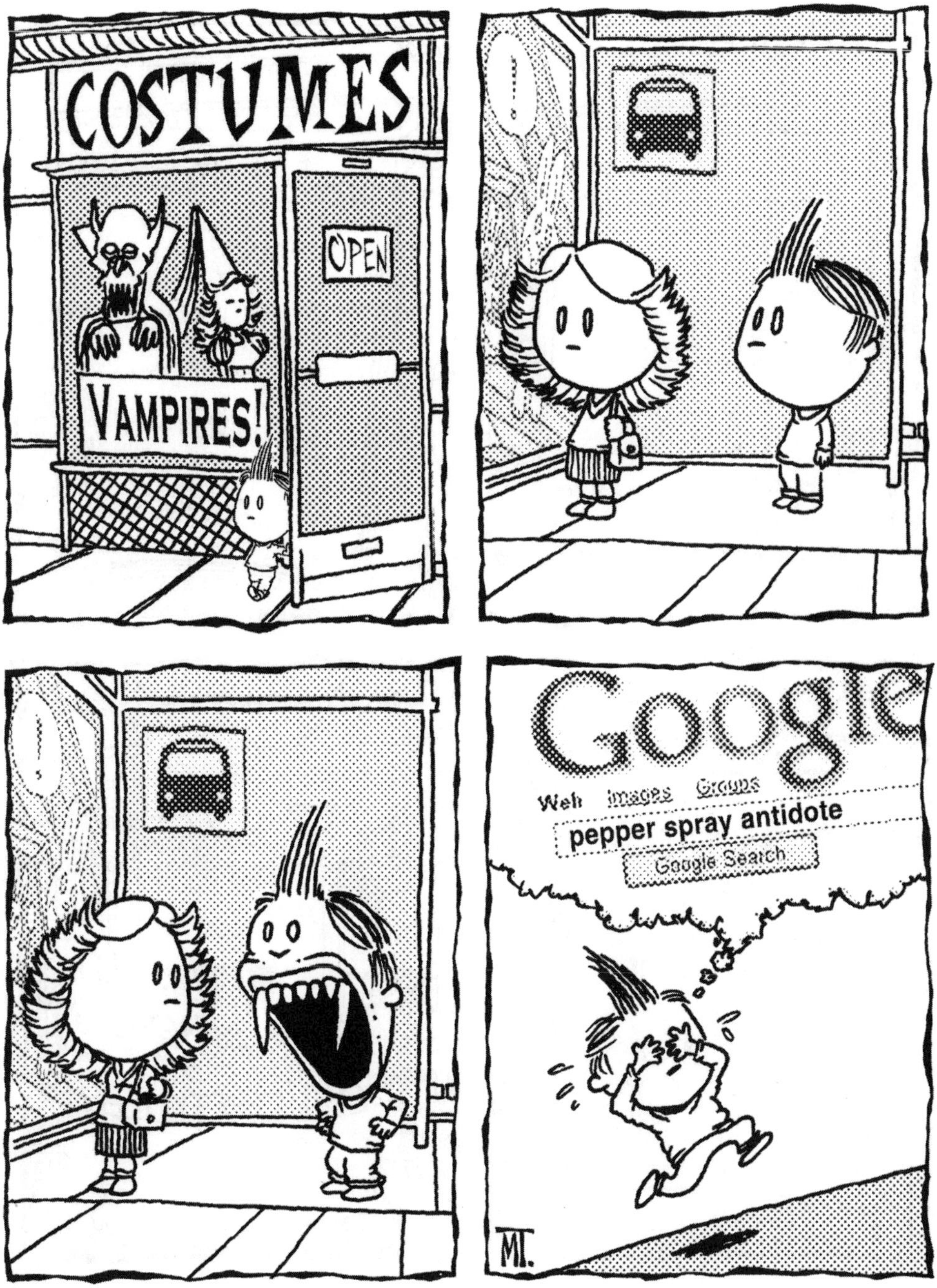
COSTUMES
OPEN
VAMPIRES!
!
!
Google
Web Images Groups
pepper spray antidote
Google Search
MI.

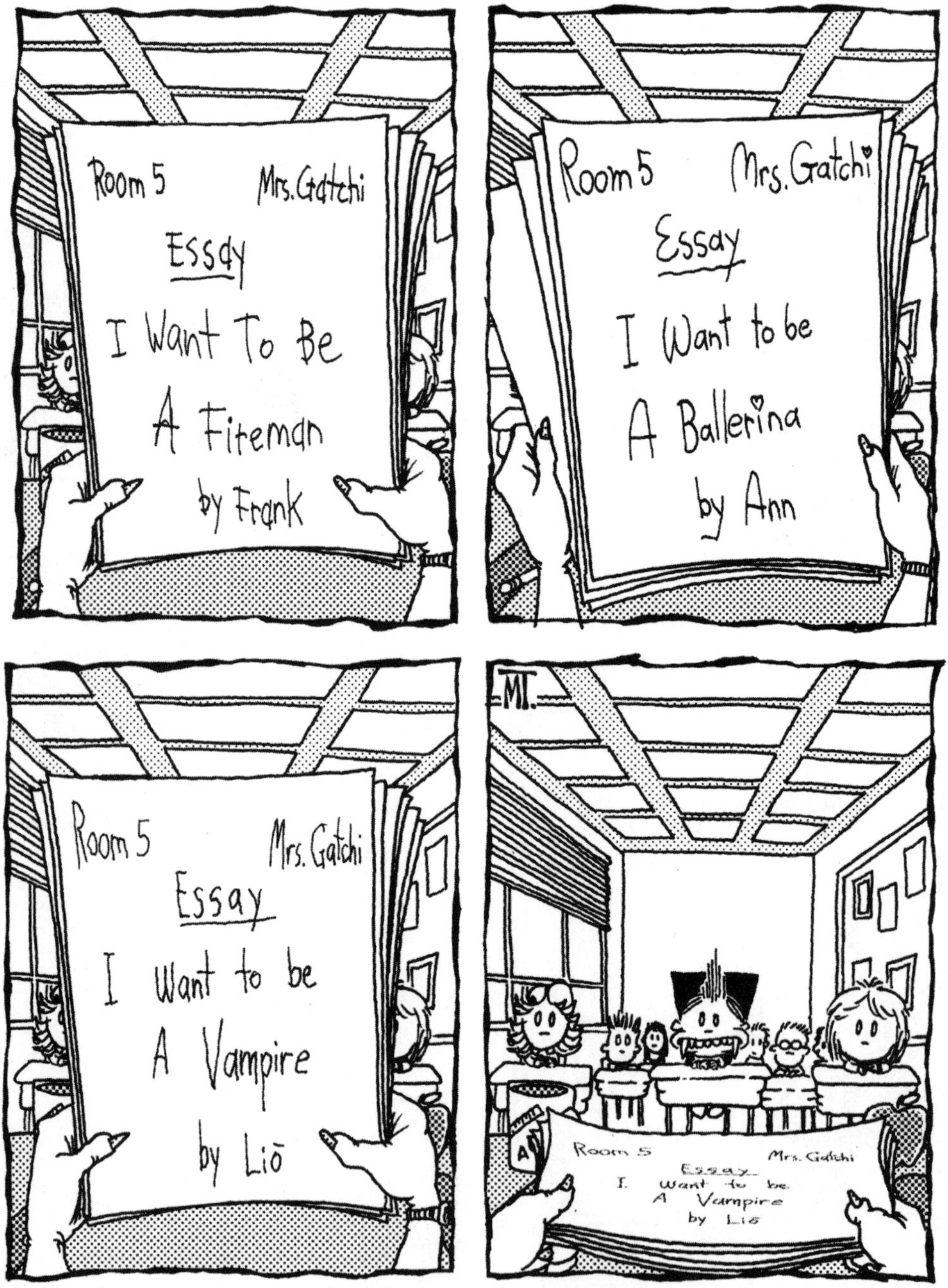
Room 5
Mrs. Gatchi
Essay
I Want To Be
A Fireman
by Frank
Room 5
Mrs. Gatchi
Essay
I Want to be
A Ballerina
by Ann
Room 5
Mrs. Gatchi
Essay
I Want to be
A Vampire
by Liō
Room 5
Mrs. Gatchi
Essay
I Want to be
A Vampire
by Liō

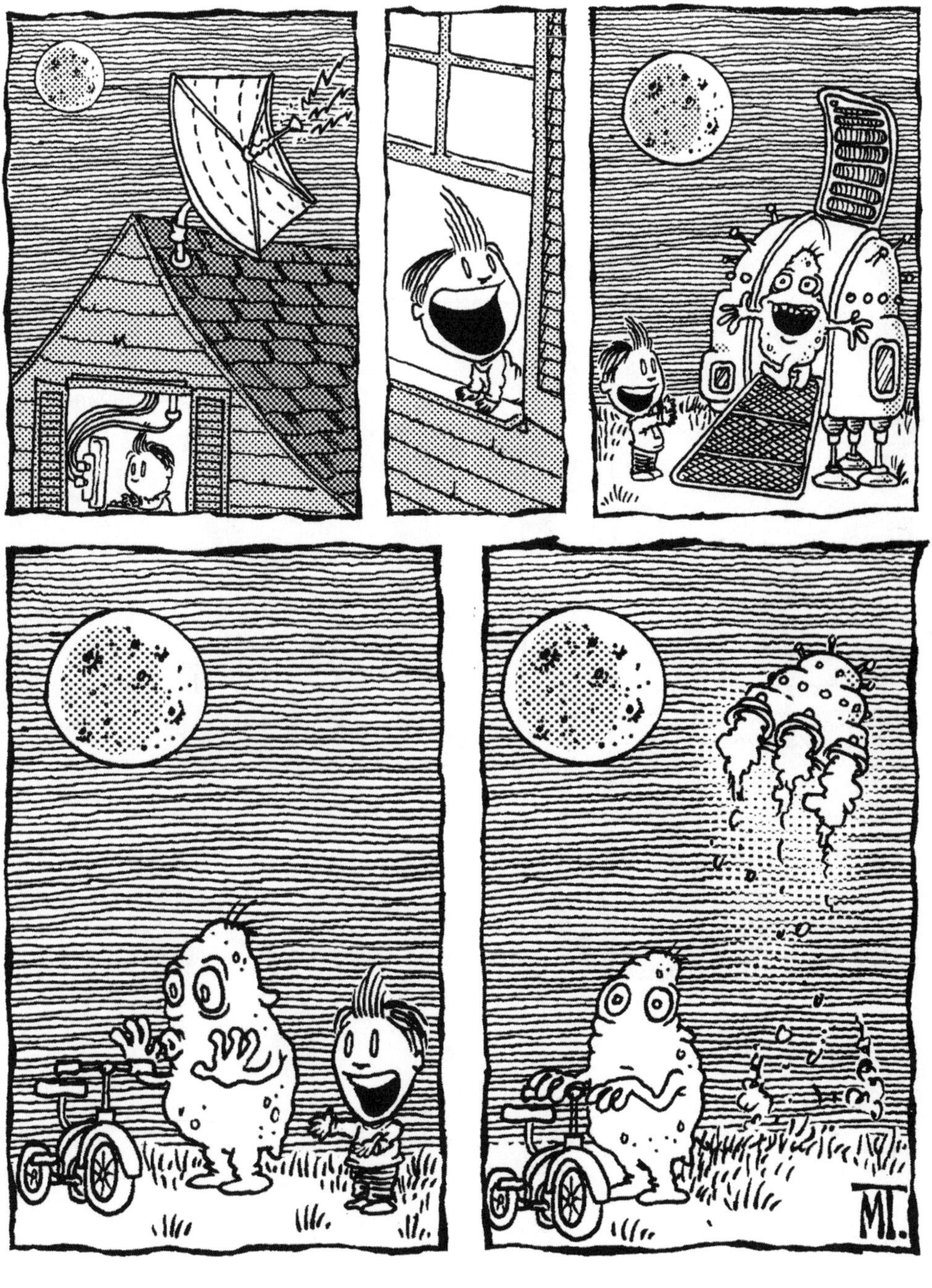
MT.

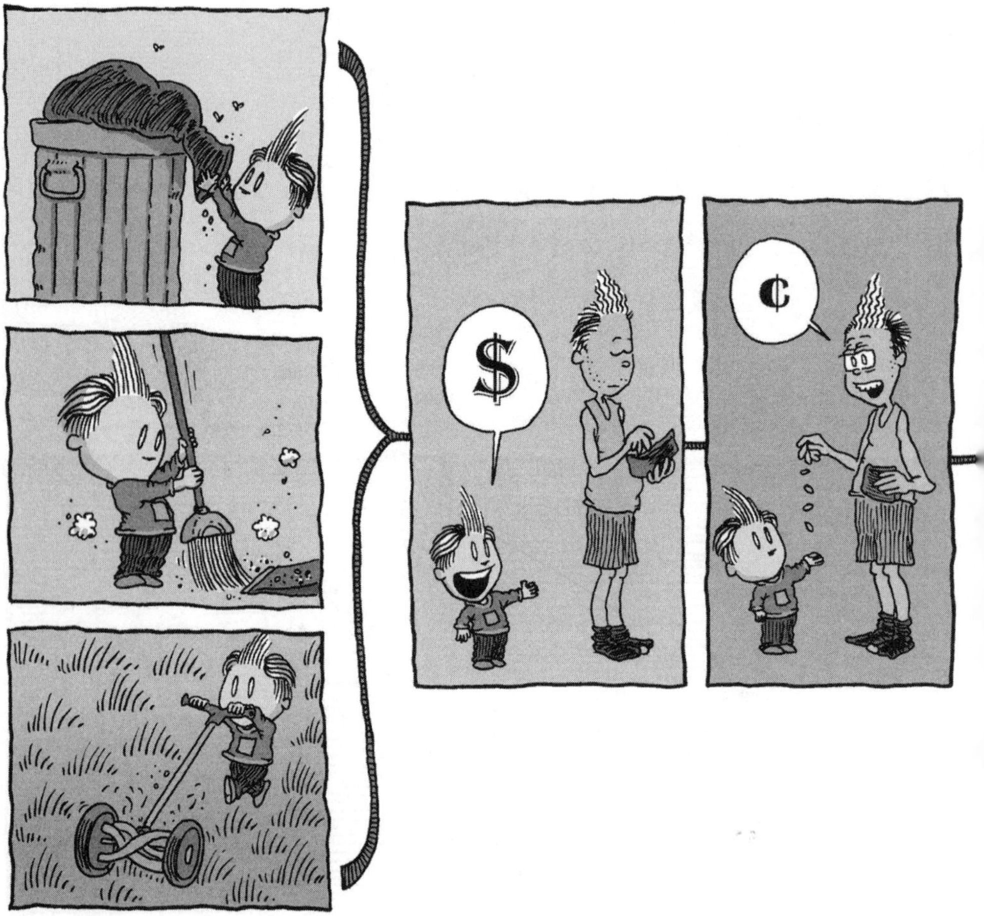
$
¢

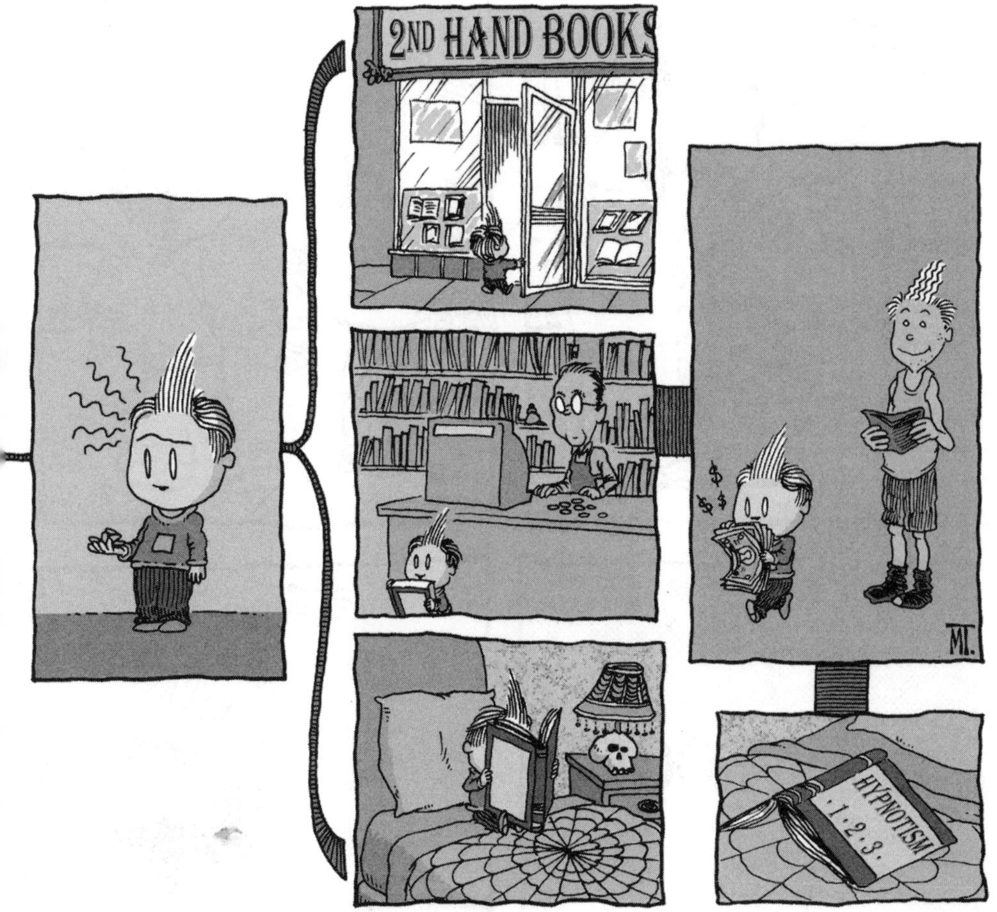
2ND HAND BOOKS
HYPNOTISM
·1·2·3·
MT.

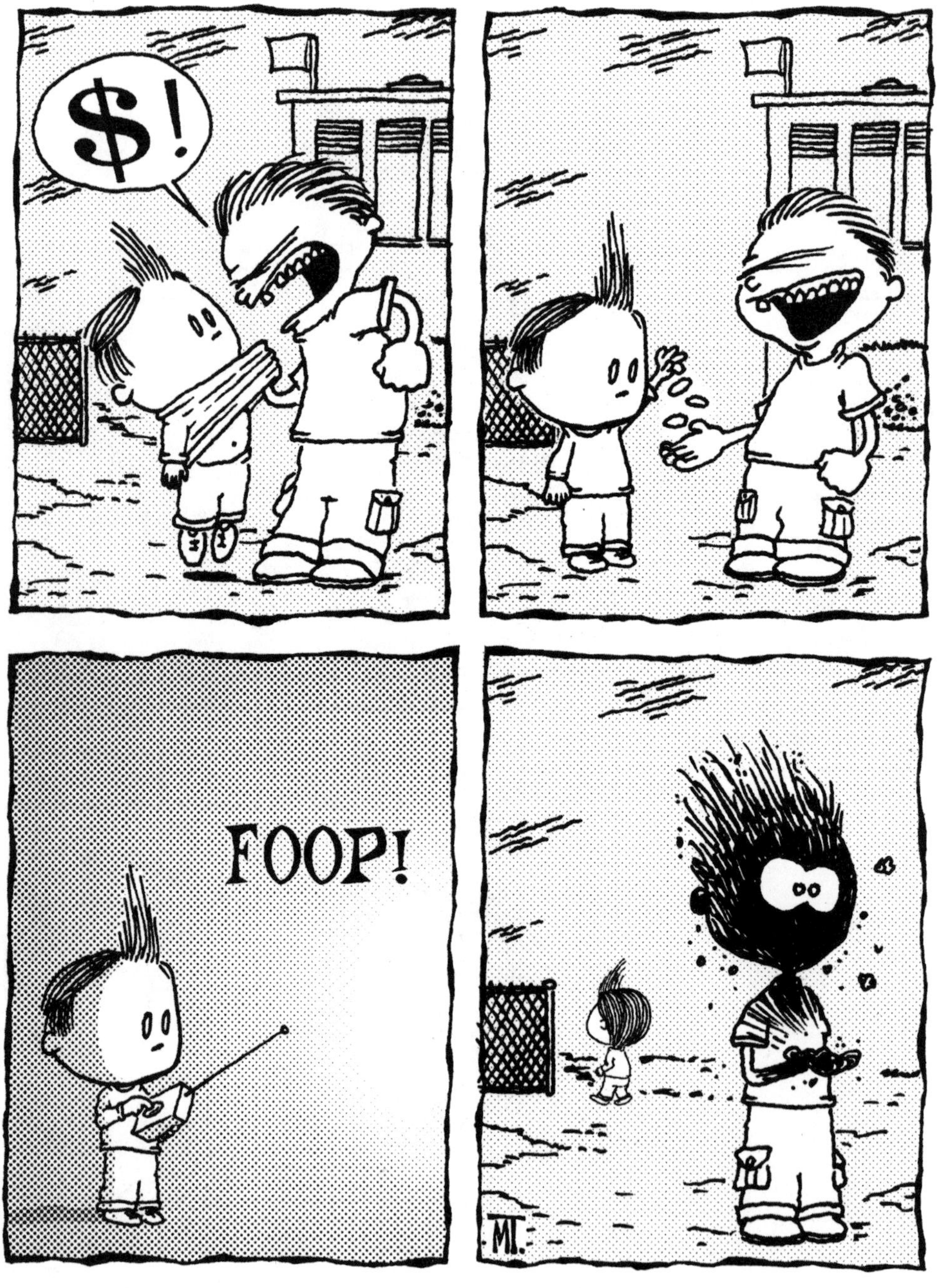
$!
FOOP!
MI.

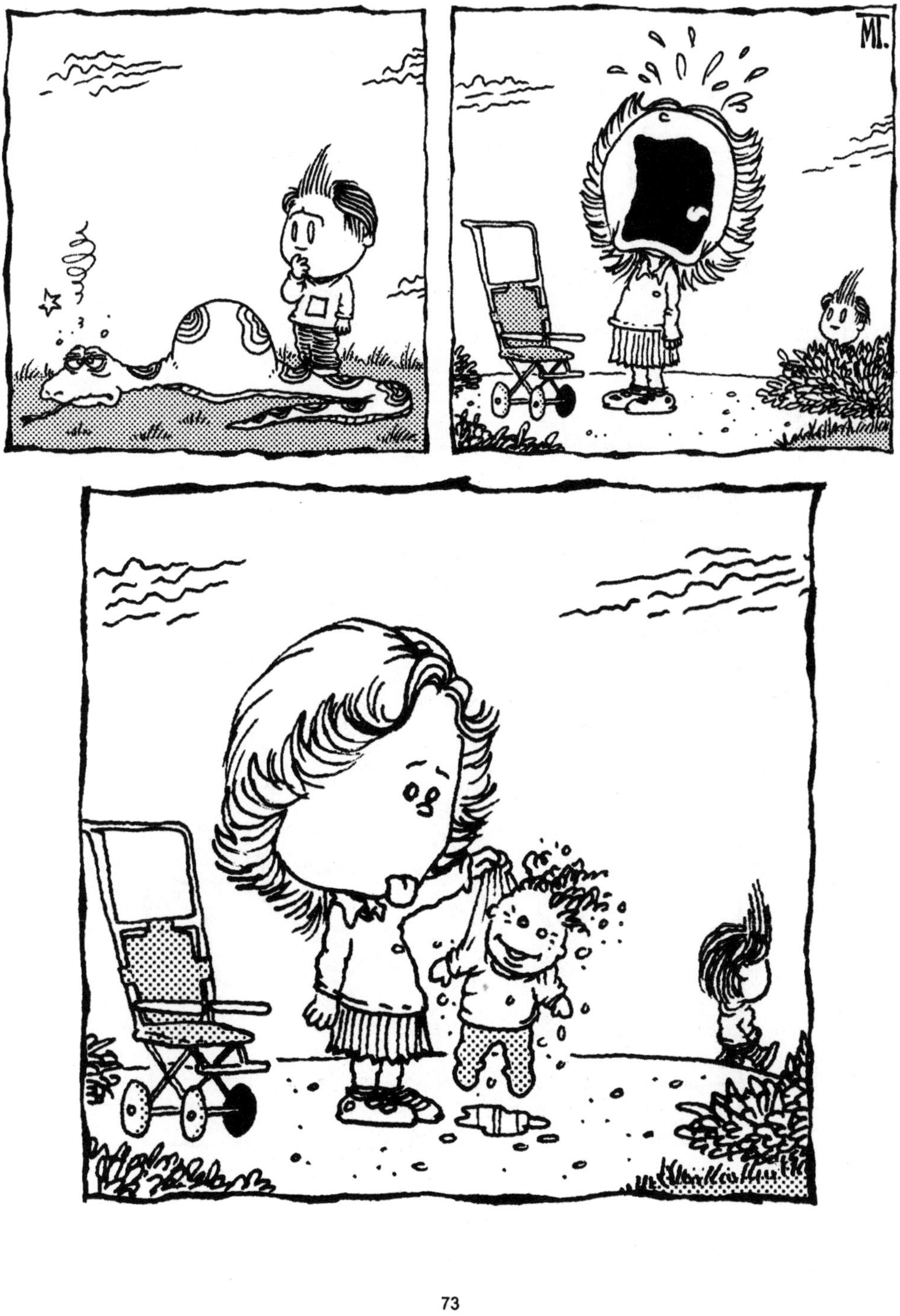

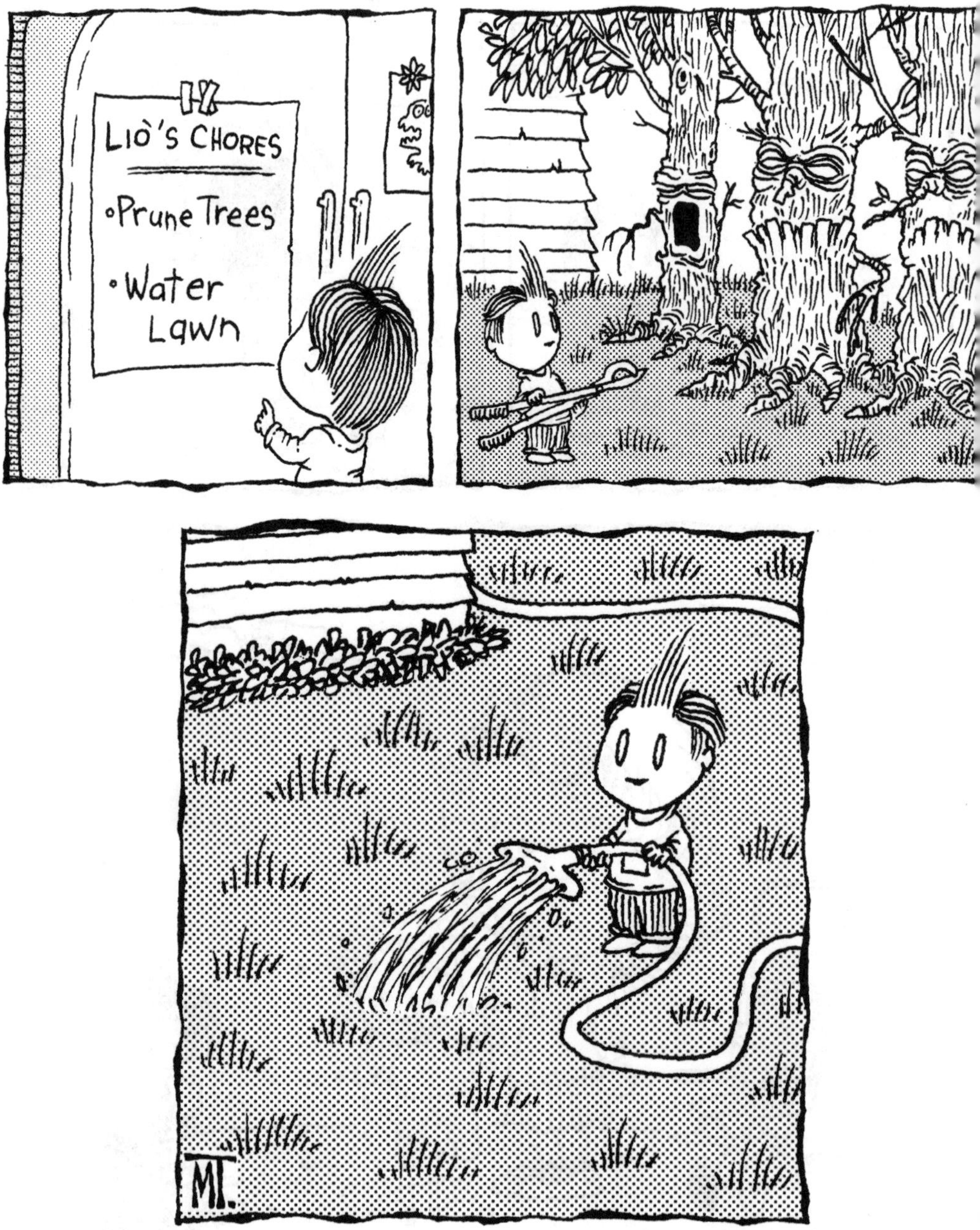
LIO'S CHORES
•Prune Trees
•Water Lawn

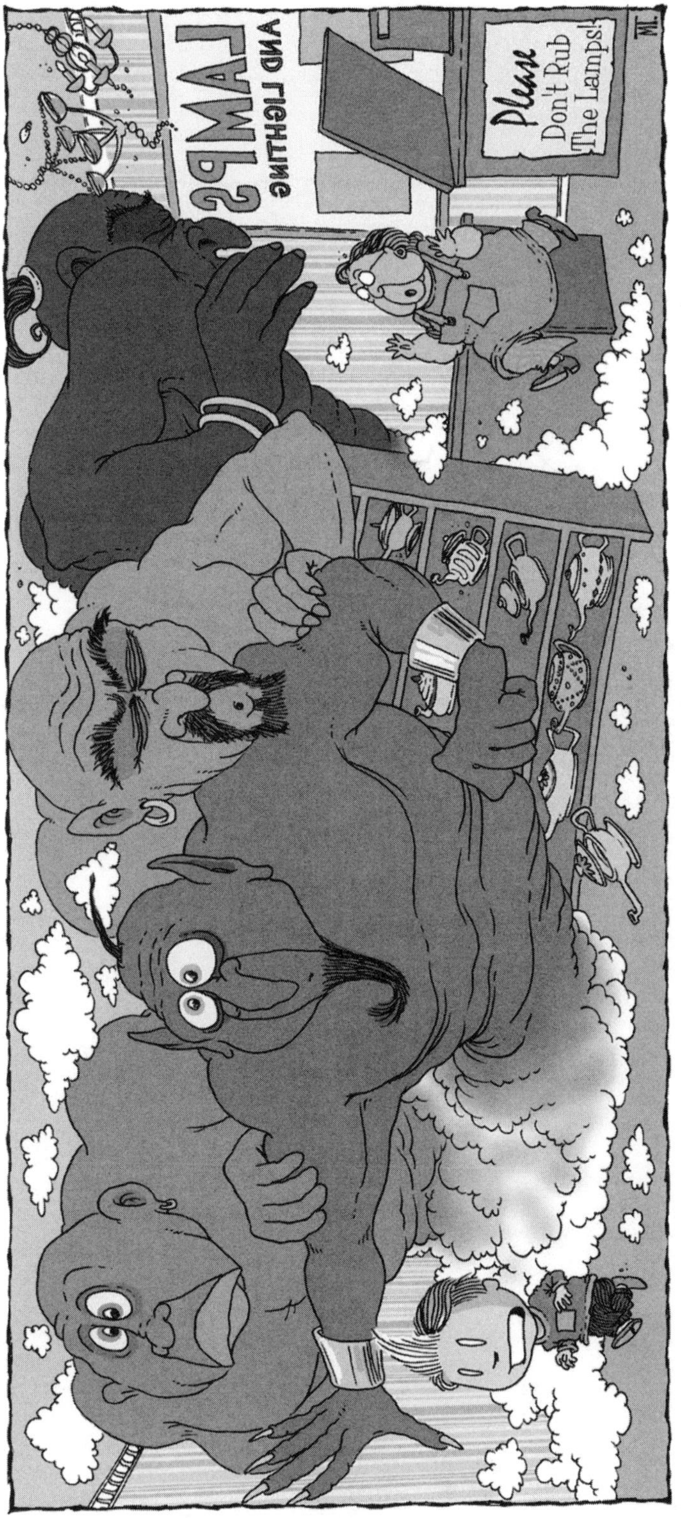
LAMPS AND LIGHTING
Please Don't Rub The Lamps!
ML

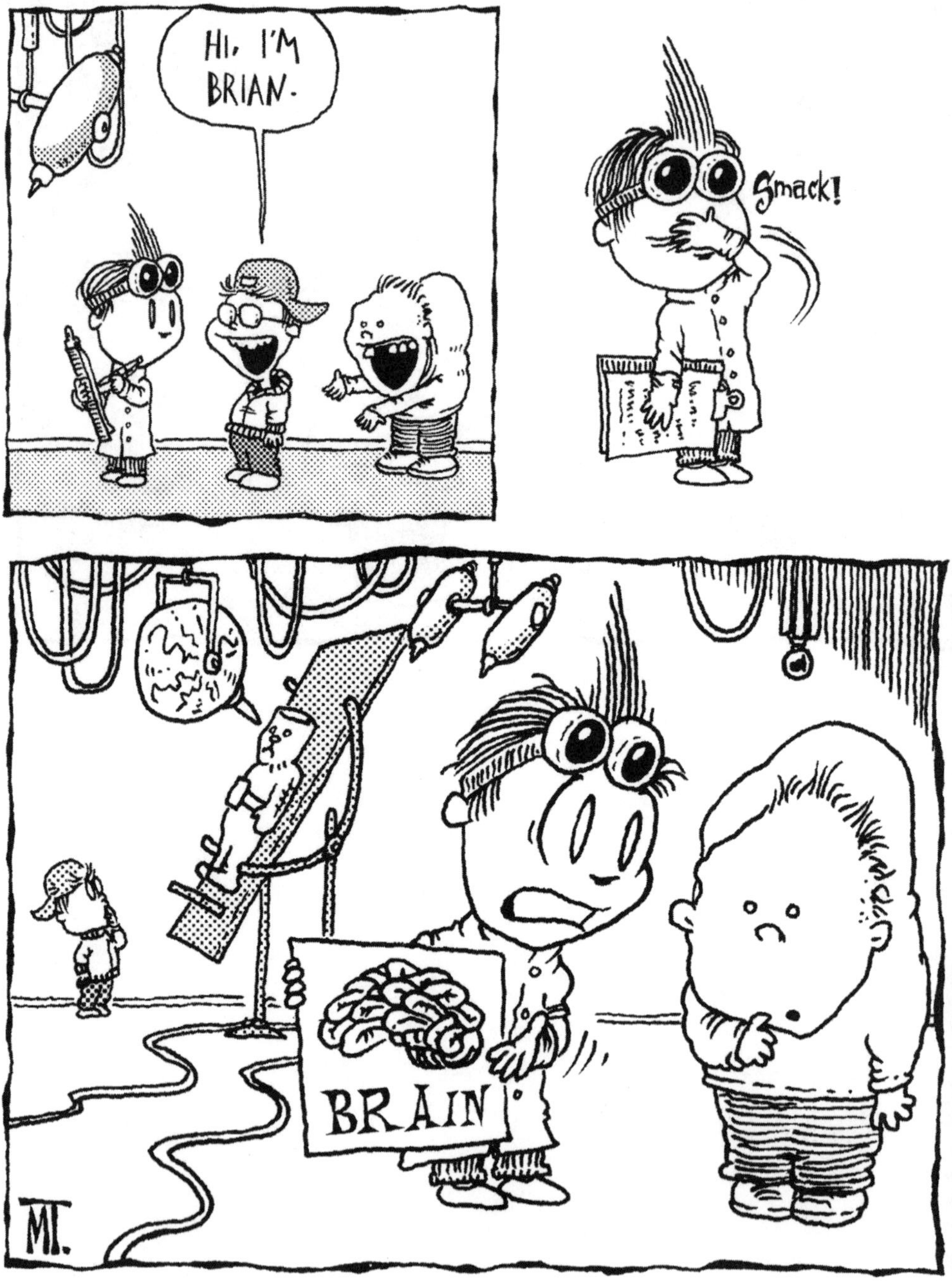
HI, I'M BRIAN.
SMACK!
BRAIN
MT.

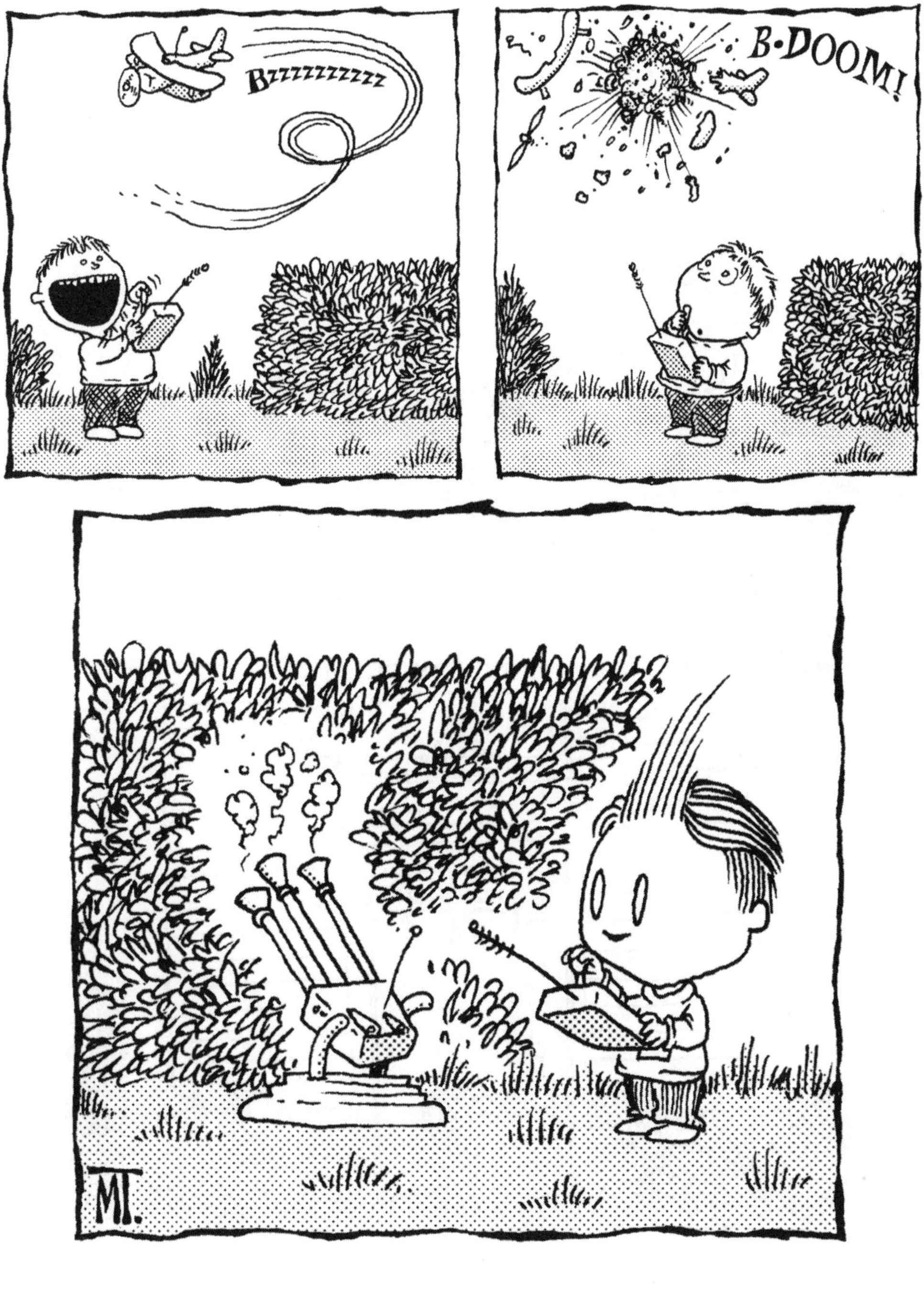
Bzzzzzzzzzzz
B•DOOM!
MT.

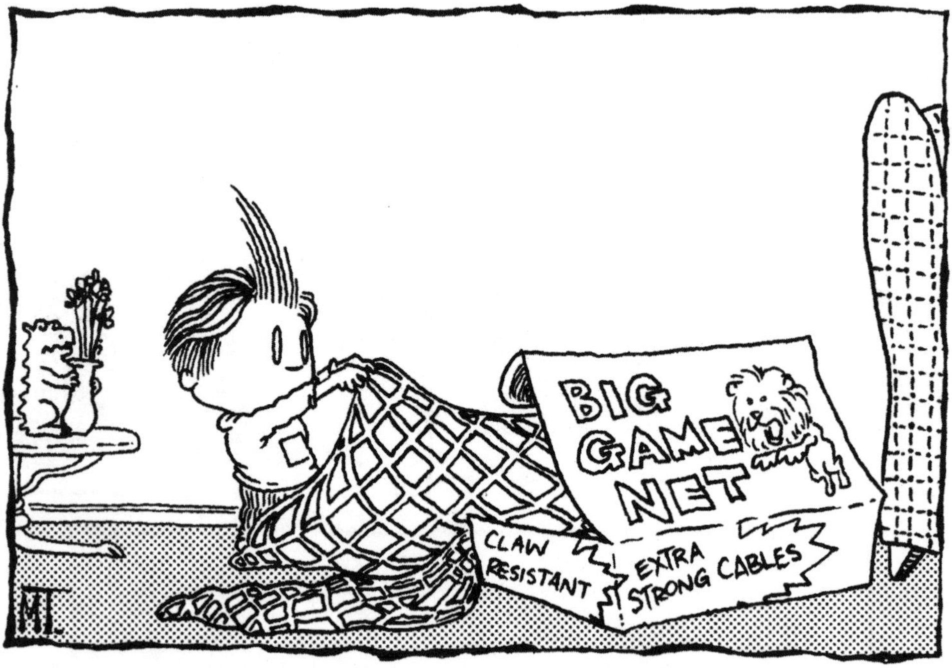
BIG GAME NET
CLAW RESISTANT
EXTRA STRONG CABLES

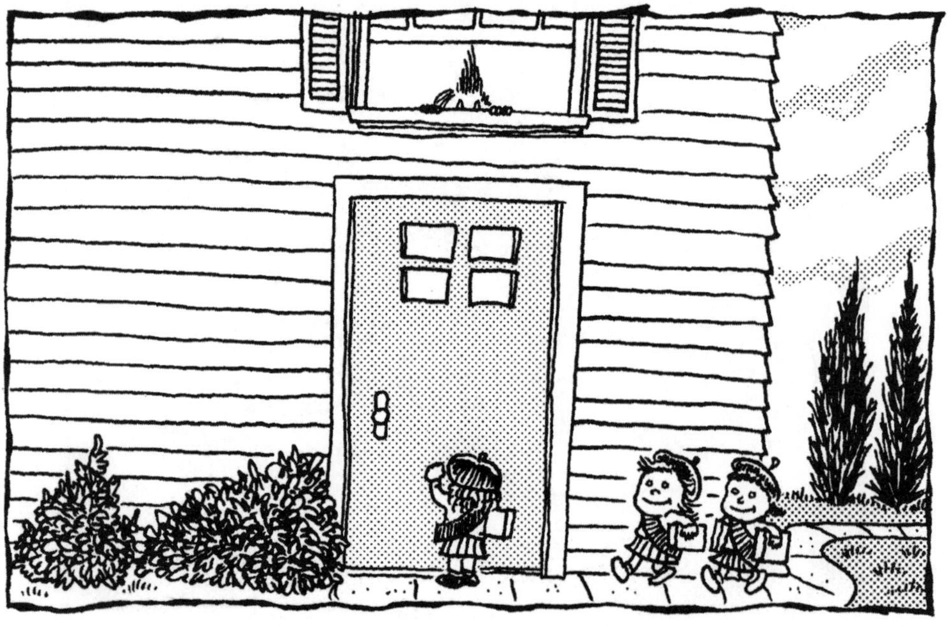

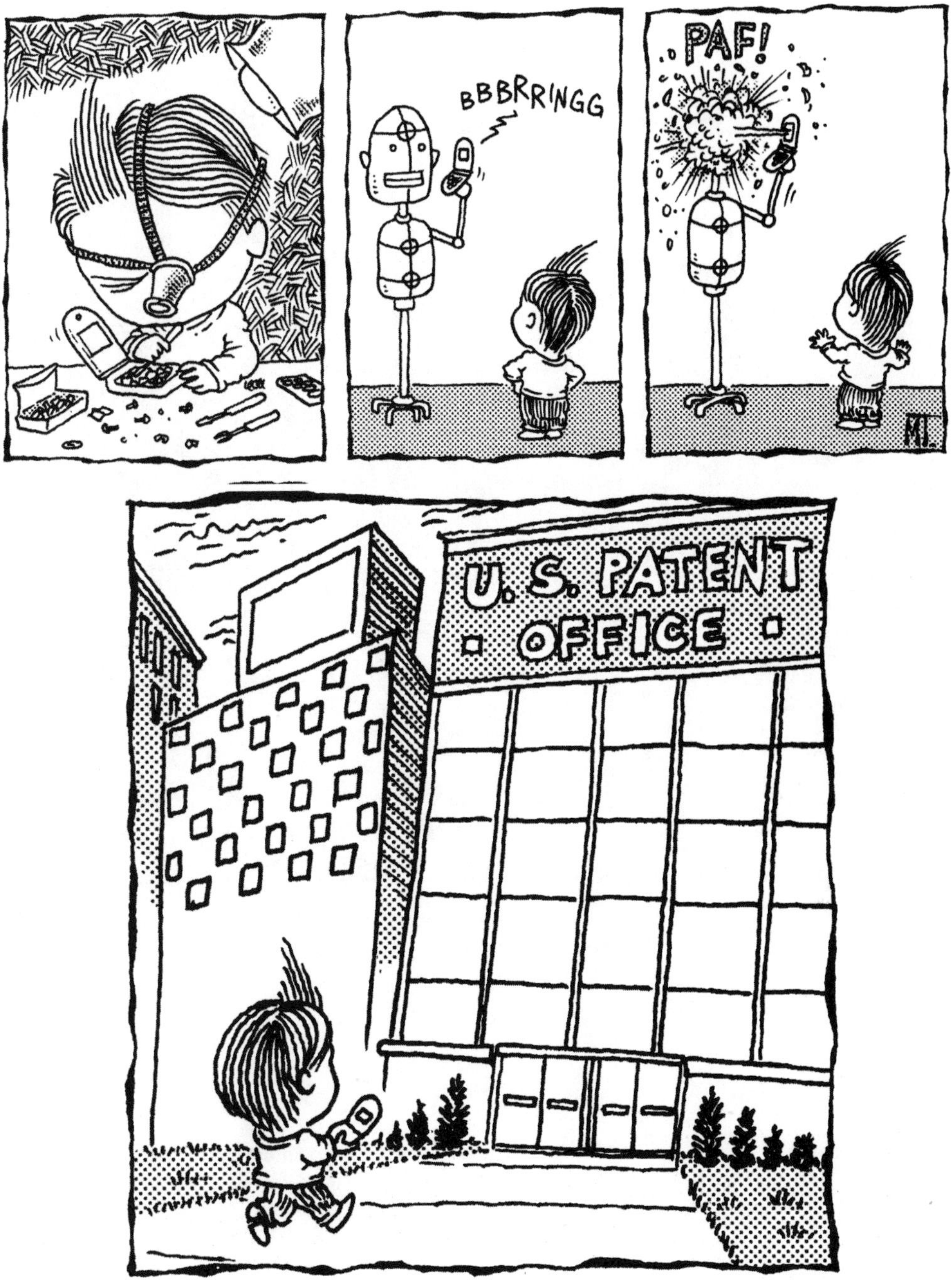
BBBRRINGG
PAF!
U.S. PATENT OFFICE

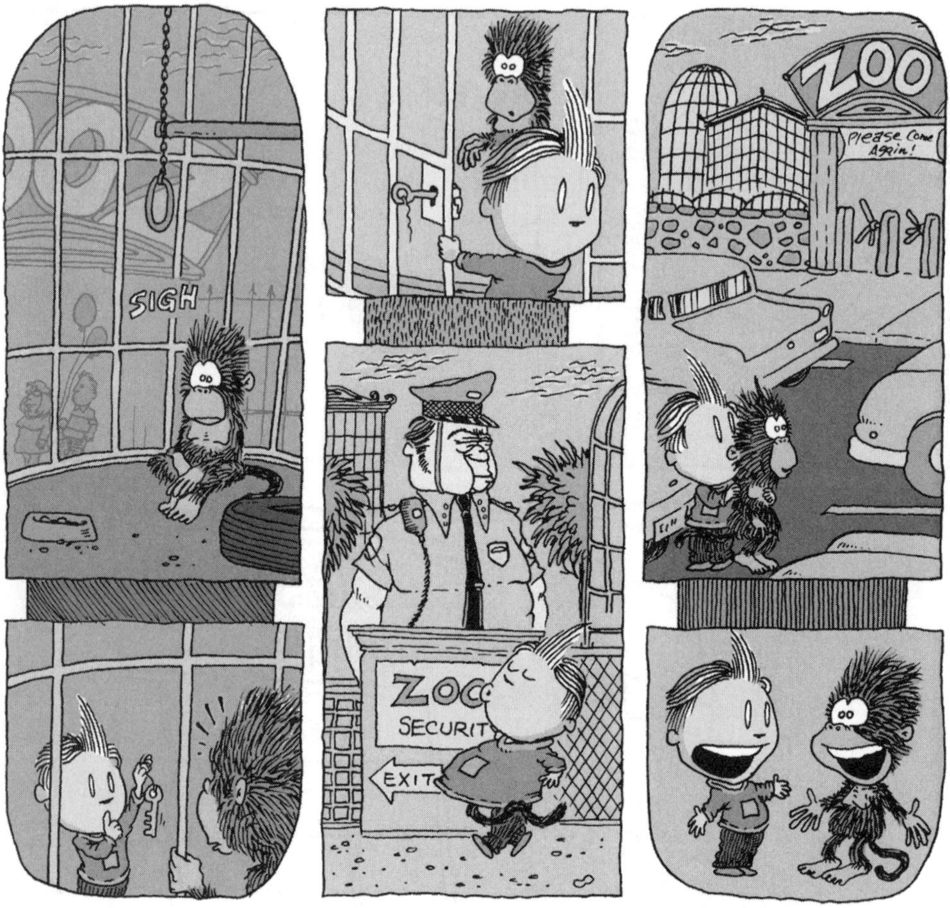
SIGH
ZOO
SECURIT
EXIT
ZOO
Please Come Again!

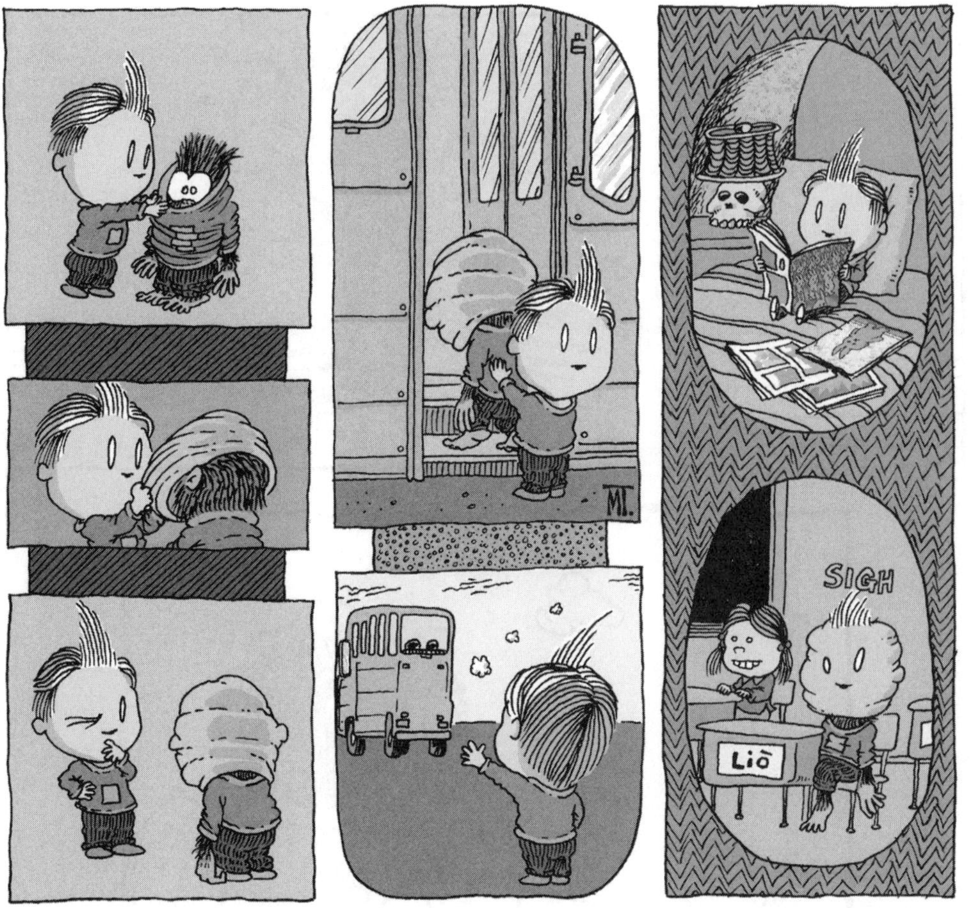
SIGH
Liò

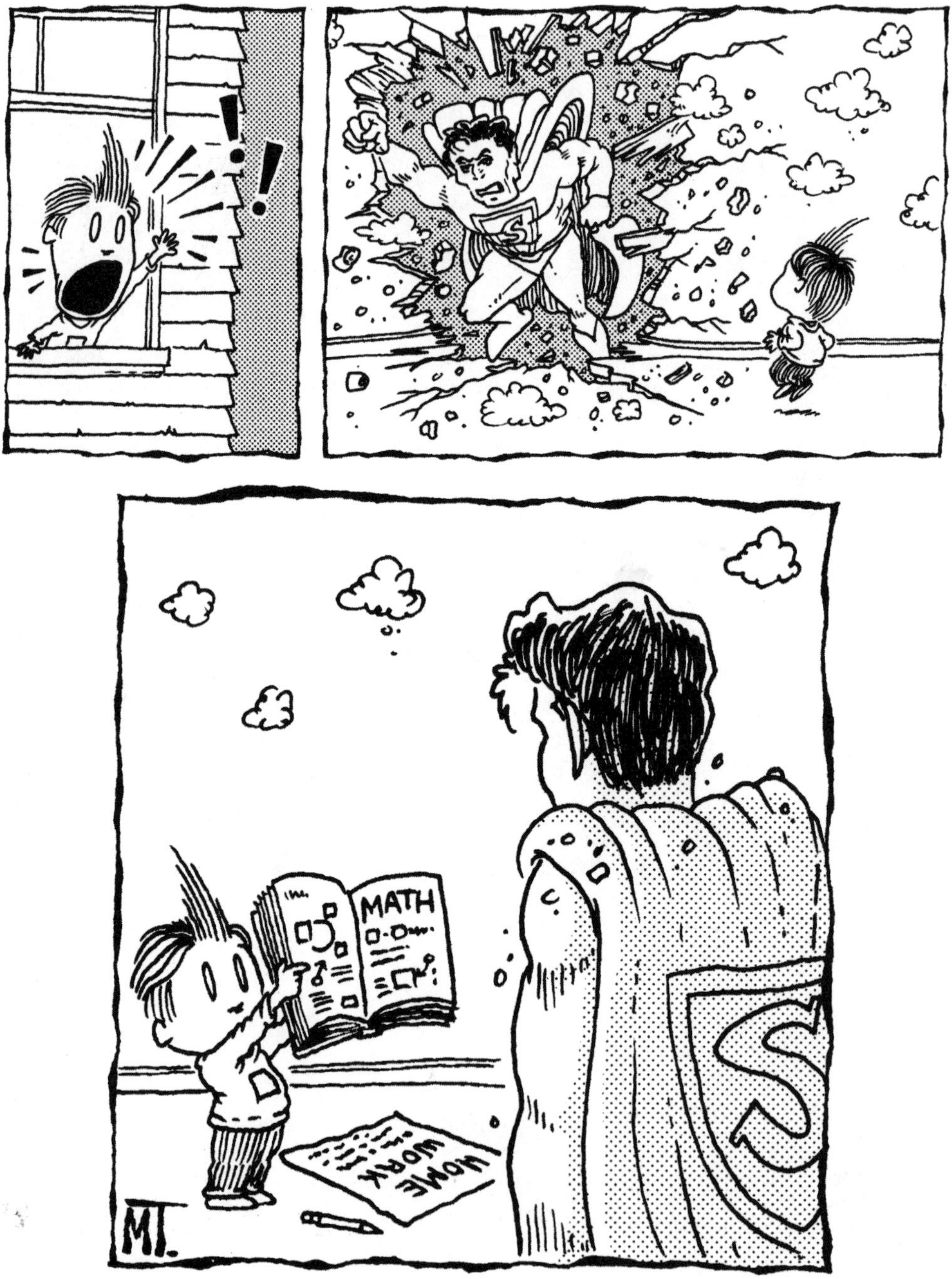
!!
MATH
HOME WORK
MT.

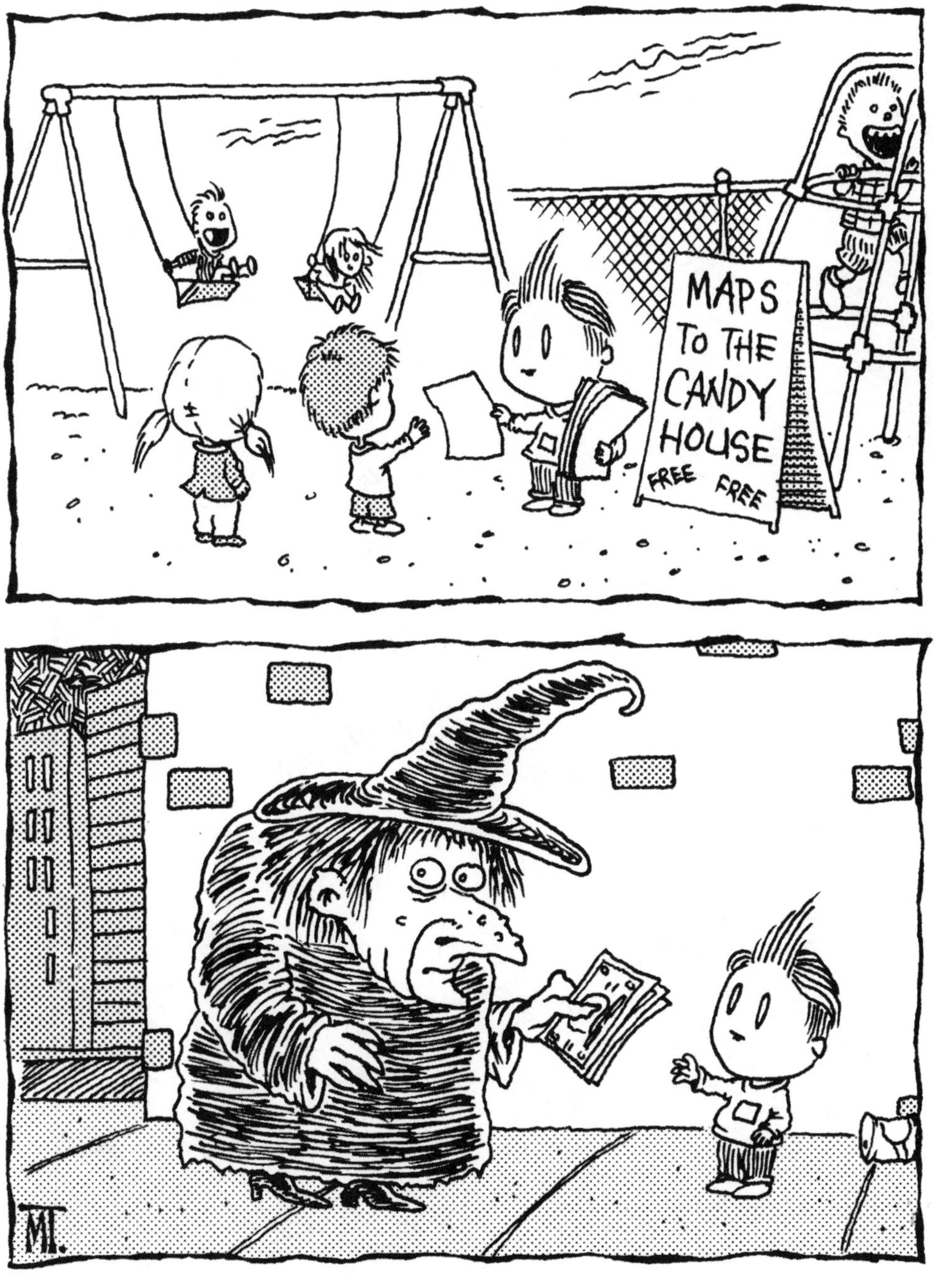
MAPS TO THE CANDY HOUSE
FREE FREE
MT.

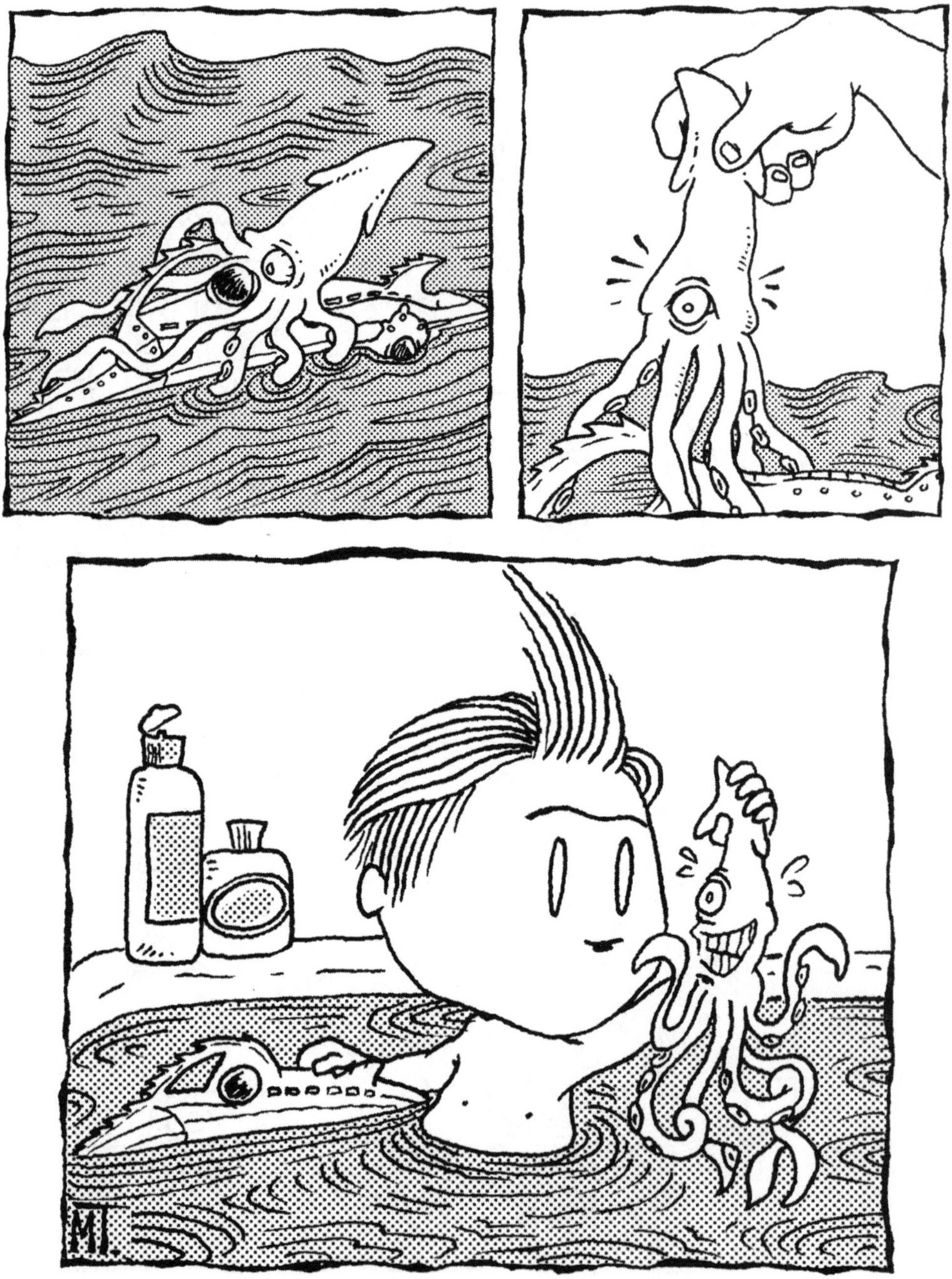

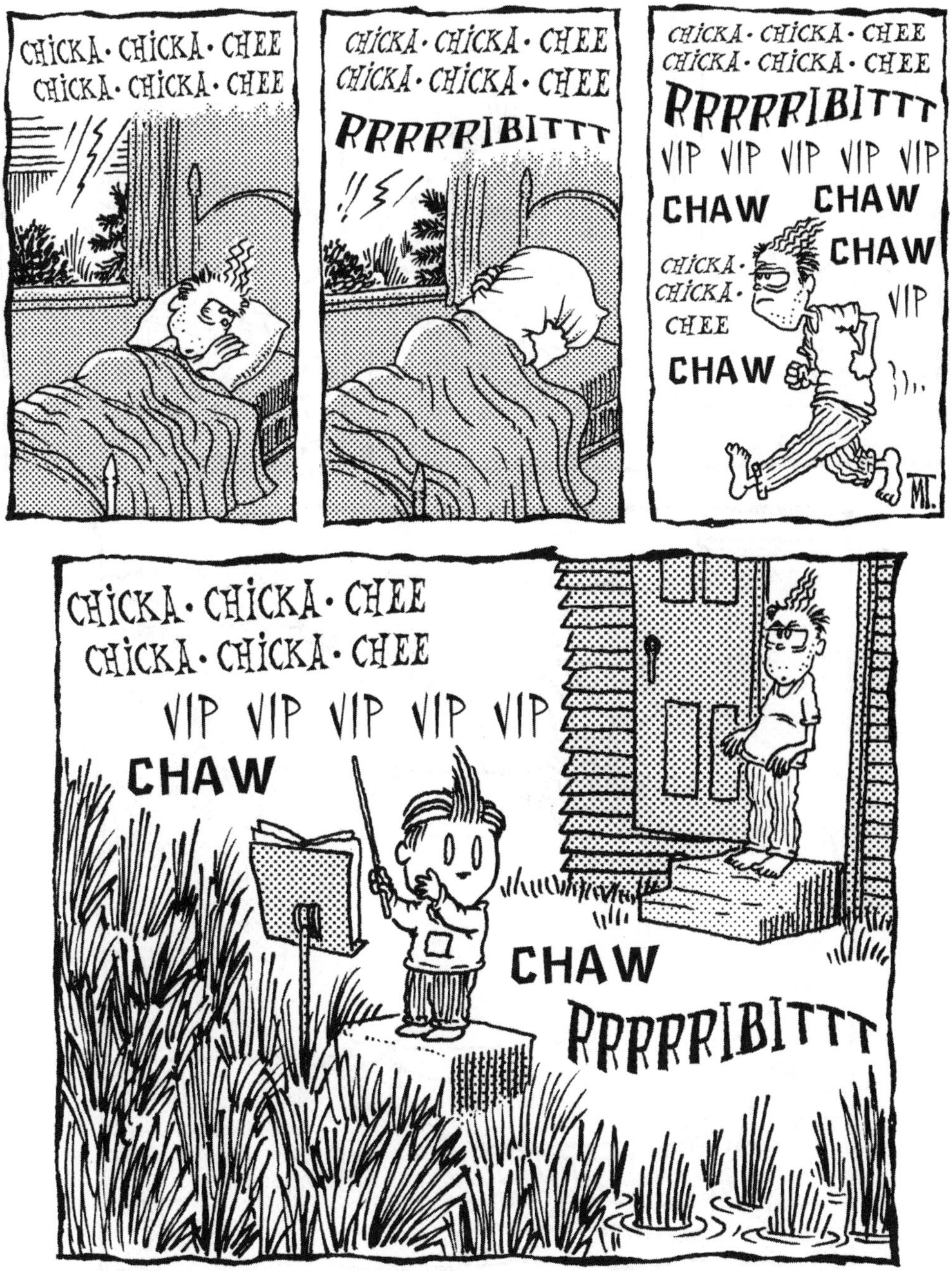
CHICKA · CHICKA · CHEE
CHICKA · CHICKA · CHEE
CHICKA · CHICKA · CHEE
CHICKA · CHICKA · CHEE
RRRRRIBITTTT
CHICKA · CHICKA · CHEE
CHICKA · CHICKA · CHEE
RRRRRIBITTTT
VIP VIP VIP VIP VIP
CHAW CHAW
CHAW
CHICKA · CHICKA · CHEE
VIP
CHAW
MT.
CHICKA · CHICKA · CHEE
CHICKA · CHICKA · CHEE
VIP VIP VIP VIP VIP
CHAW
CHAW
RRRRRIBITTT

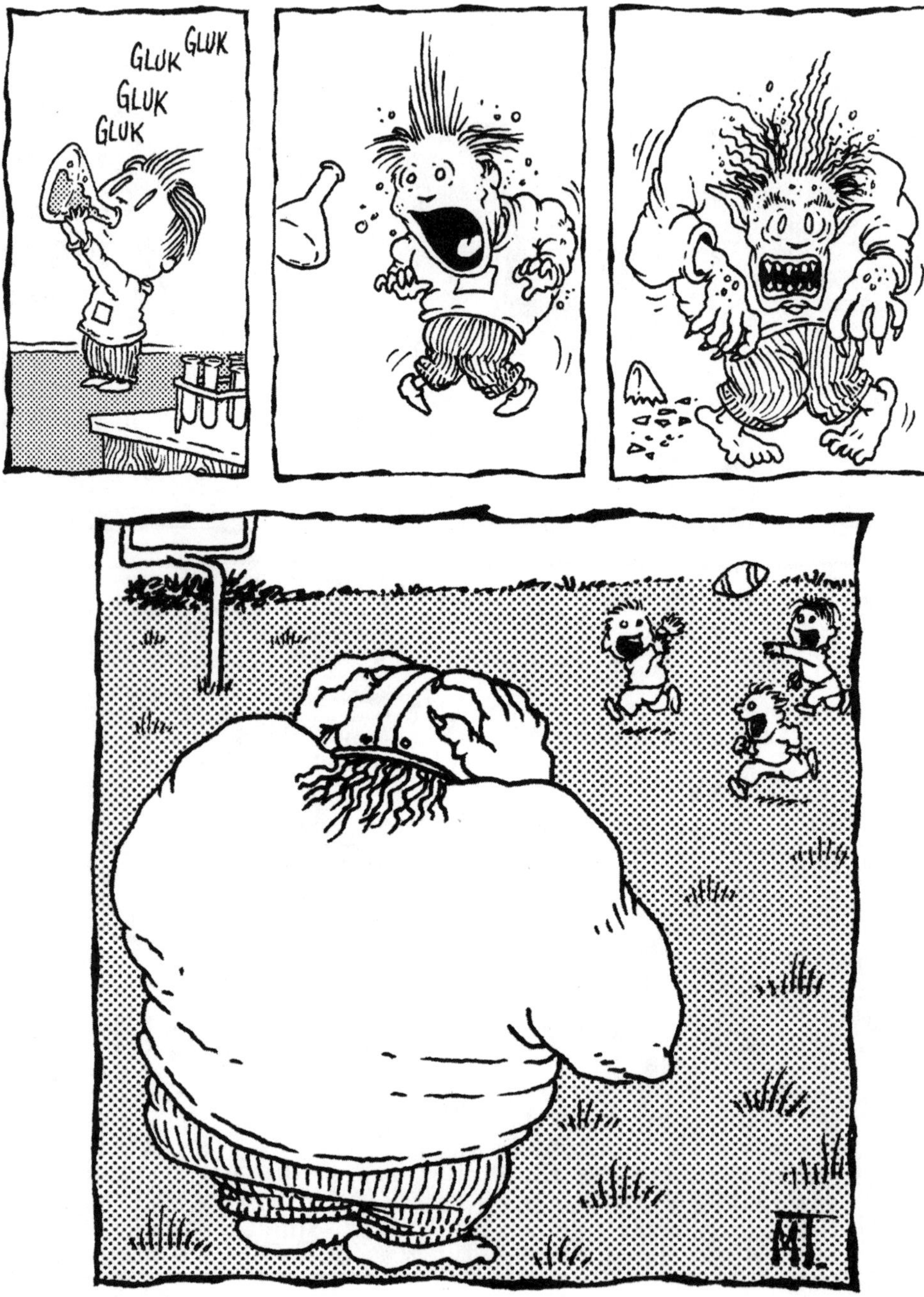
GLUK
GLUK
GLUK
GLUK
ML

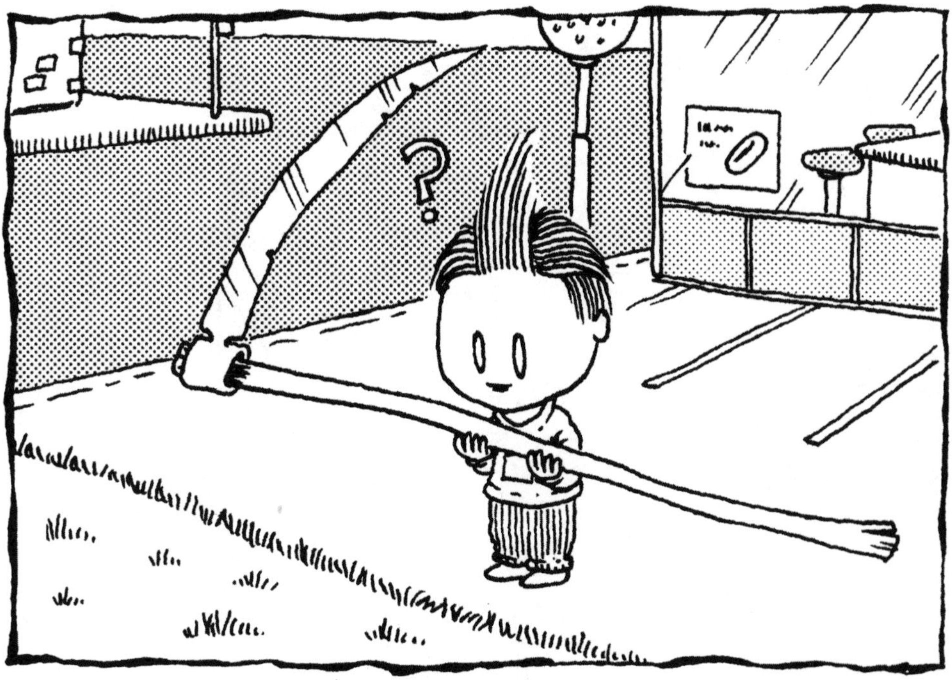
?

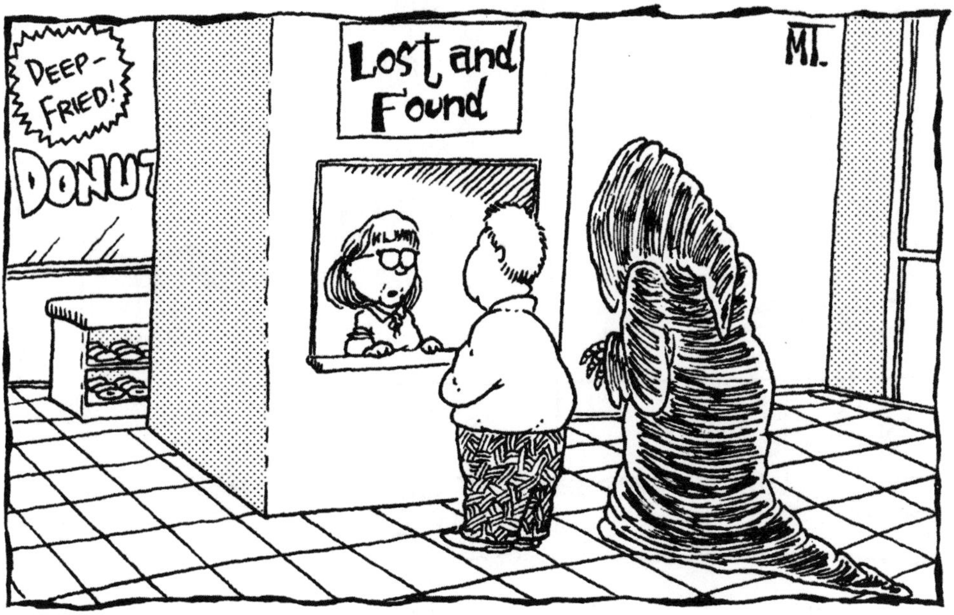
DEEP-FRIED!
DONUT
Lost and Found
MT.

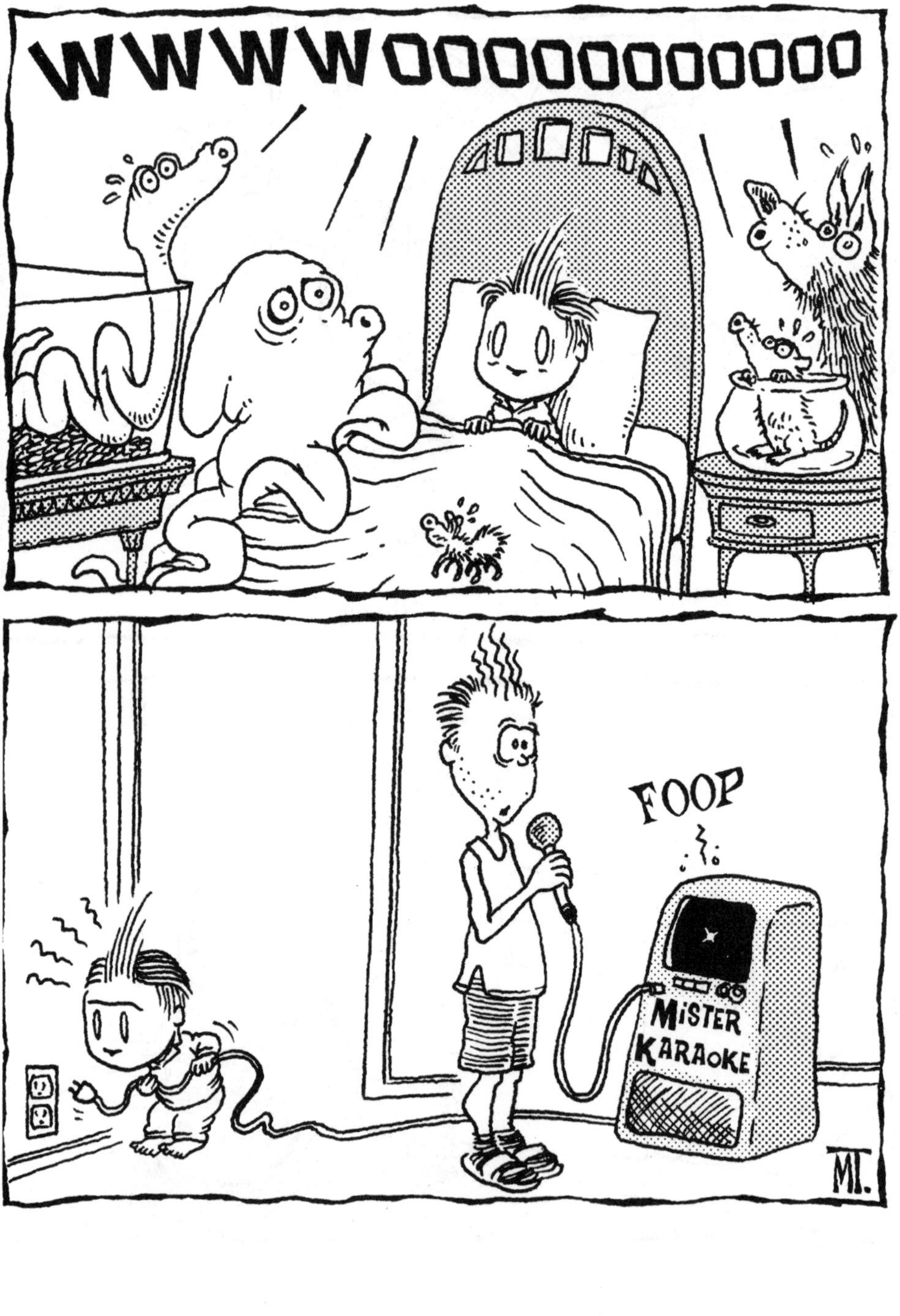
WWWWOOOOOOOOOOO
FOOP
MISTER KARAOKE
MT.

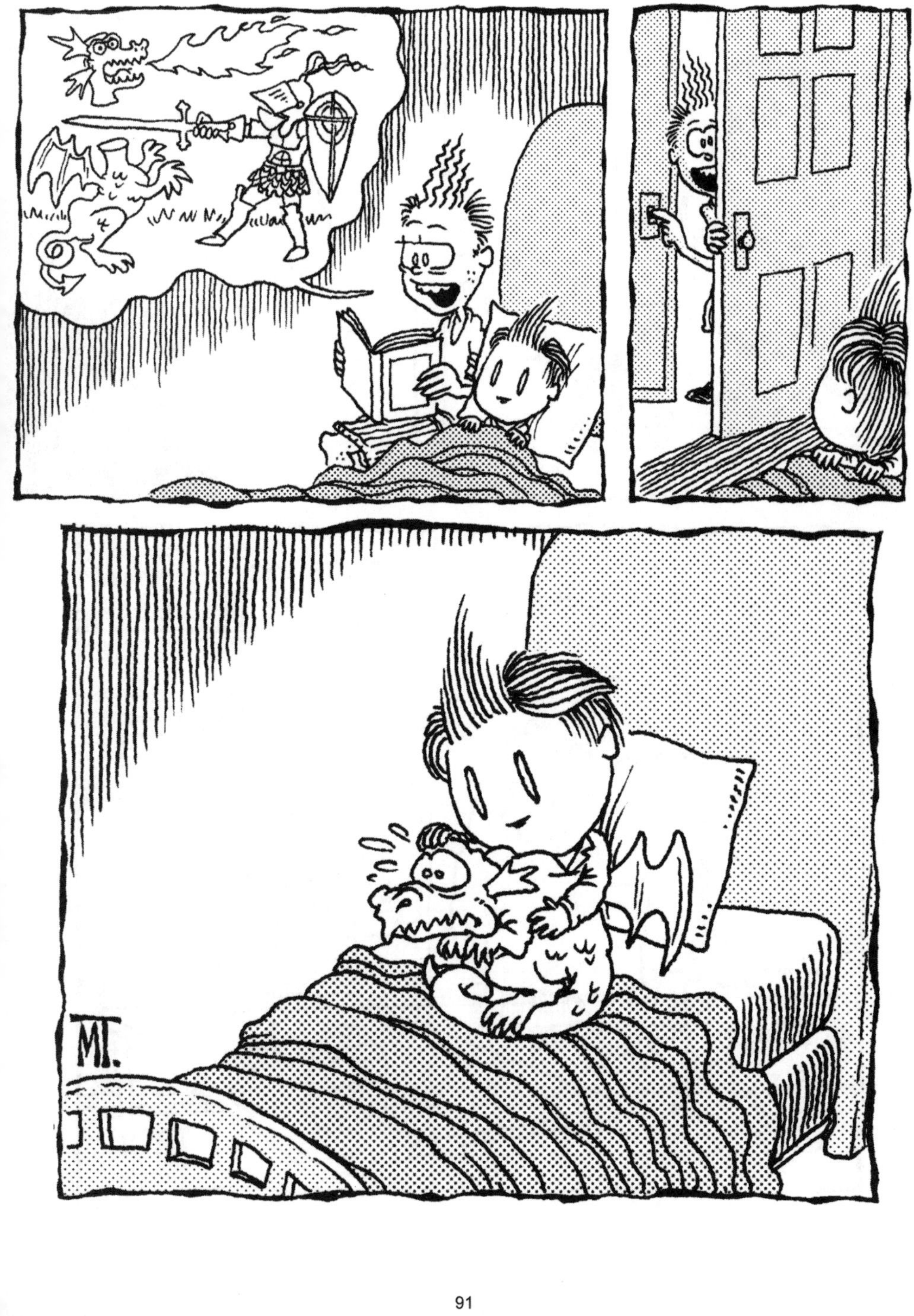
MT.

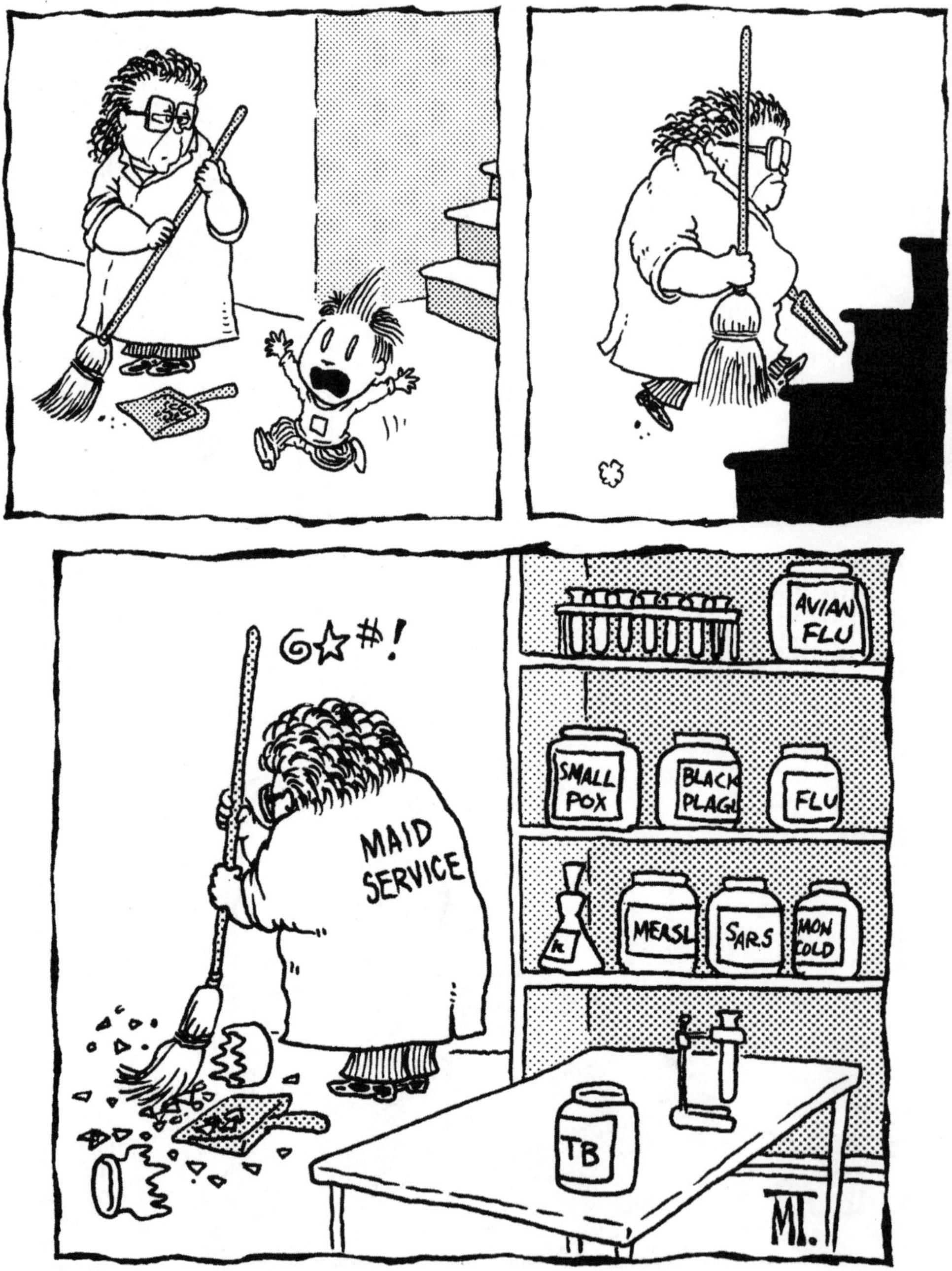
MAID
SERVICE
AVIAN
FLU
SMALL
POX
BLACK
PLAGU
FLU
MEASL
SARS
MON
COLD
TB
MI.

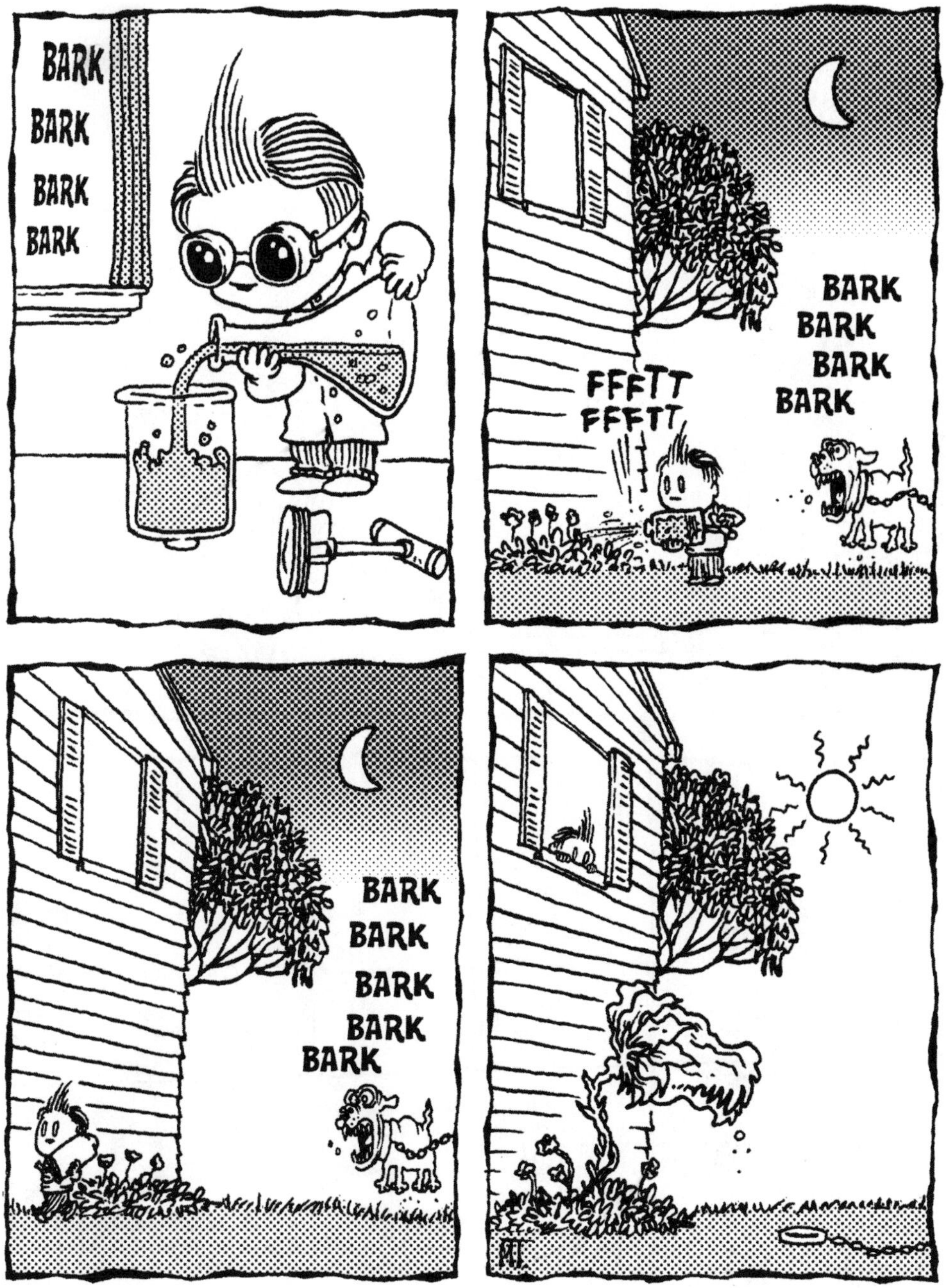
BARK
BARK
BARK
BARK
FFFTT
FFFTT
BARK
BARK
BARK
BARK
BARK
BARK
BARK
BARK
BARK

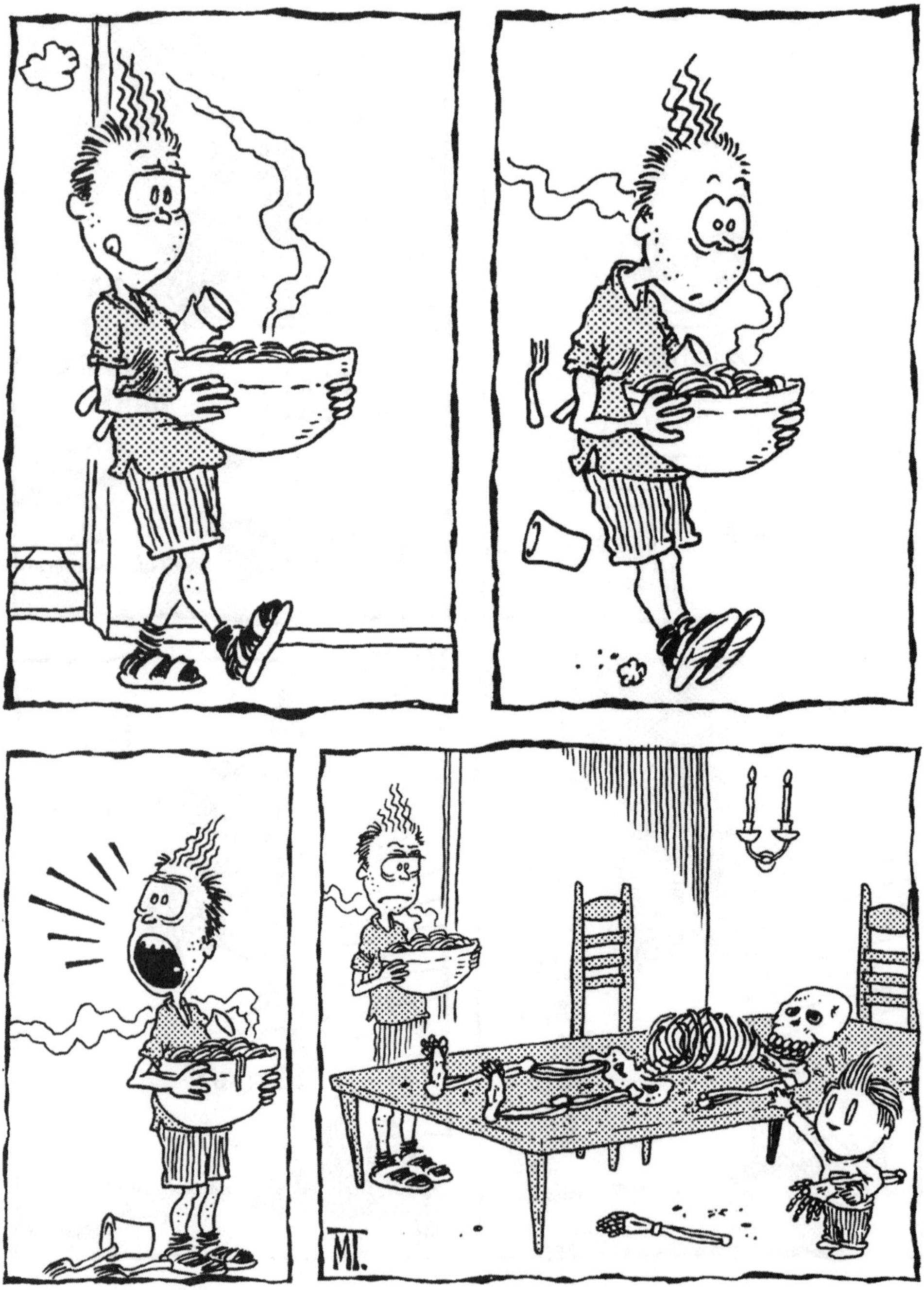
MT.

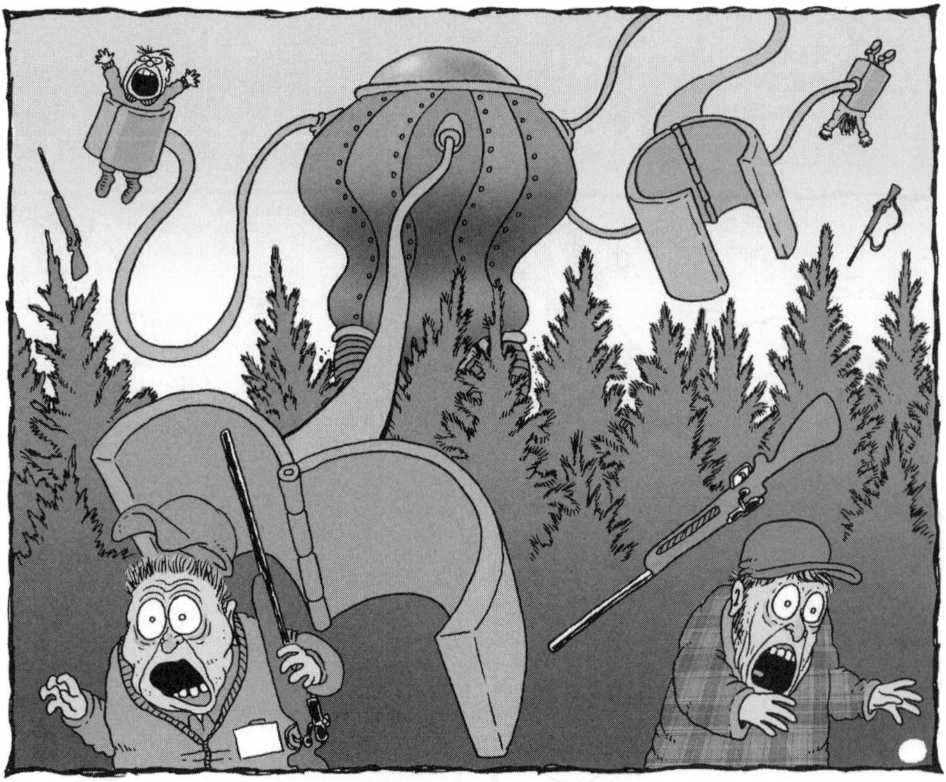

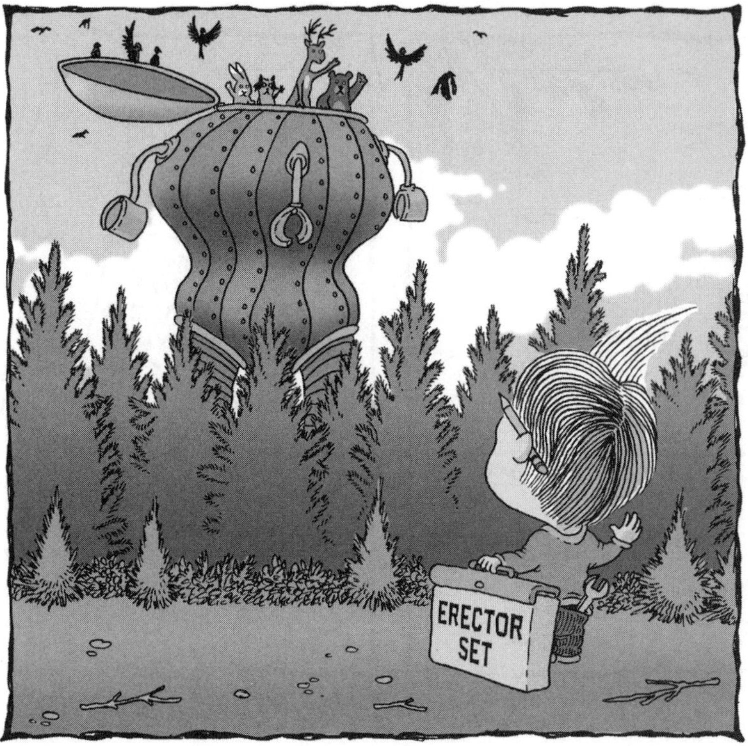
ERECTOR
SET

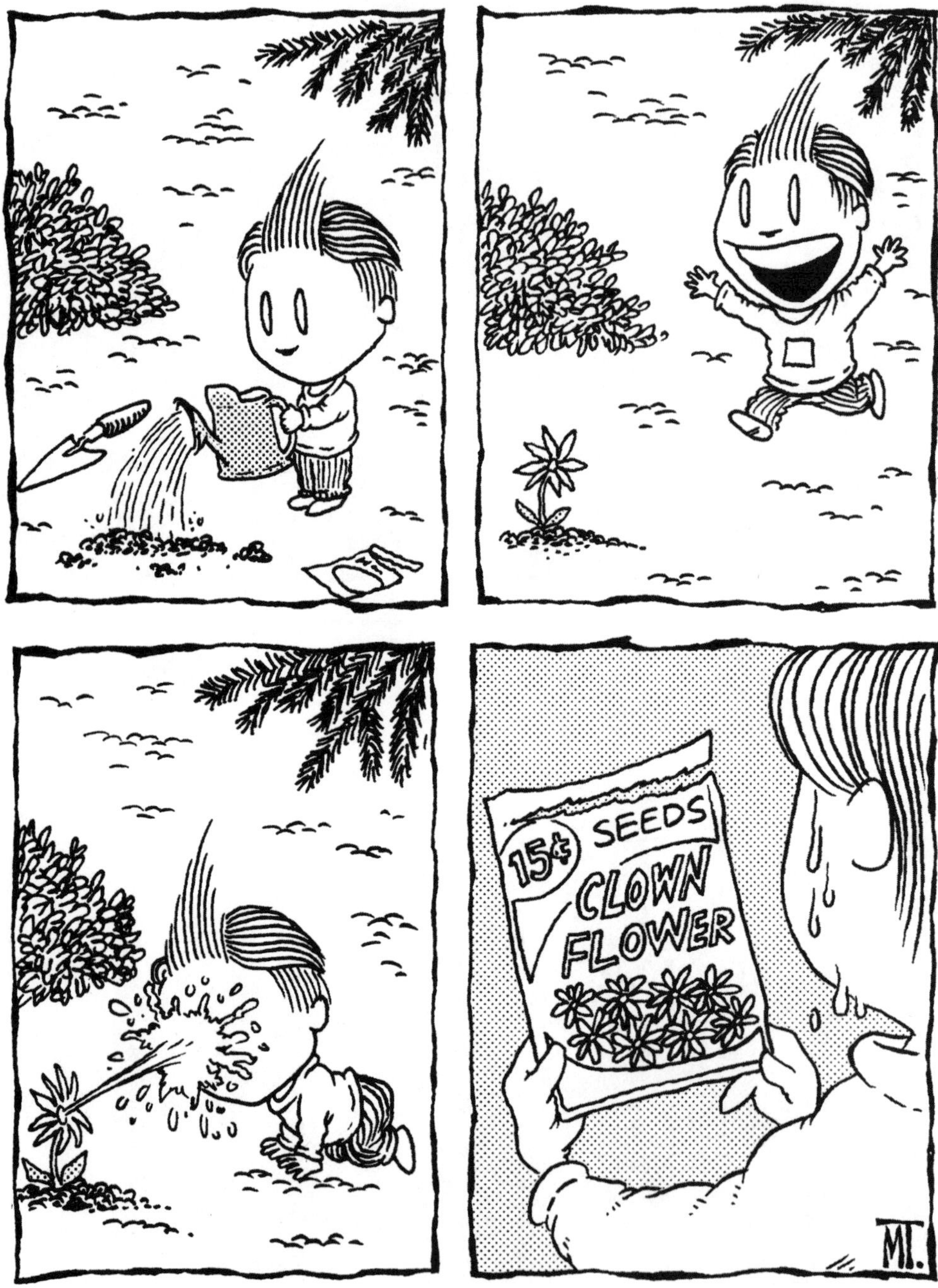
15¢
SEEDS
CLOWN
FLOWER
MI.

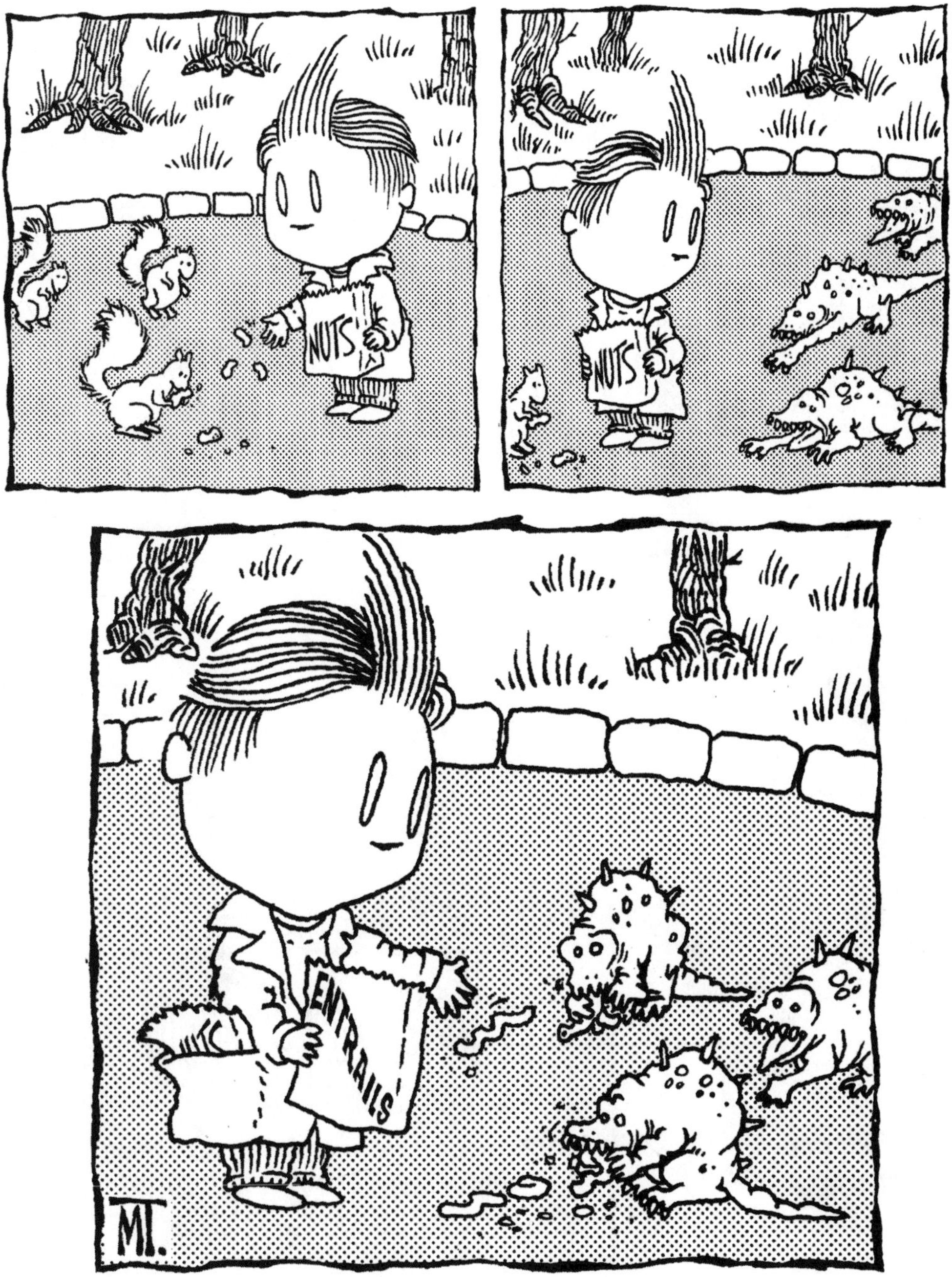
NUTS
NUTS
ENTRAILS
MT.

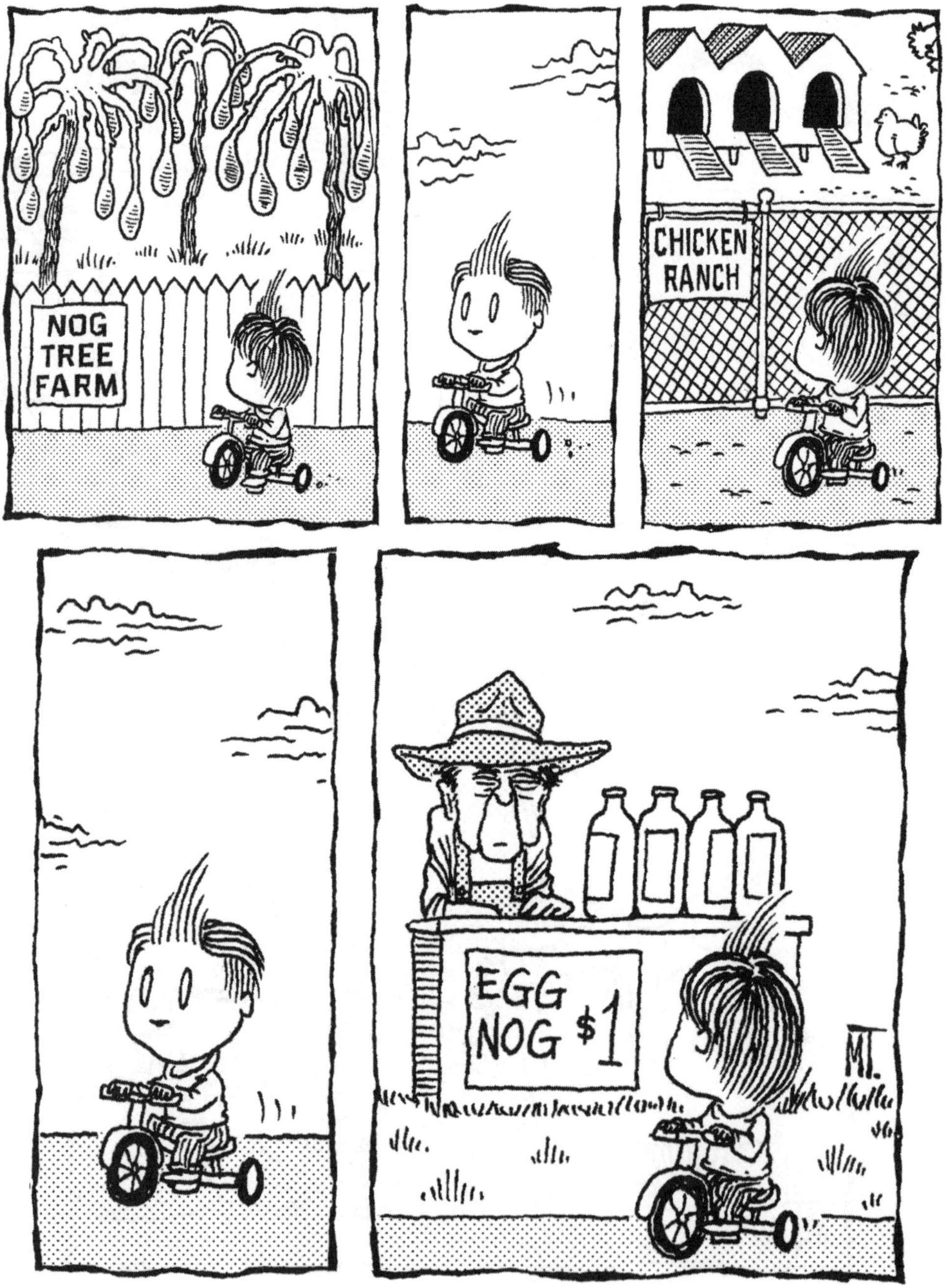
NOG
TREE
FARM
CHICKEN
RANCH
EGG
NOG $1
MT.

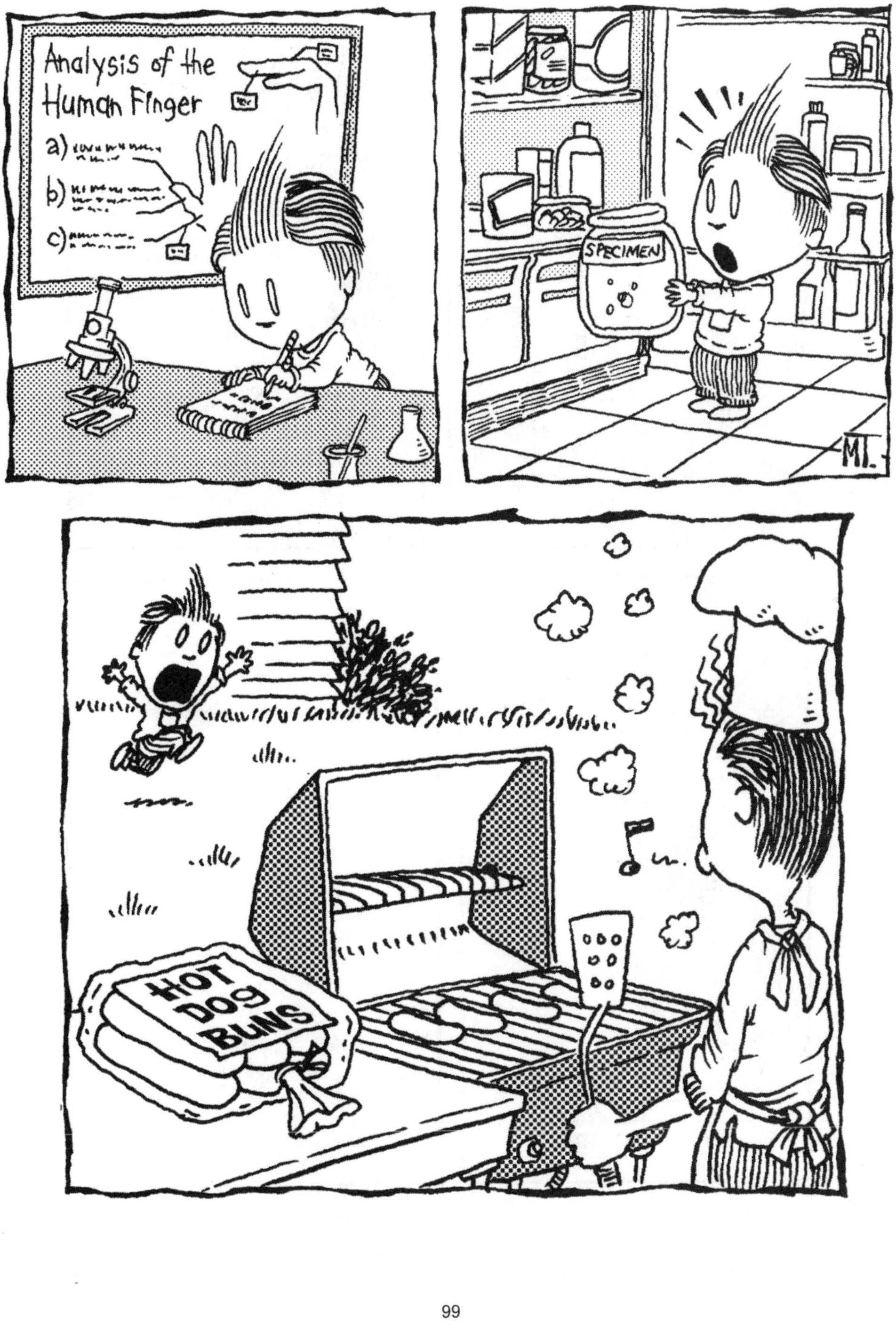
Analysis of the Human Finger
a)
b)
c)
SPECIMEN
ML
HOT DOG BUNS

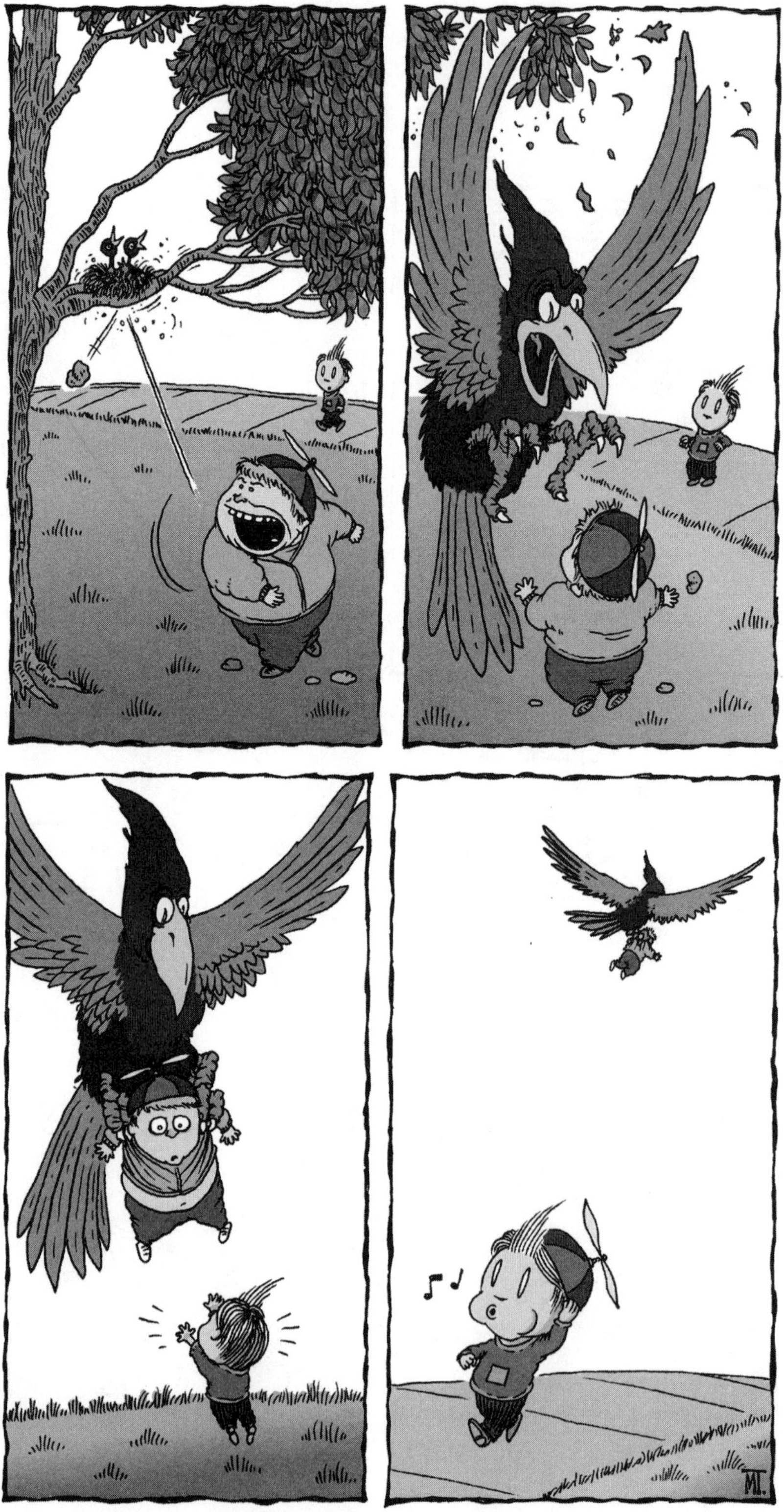

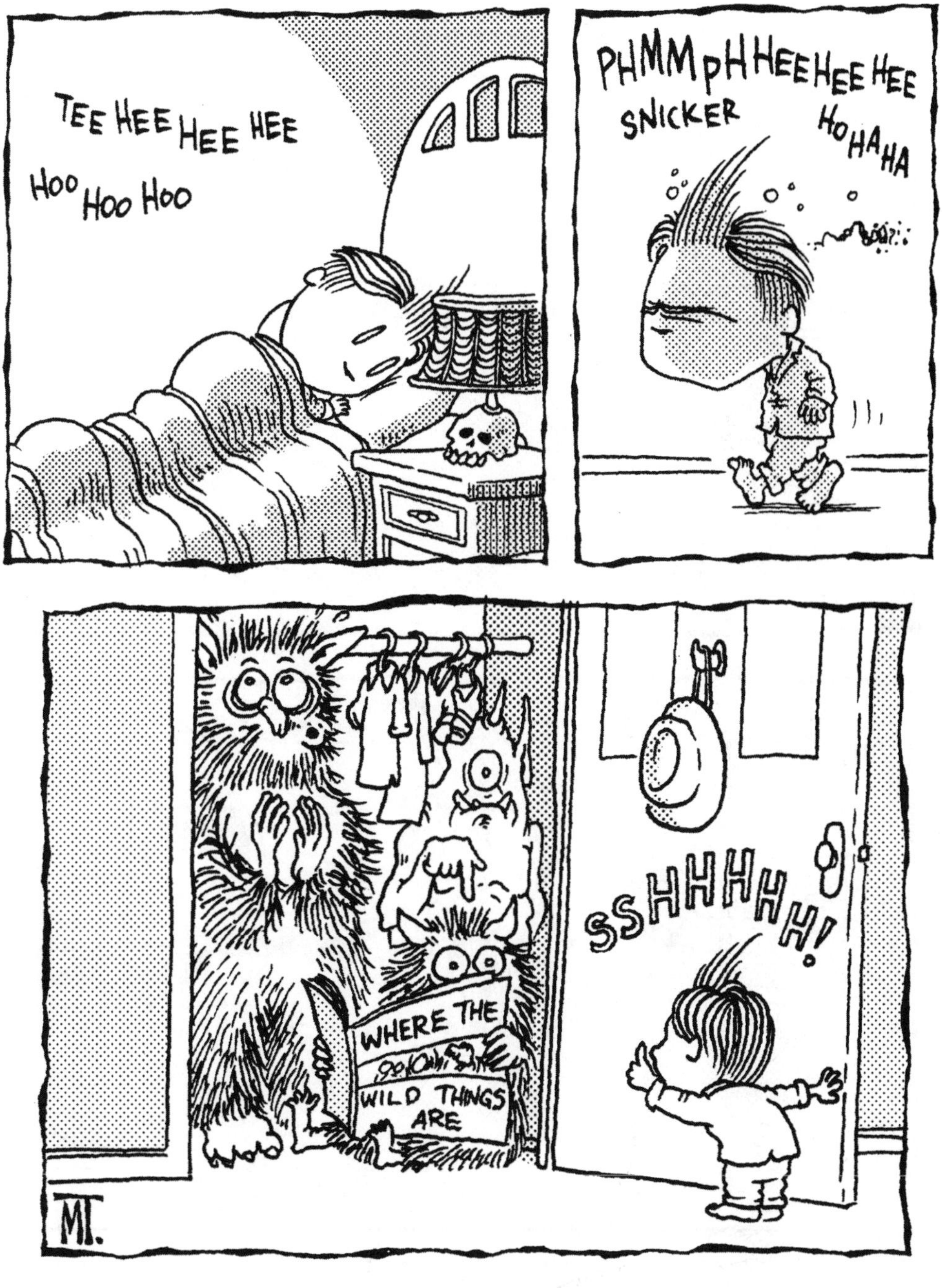
TEE HEE HEE HEE
HOO HOO HOO
PHMM pH HEE HEE HEE
SNICKER
HO HA HA
WHERE THE WILD THINGS ARE
SSHHHHHH!
MT.

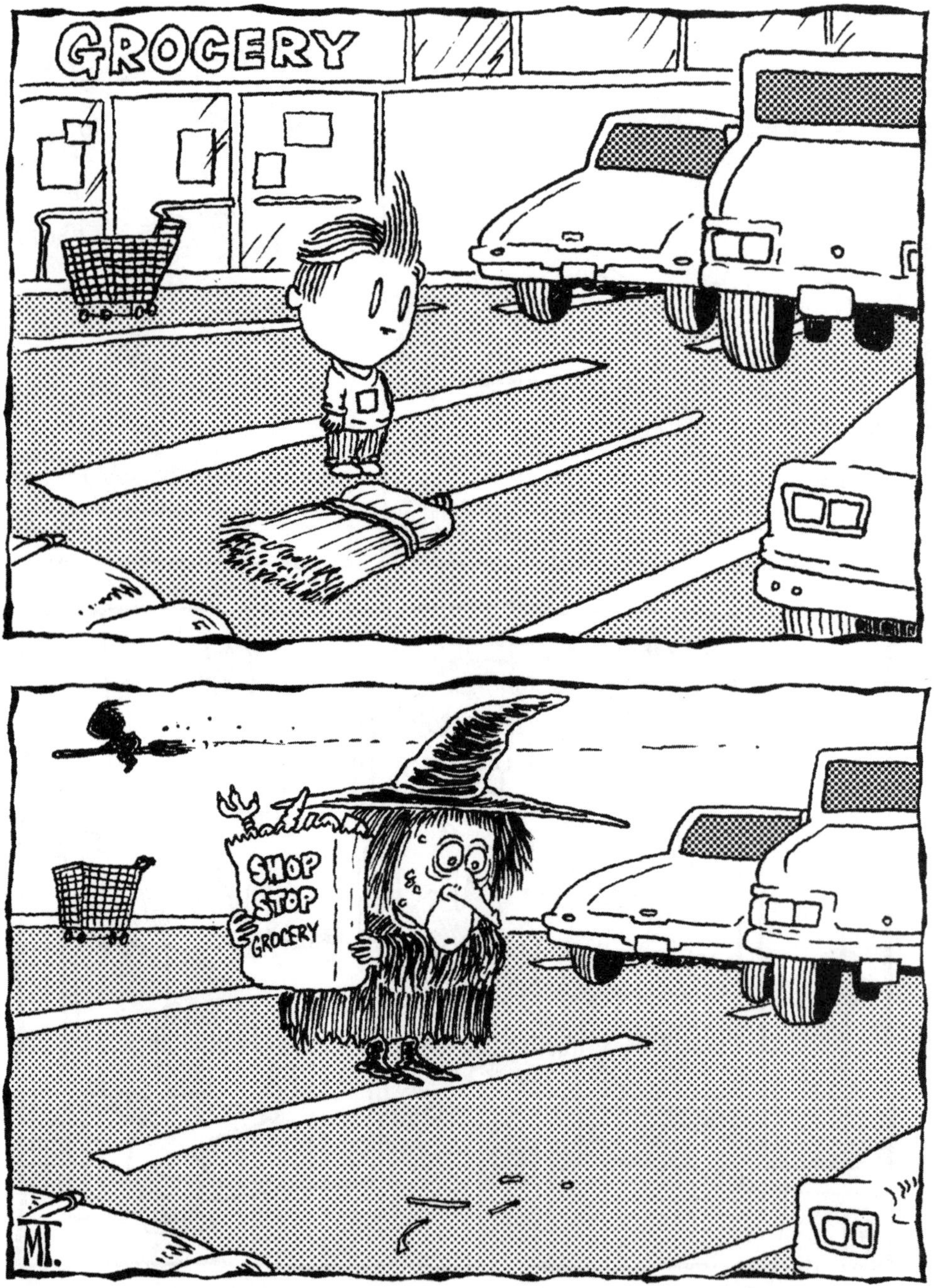
GROCERY
SHOP
STOP
GROCERY
MI.

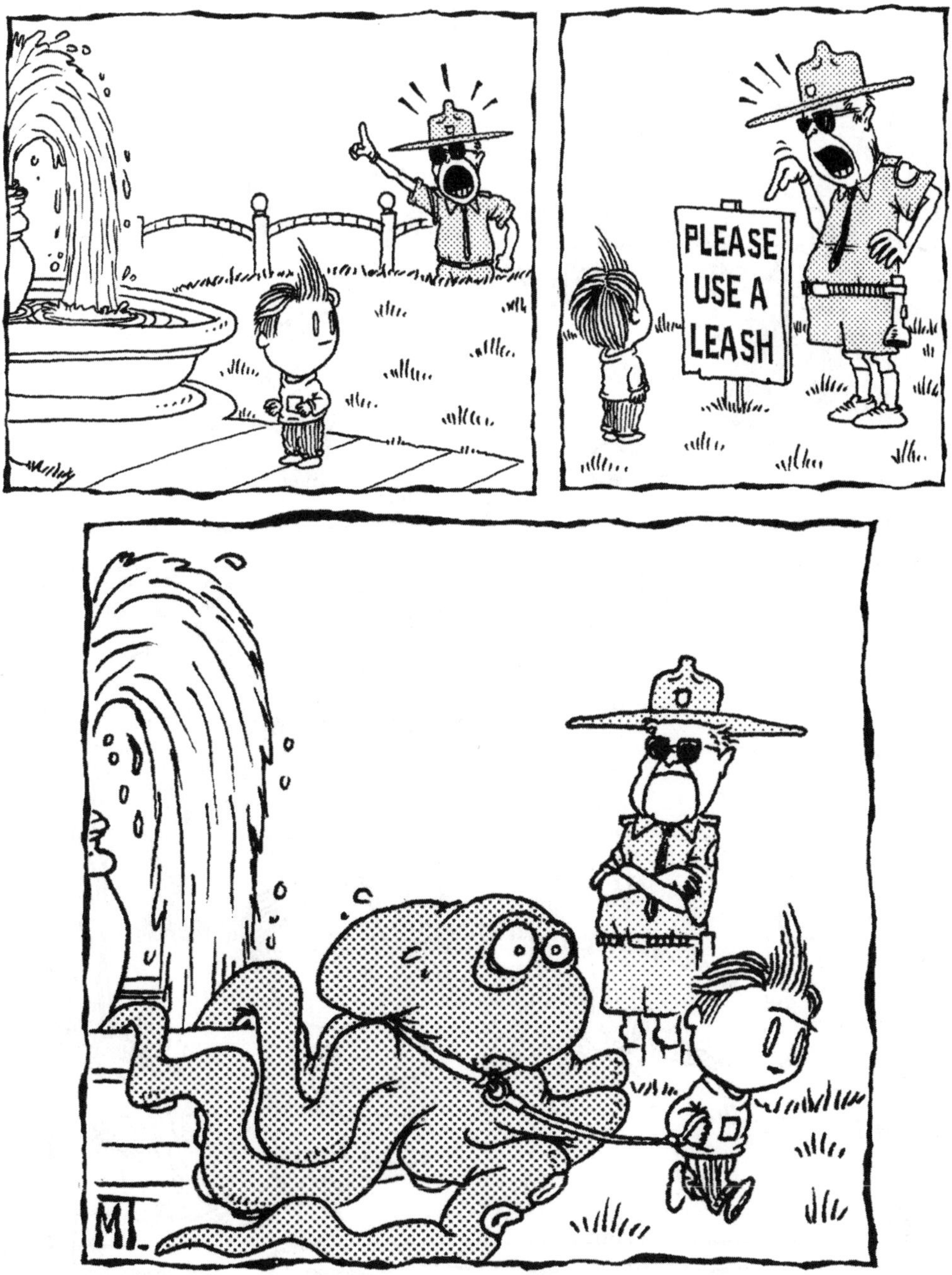
PLEASE USE A LEASH
MI

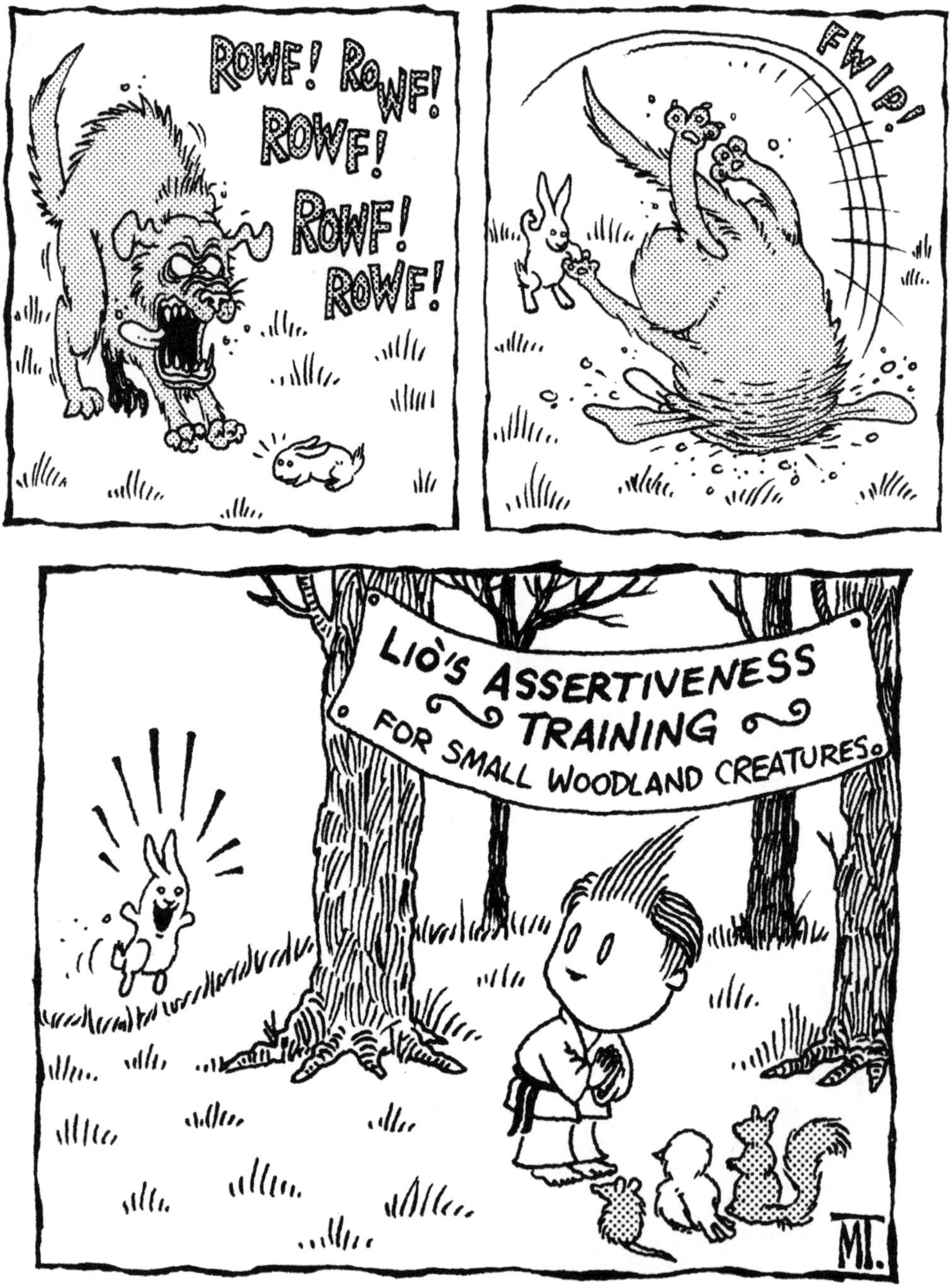
ROWF! ROWF!
ROWF!
ROWF!
ROWF!
FWIP!
LIO'S ASSERTIVENESS
TRAINING
FOR SMALL WOODLAND CREATURES
MT.

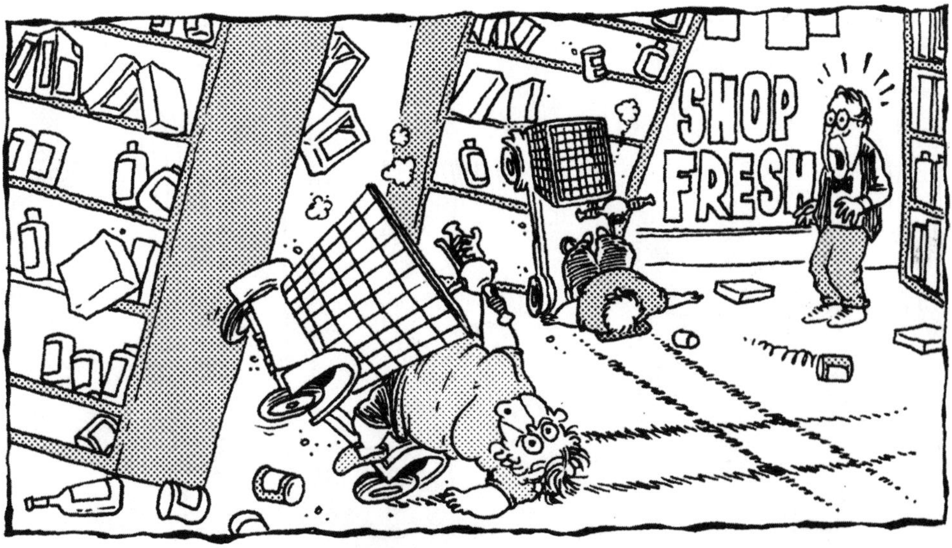
SHOP
FRESH

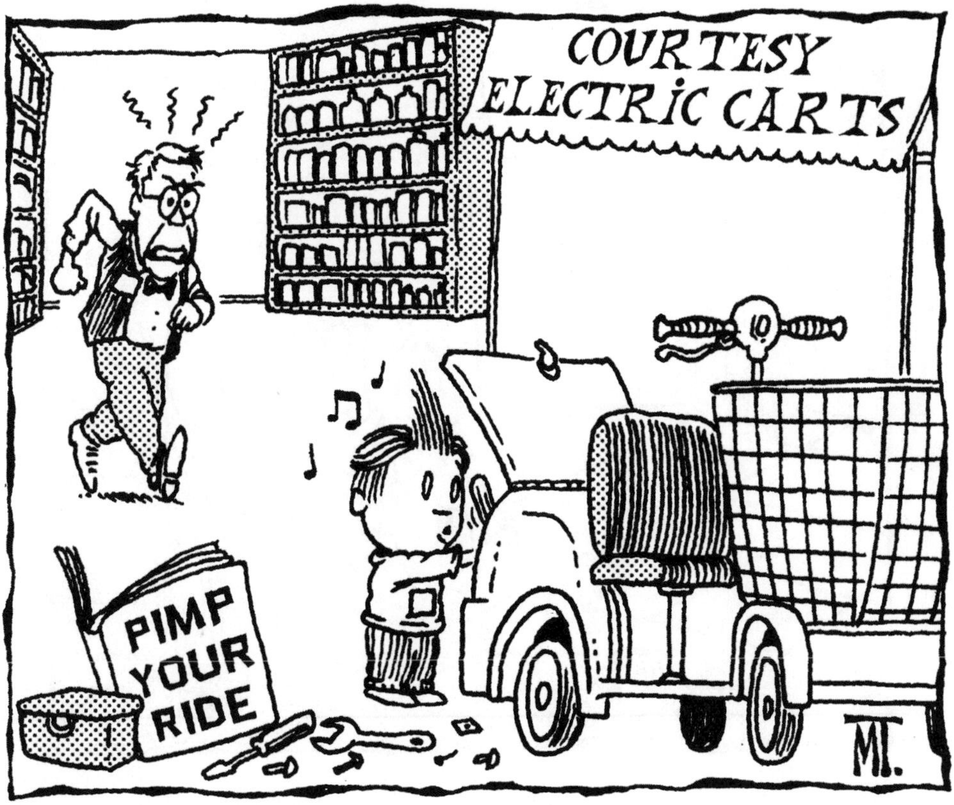
COURTESY
ELECTRIC CARTS
10
PIMP
YOUR
RIDE
MT.

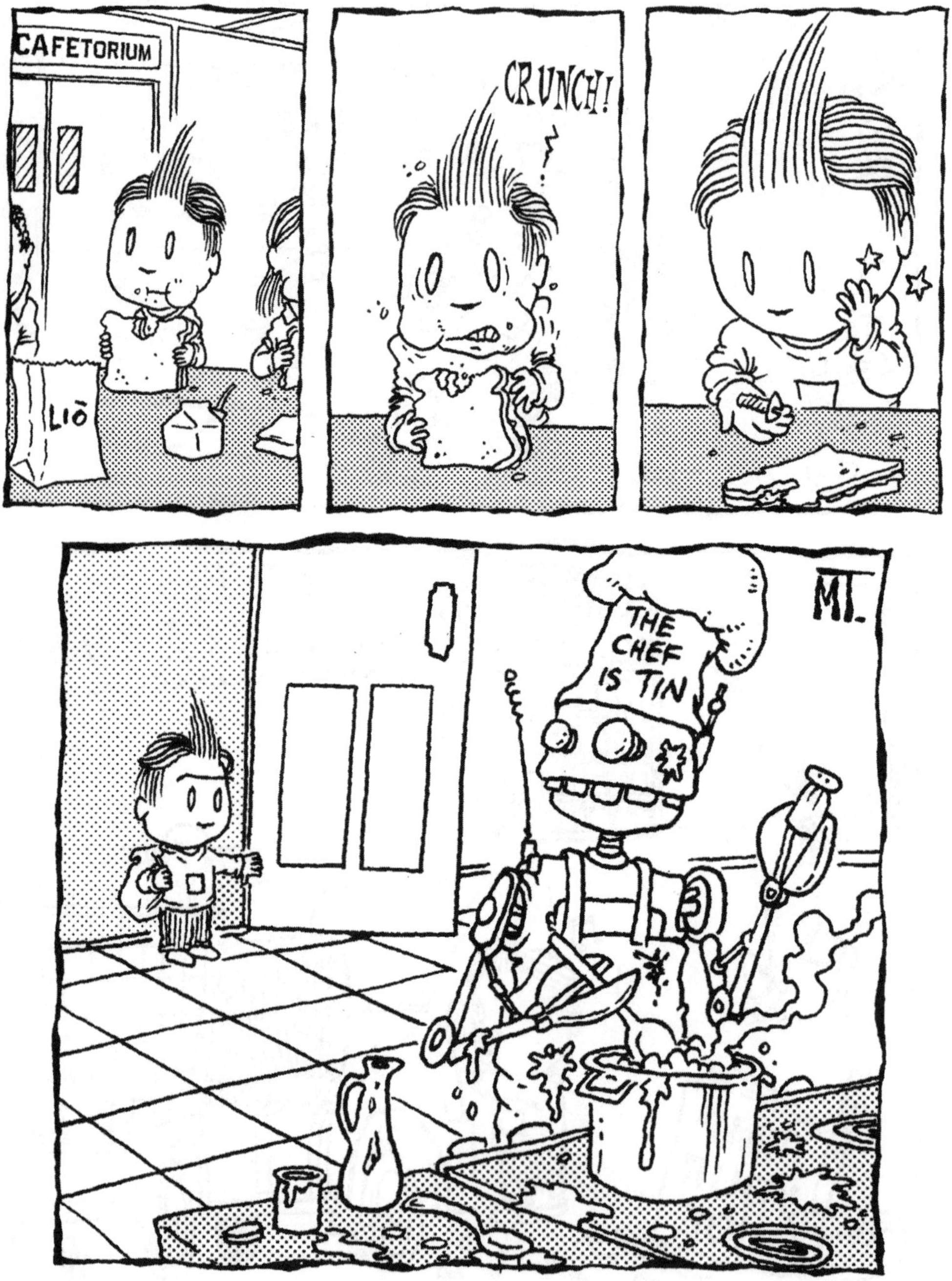
CAFETORIUM
LIO
CRUNCH!
MT.
THE CHEF IS TIN

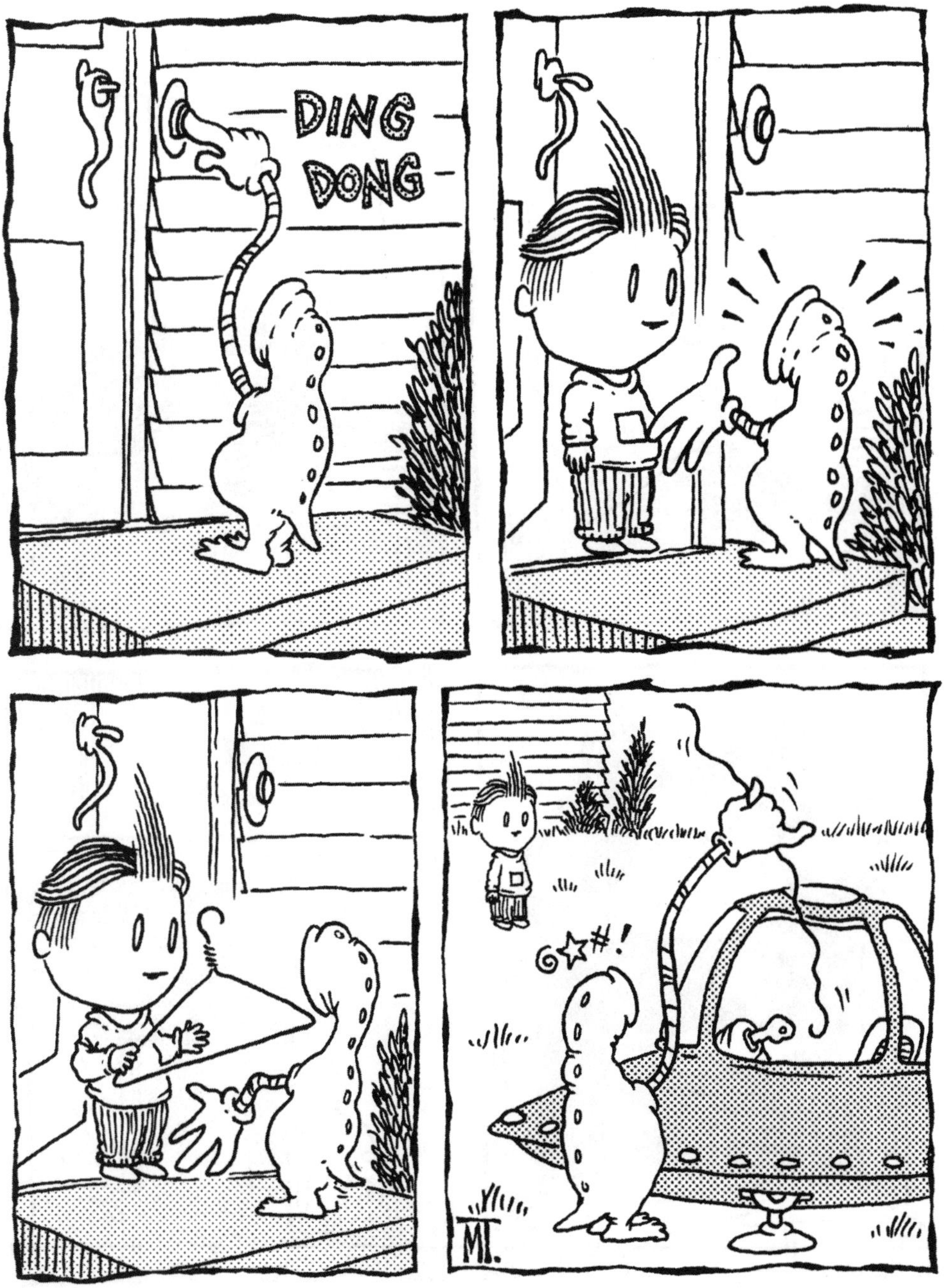
DING
DONG
@☆#!

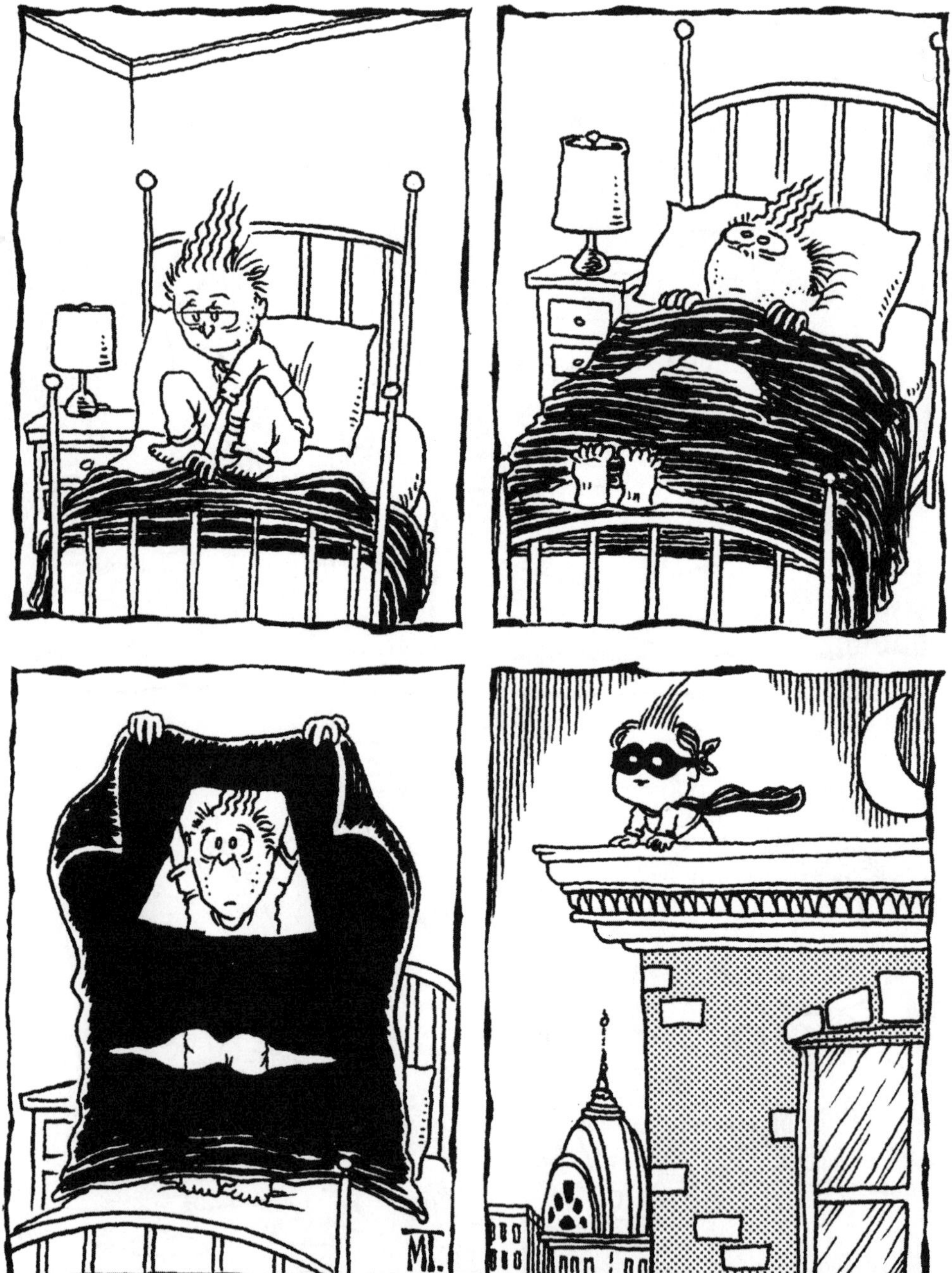

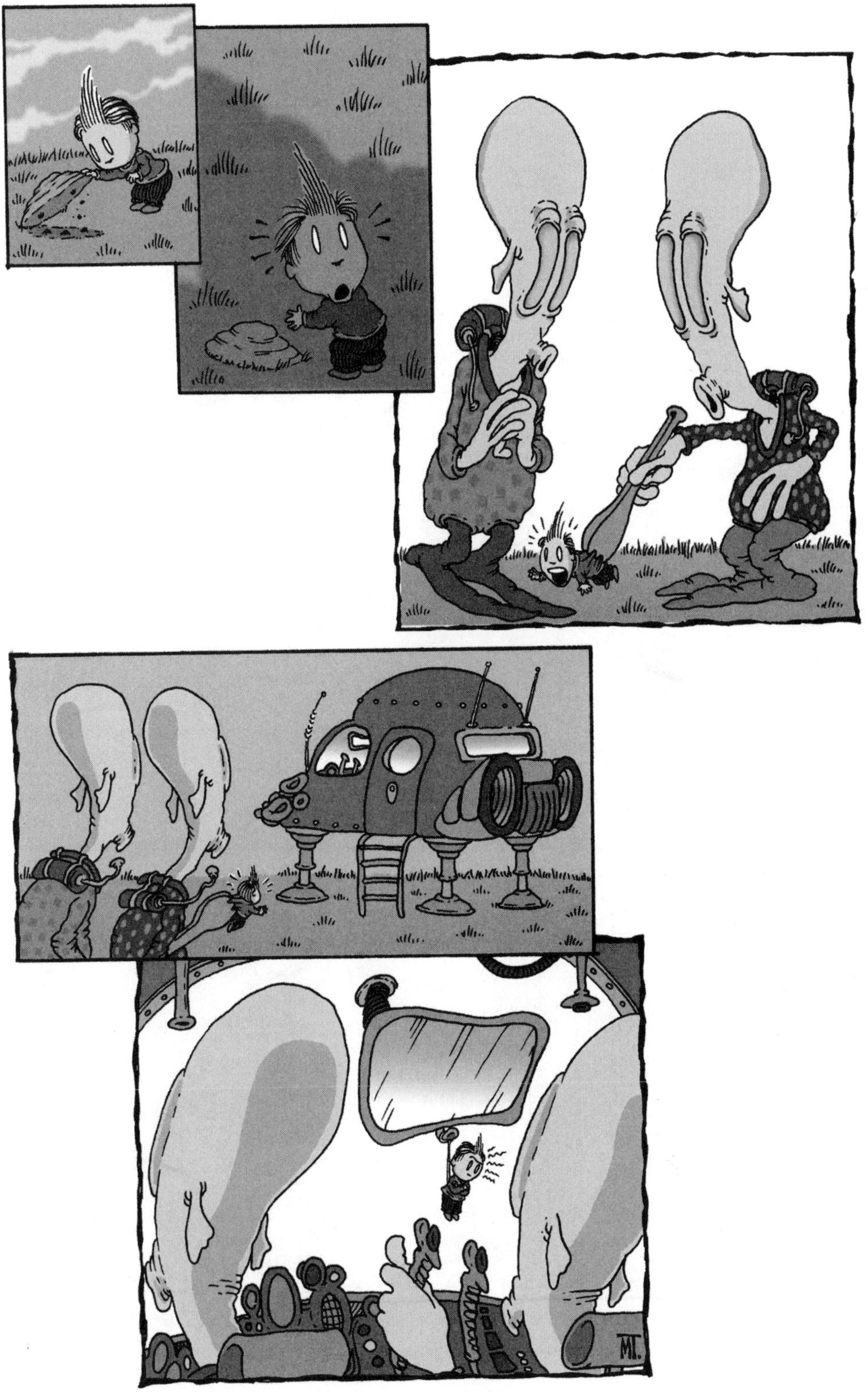

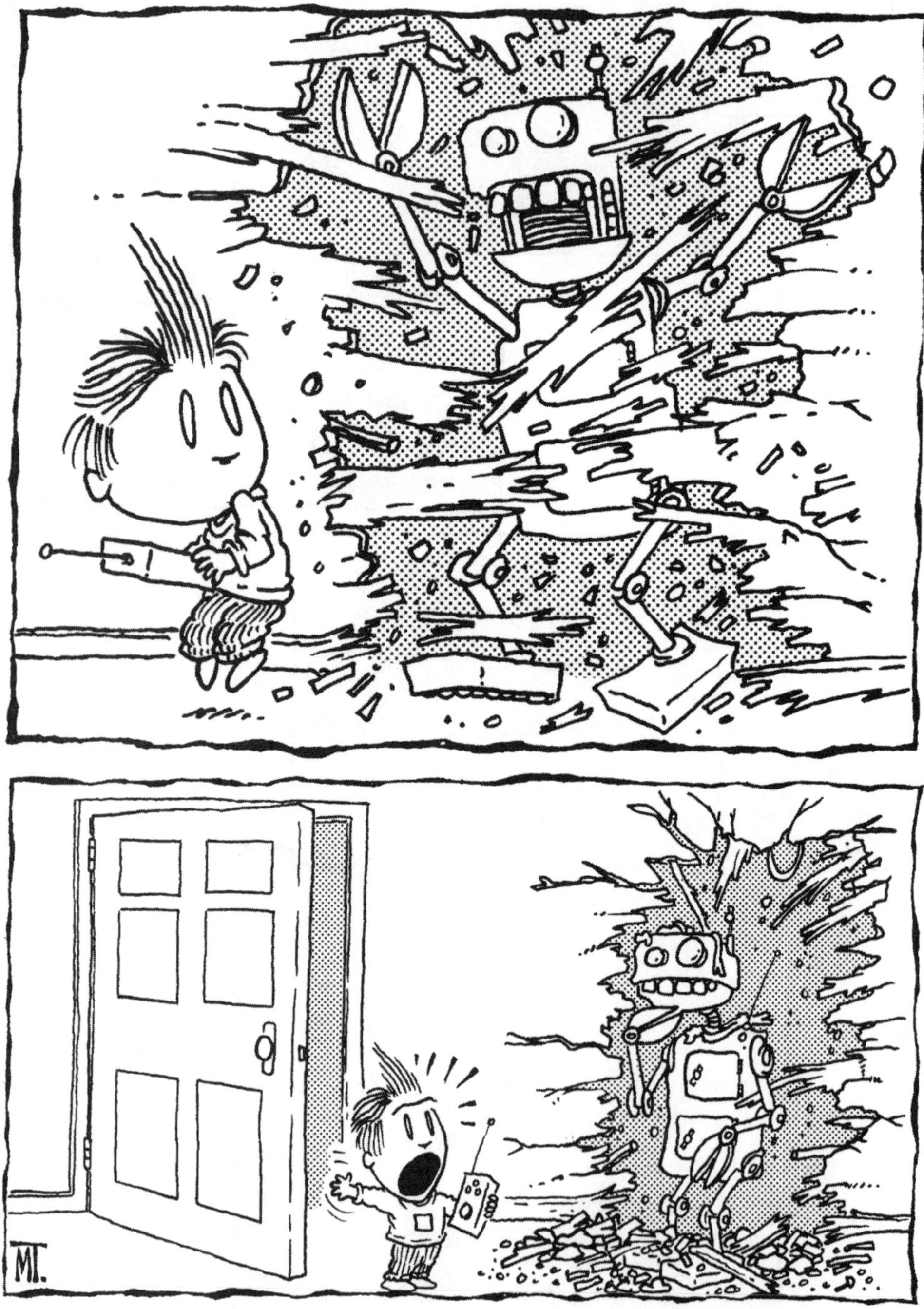

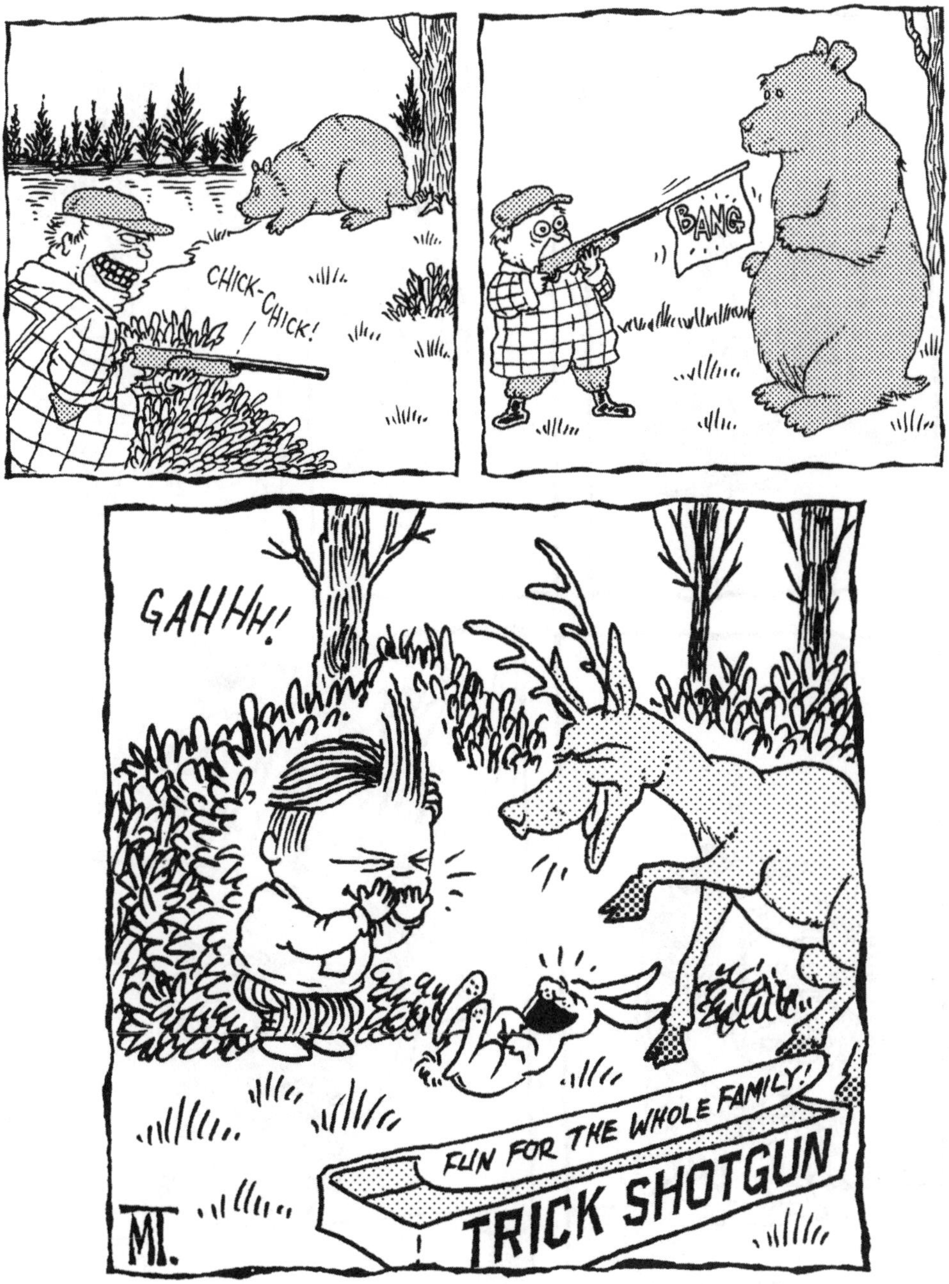
CHICK-CHICK!
BANG
GAHHH!
FUN FOR THE WHOLE FAMILY!
TRICK SHOTGUN
MT.

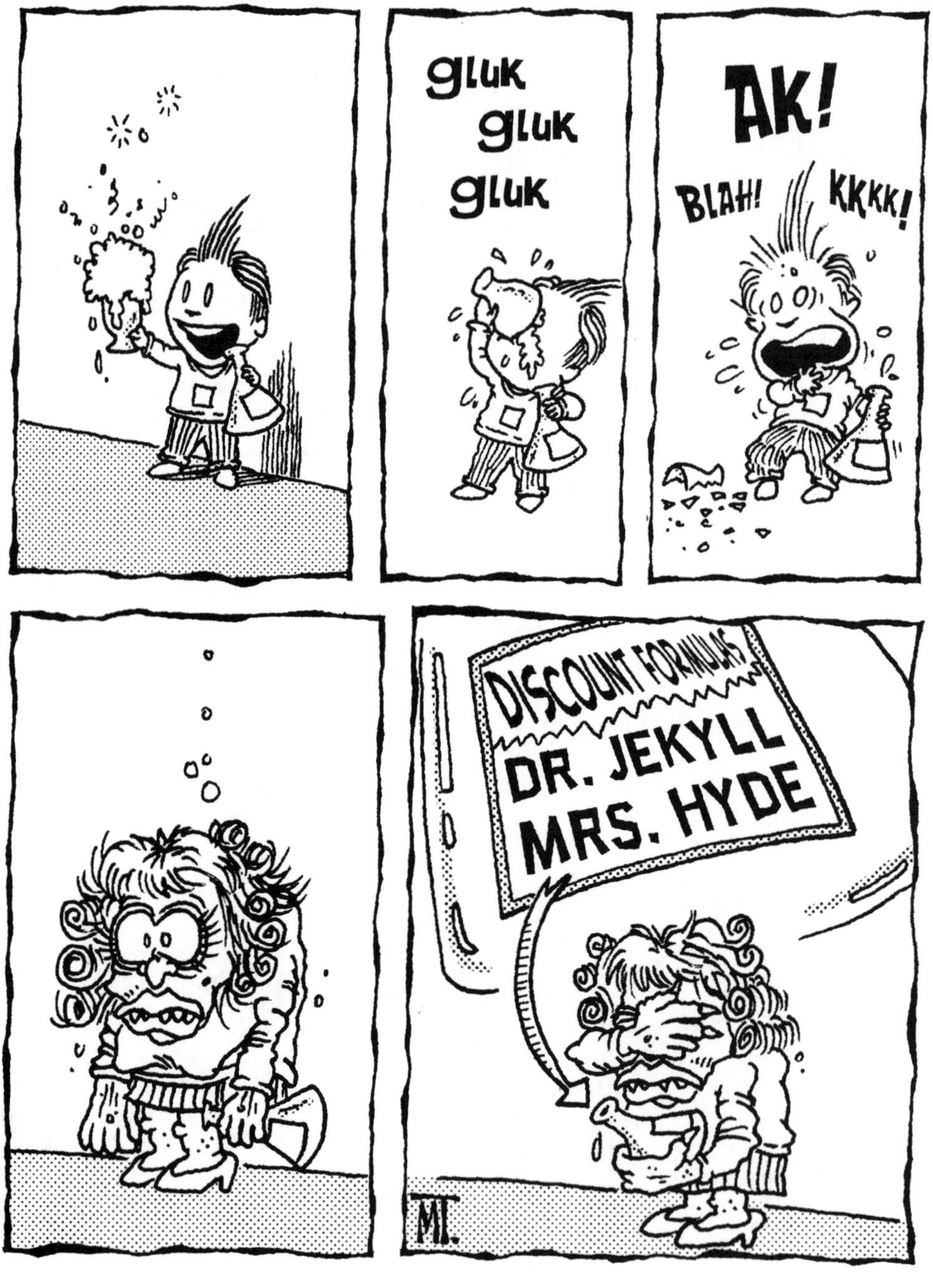
gluk
gluk
gluk
AK!
BLAH!
KKKK!
DISCOUNT FORMULAS
DR. JEKYLL
MRS. HYDE
MT.

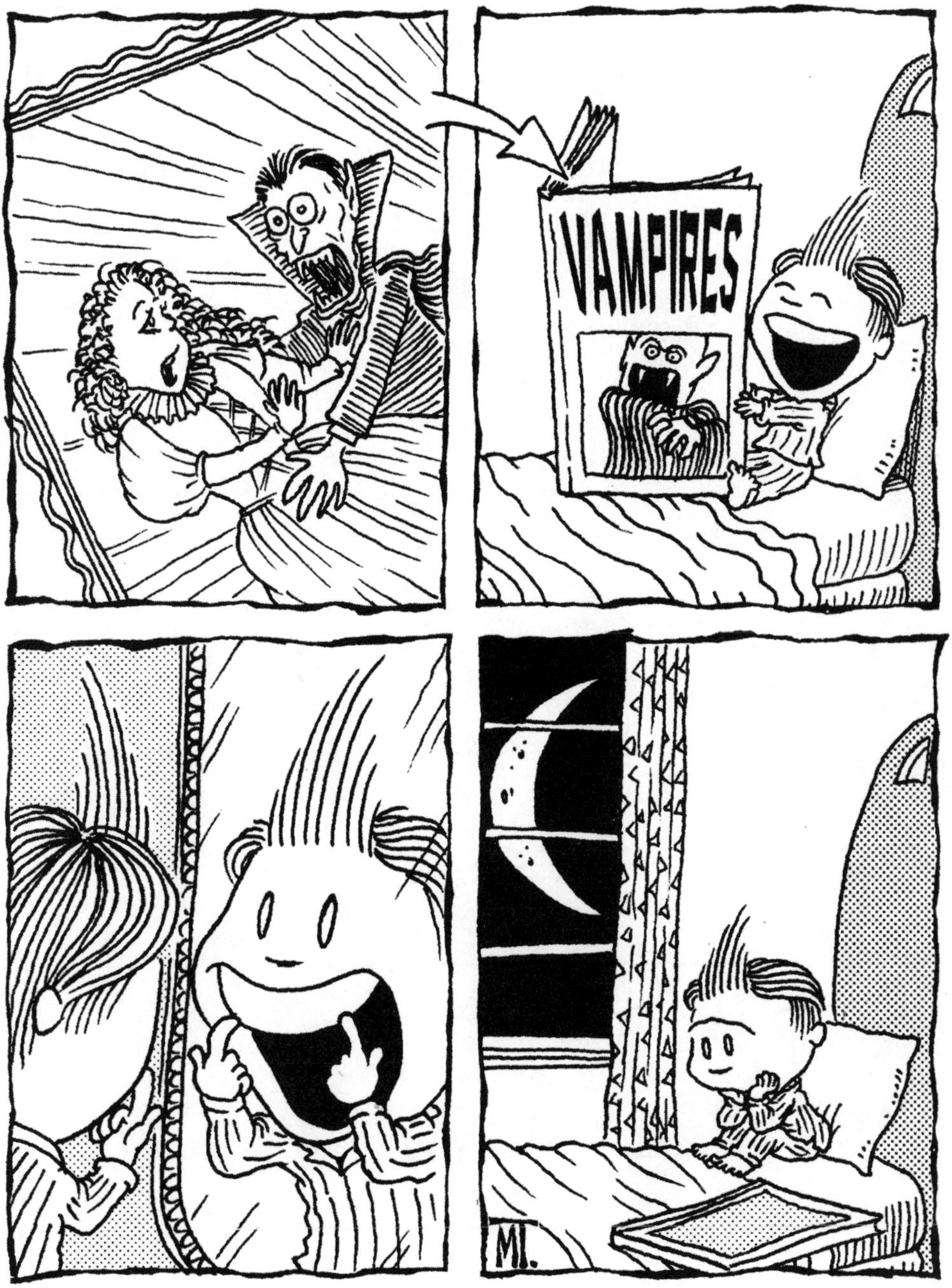
VAMPIRES
MI.

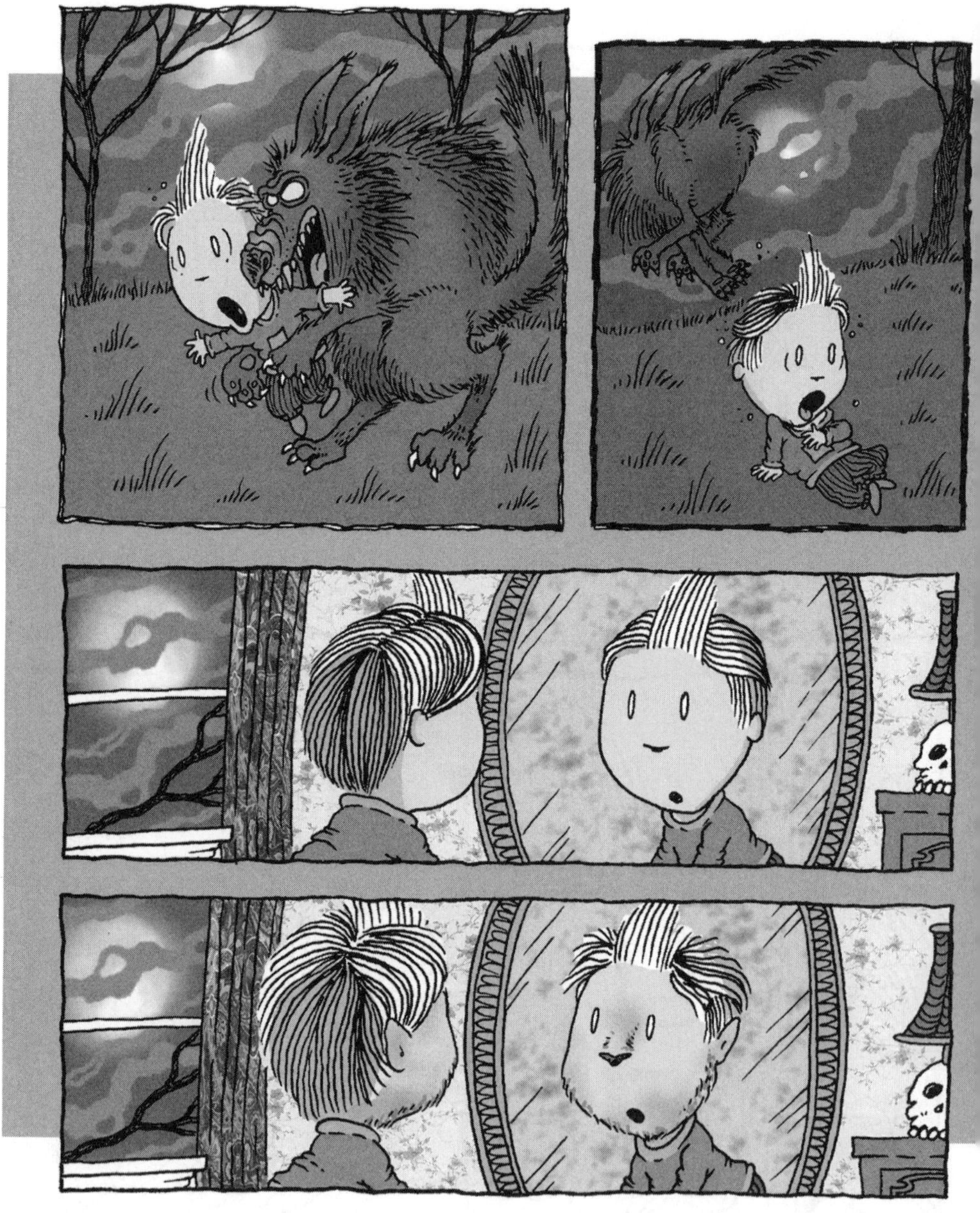

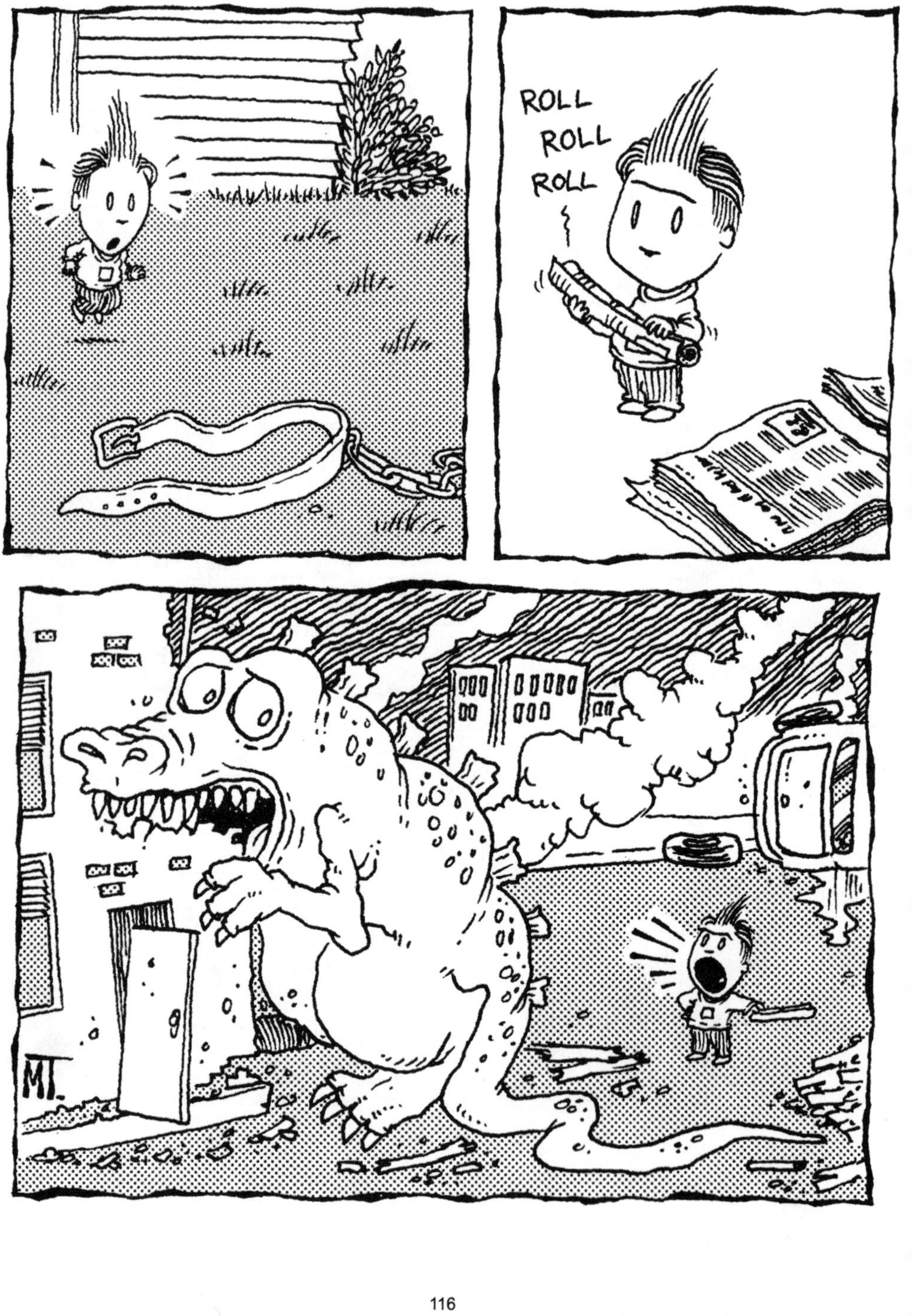
ROLL
ROLL
ROLL

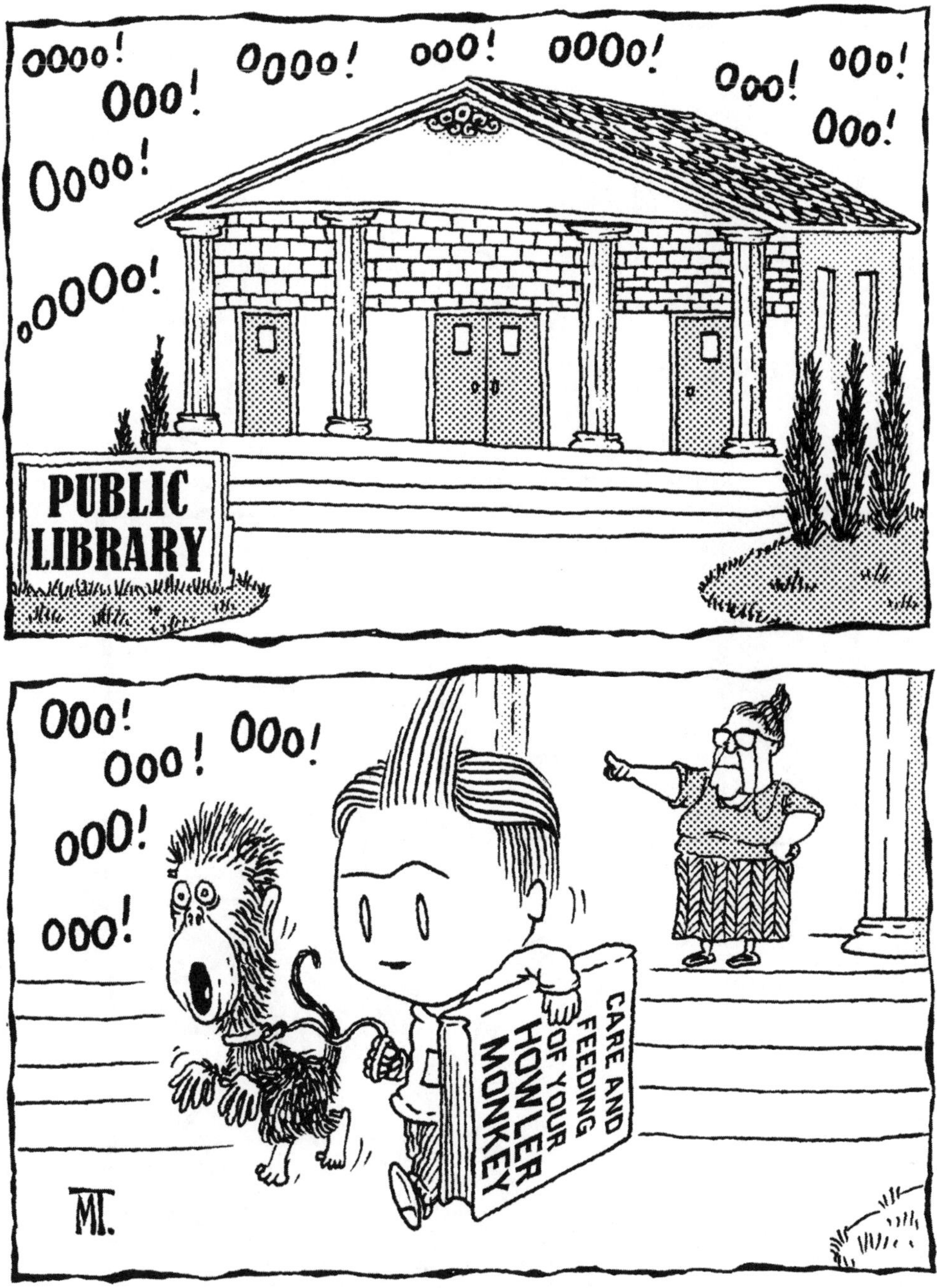
OOOO!
OOO!
OOOO!
OOOO!
OOOO!
OOO!
OOOO!
OOO!
OOO!
OOO!
PUBLIC LIBRARY
OOO!
OOO!
OOO!
OOO!
OOO!
CARE AND FEEDING OF YOUR HOWLER MONKEY

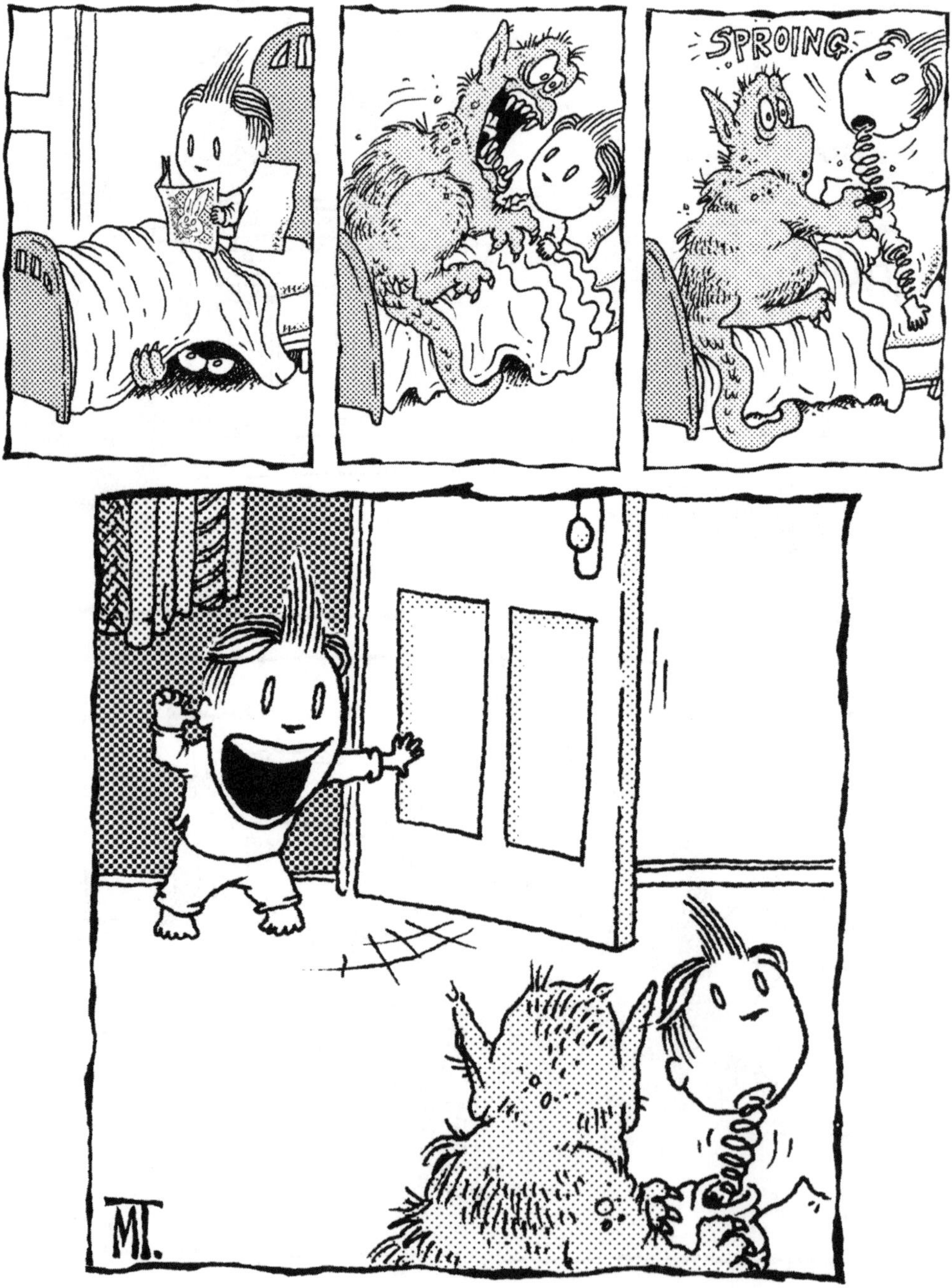
SPROING
MT.

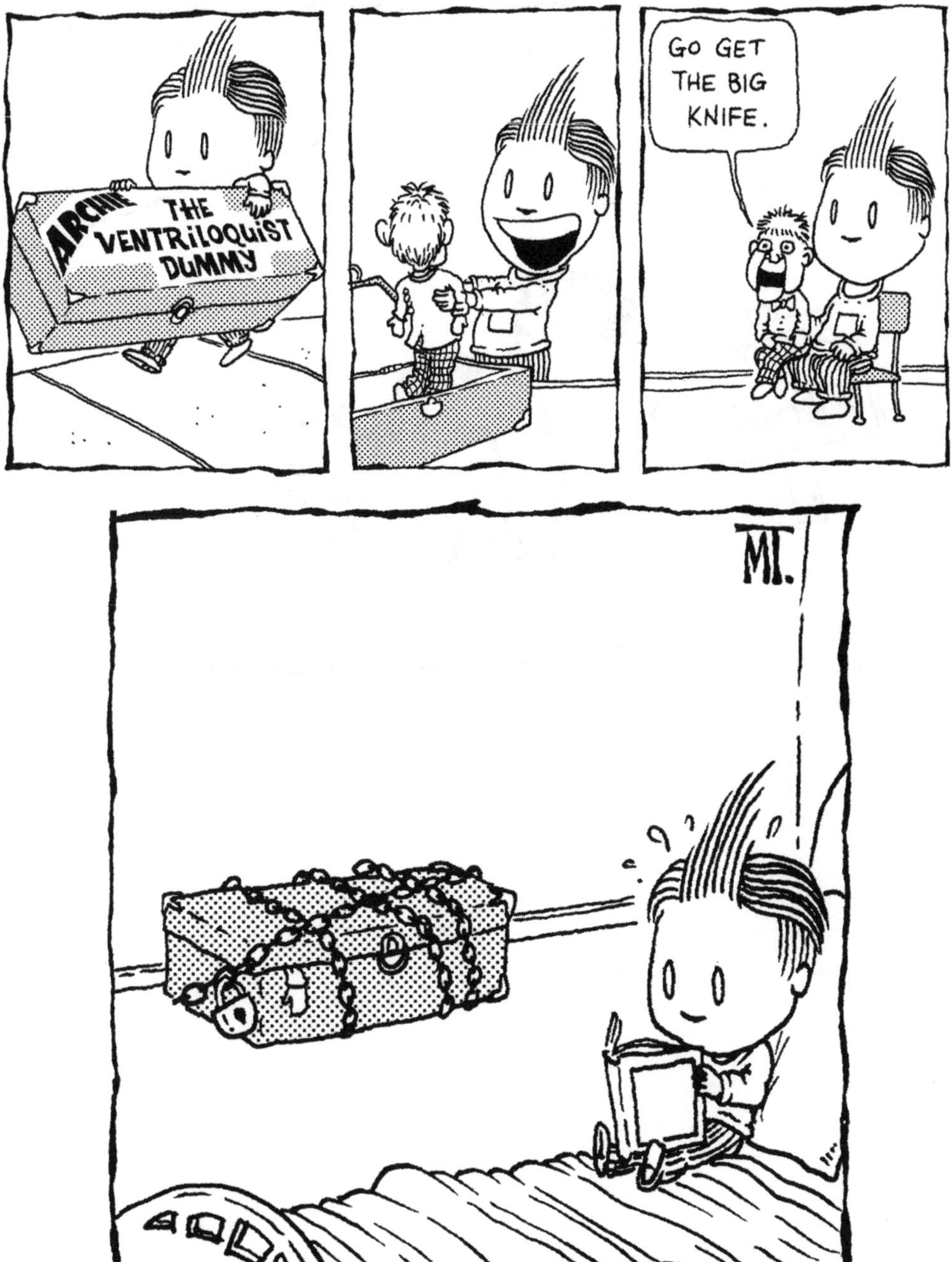
ARCHIE THE VENTRILOQUIST DUMMY
GO GET THE BIG KNIFE.
MT.

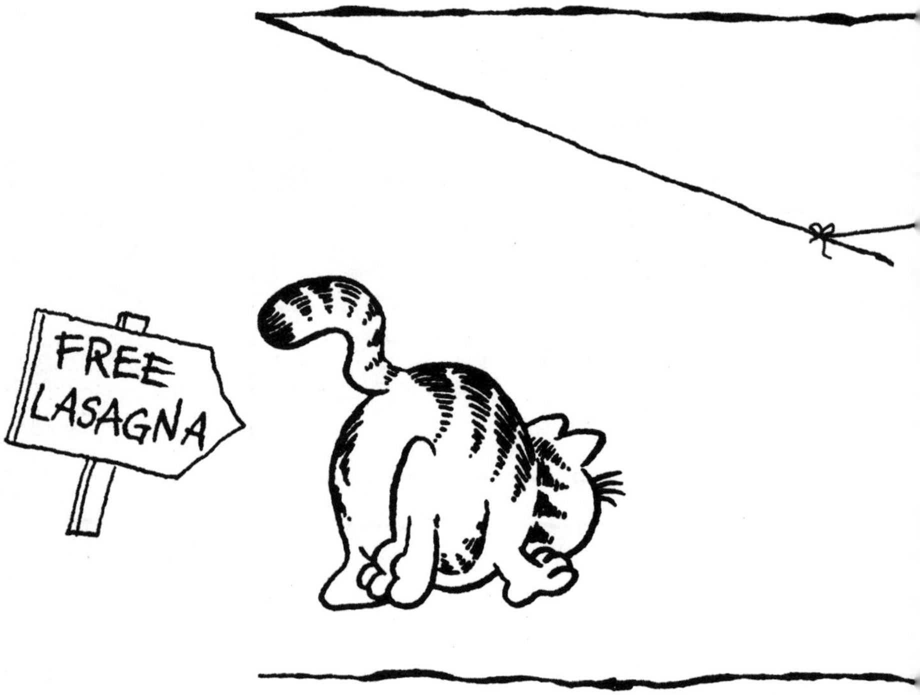
FREE
LASAGNA

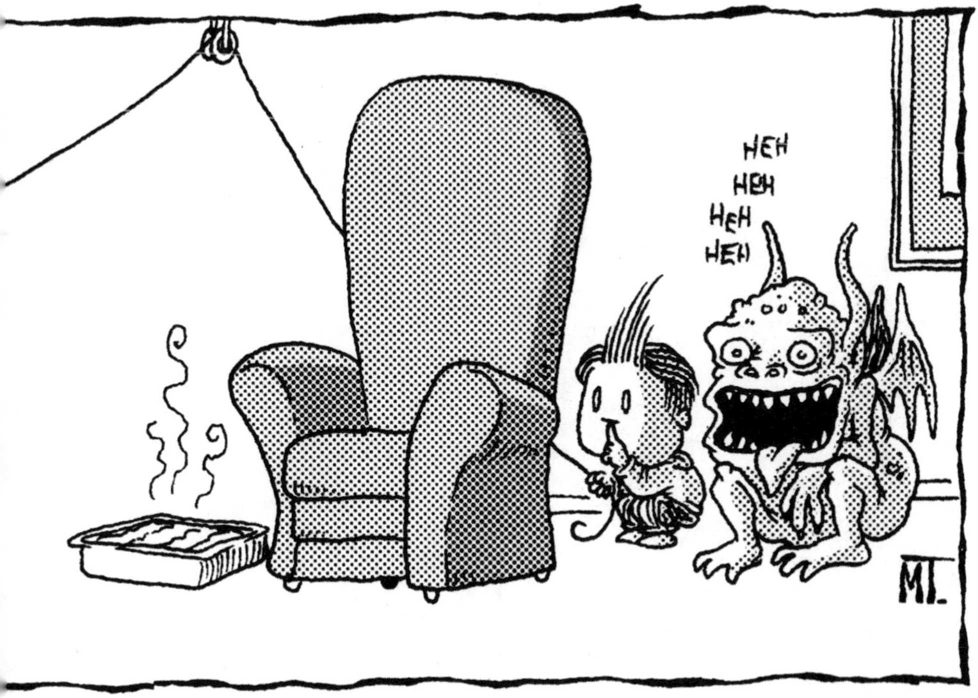
HEH
HEH
HEH
HEH
MT

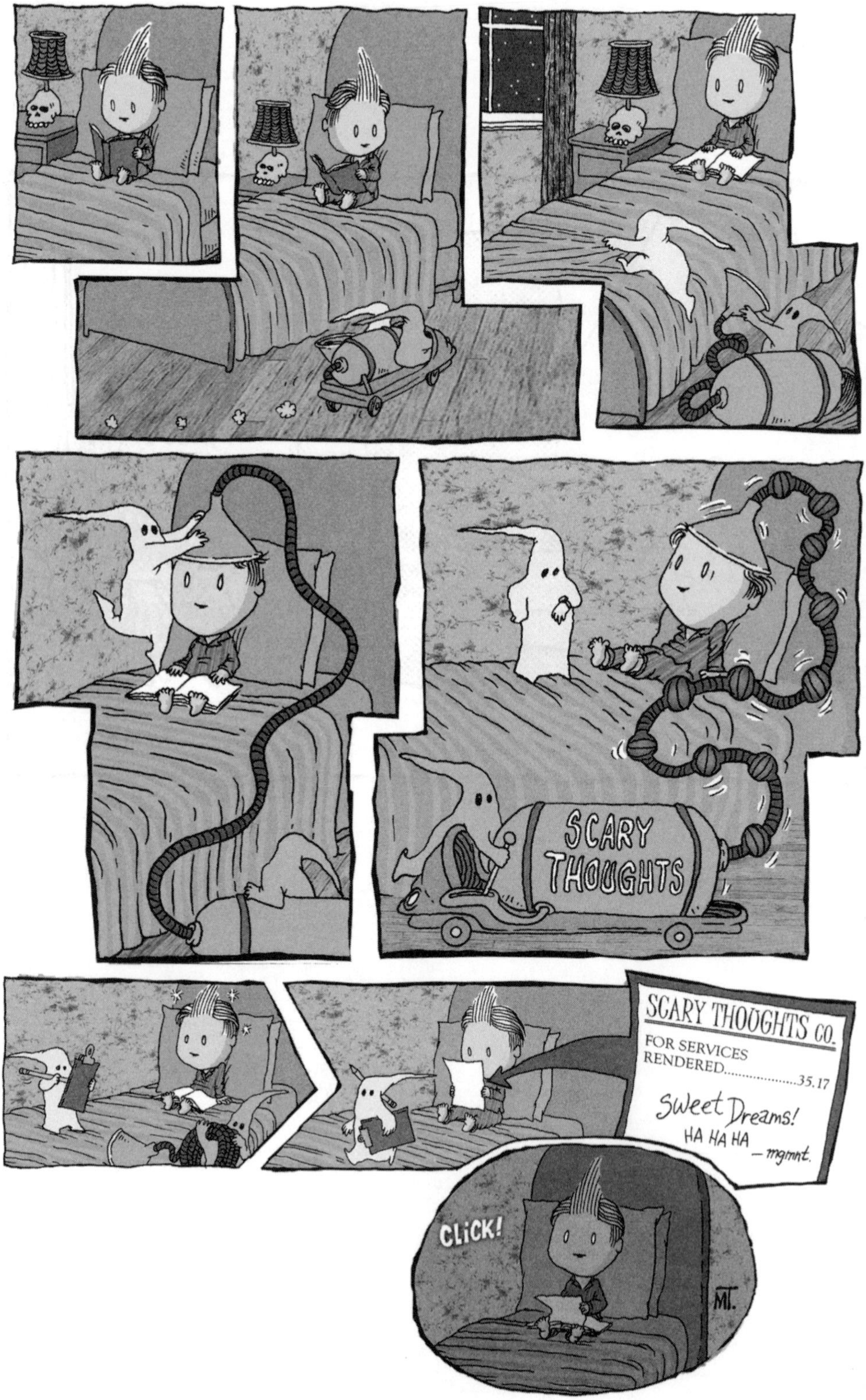
SCARY THOUGHTS
SCARY THOUGHTS CO.
FOR SERVICES RENDERED....................35.17
Sweet Dreams!
HA HA HA — mgmnt.
CLICK!
MT.

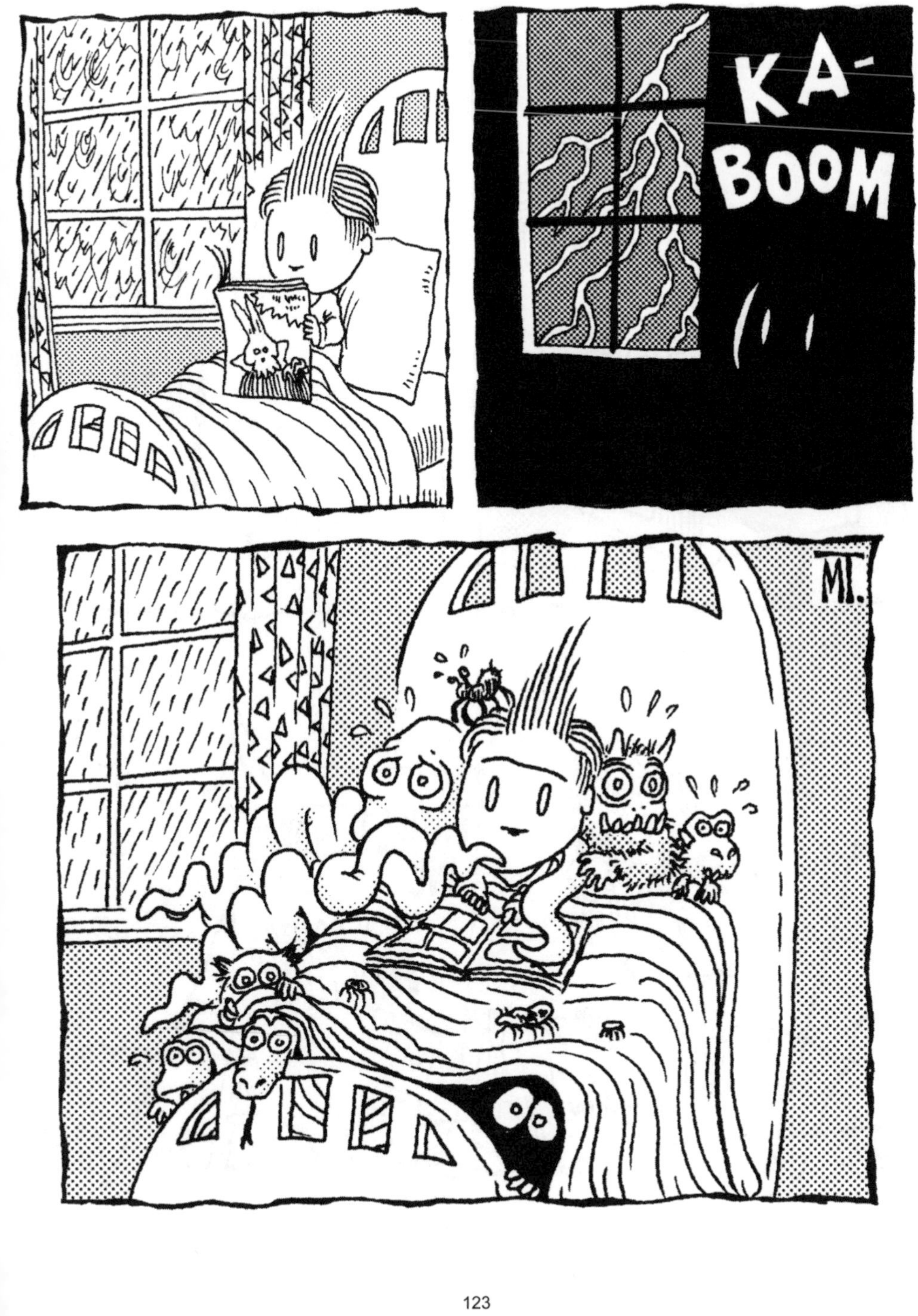
KA-
BOOM
MT.

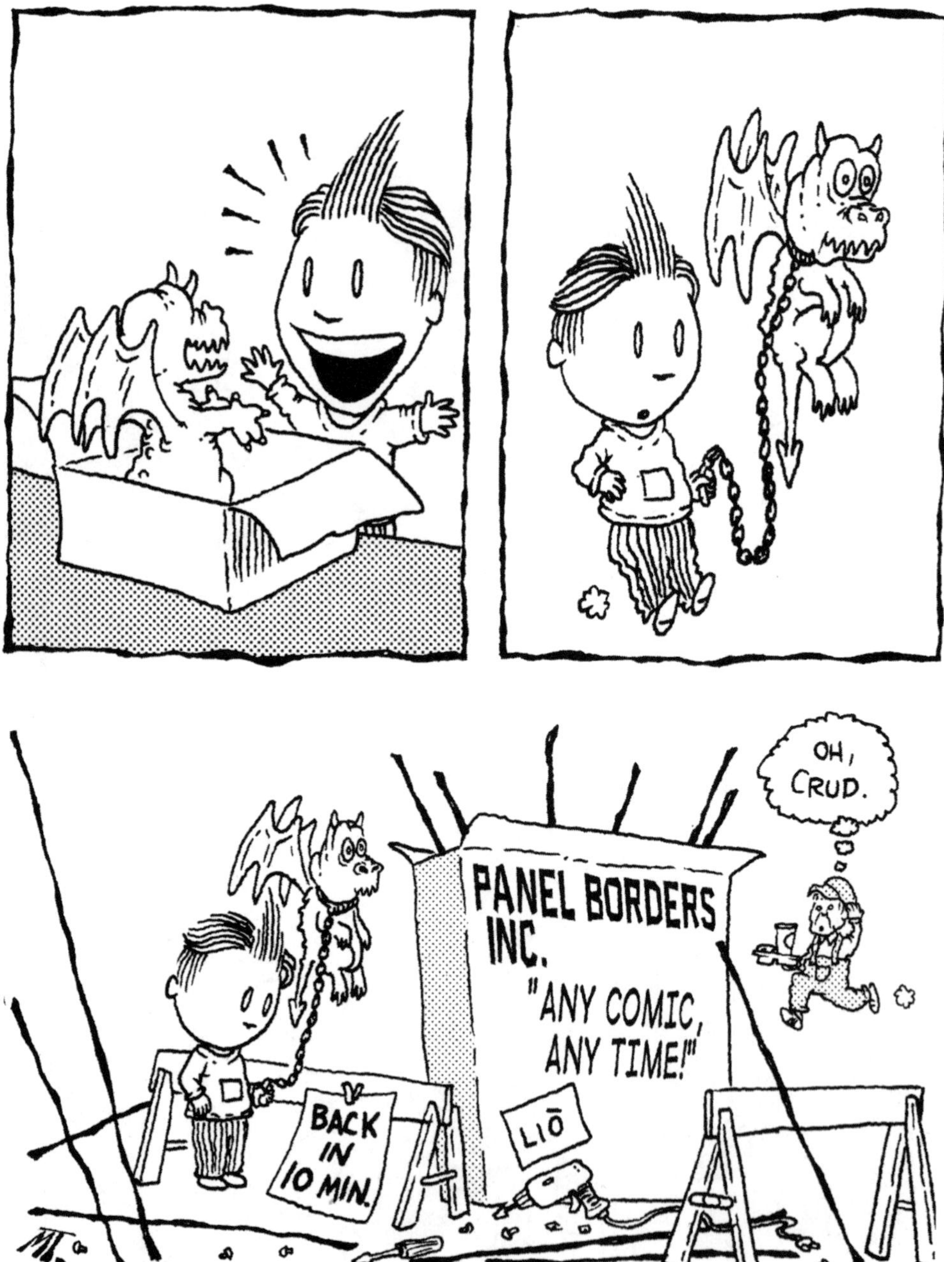
OH, CRUD.
PANEL BORDERS INC.
"ANY COMIC, ANY TIME!"
BACK IN 10 MIN.
LIO

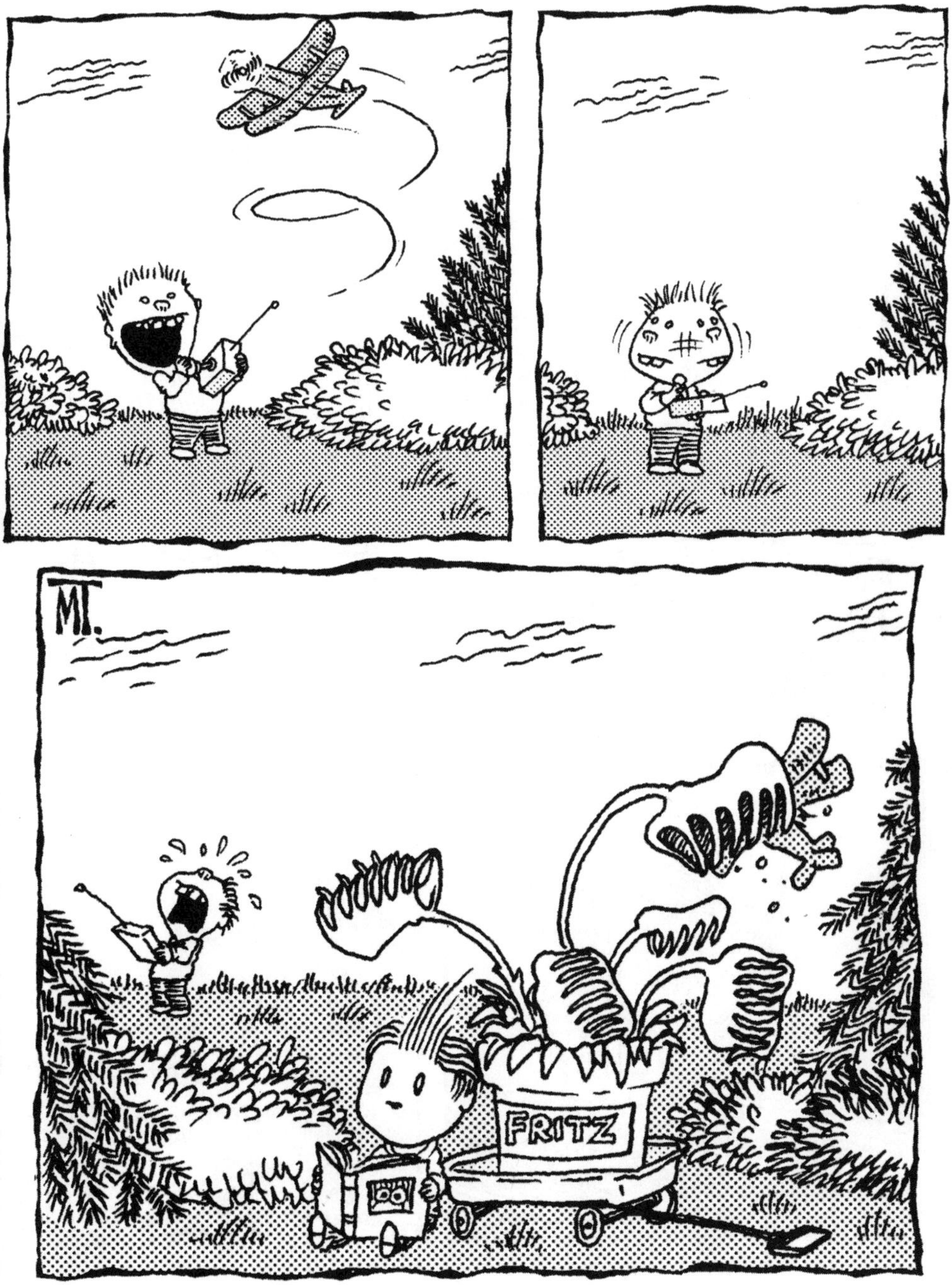
FRITZ

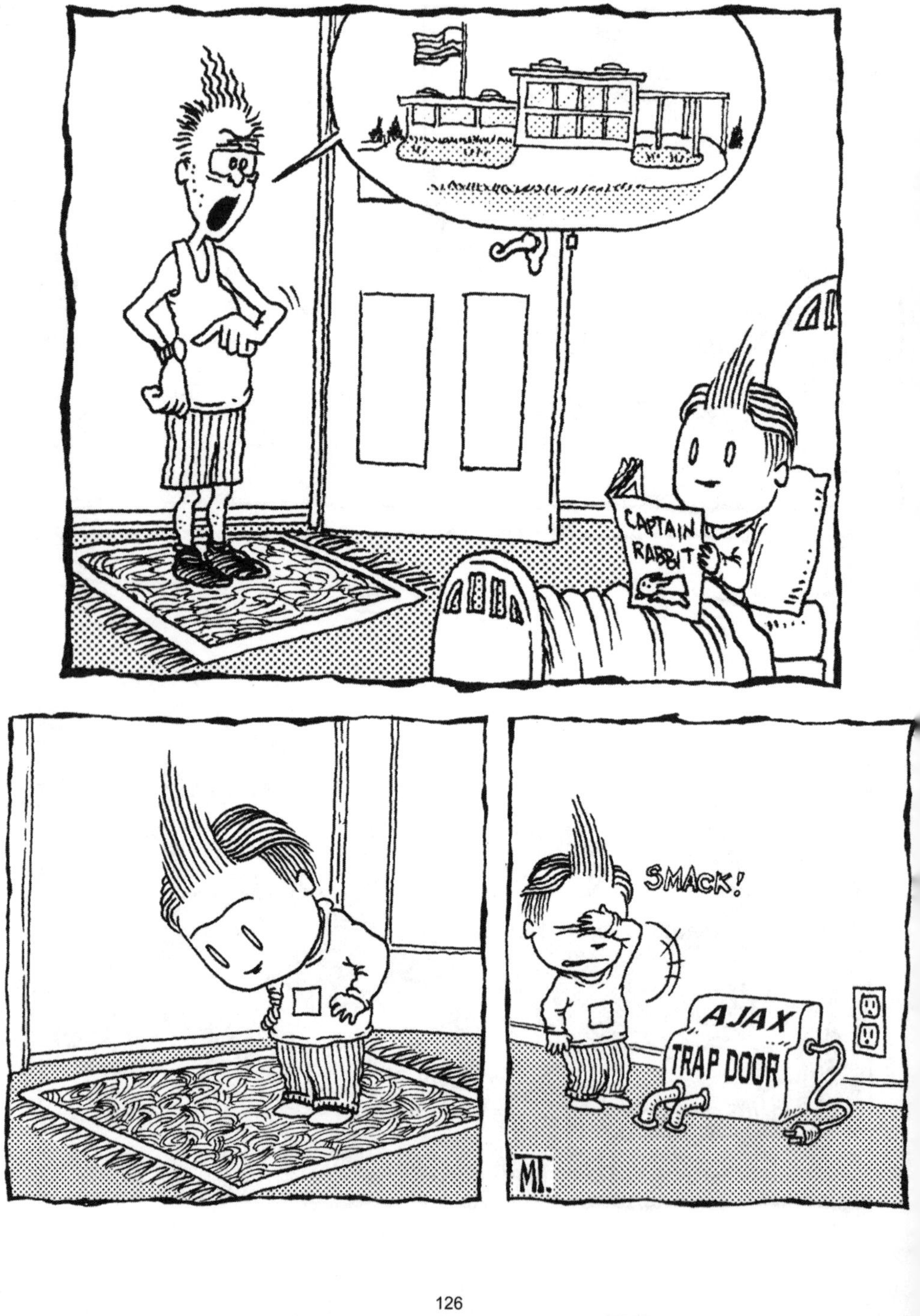
CAPTAIN RABBIT
SMACK!
AJAX
TRAP DOOR
MI.

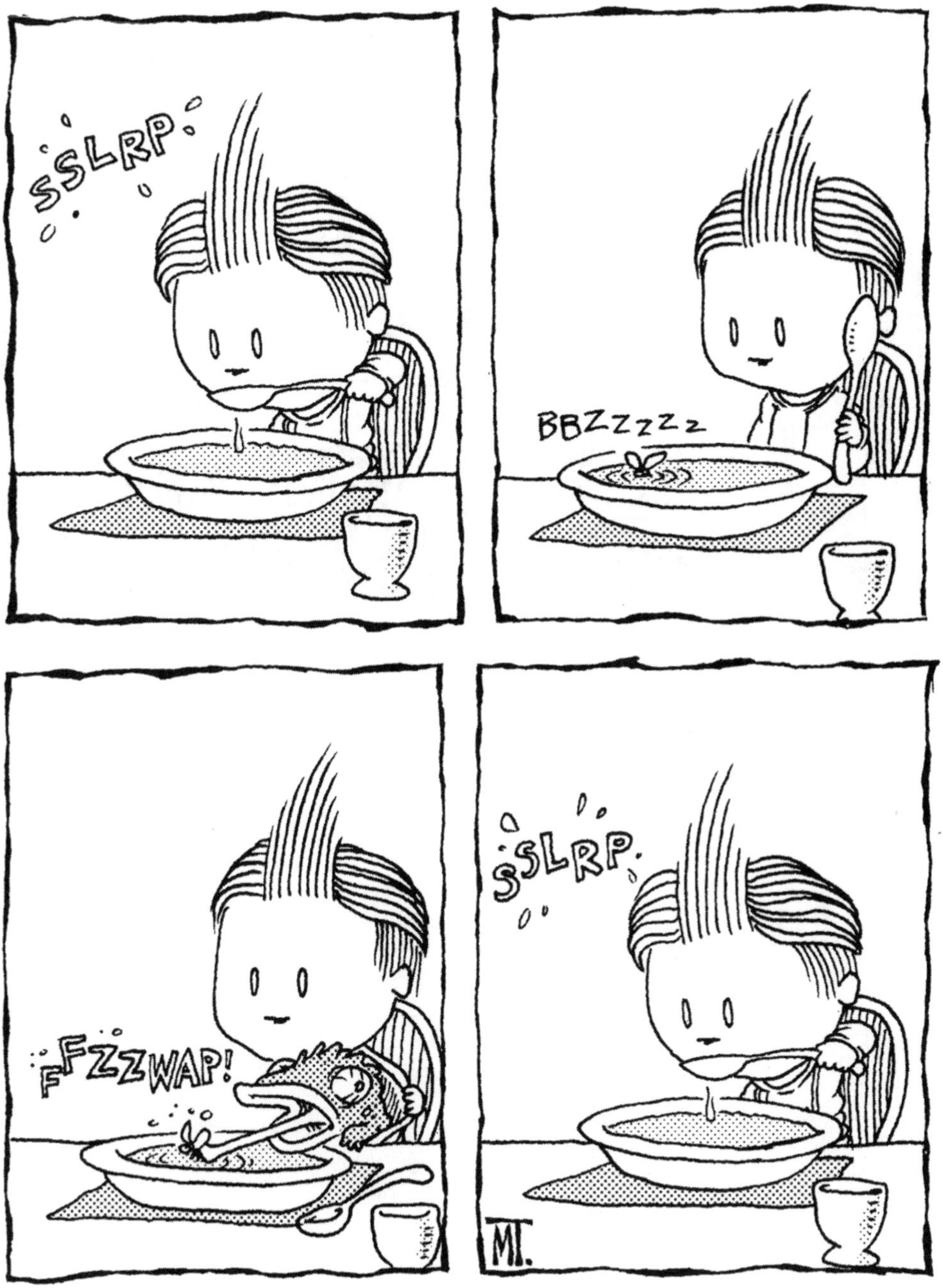
SSLRP
BBZzzzz
FFZZWAP!
SSLRP
MT.

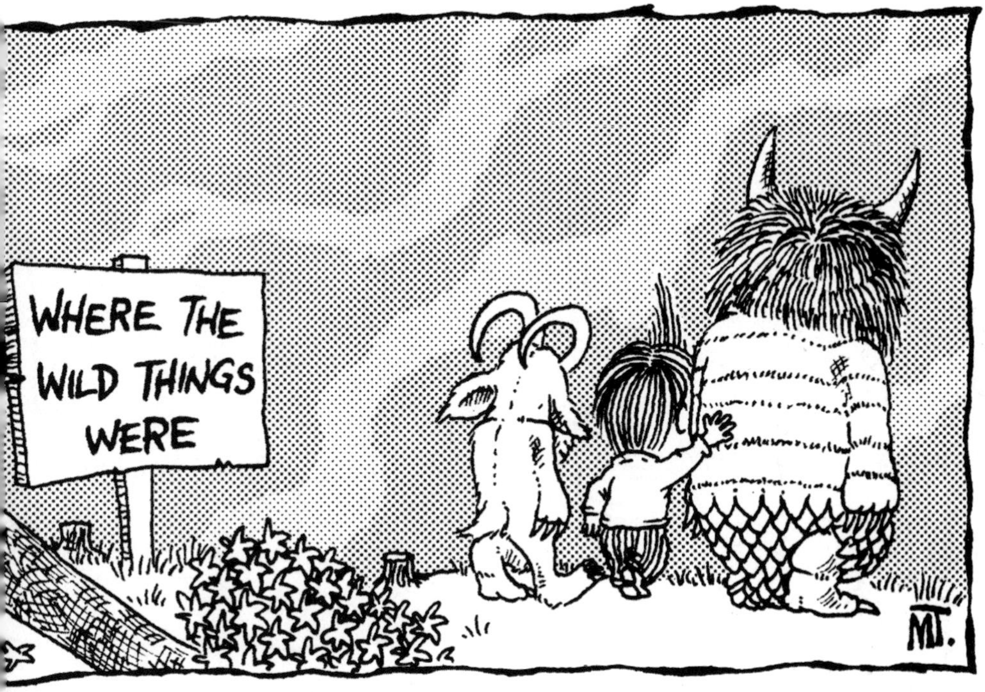
WHERE THE
WILD THINGS
WERE
MT.

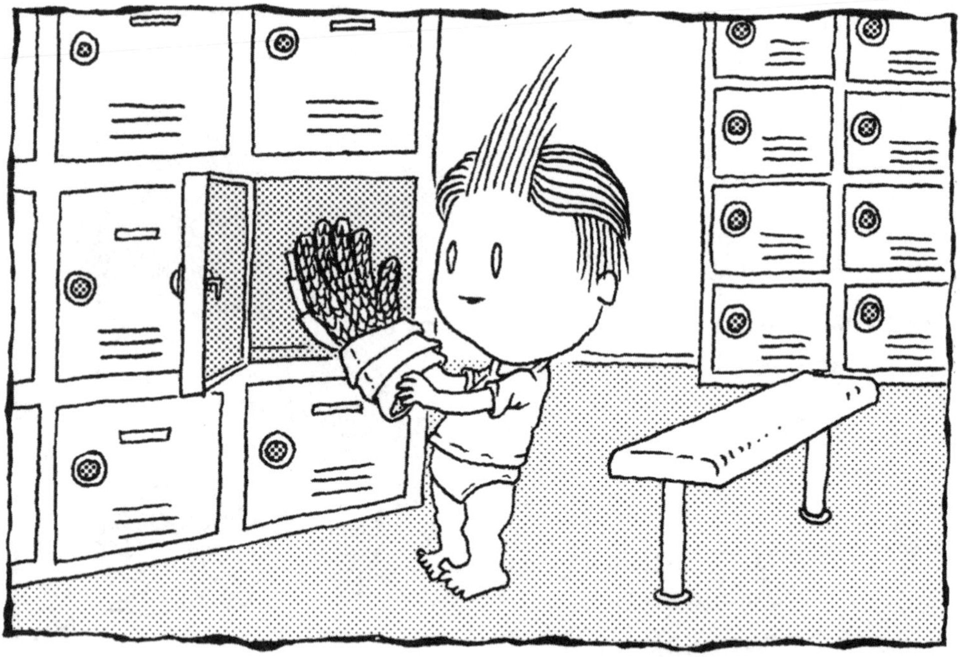

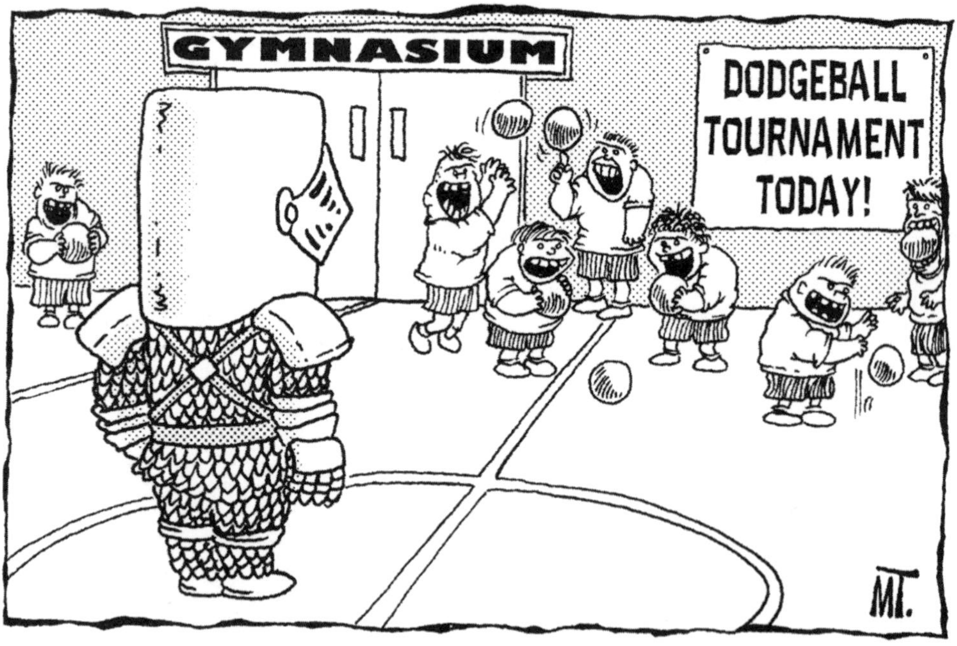
GYMNASIUM
DODGEBALL TOURNAMENT TODAY!
MT.

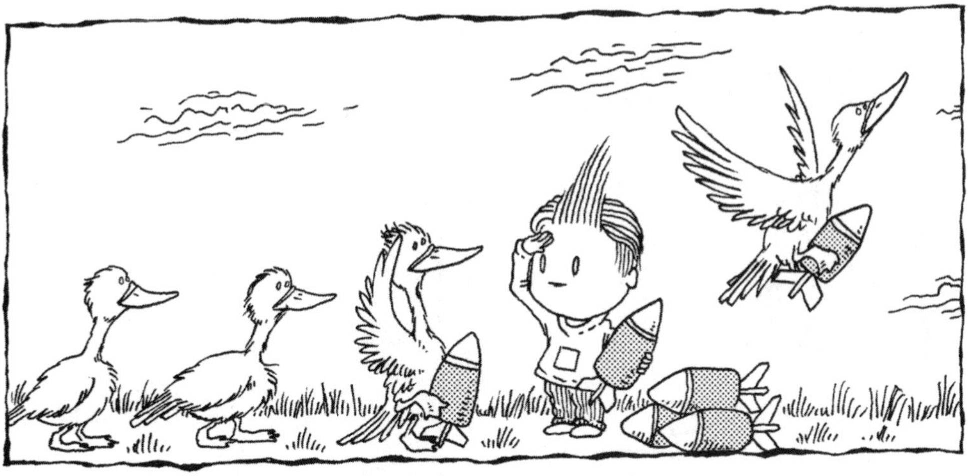

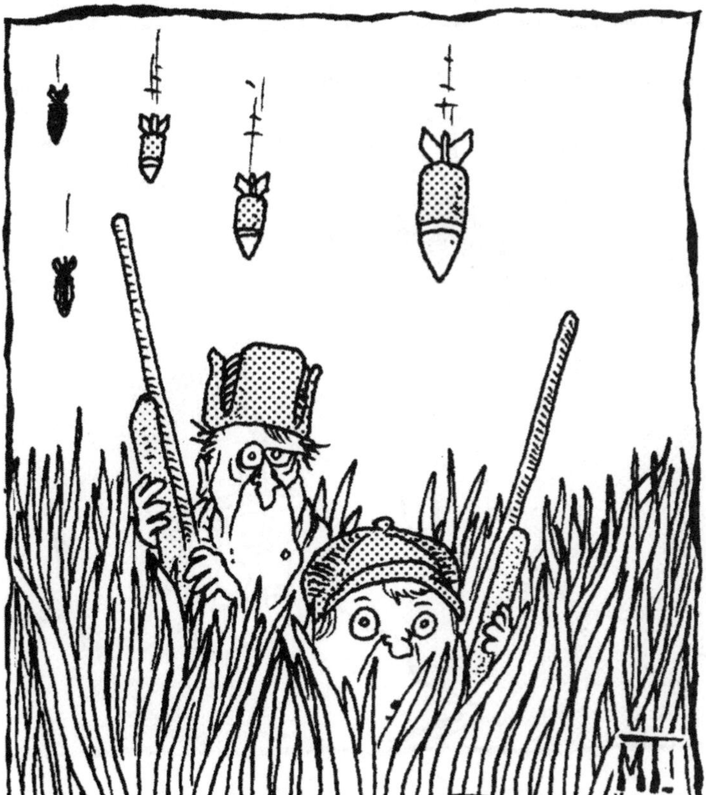

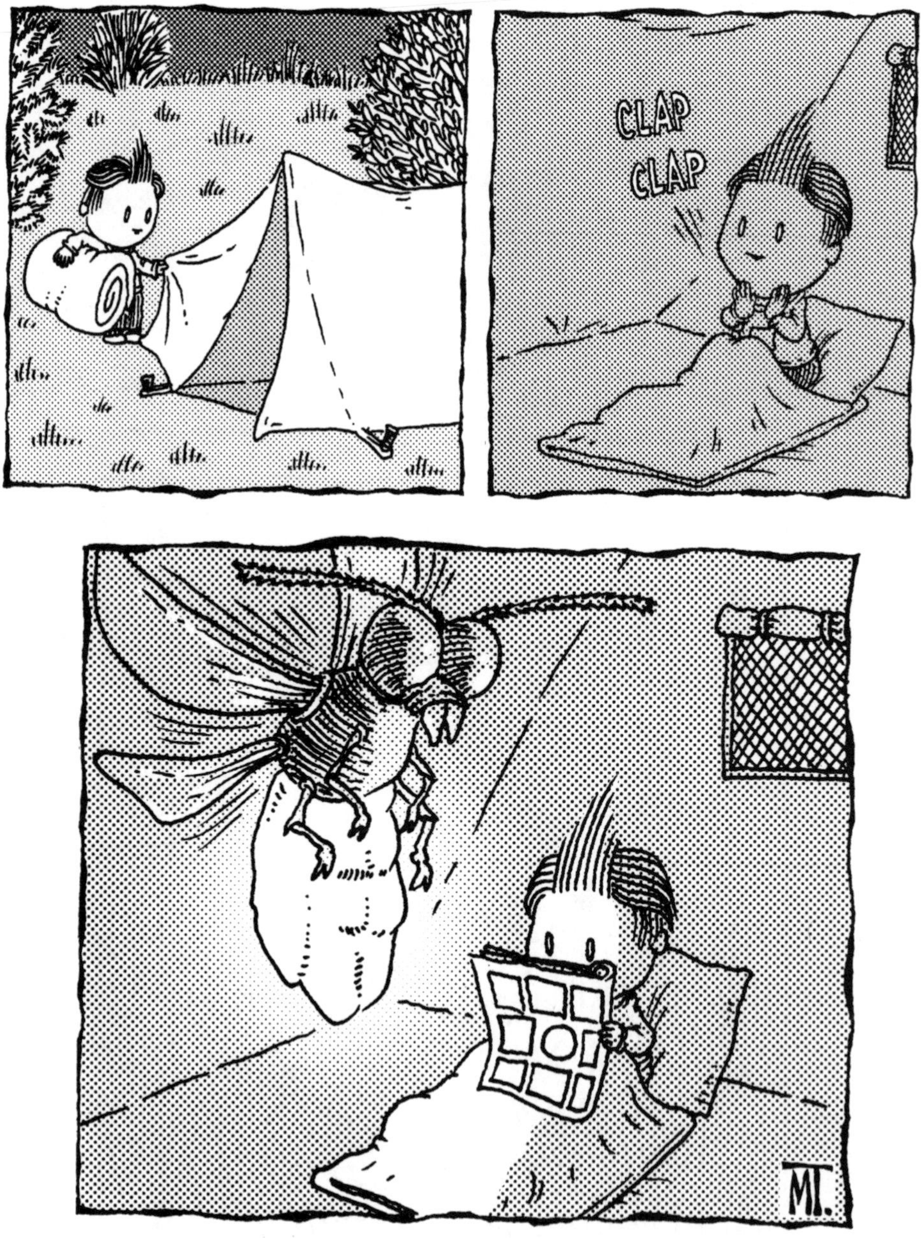
CLAP
CLAP
MT.

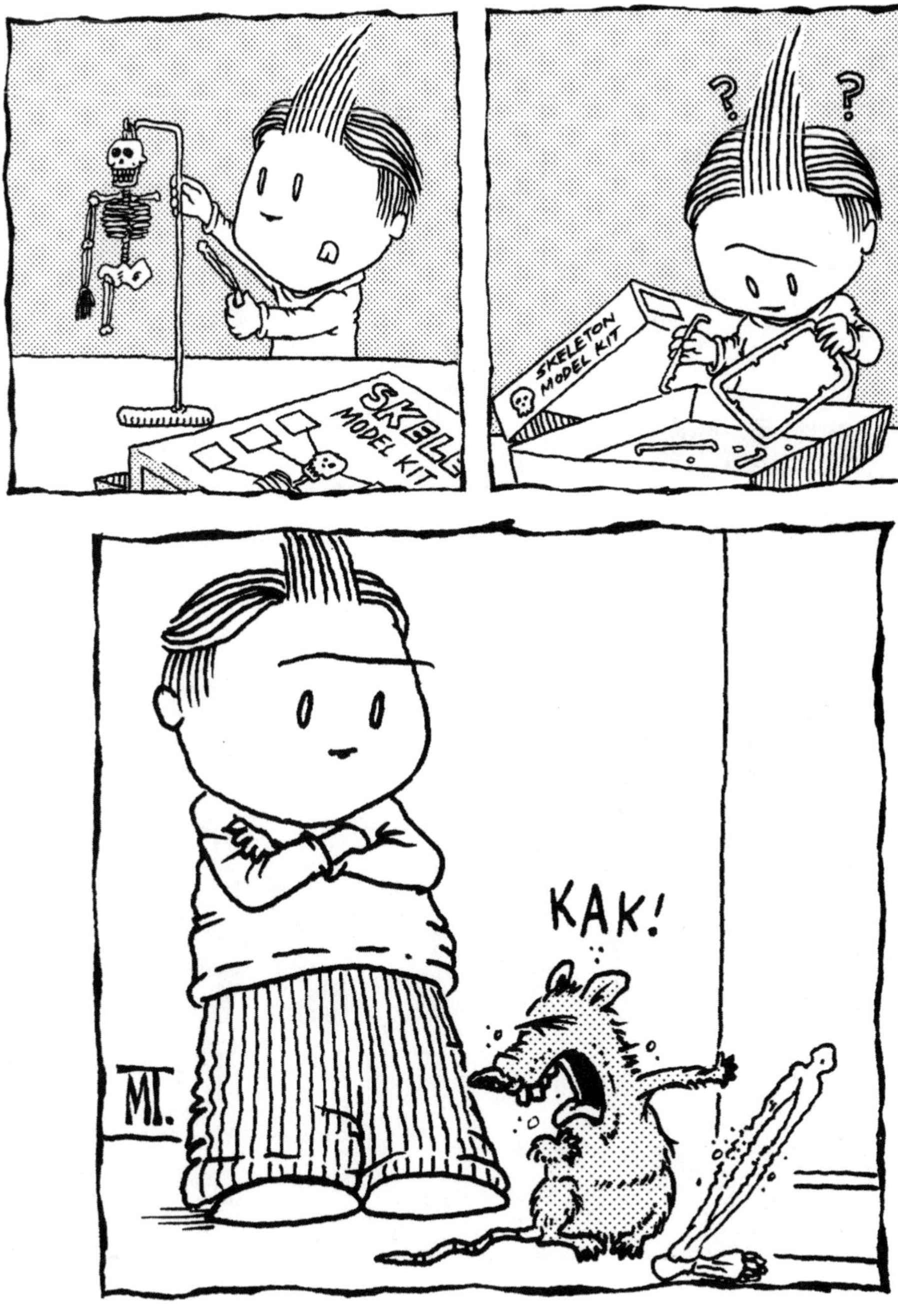
SKELE
MODEL KIT
?
?
SKELETON
MODEL KIT
KAK!
MT.

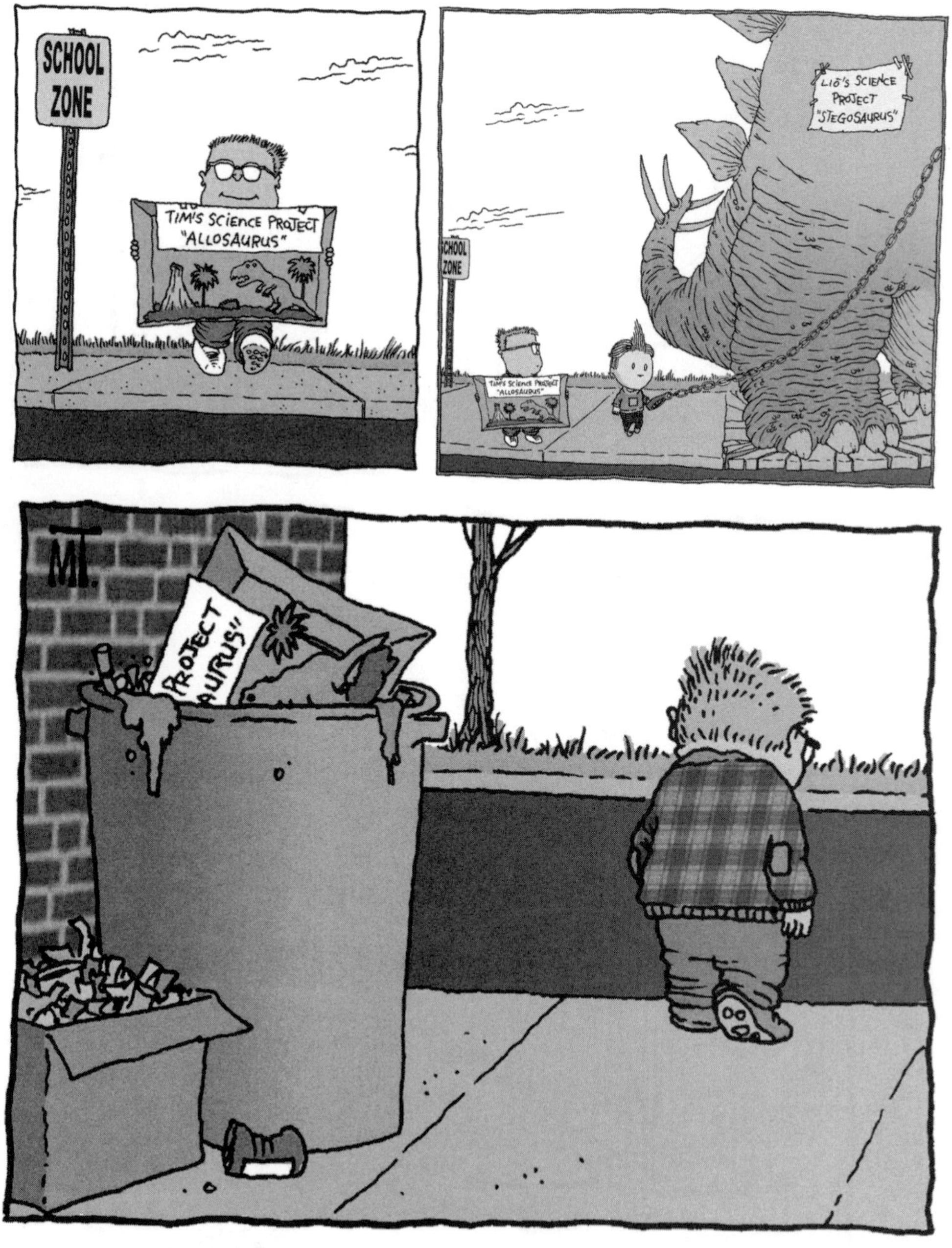
SCHOOL ZONE
TIM'S SCIENCE PROJECT "ALLOSAURUS"
SCHOOL ZONE
TIM'S SCIENCE PROJECT "ALLOSAURUS"
LIŌ'S SCIENCE PROJECT "STEGOSAURUS"
PROJECT
AURUS"

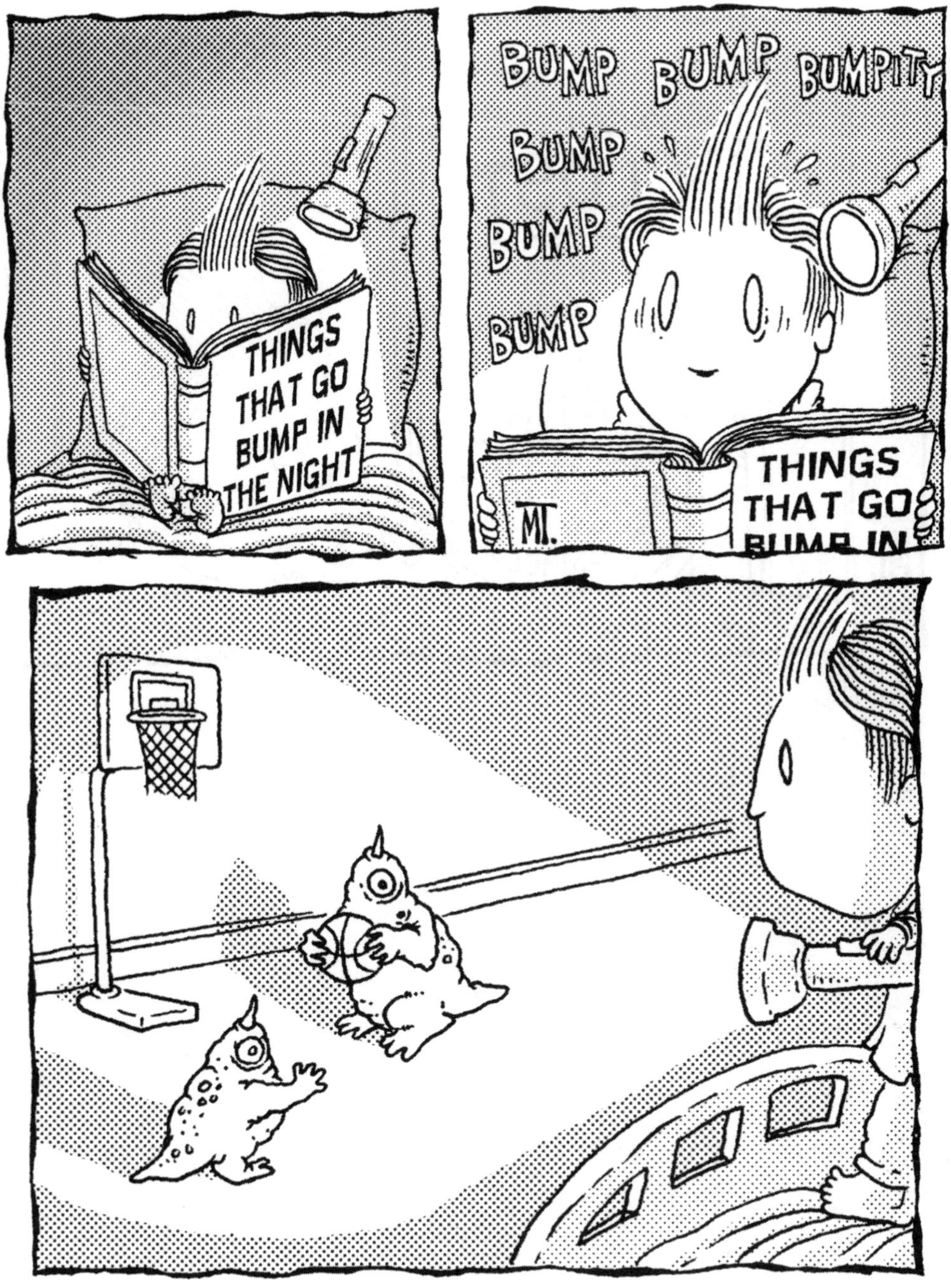
THINGS THAT GO BUMP IN THE NIGHT
BUMP BUMP BUMPITY
BUMP
BUMP
BUMP
THINGS THAT GO
MT.

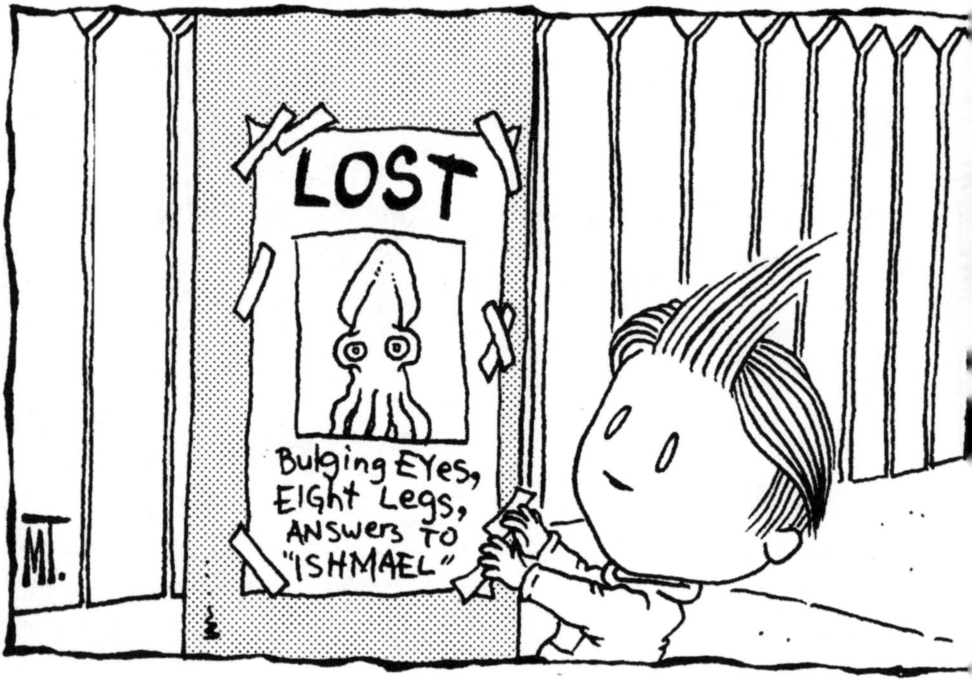
LOST
Bulging Eyes, Eight Legs, Answers to "ISHMAEL"
MT.

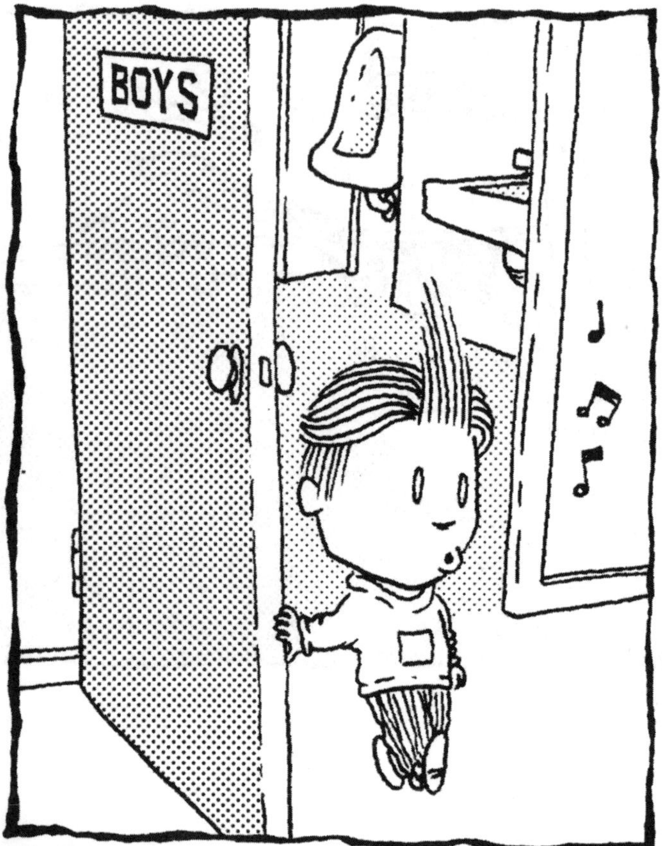
BOYS

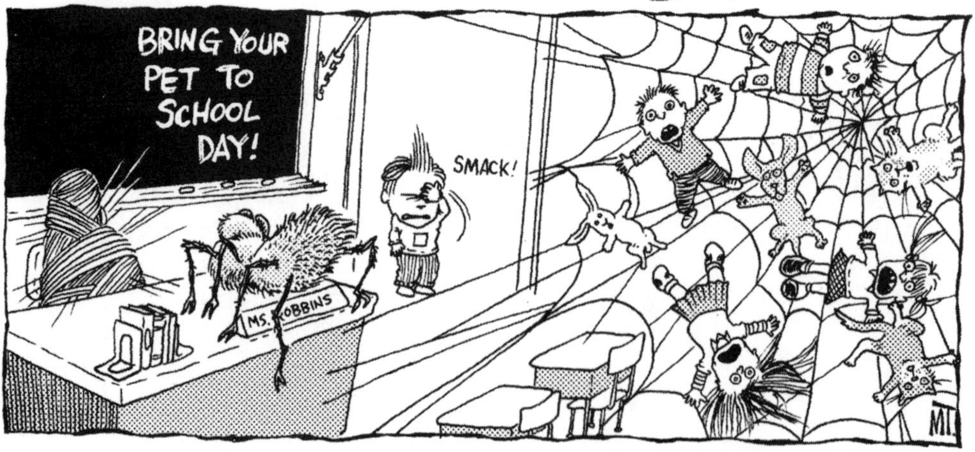
BRING YOUR PET TO SCHOOL DAY!
SMACK!
MS. ROBBINS

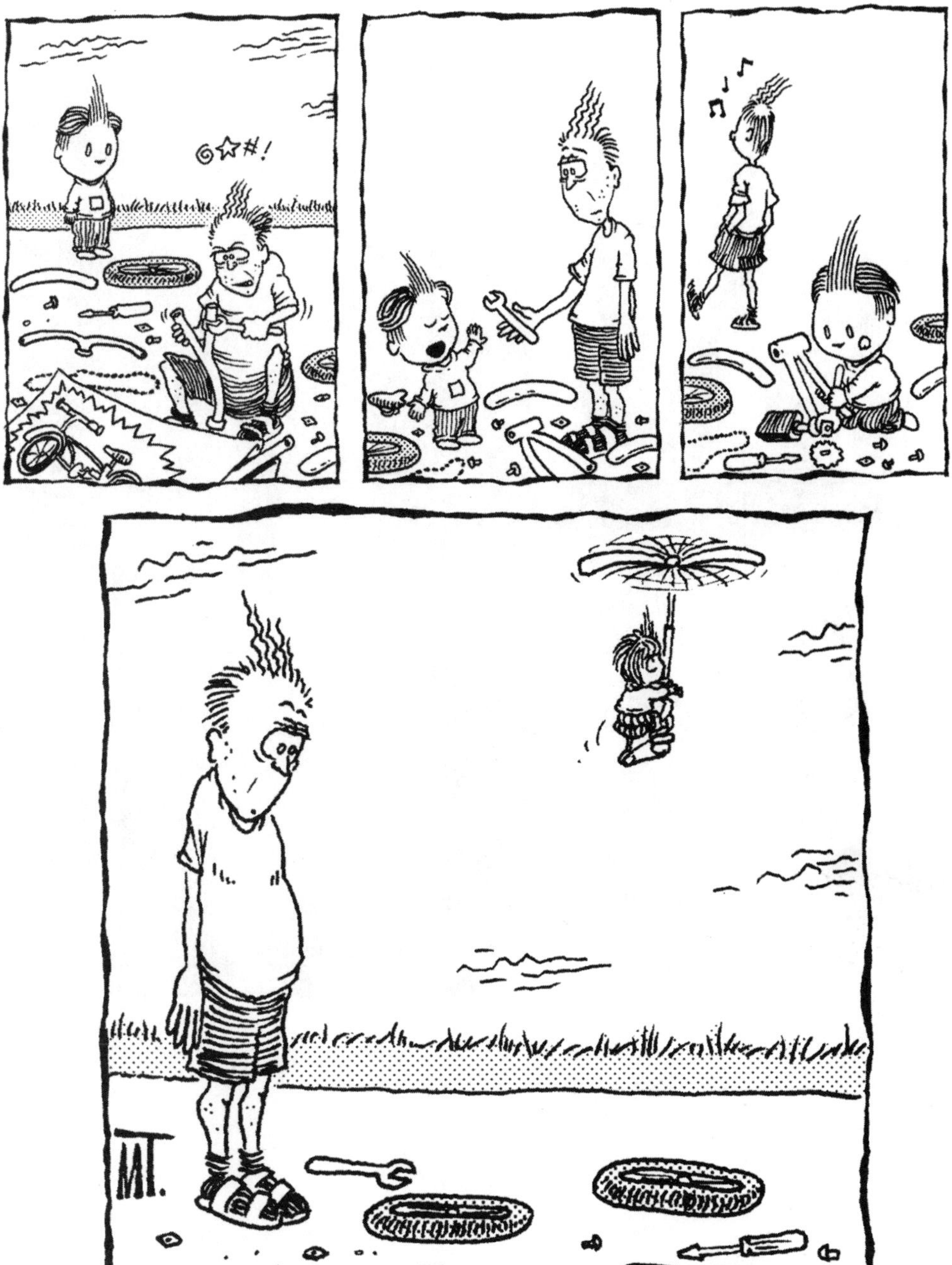
@☆#!
MT.

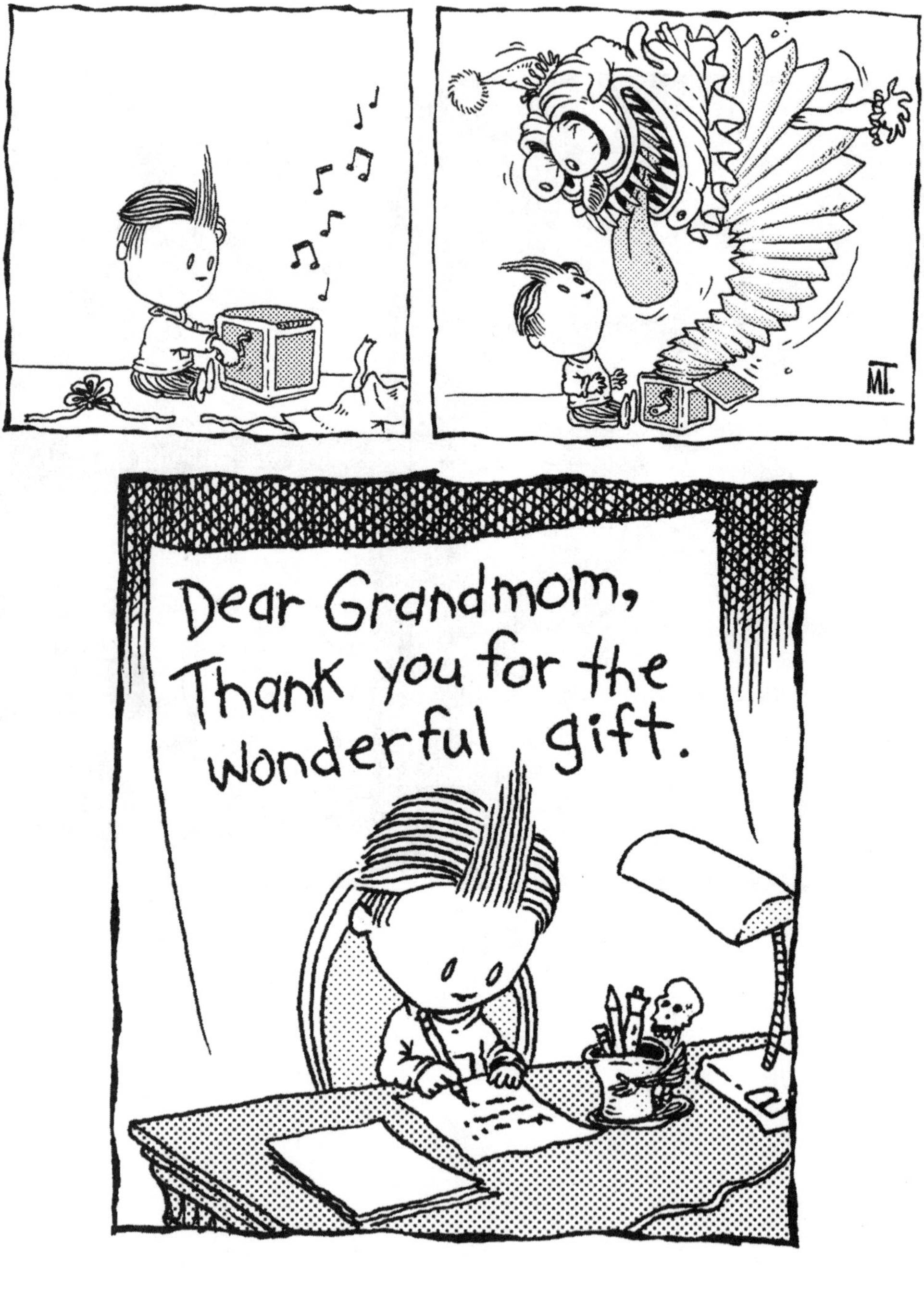
MT.
Dear Grandmom,
Thank you for the
wonderful gift.

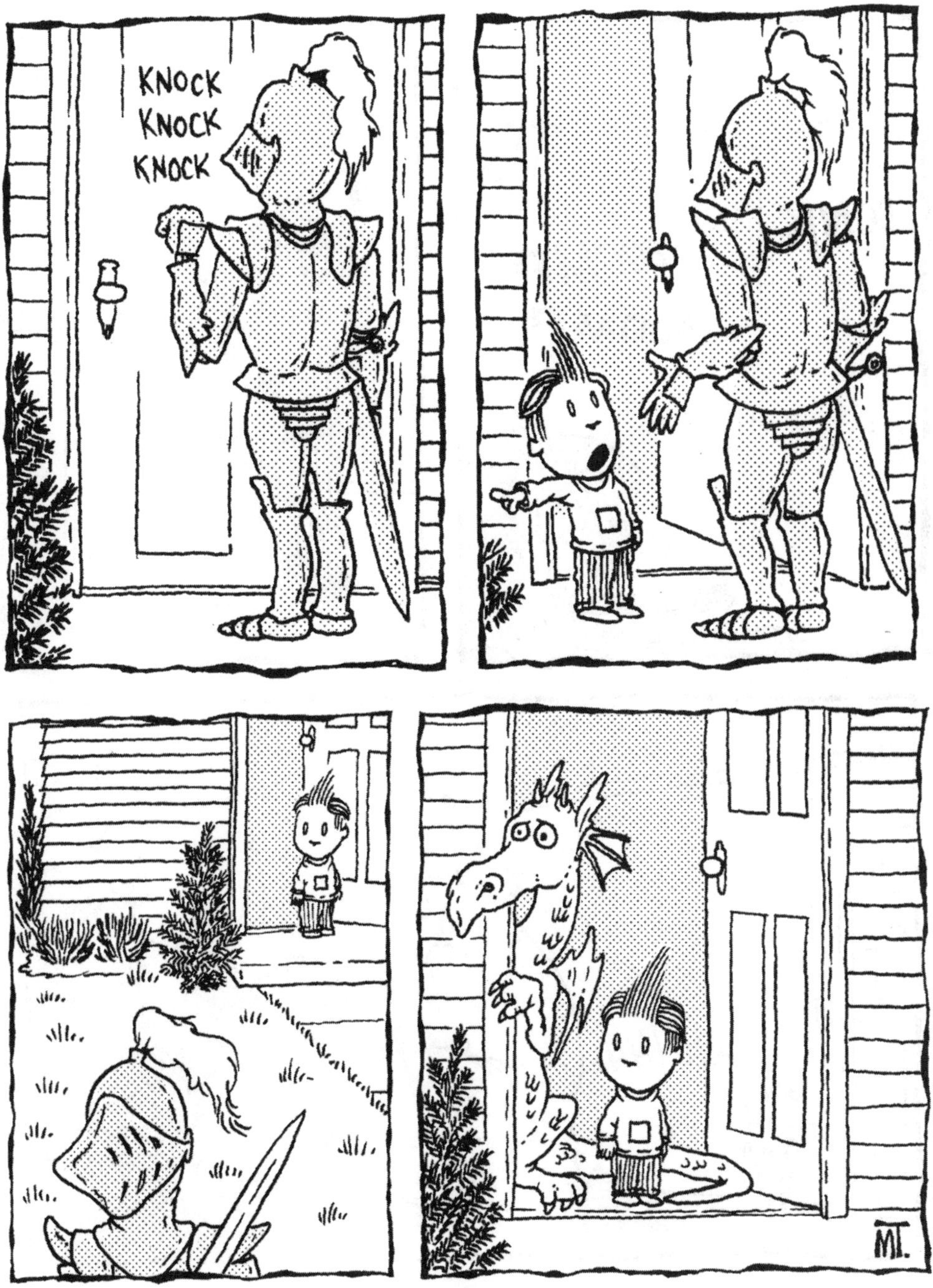
KNOCK
KNOCK
KNOCK
MT.

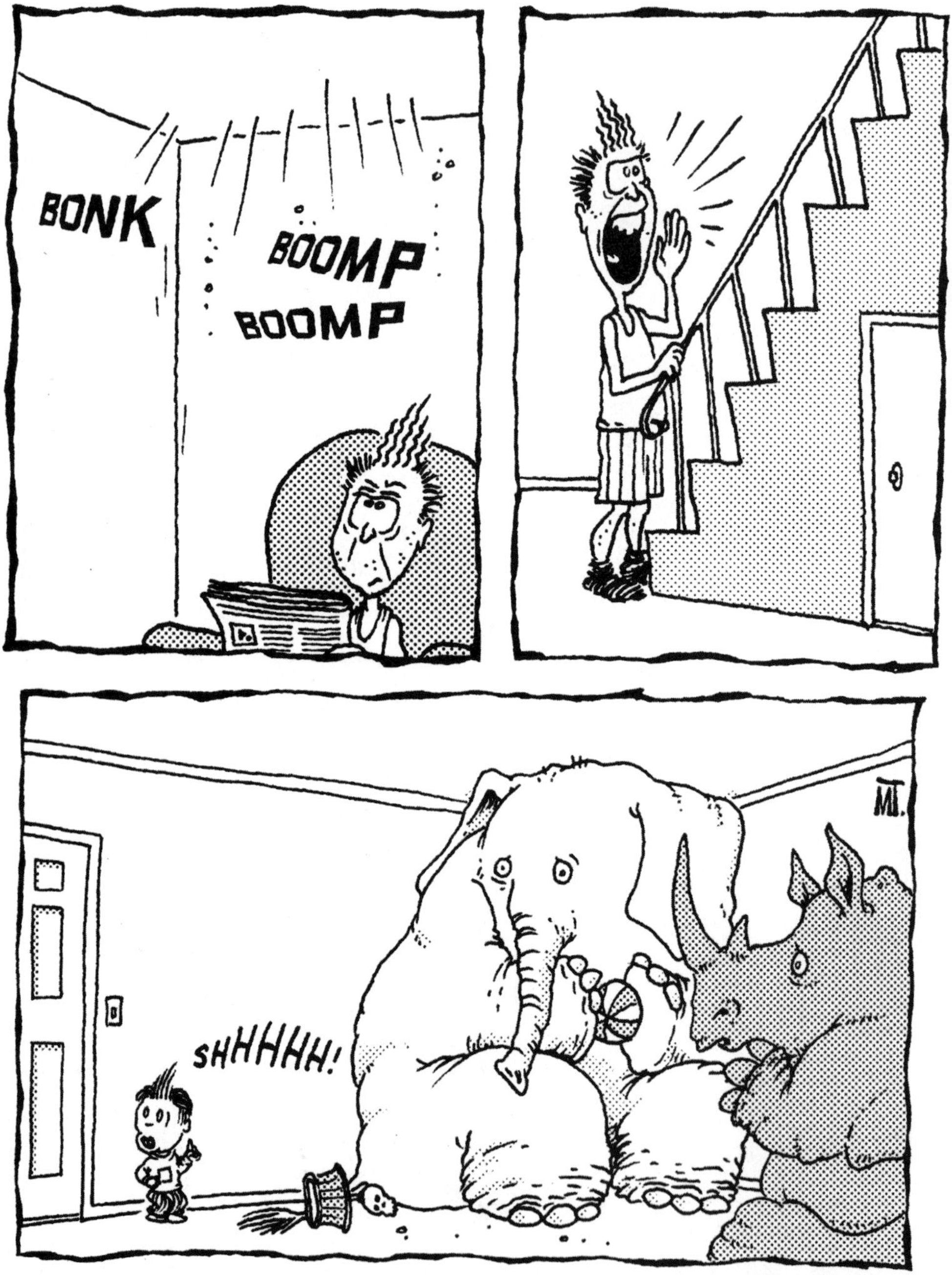
BONK
BOOMP
BOOMP
MT.
SHHHHH!

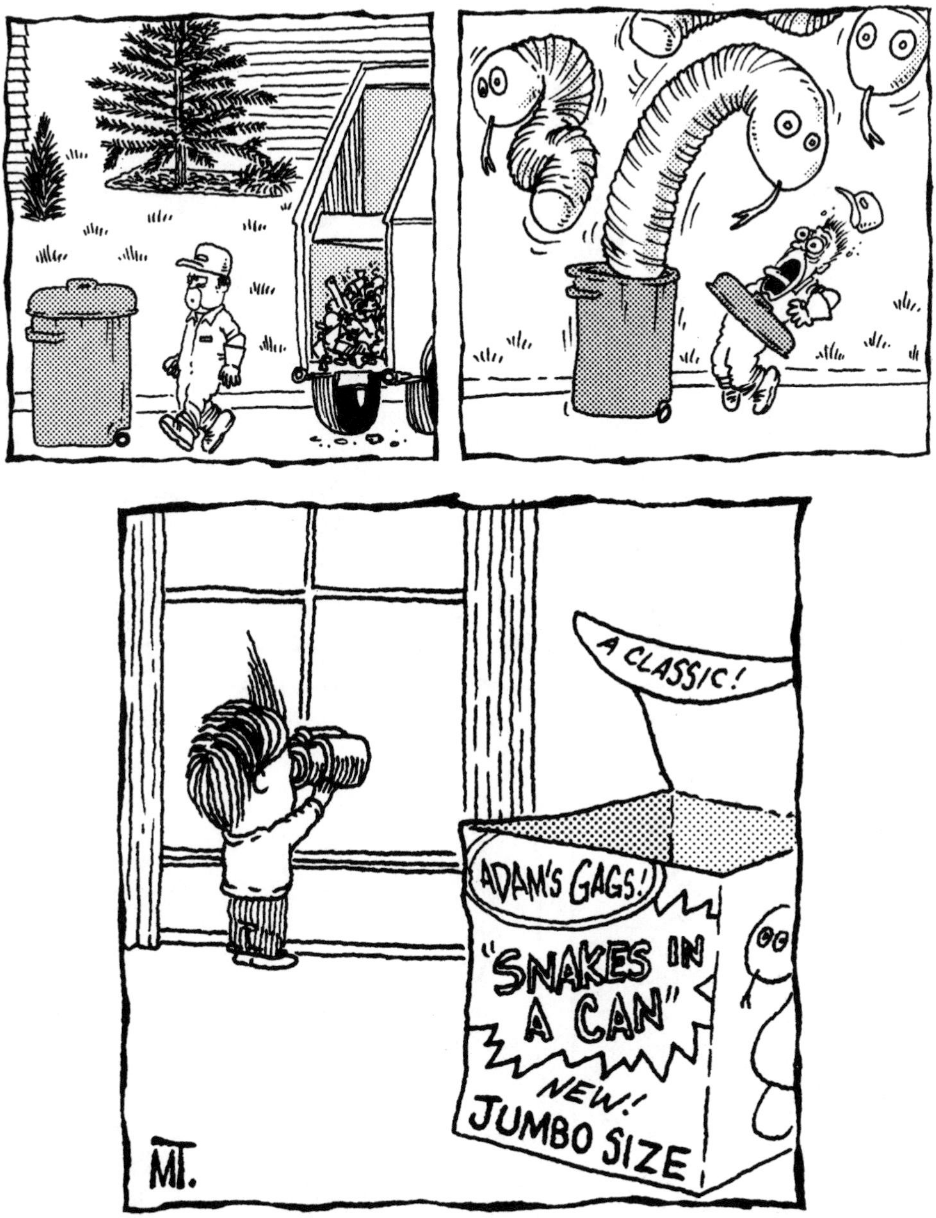
A CLASSIC!
ADAM'S GAGS!
"SNAKES IN A CAN"
NEW!
JUMBO SIZE
MT.

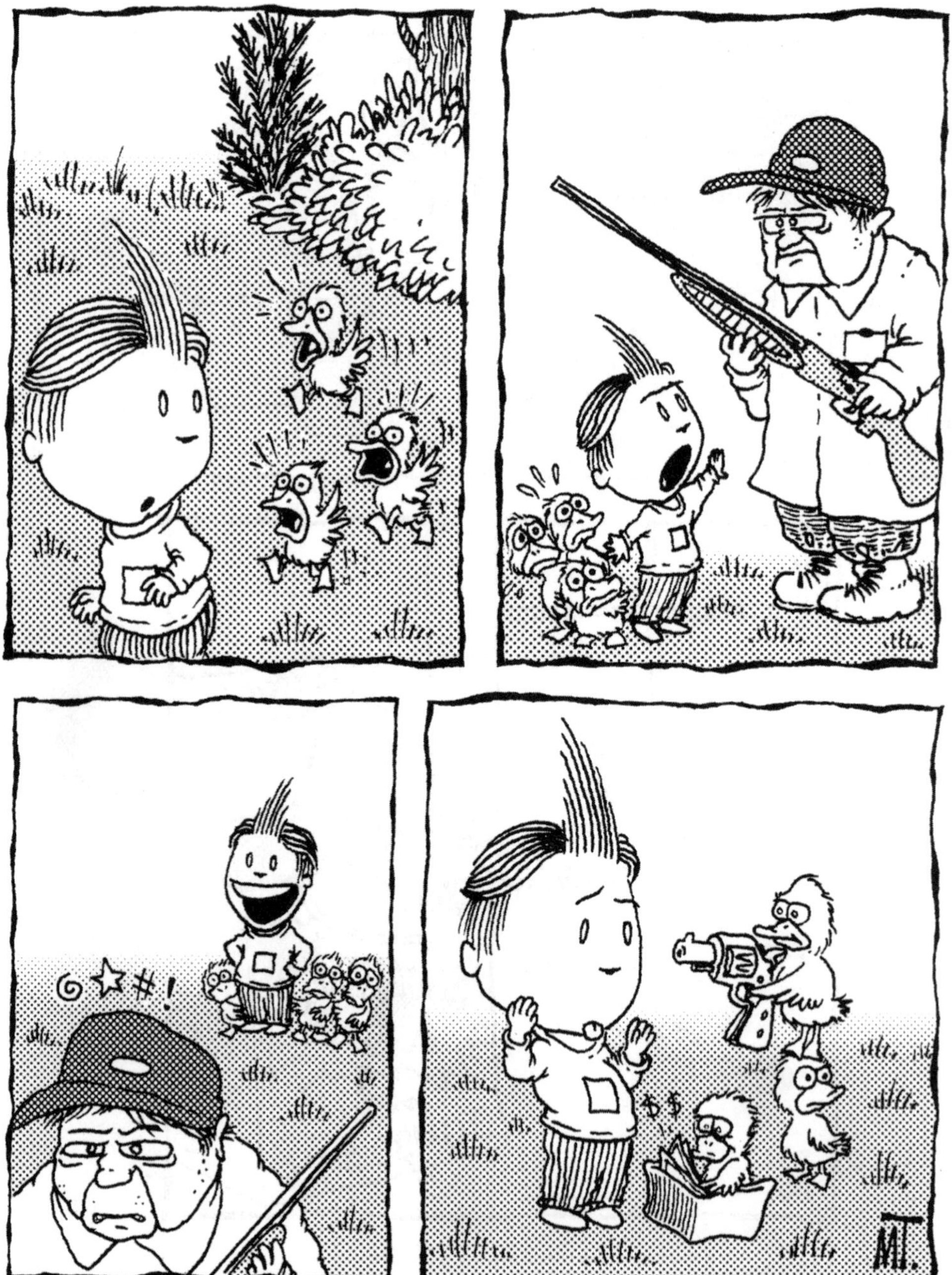

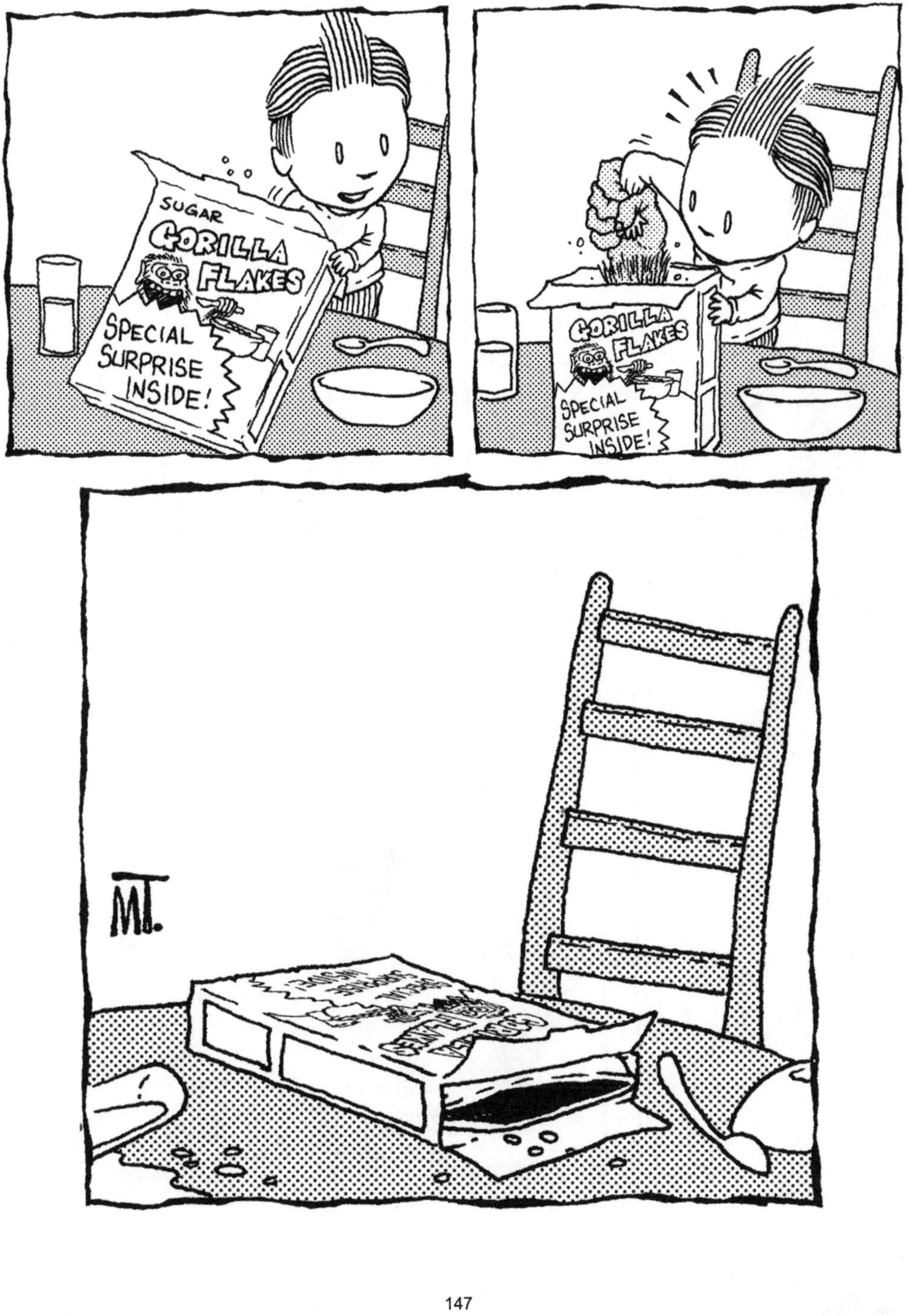

SUGAR
GORILLA
FLAKES
SPECIAL SURPRISE INSIDE!
GORILLA
FLAKES
SPECIAL SURPRISE INSIDE!
MT.

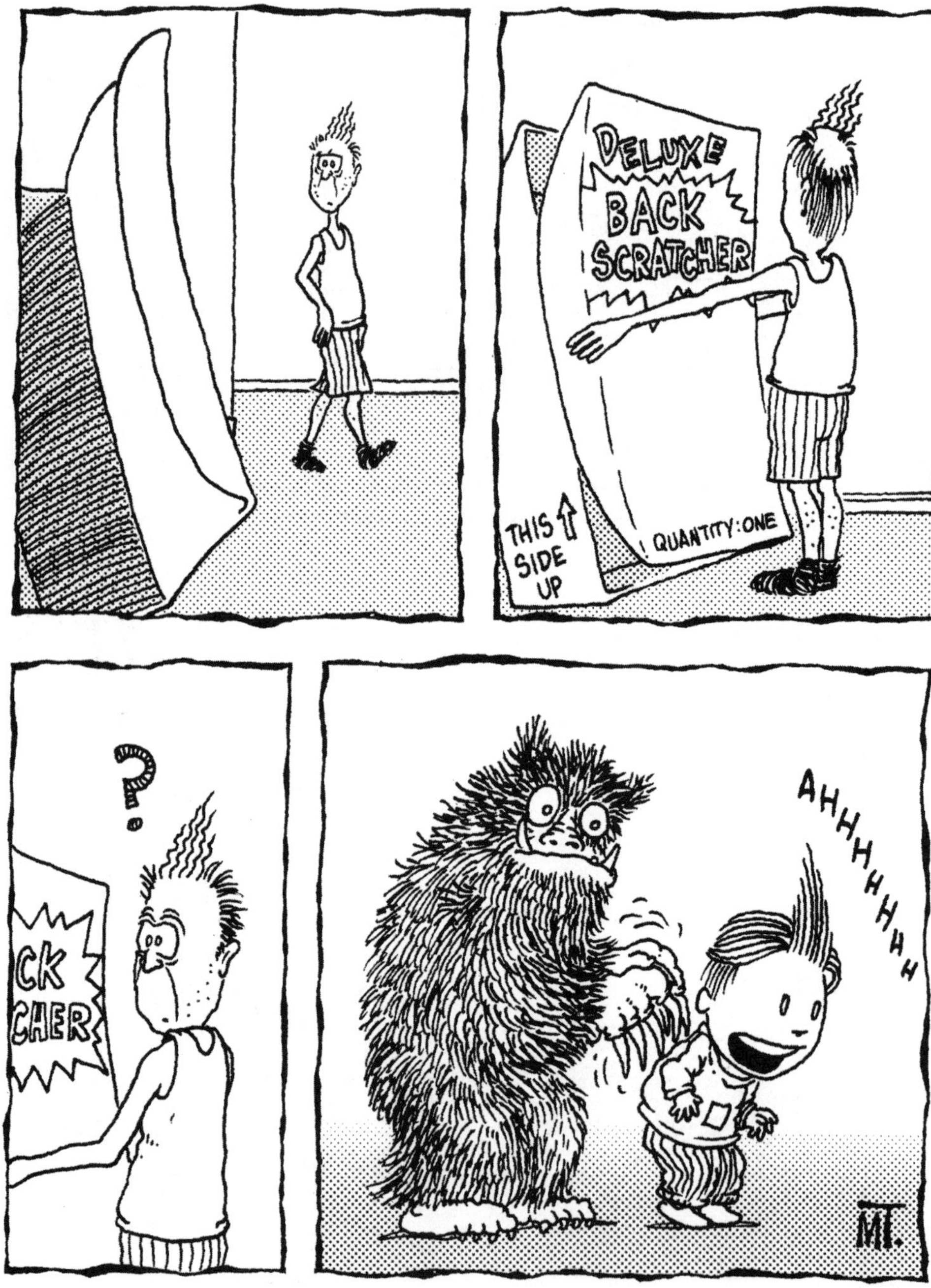
DELUXE
BACK
SCRATCHER
THIS SIDE UP
QUANTITY: ONE
?
CK
CHER
AHHHHHHH
MT.

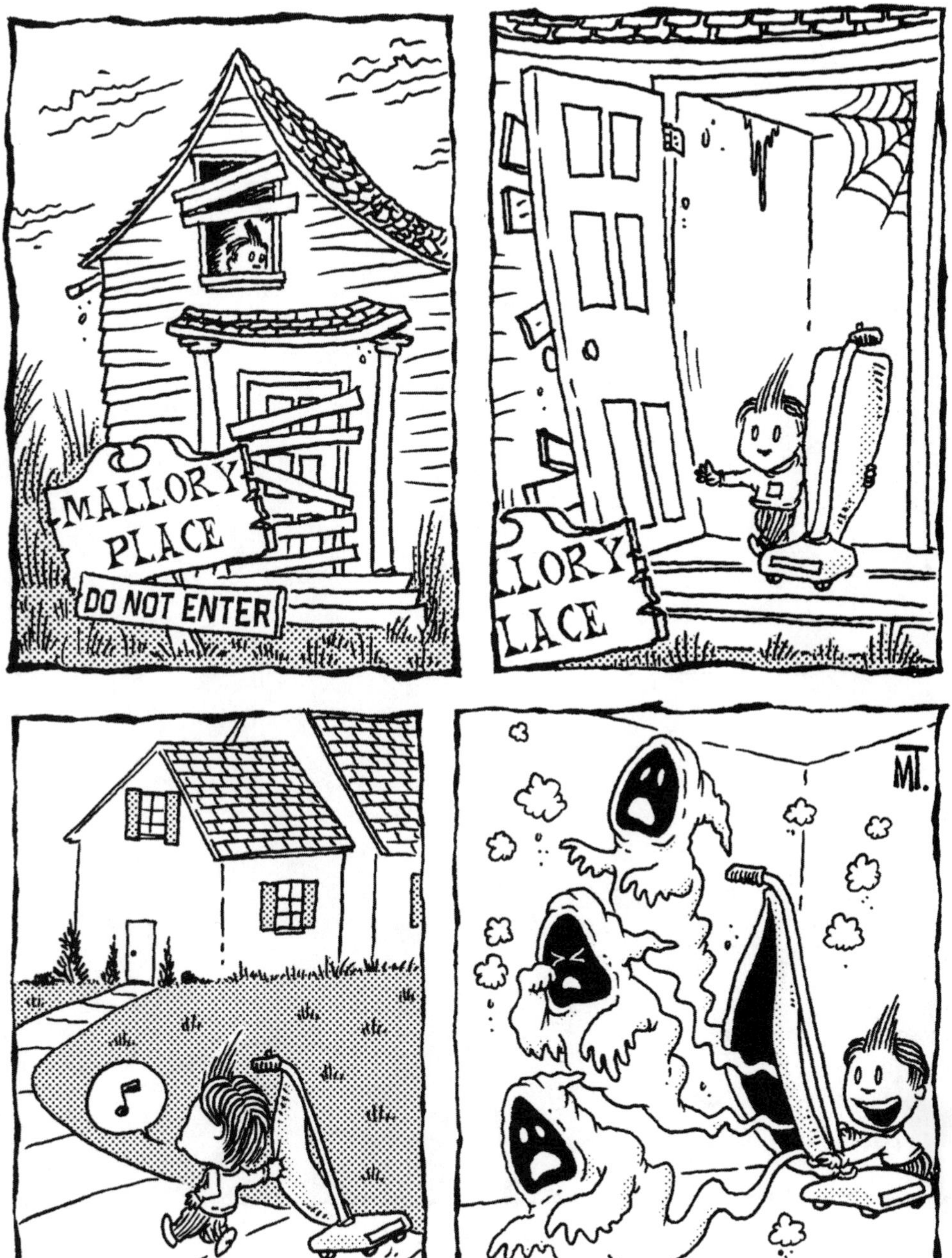
MALLORY
PLACE
DO NOT ENTER
LLORY
LACE
MT.

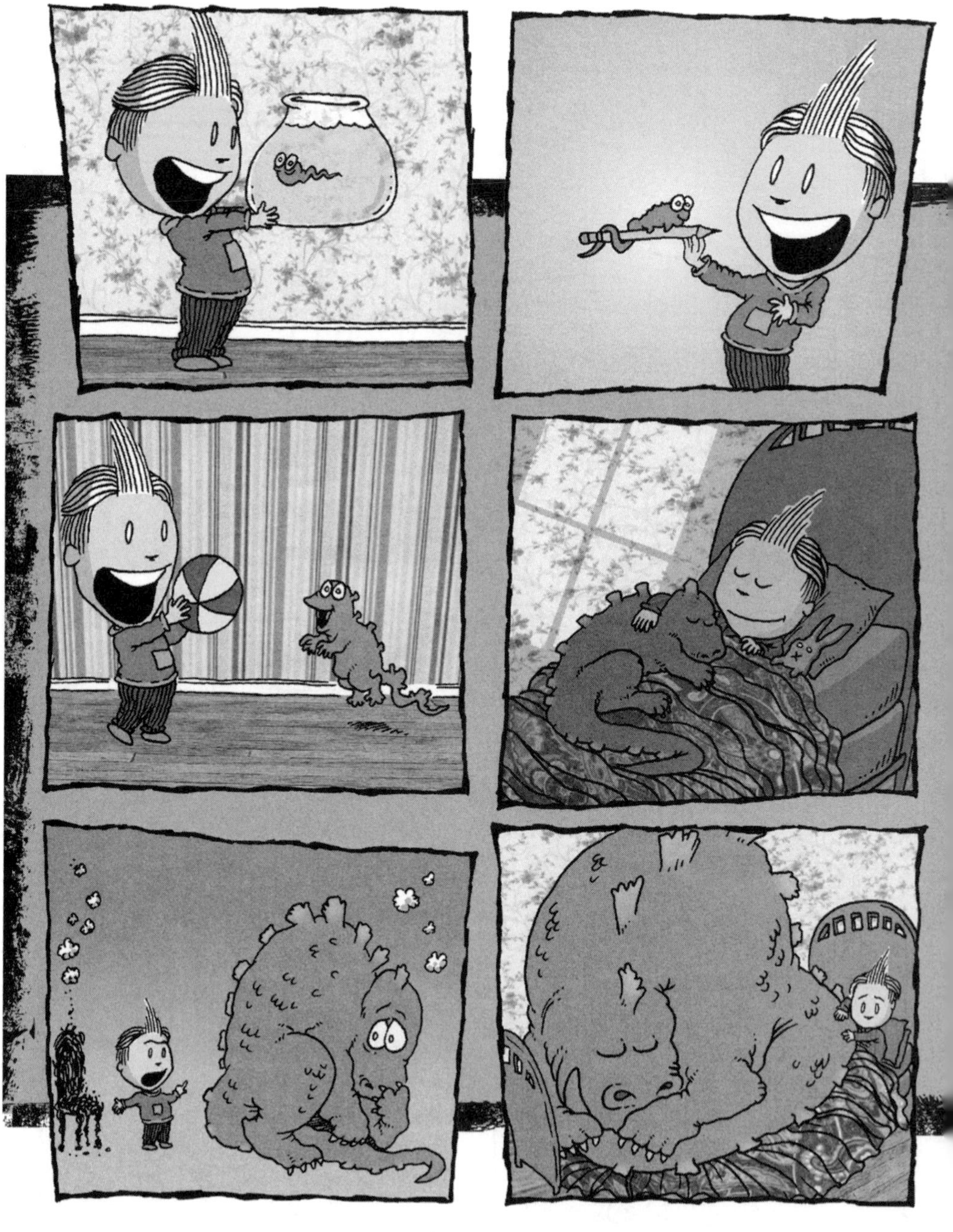

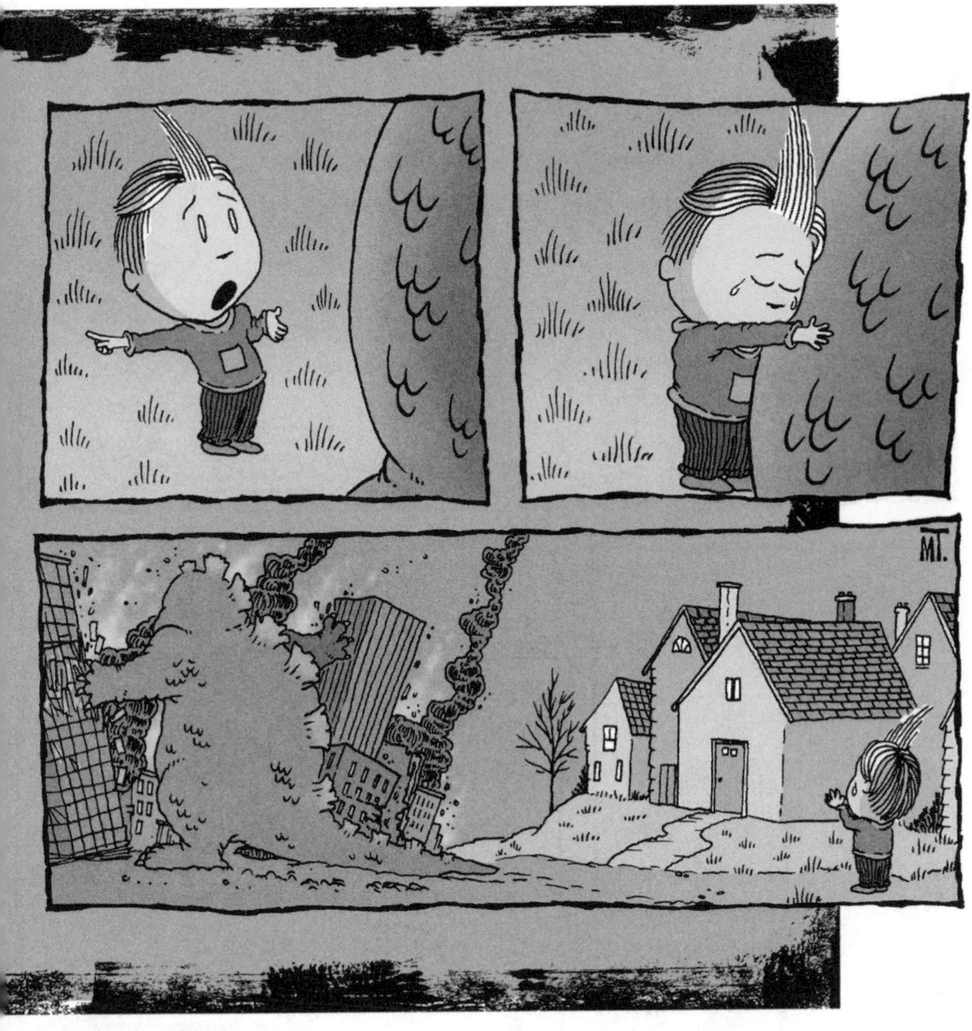
MT.

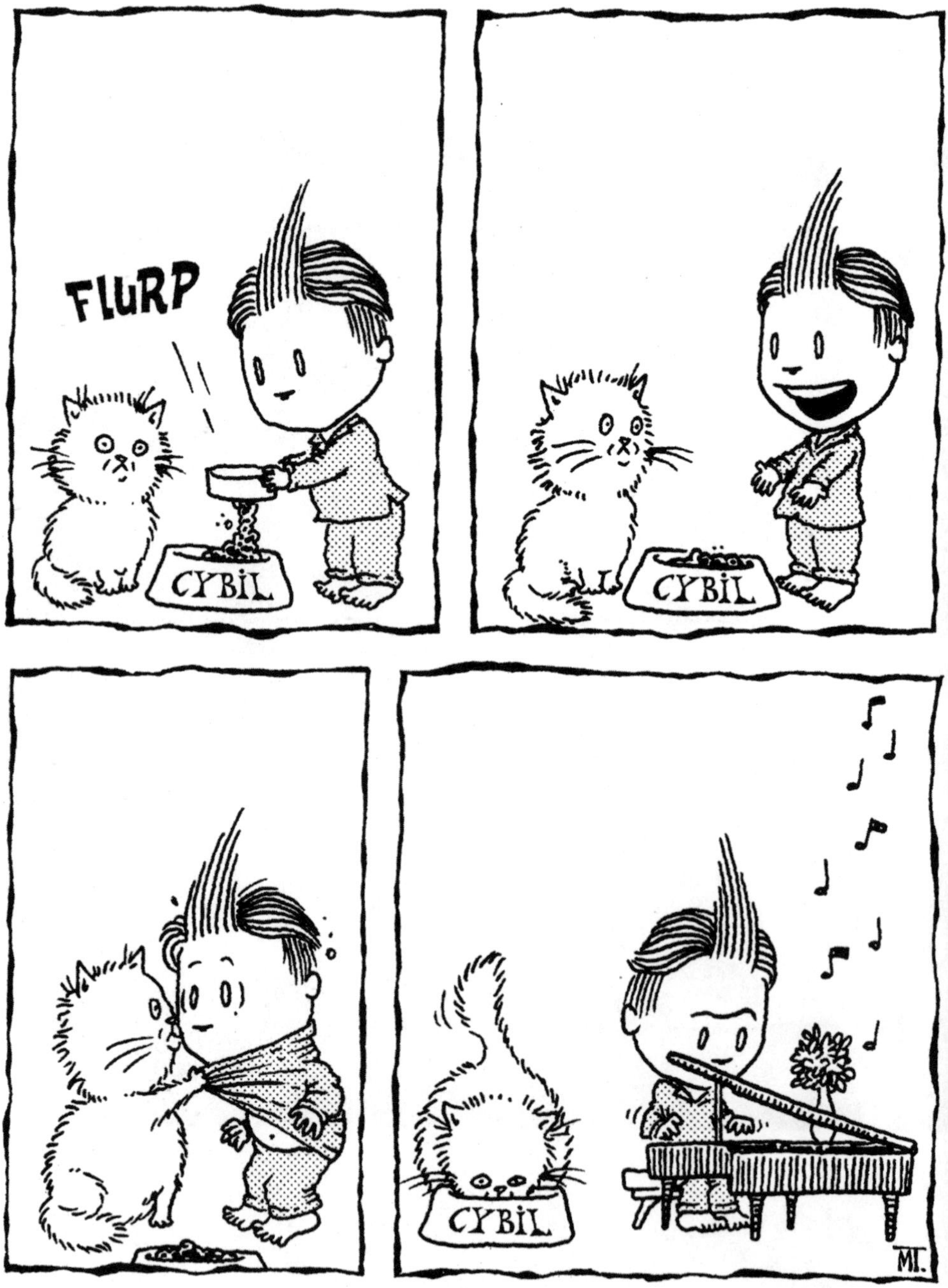
FLURP
CYBIL
CYBIL
CYBIL
MT.

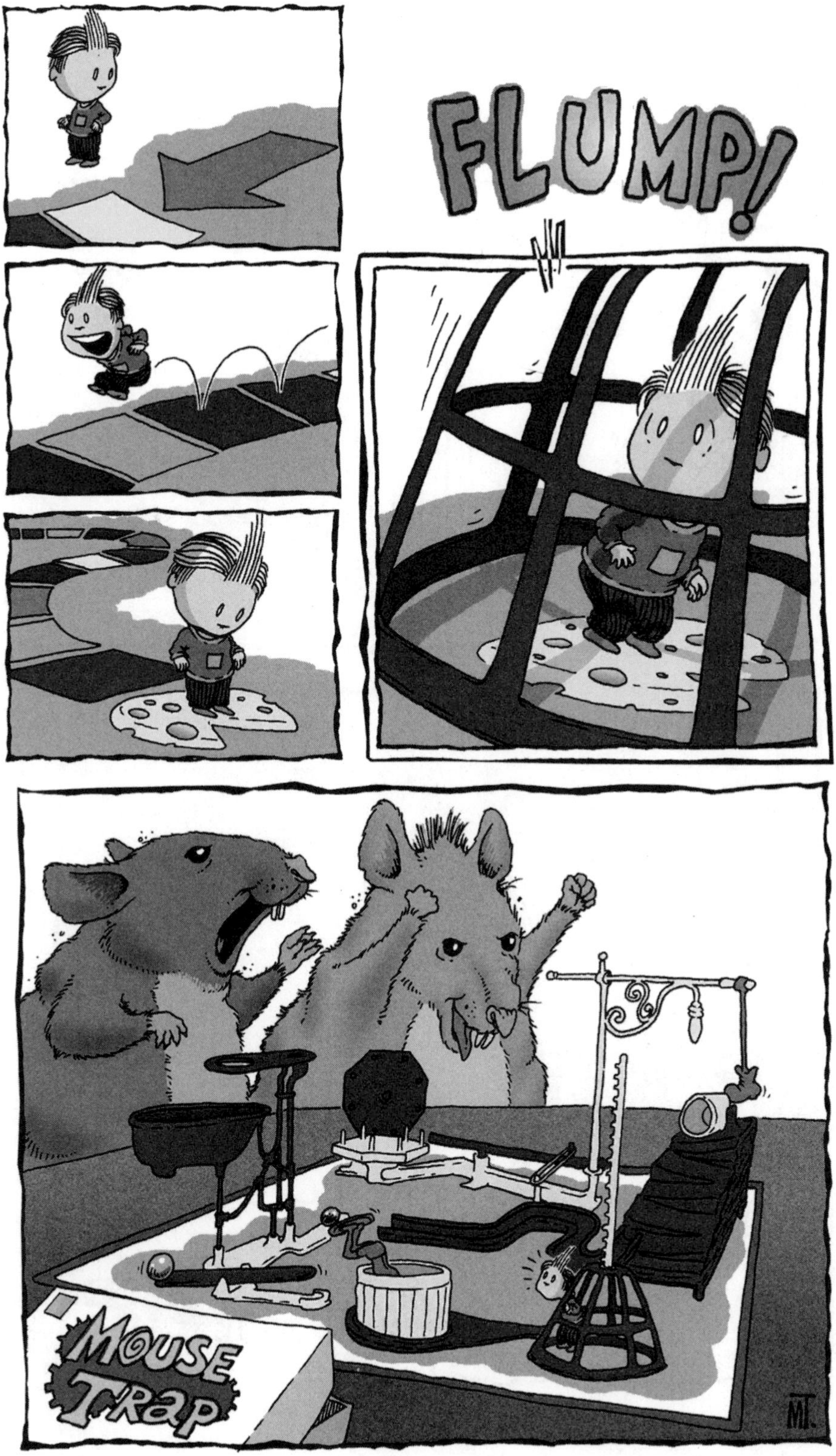
FLUMP!
MOUSE TRAP
MT.

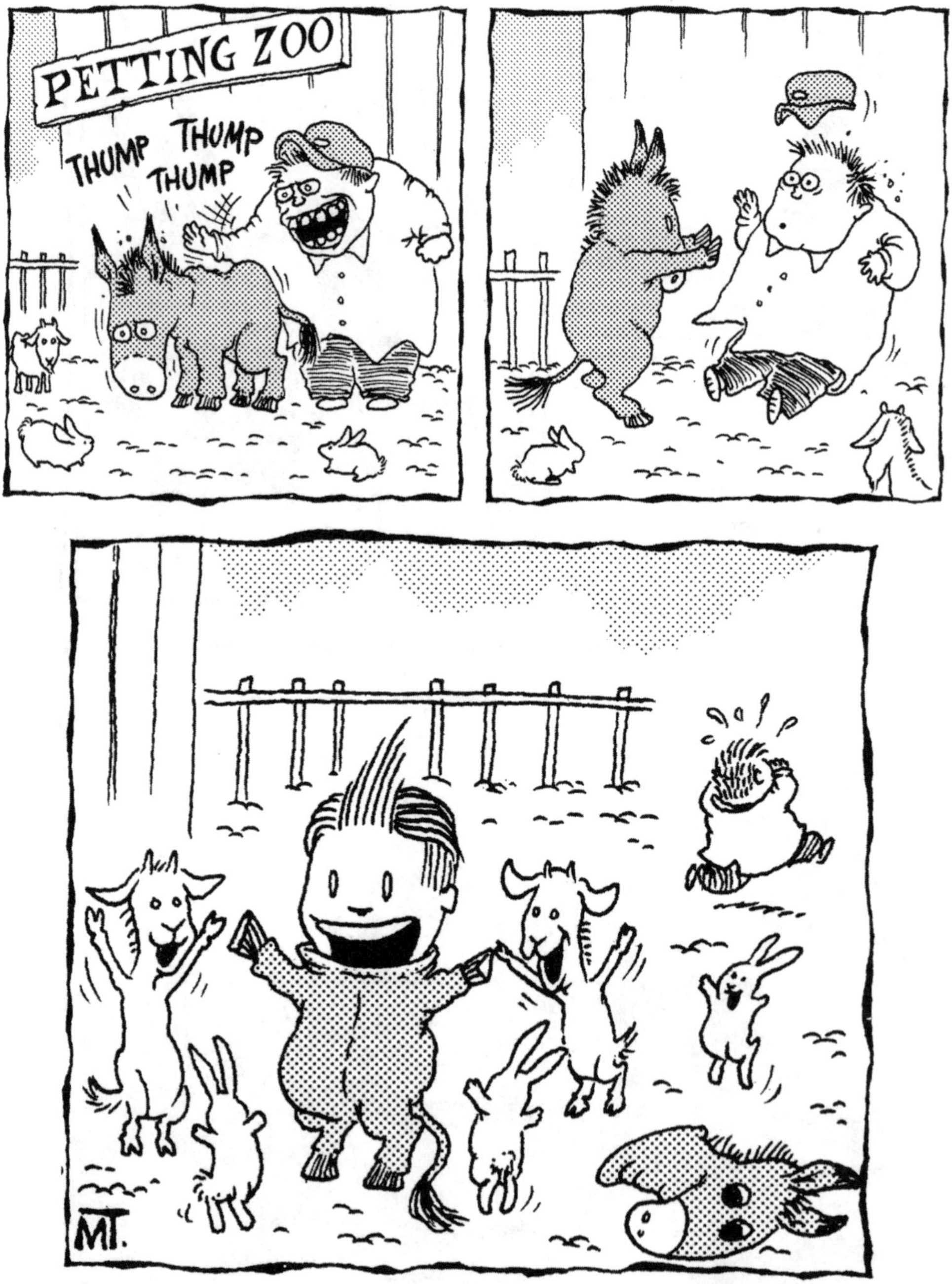
PETTING ZOO
THUMP THUMP
THUMP
MT.

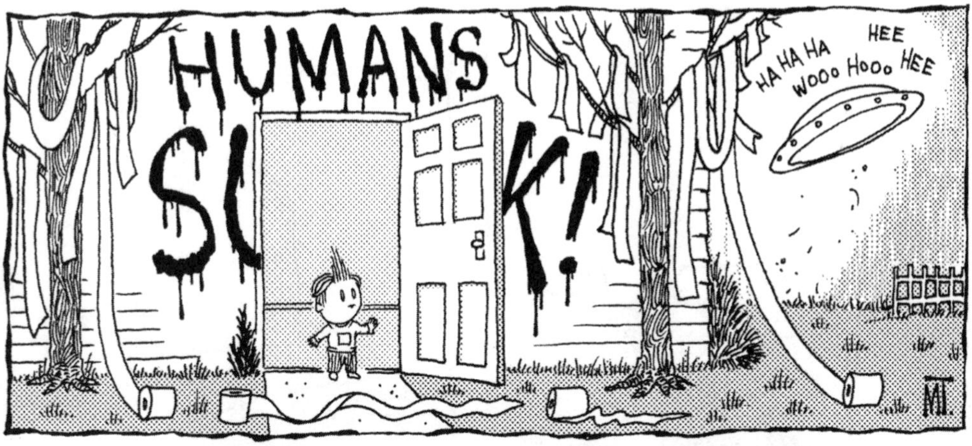
HUMANS
SUCK!
HA HA HA
HEE
WOOO HOOO
HEE
MT.

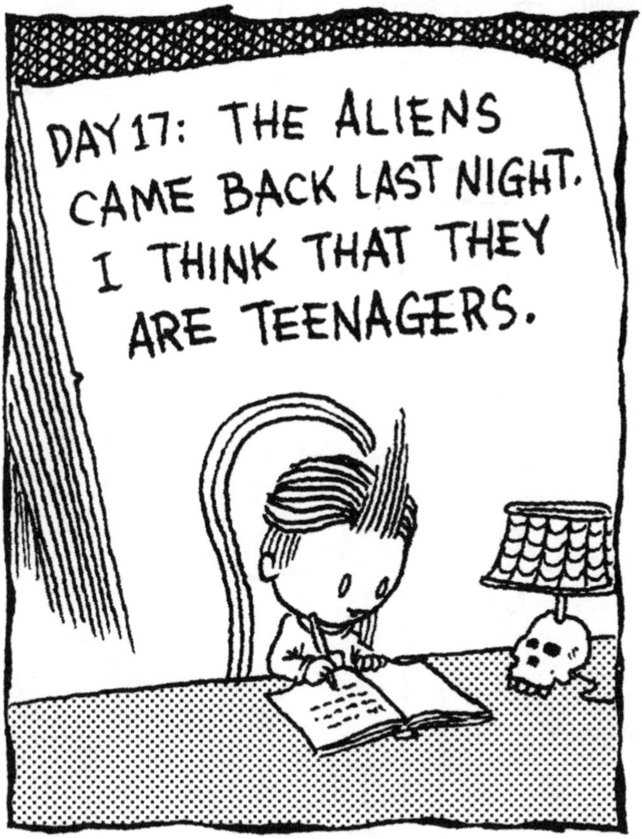
DAY 17: THE ALIENS CAME BACK LAST NIGHT. I THINK THAT THEY ARE TEENAGERS.

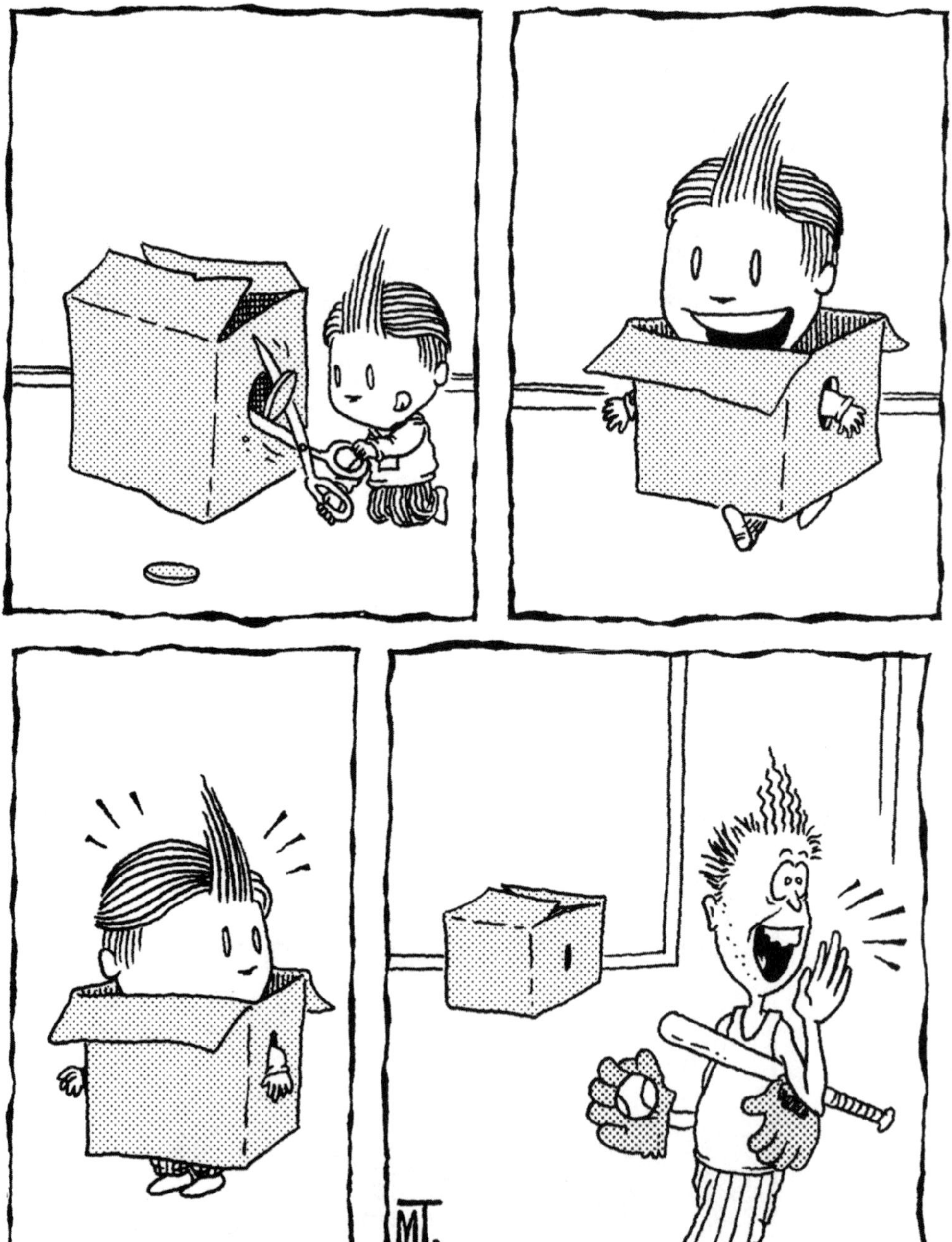
MT.

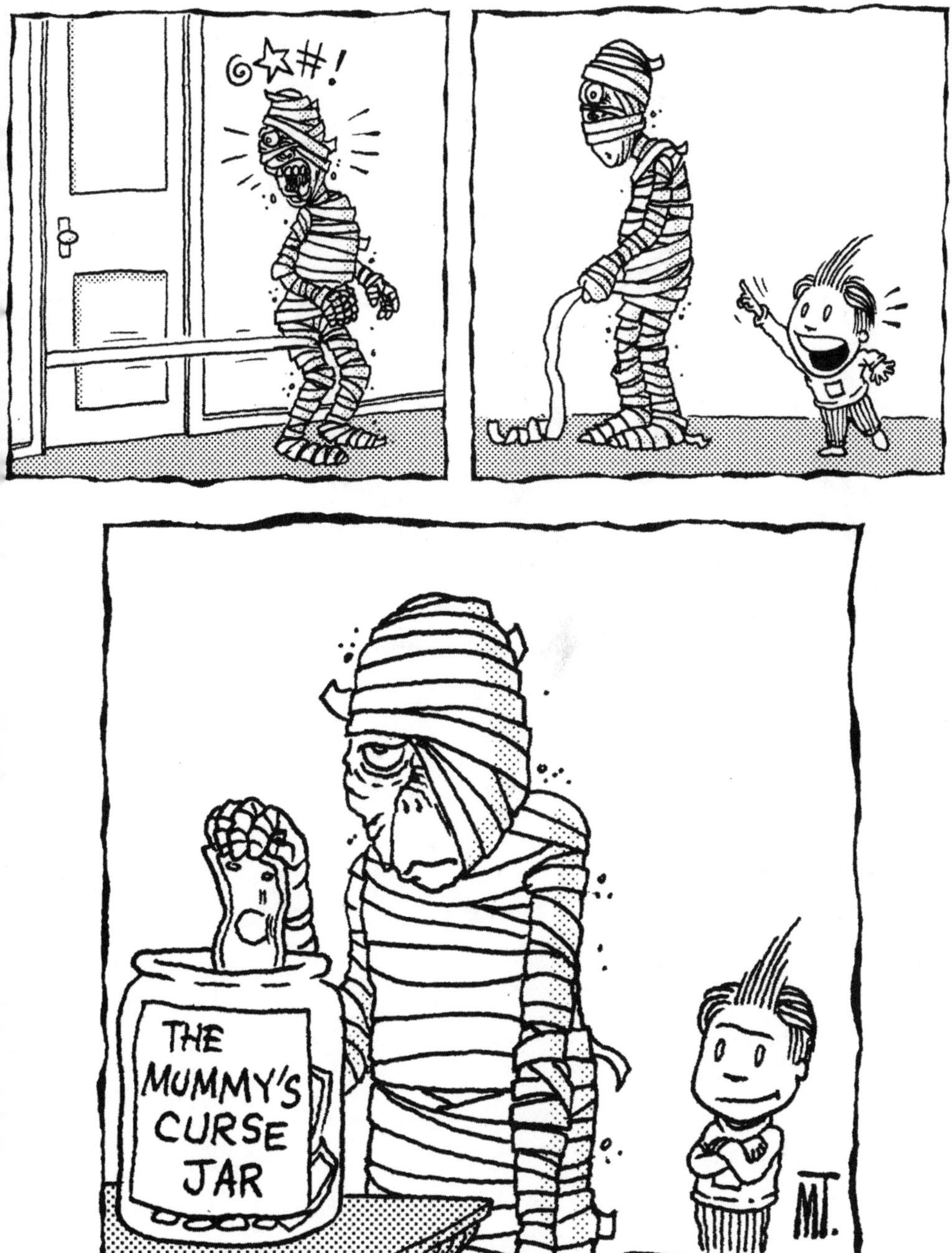
@☆#!
THE MUMMY'S CURSE JAR
MT.

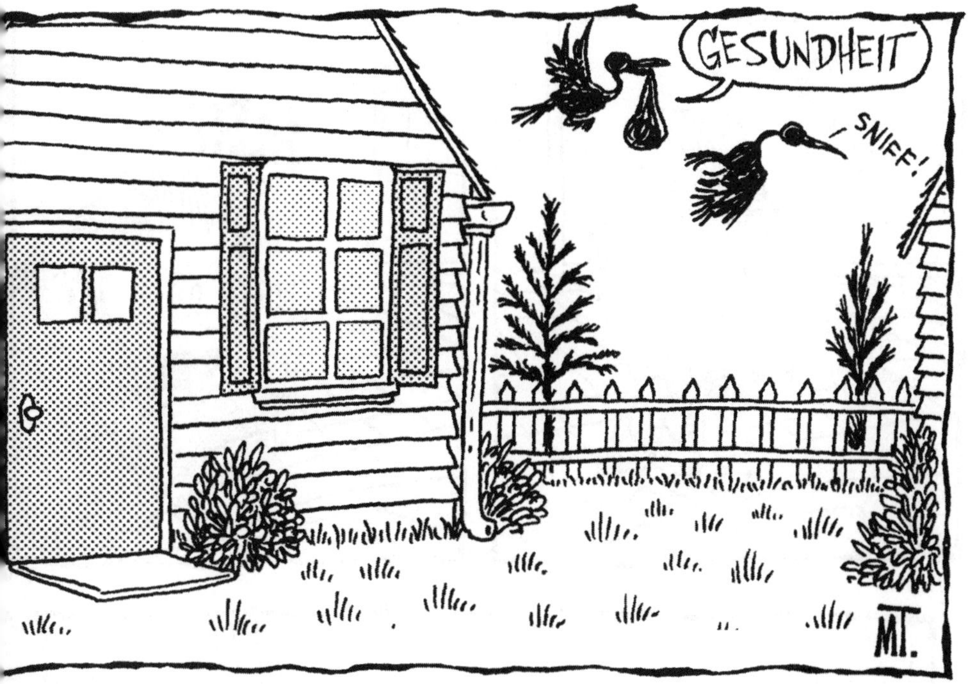
GESUNDHEIT
SNIFF!
MT.

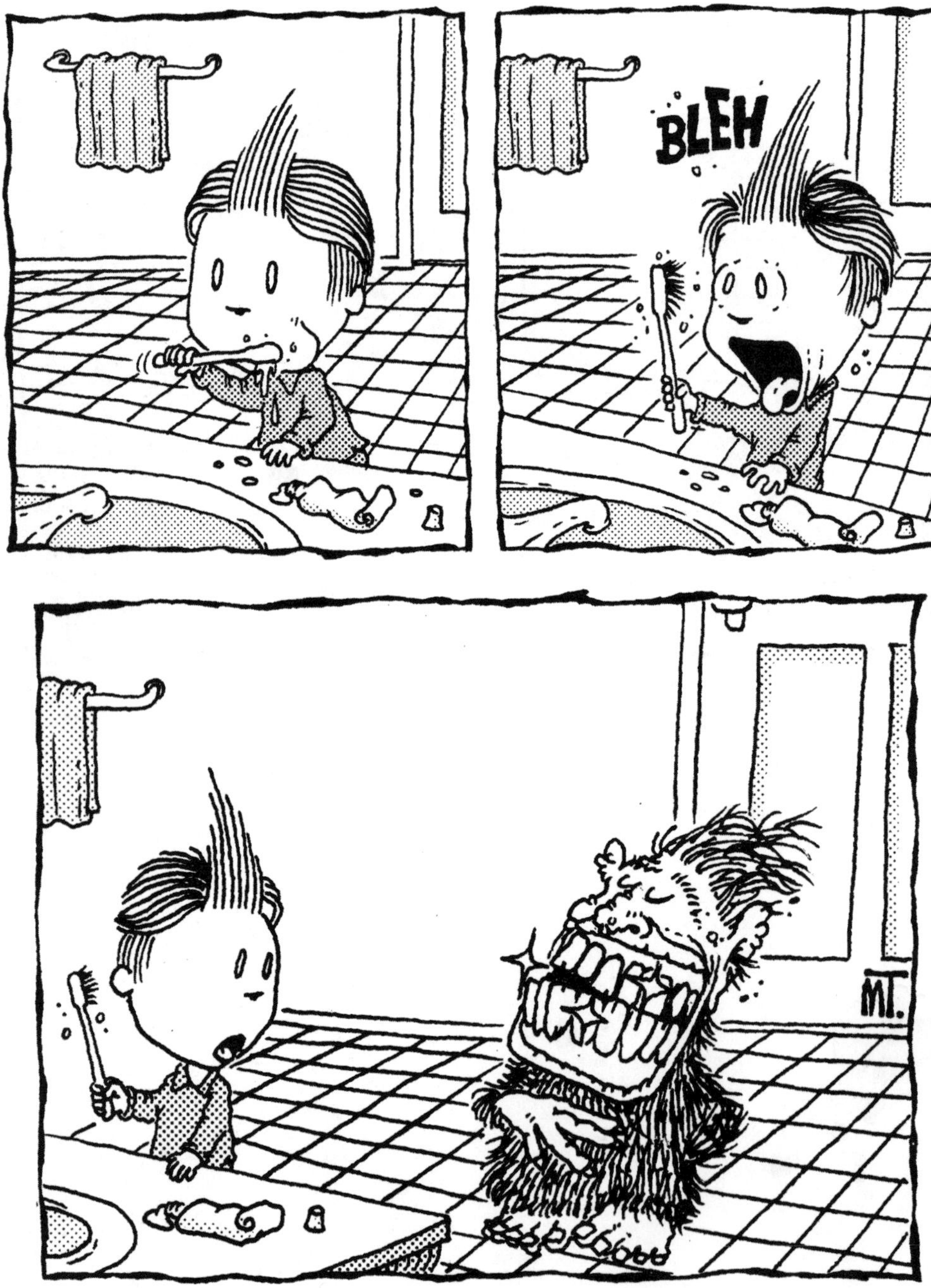
BLEH
MT.

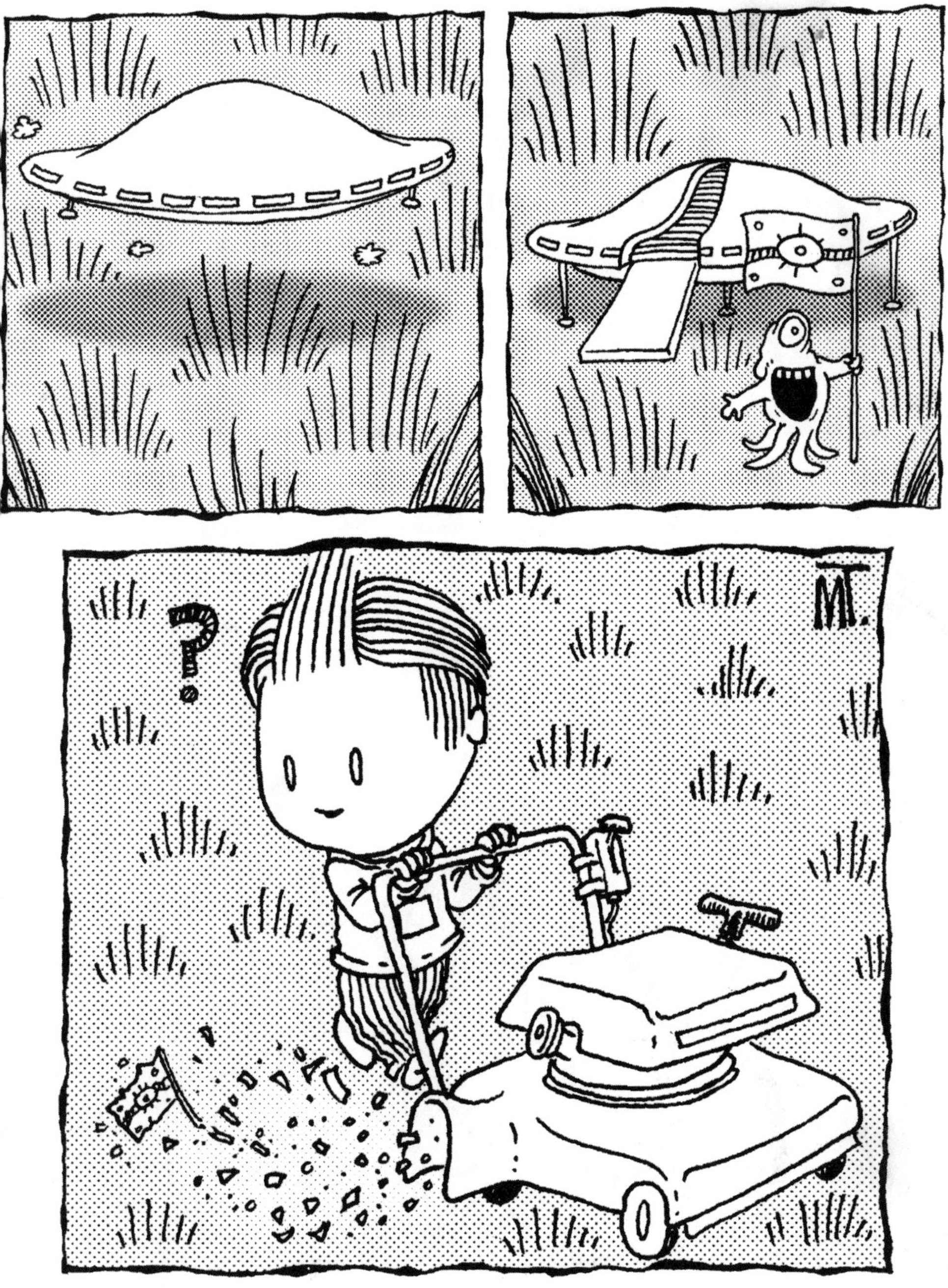

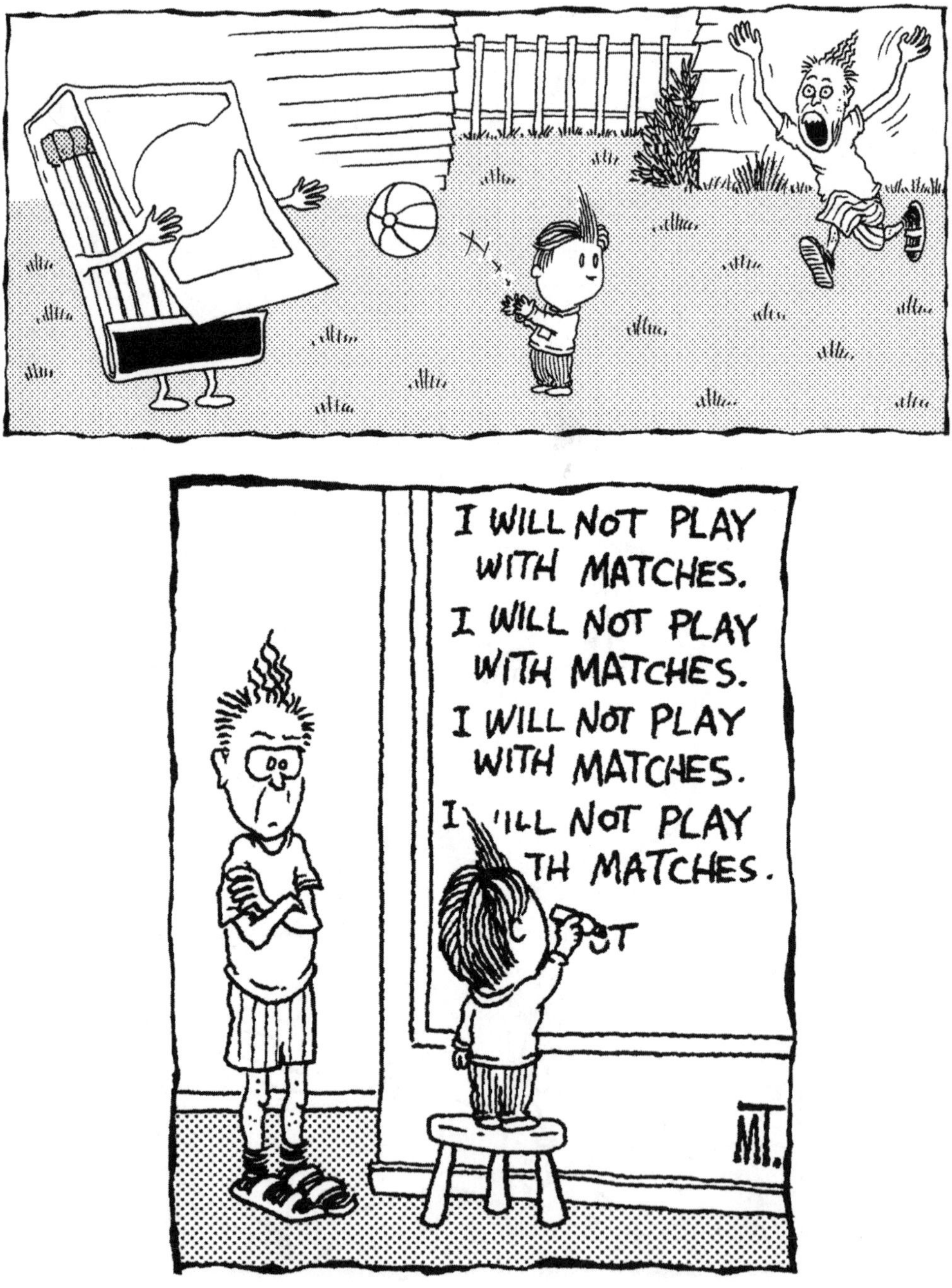

I WILL NOT PLAY WITH MATCHES.
I WILL NOT PLAY WITH MATCHES.
I WILL NOT PLAY WITH MATCHES.
MT.

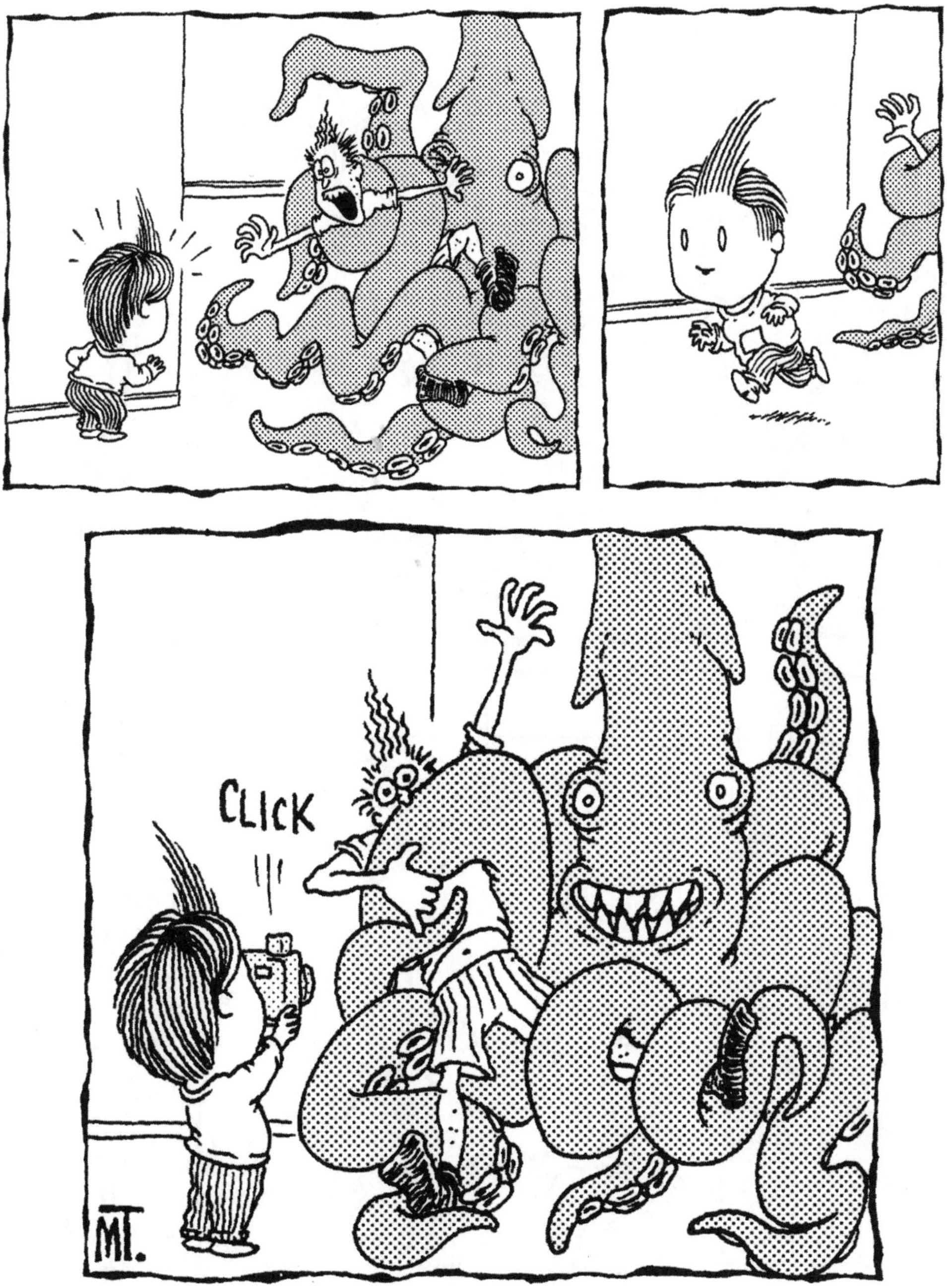
CLICK
MT.

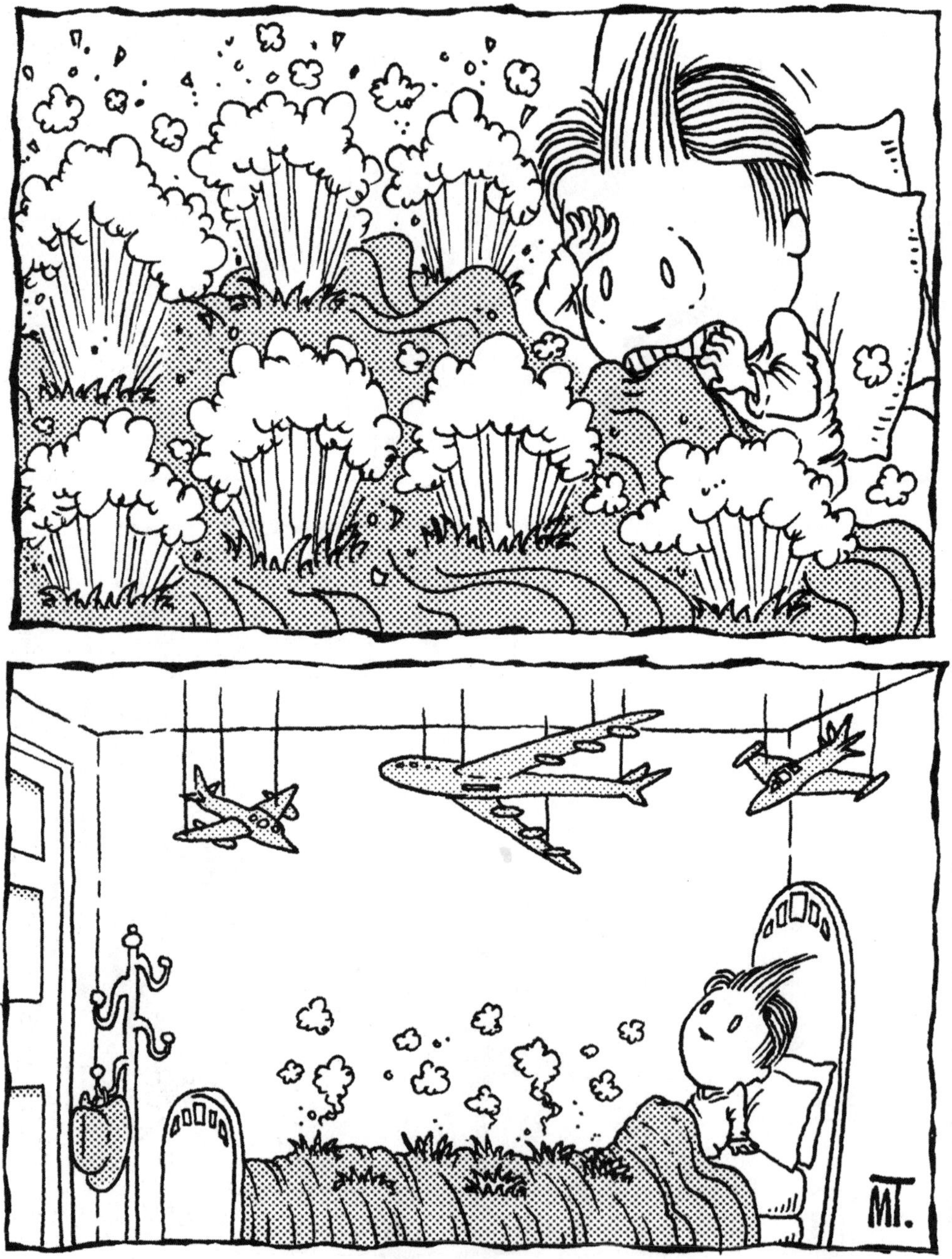
MT.

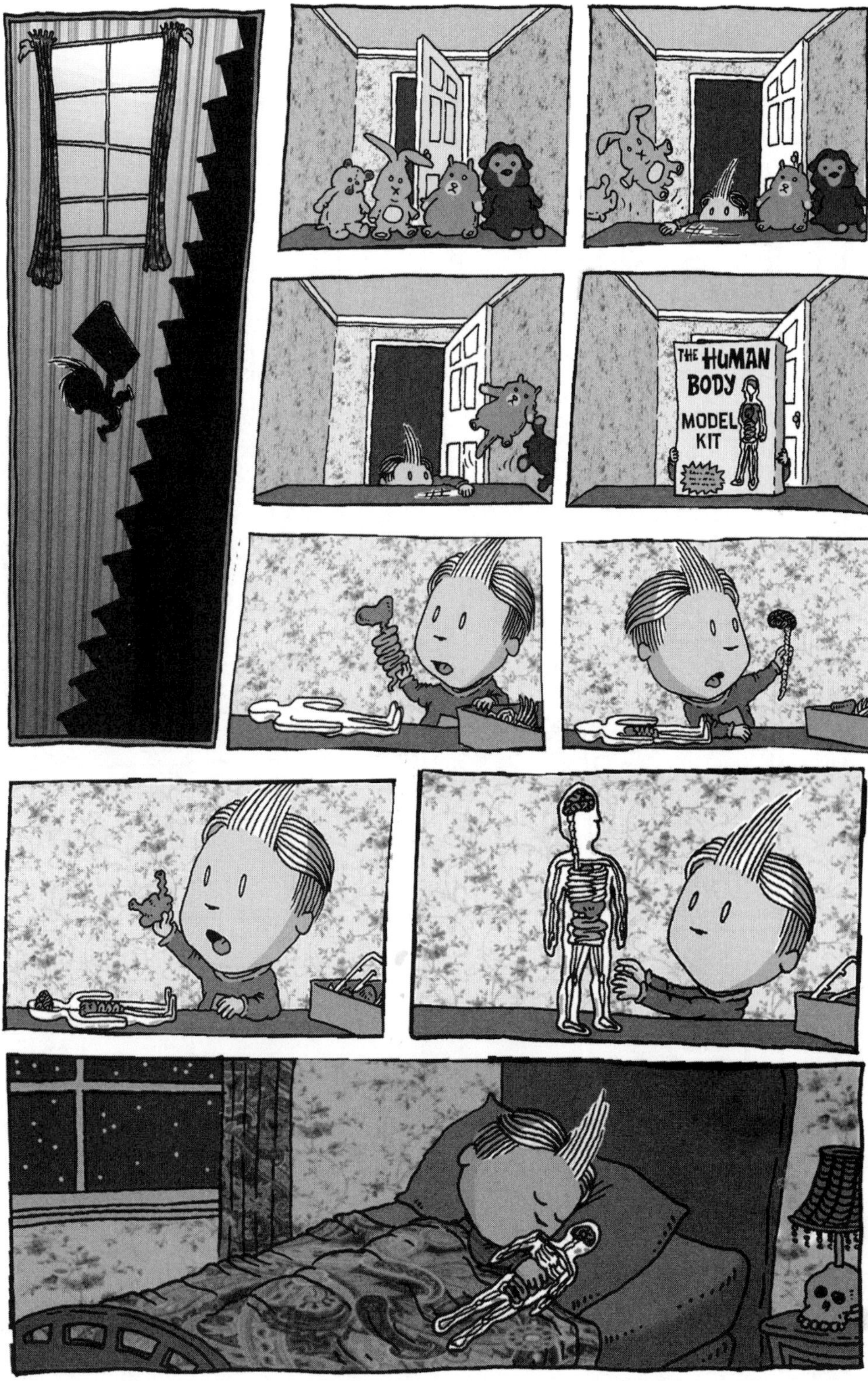
THE HUMAN BODY
MODEL KIT

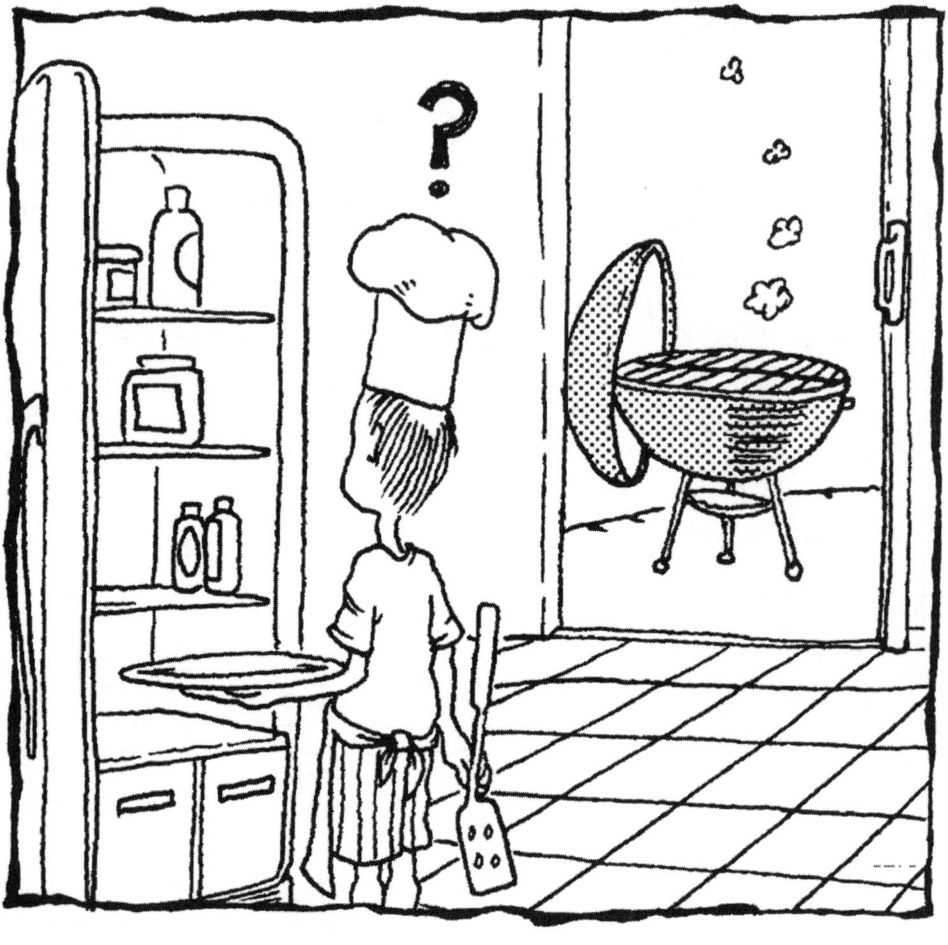
?

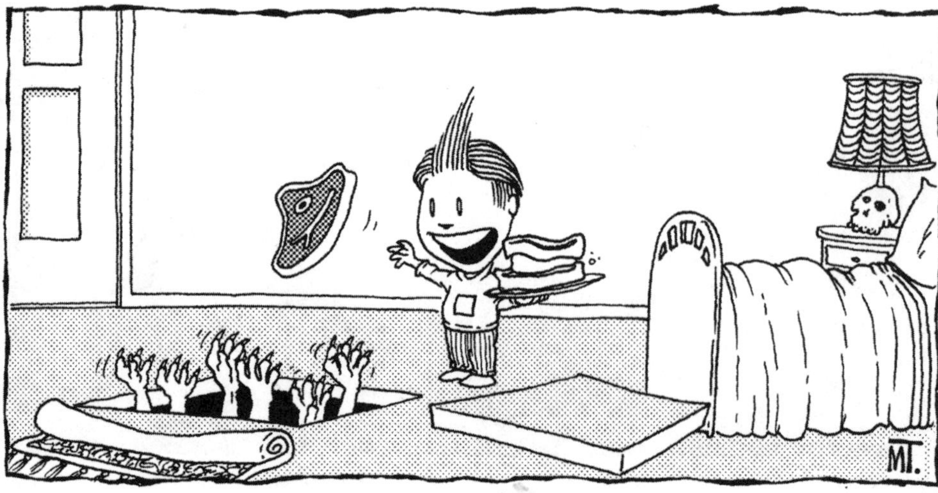
MT.

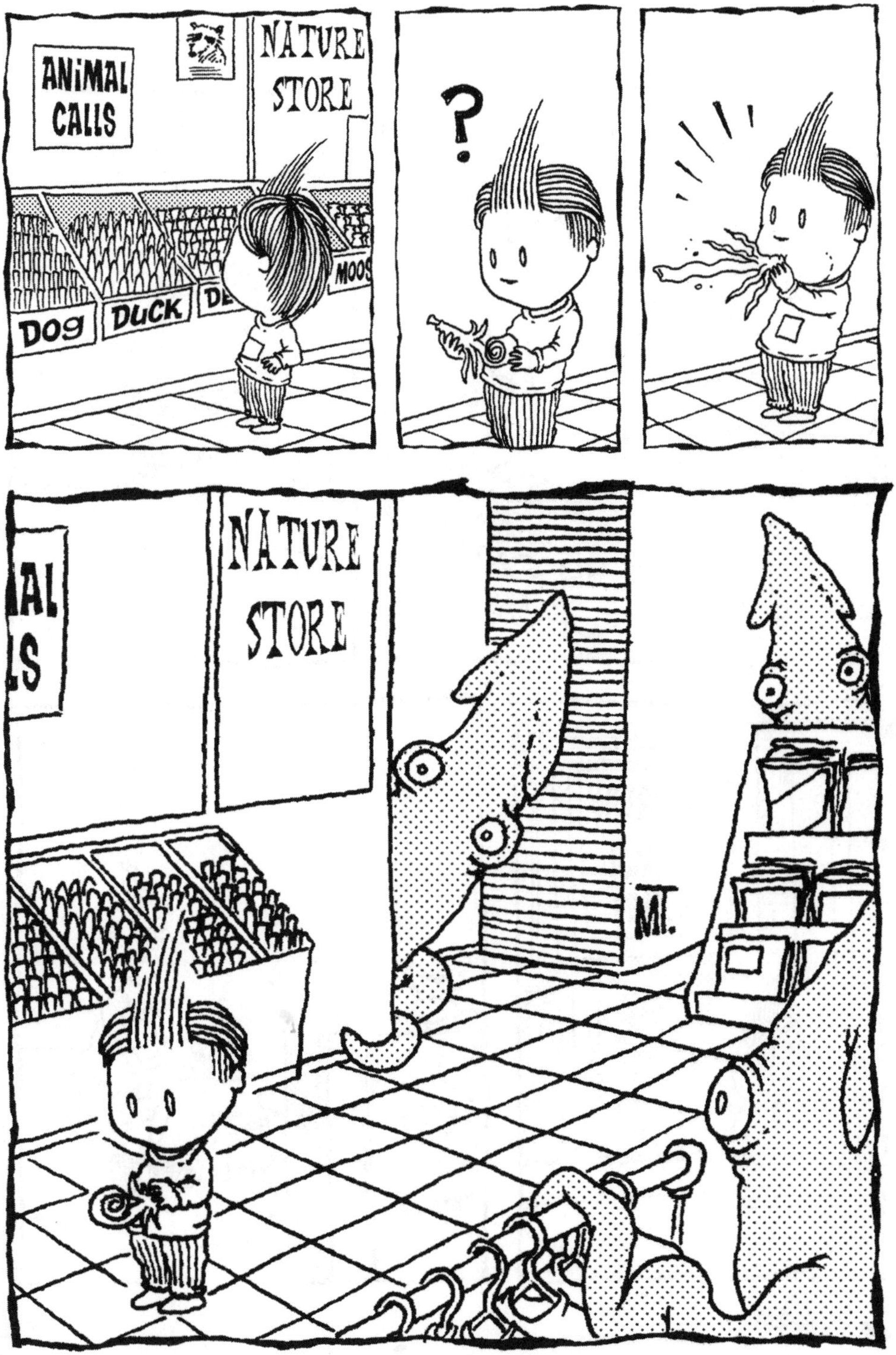

ANIMAL CALLS
NATURE STORE
DOG
DUCK
?
NATURE STORE
MT.

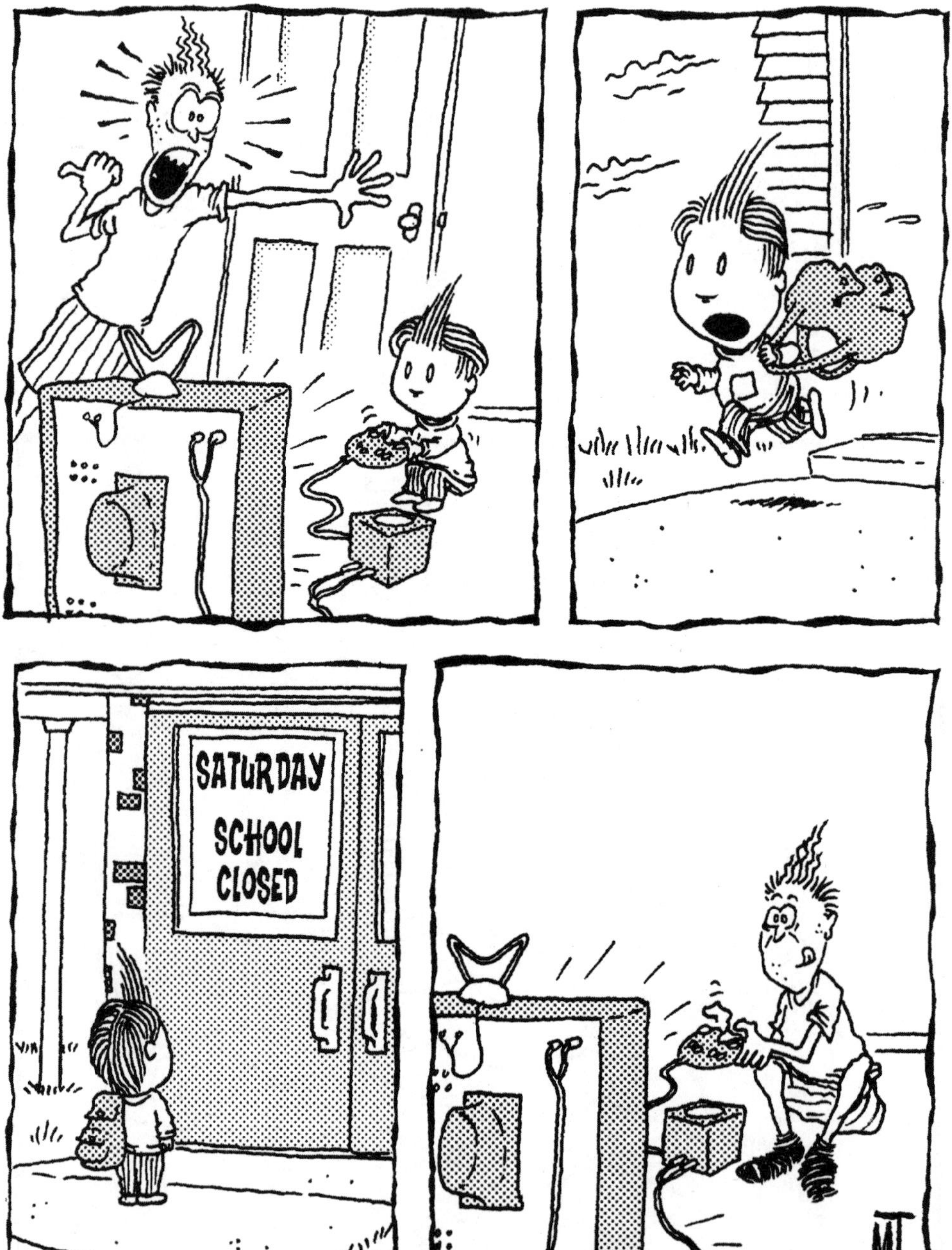
SATURDAY
SCHOOL CLOSED
MT.

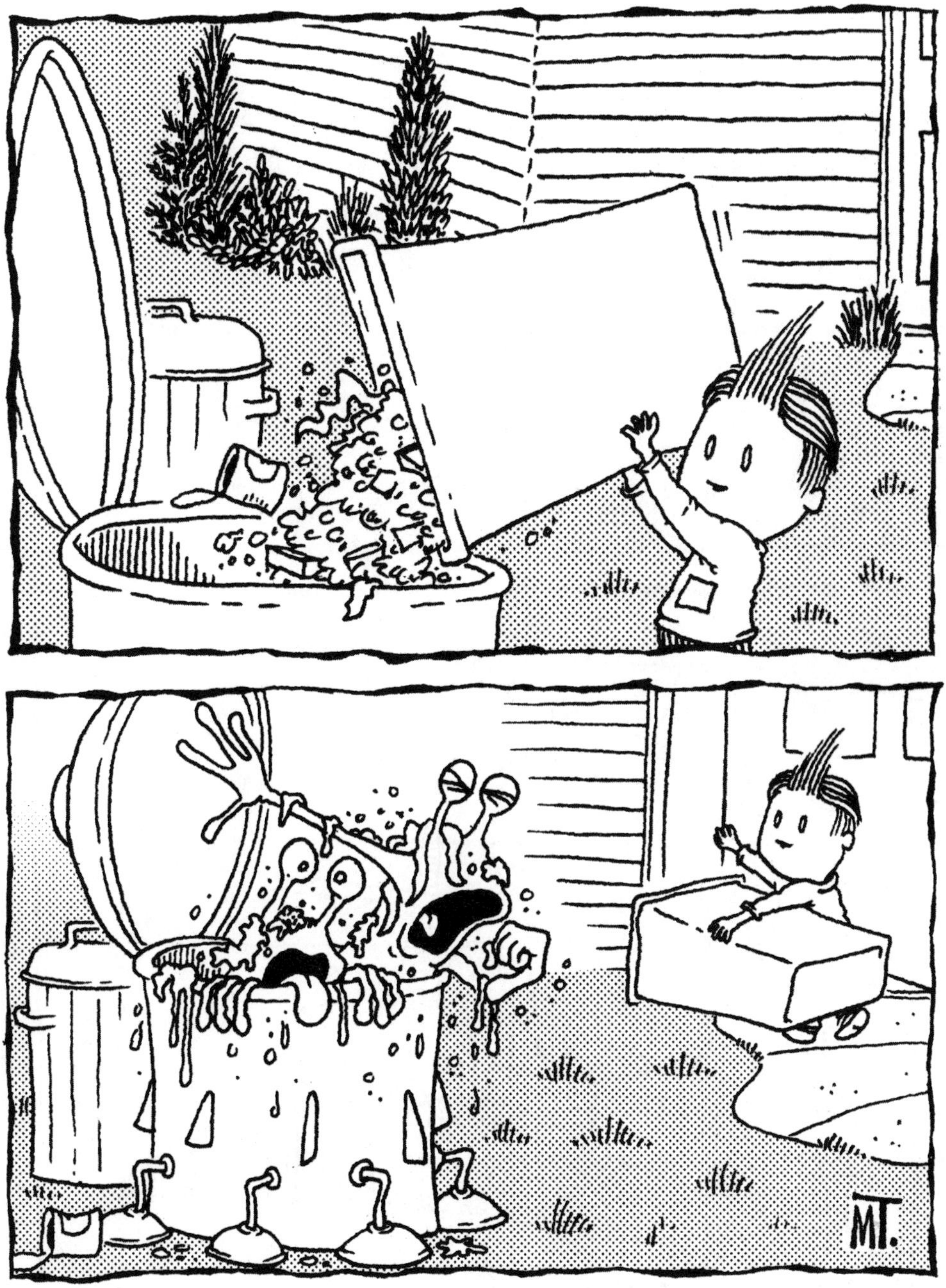
MT.

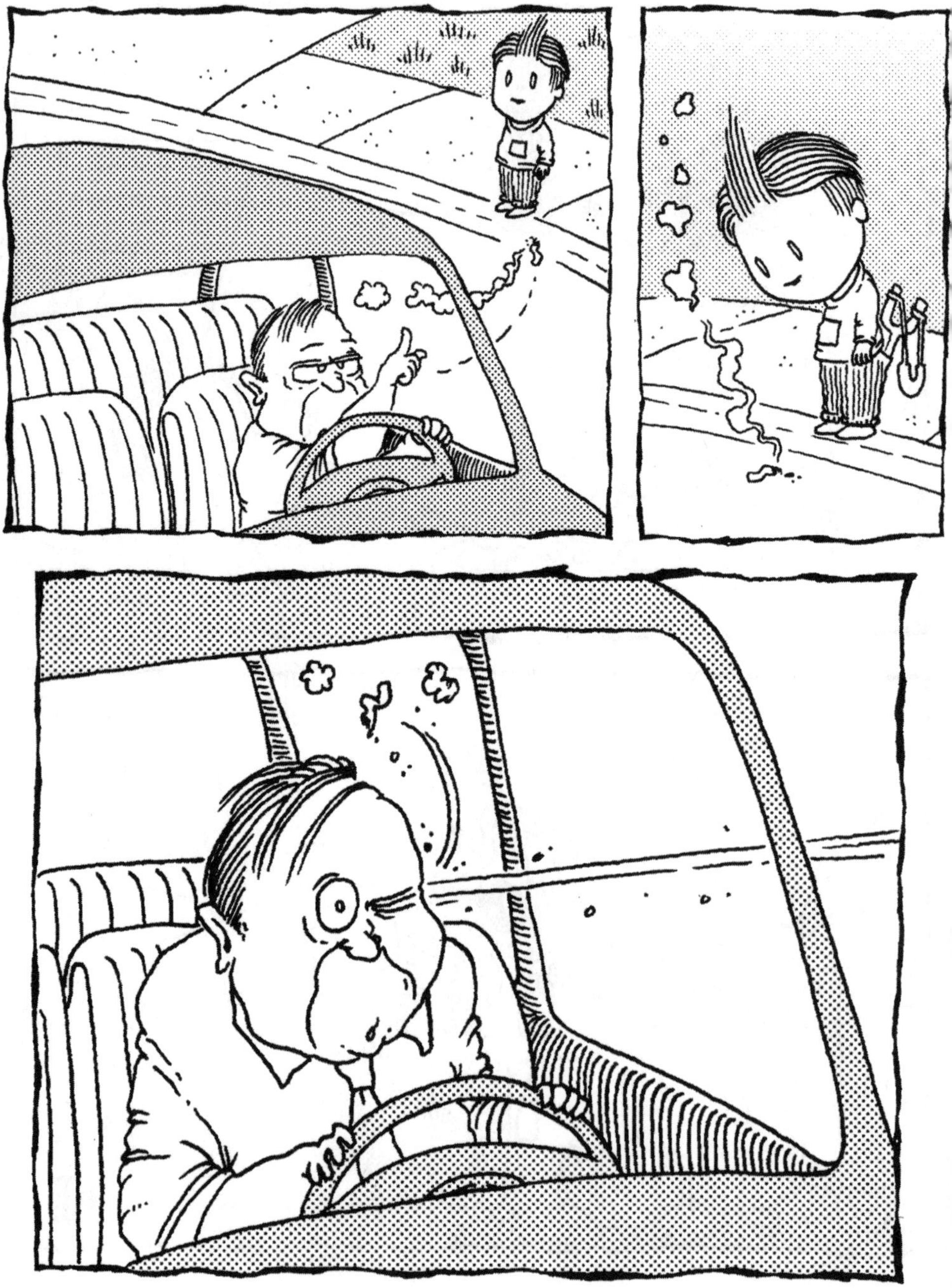

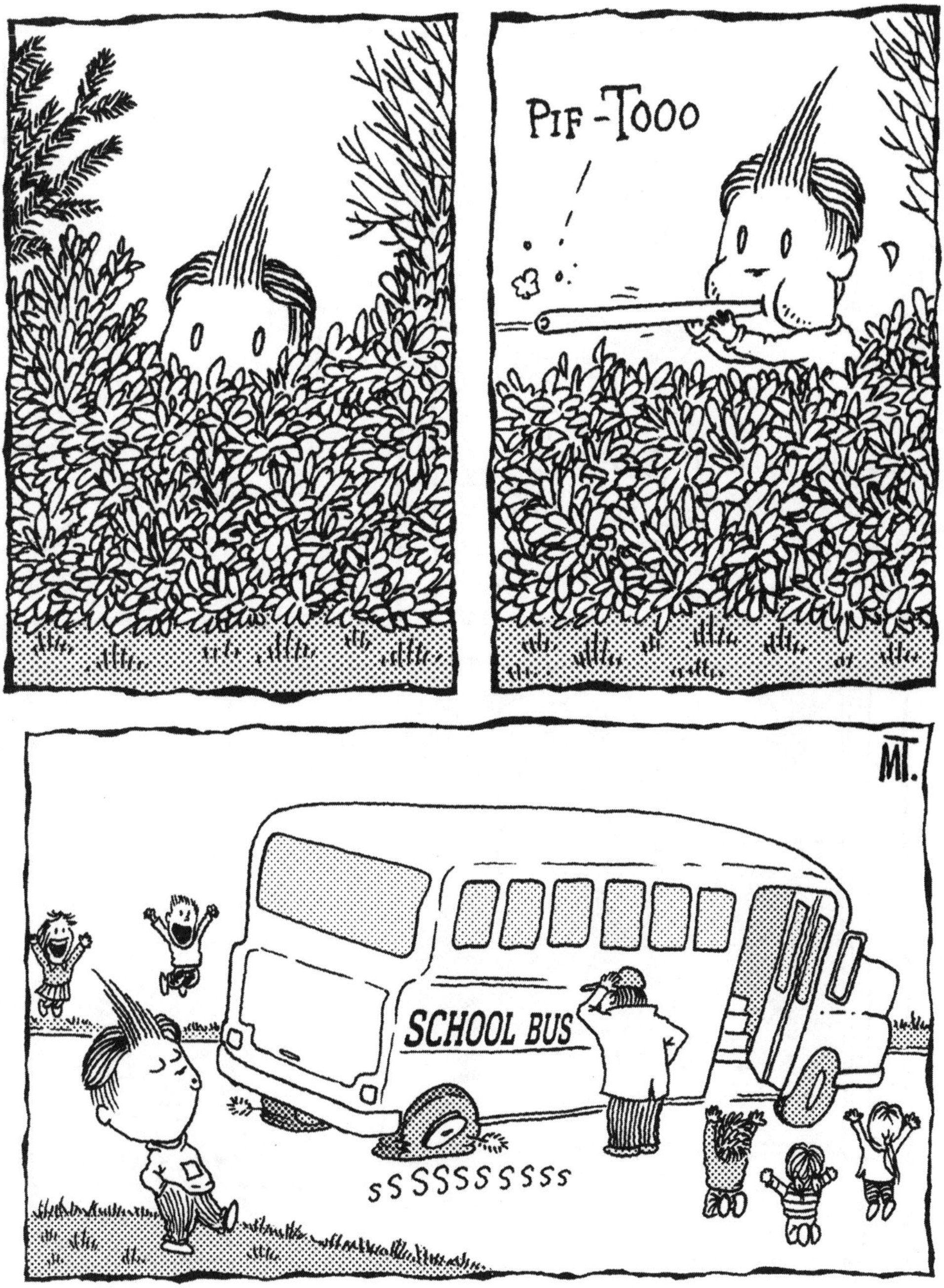
PIF-TOOO
SCHOOL BUS
sSSSSSSSSs
MT.

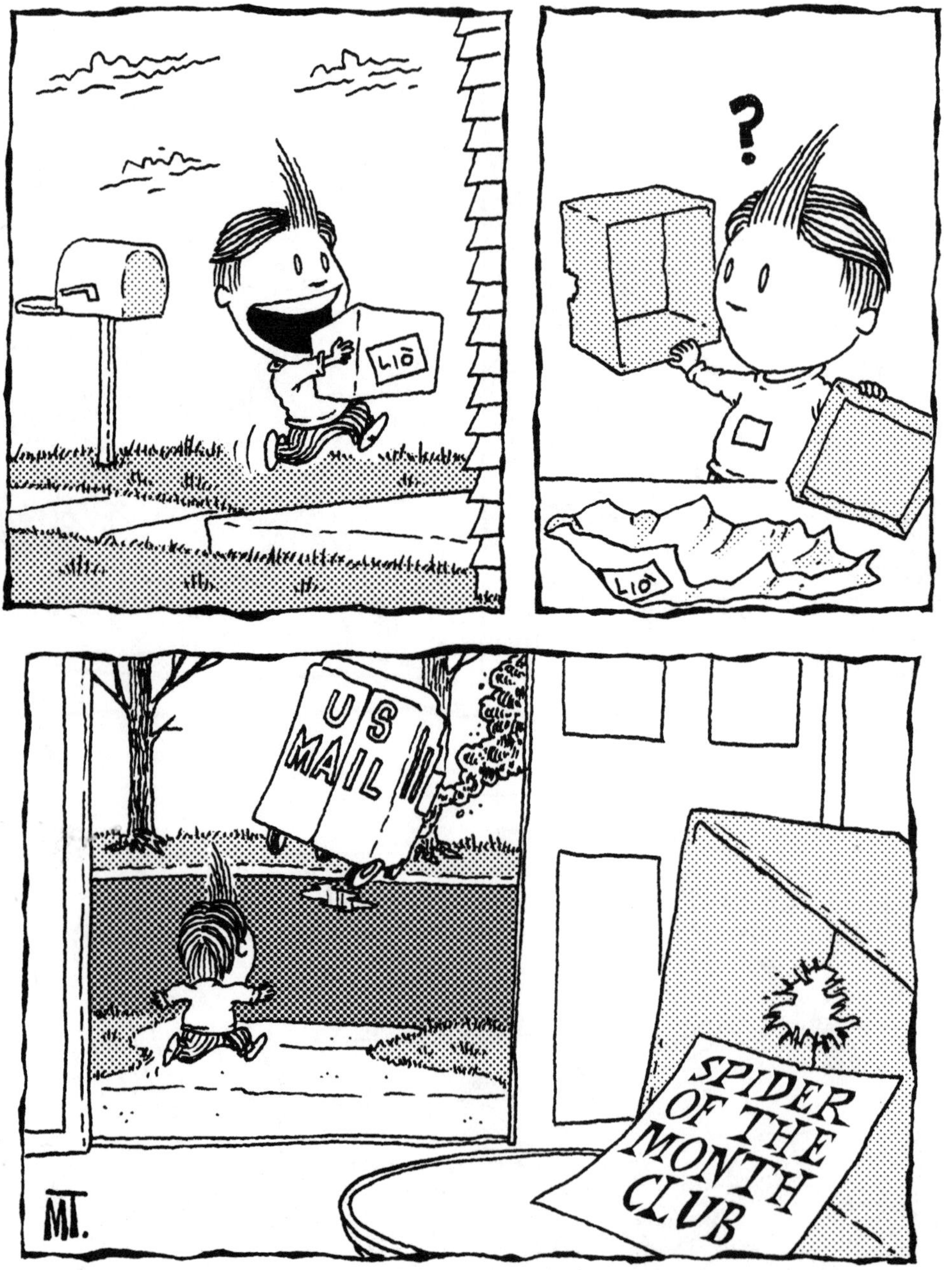
LIO
?
LIO
US MAIL
SPIDER OF THE MONTH CLUB
MT.

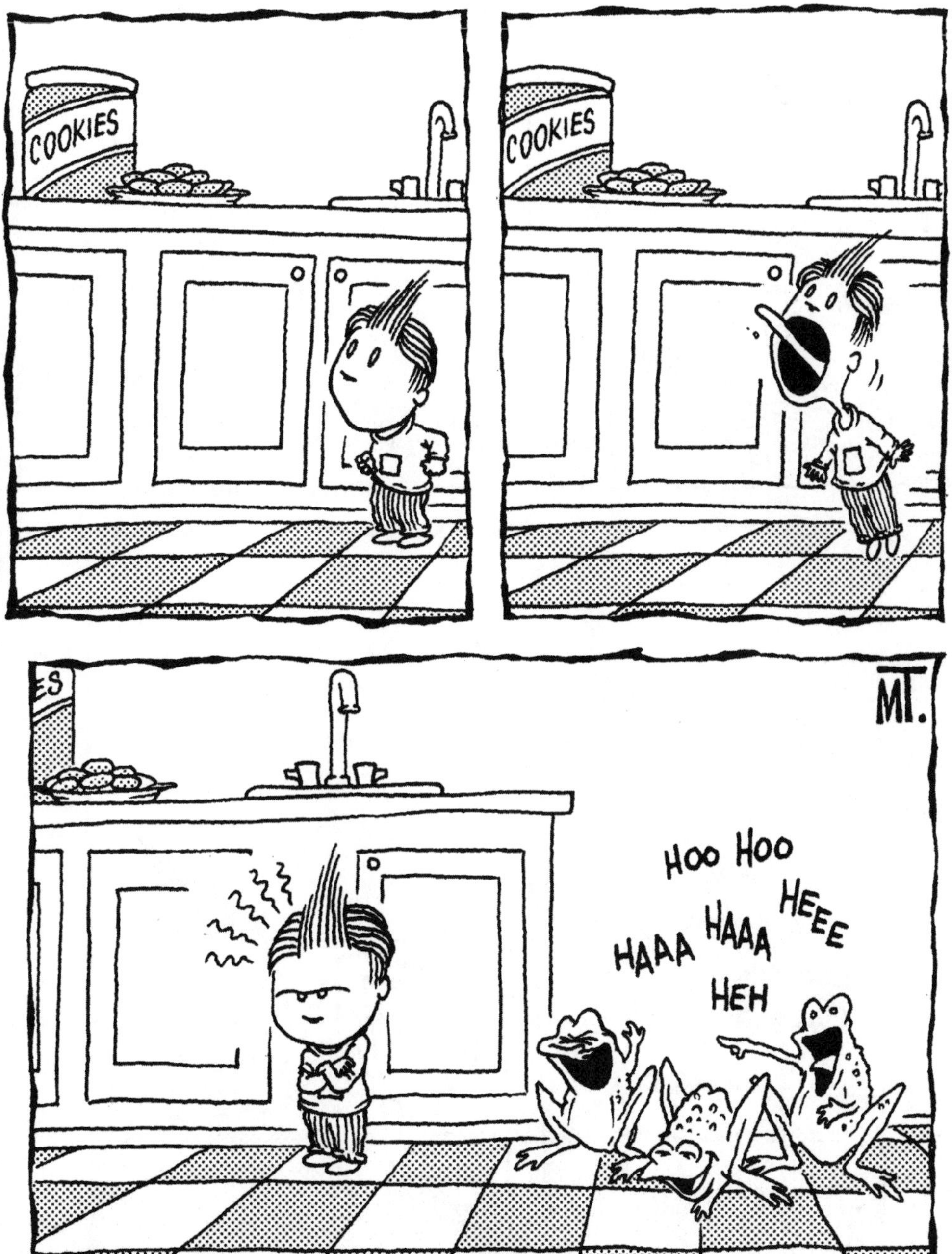
COOKIES
COOKIES
HOO HOO
HEEE
HAAA HAAA
HEH
MT.

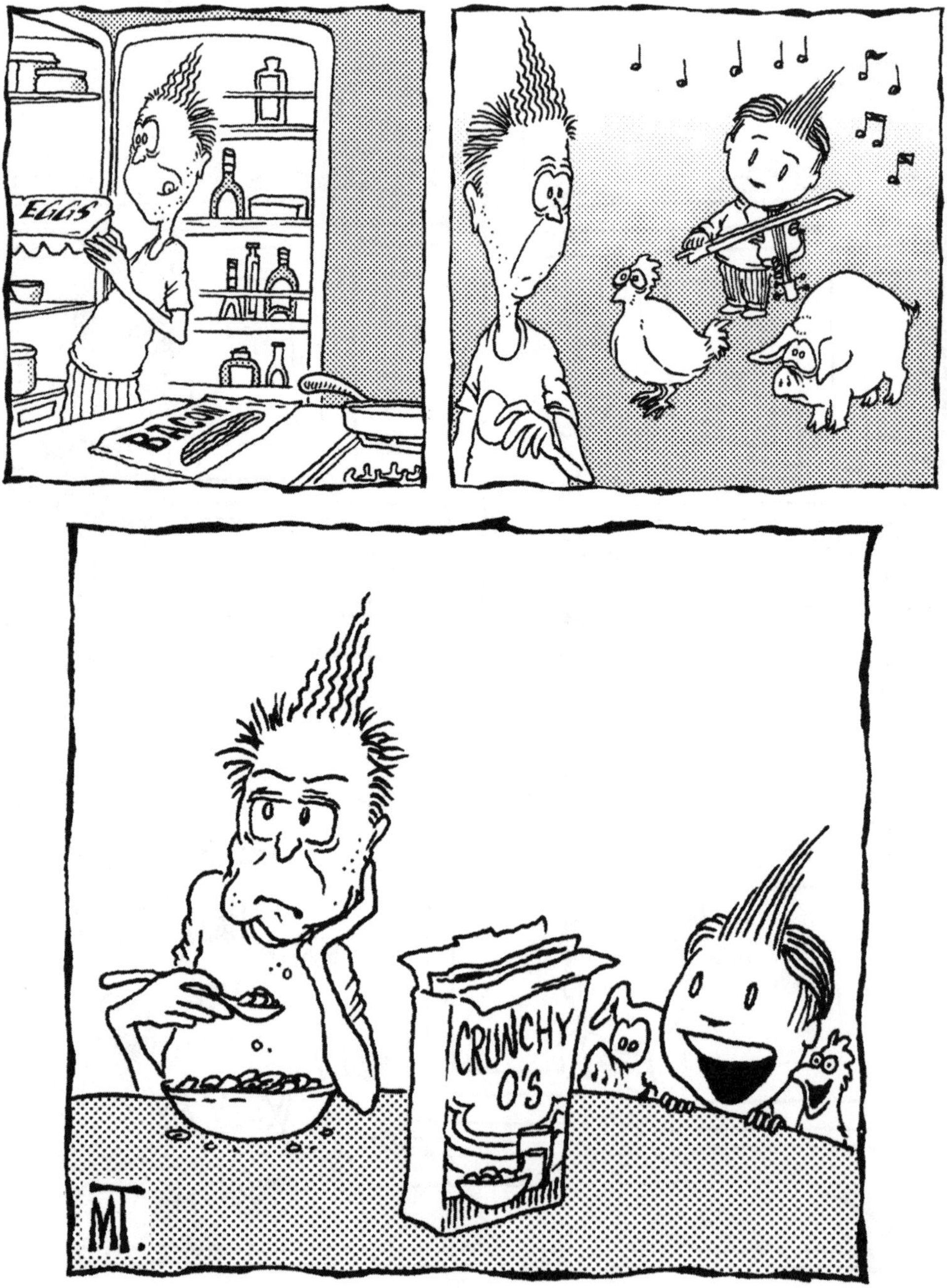
EGGS
BACON
CRUNCHY
O'S
MT.

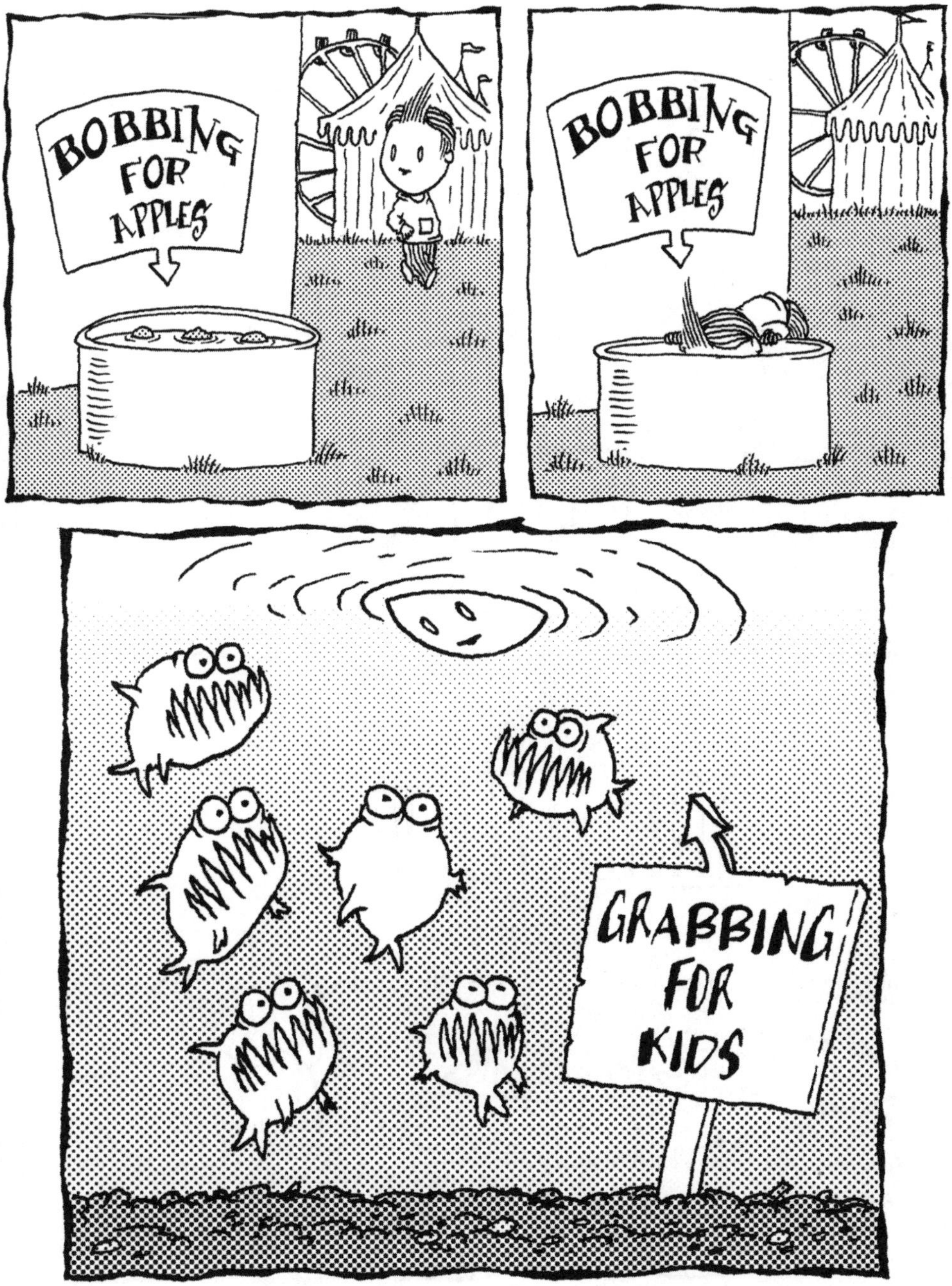
BOBBING FOR APPLES
BOBBING FOR APPLES
GRABBING FOR KIDS

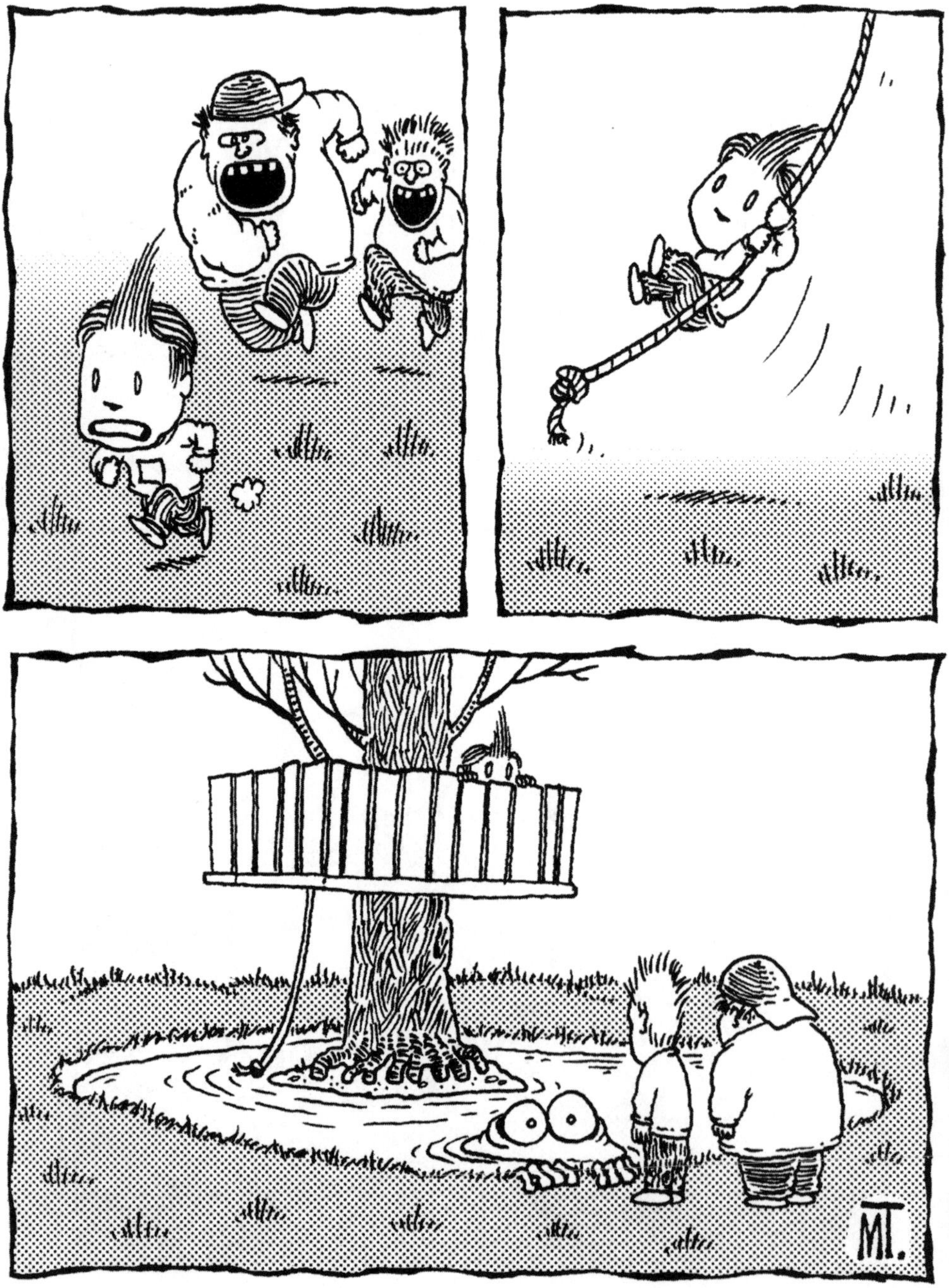
MT.

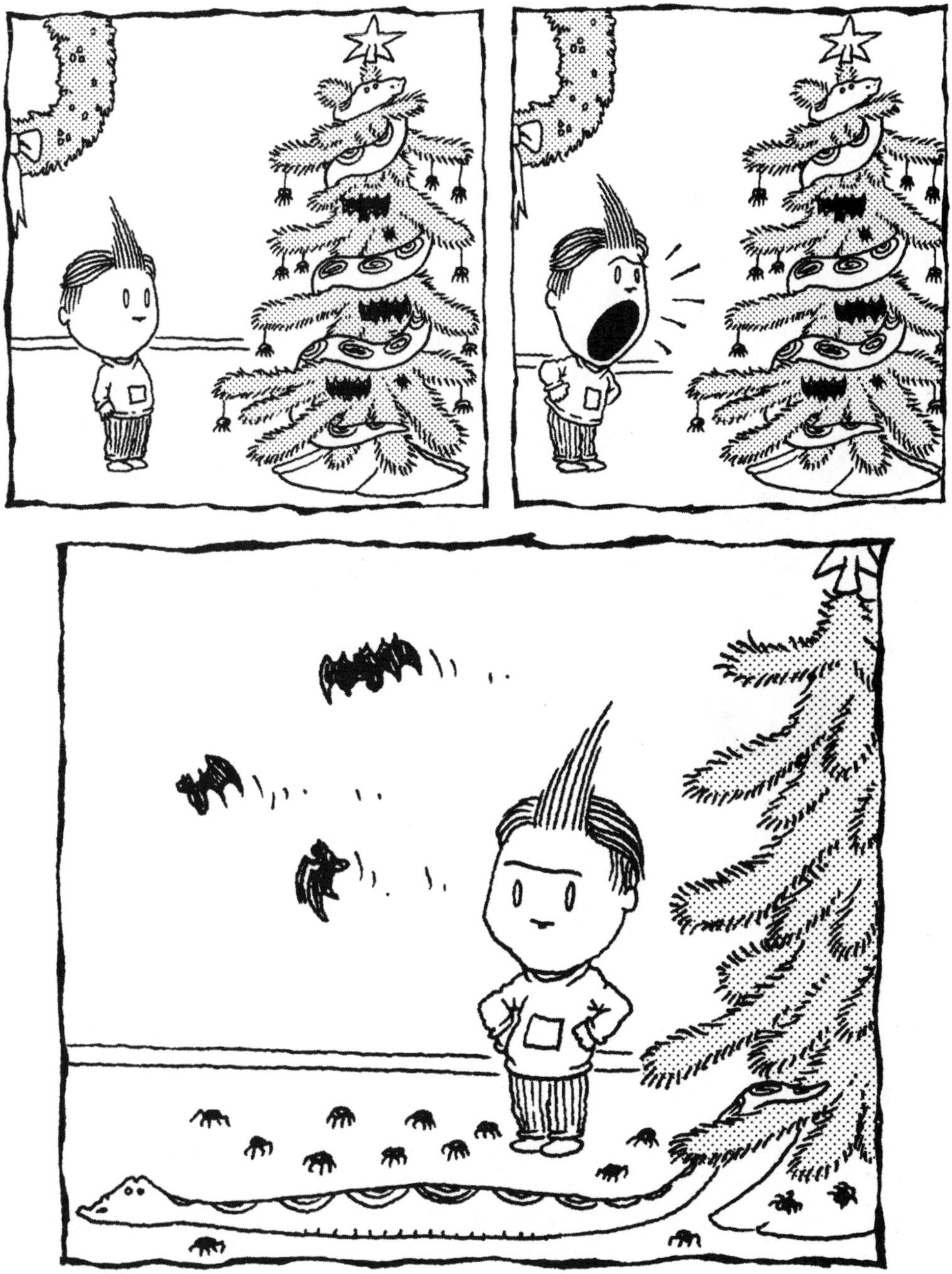

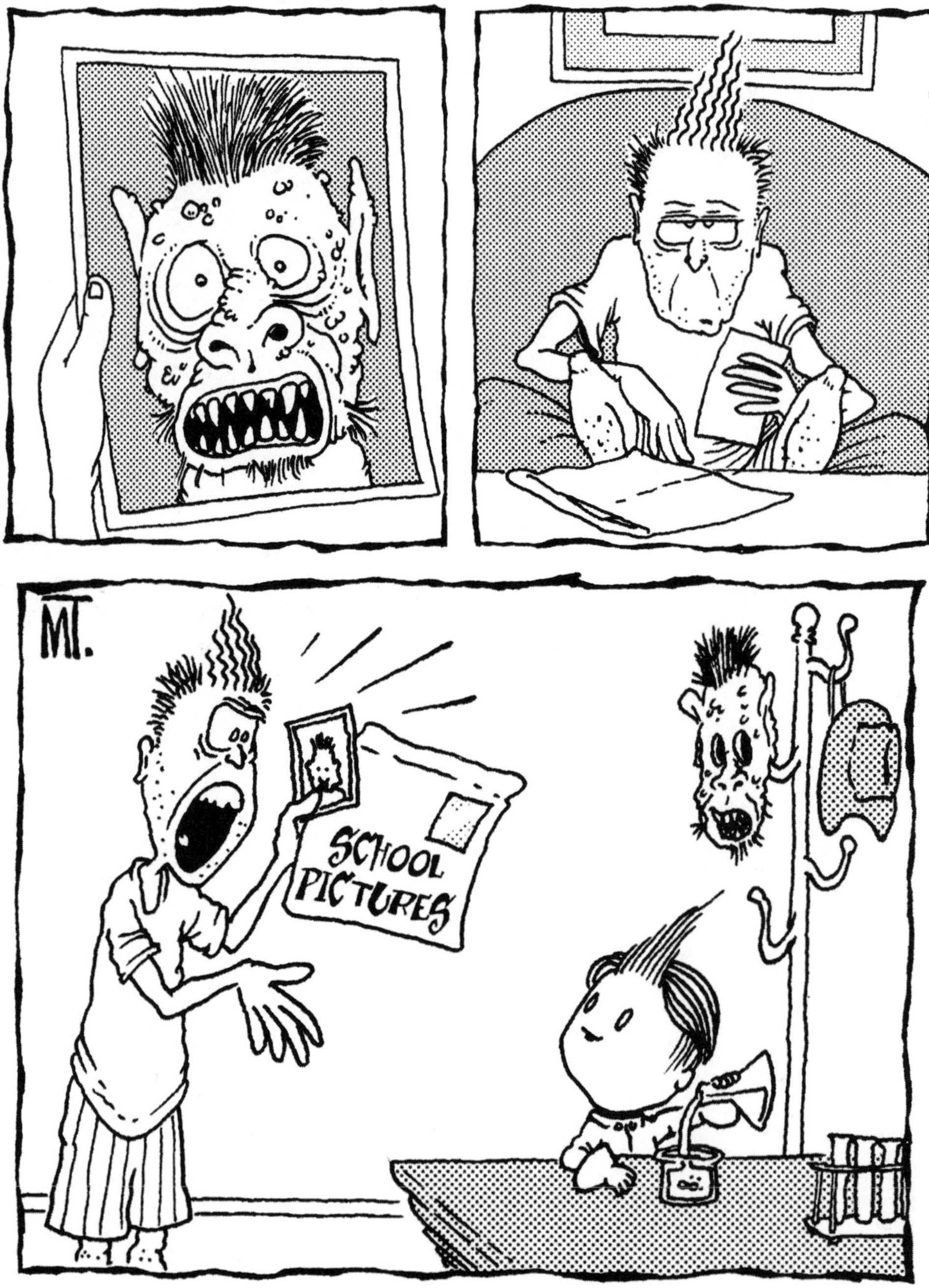
MT.
SCHOOL PICTURES

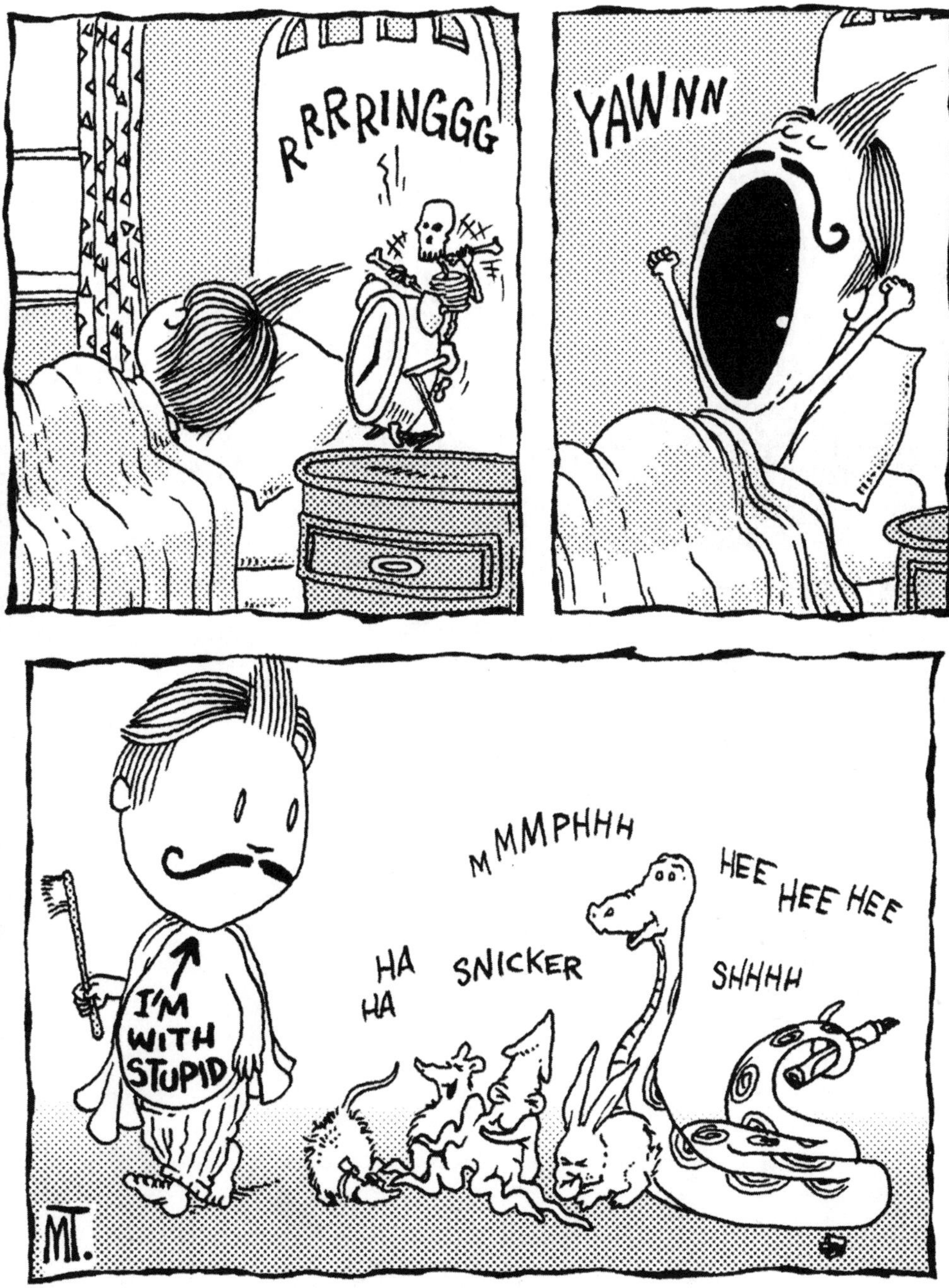
RRRRINGGG
YAWNN
I'M WITH STUPID
MMMPHHH
HEE HEE HEE
HA HA
SNICKER
SHHHH
MT.

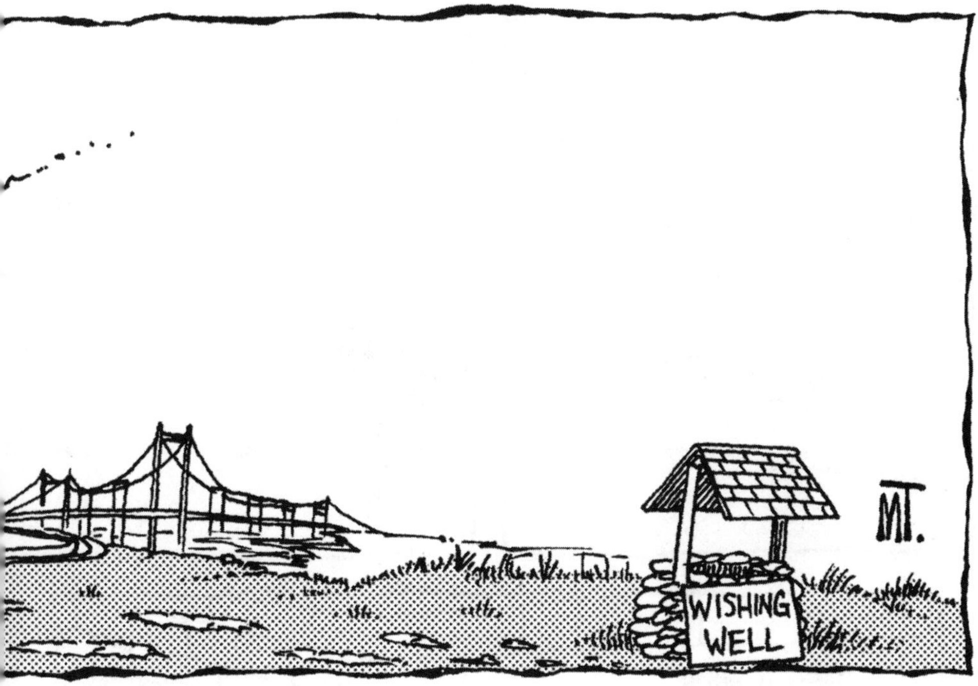
WISHING
WELL
MT.

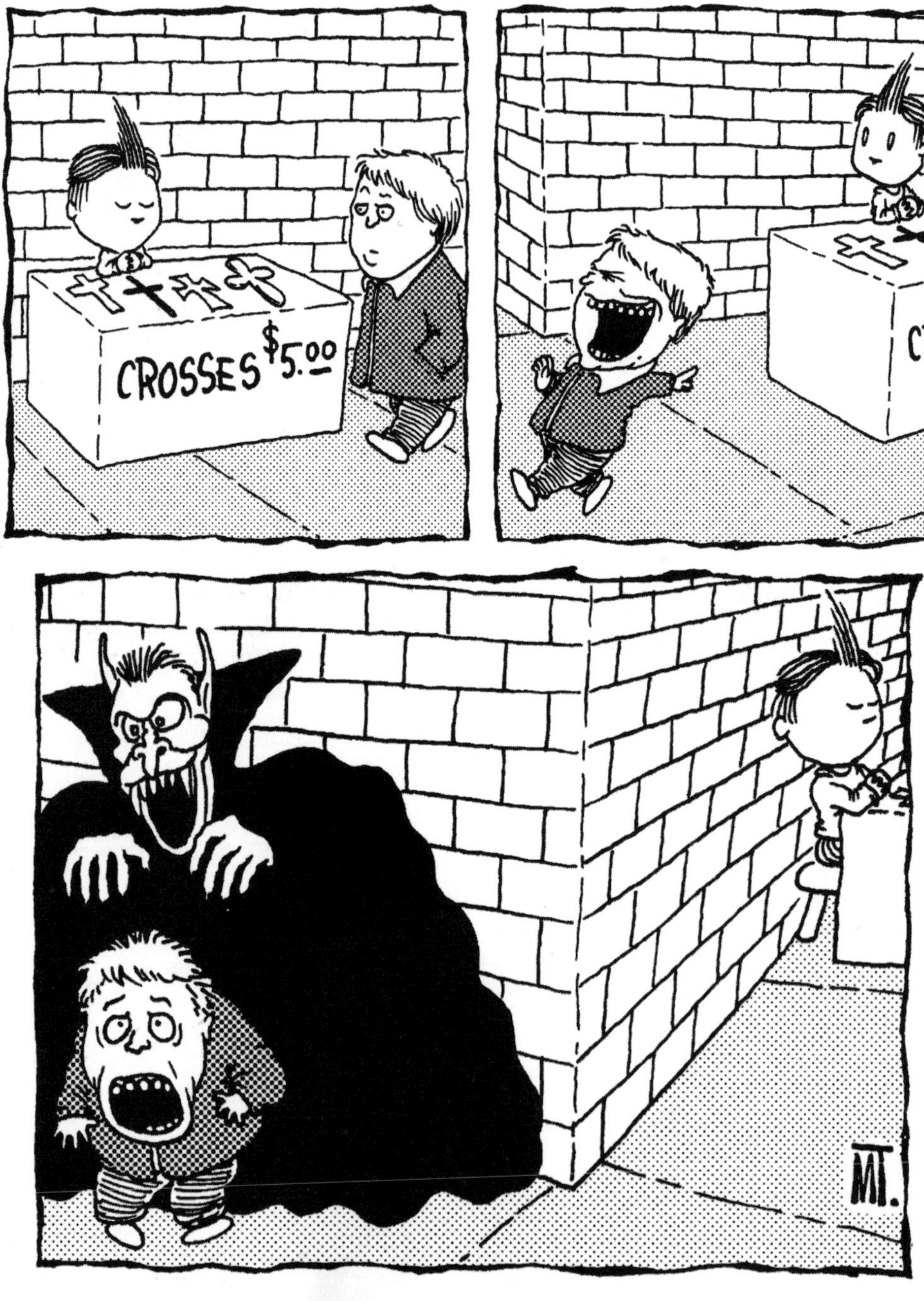
CROSSES $5.00
CR
MT.

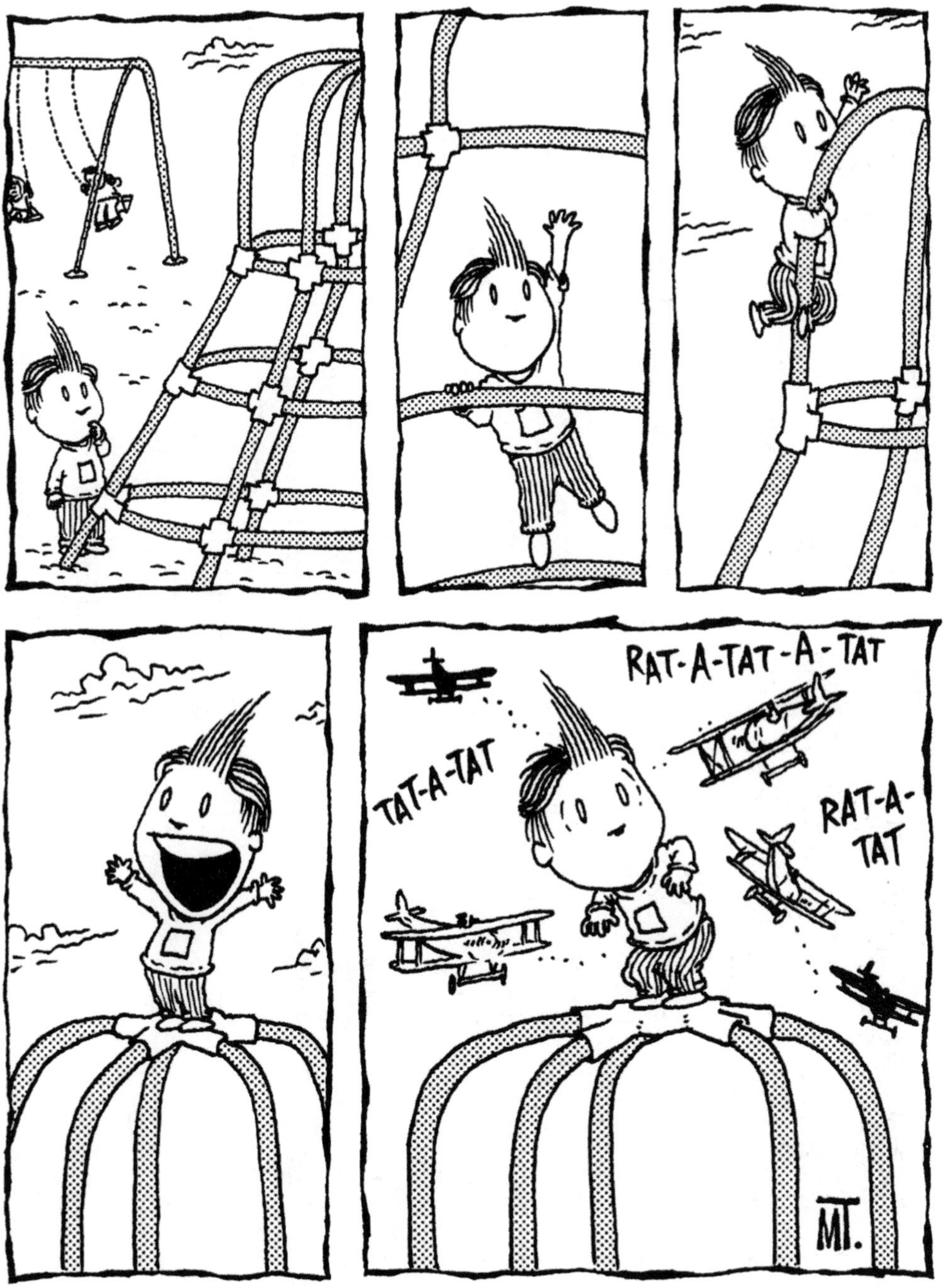

RAT-A-TAT-A-TAT
TAT-A-TAT
RAT-A-TAT
MT.

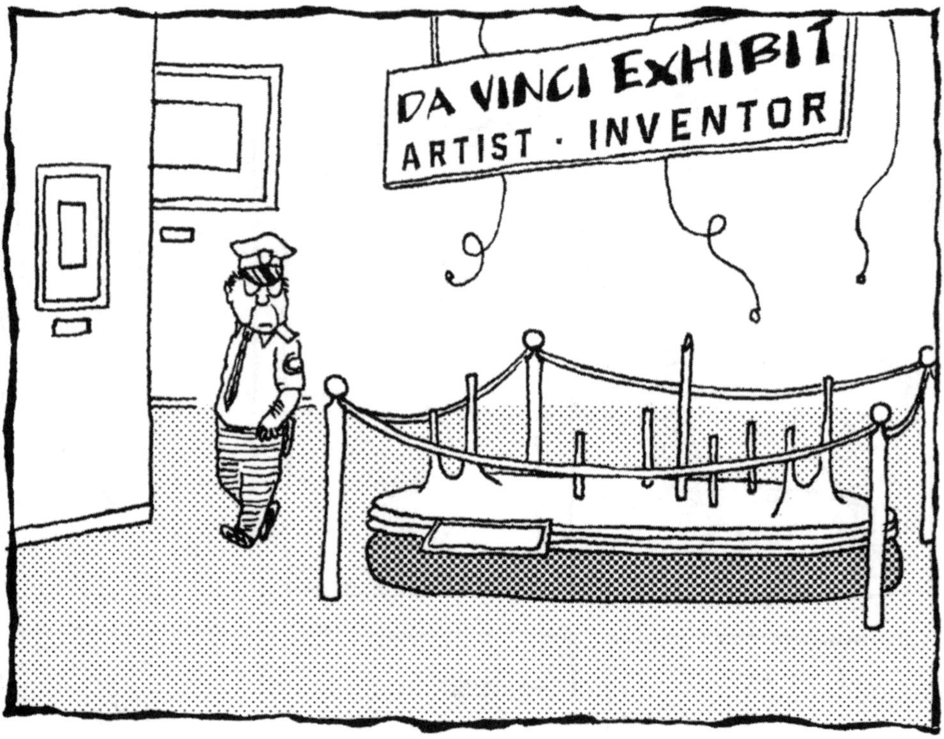
DA VINCI EXHIBIT
ARTIST · INVENTOR

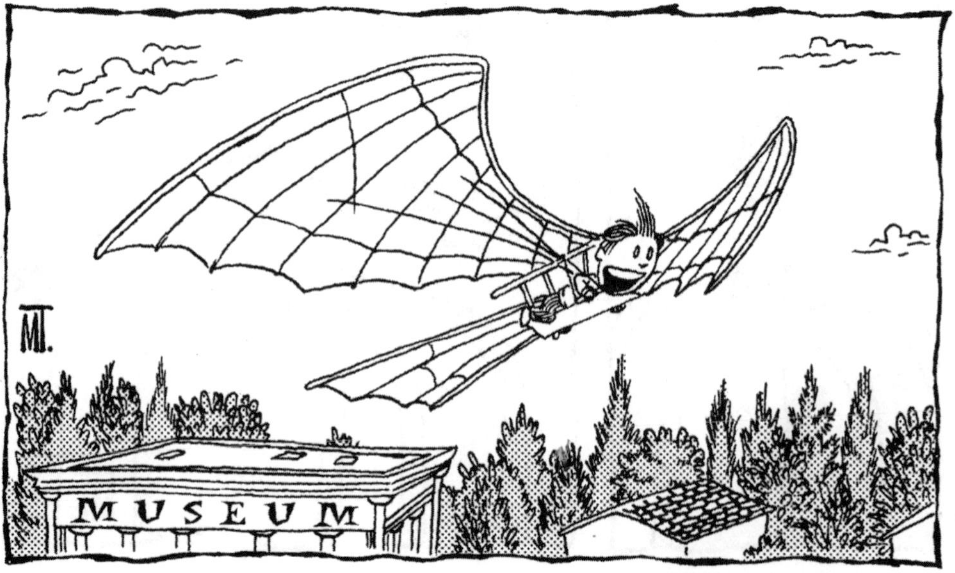
MUSEUM

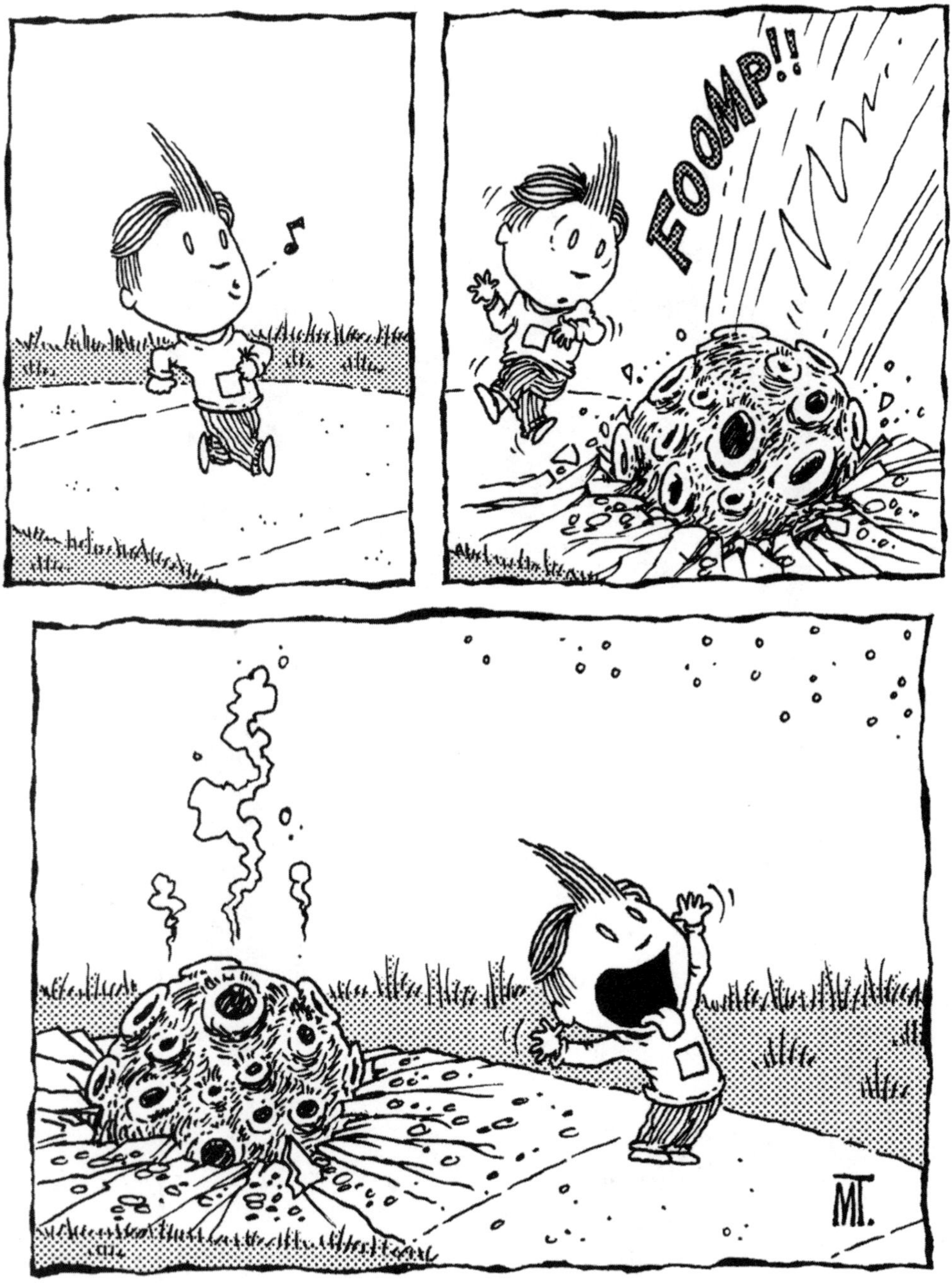
FOOMP!!
MT.

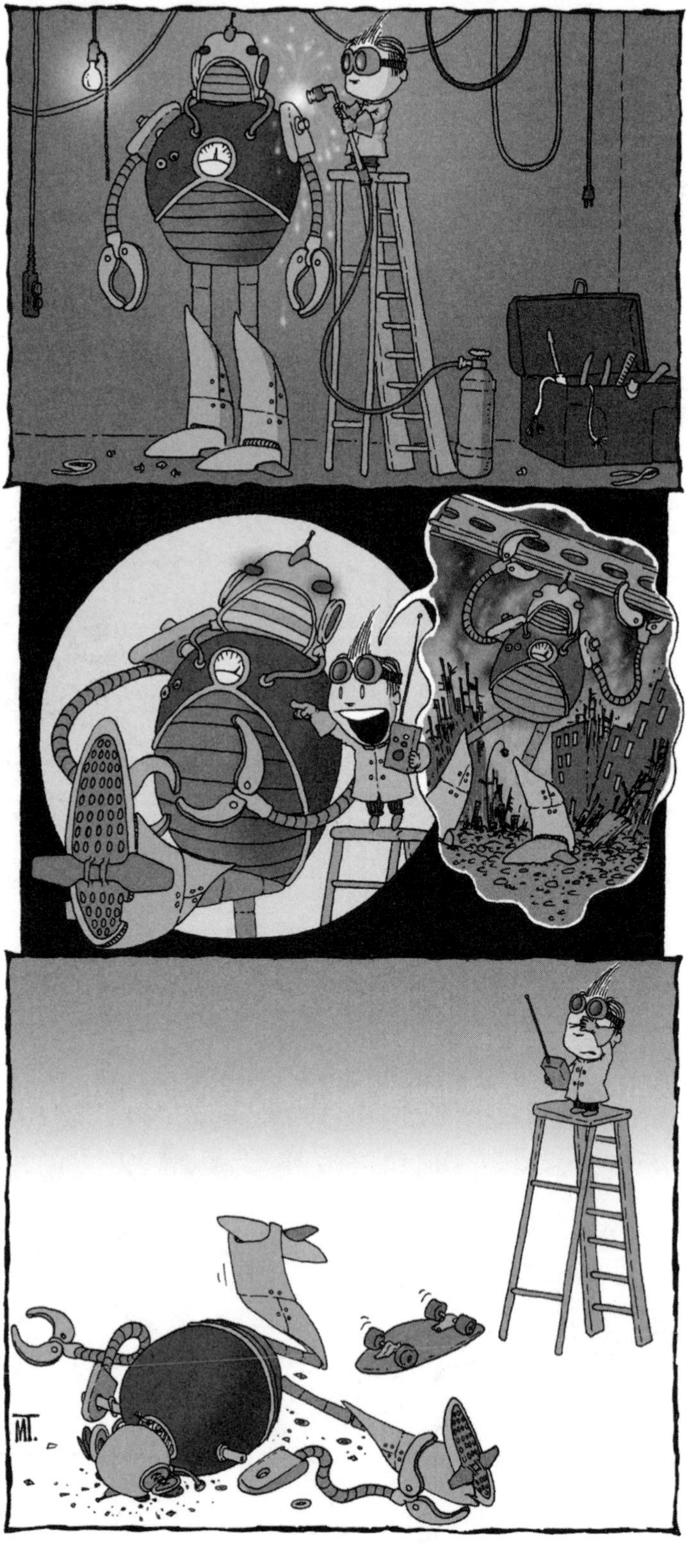

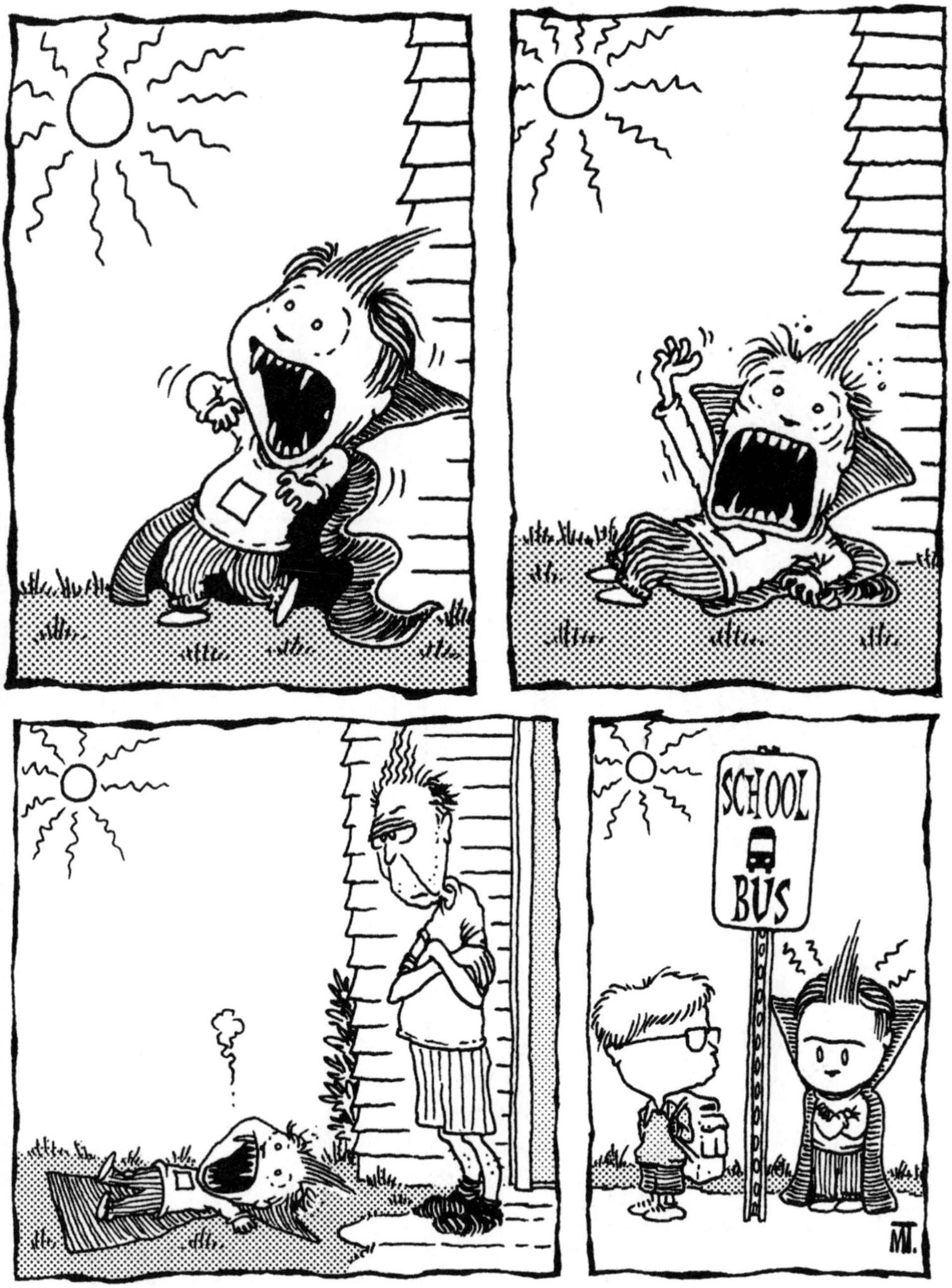
SCHOOL
BUS
MT.

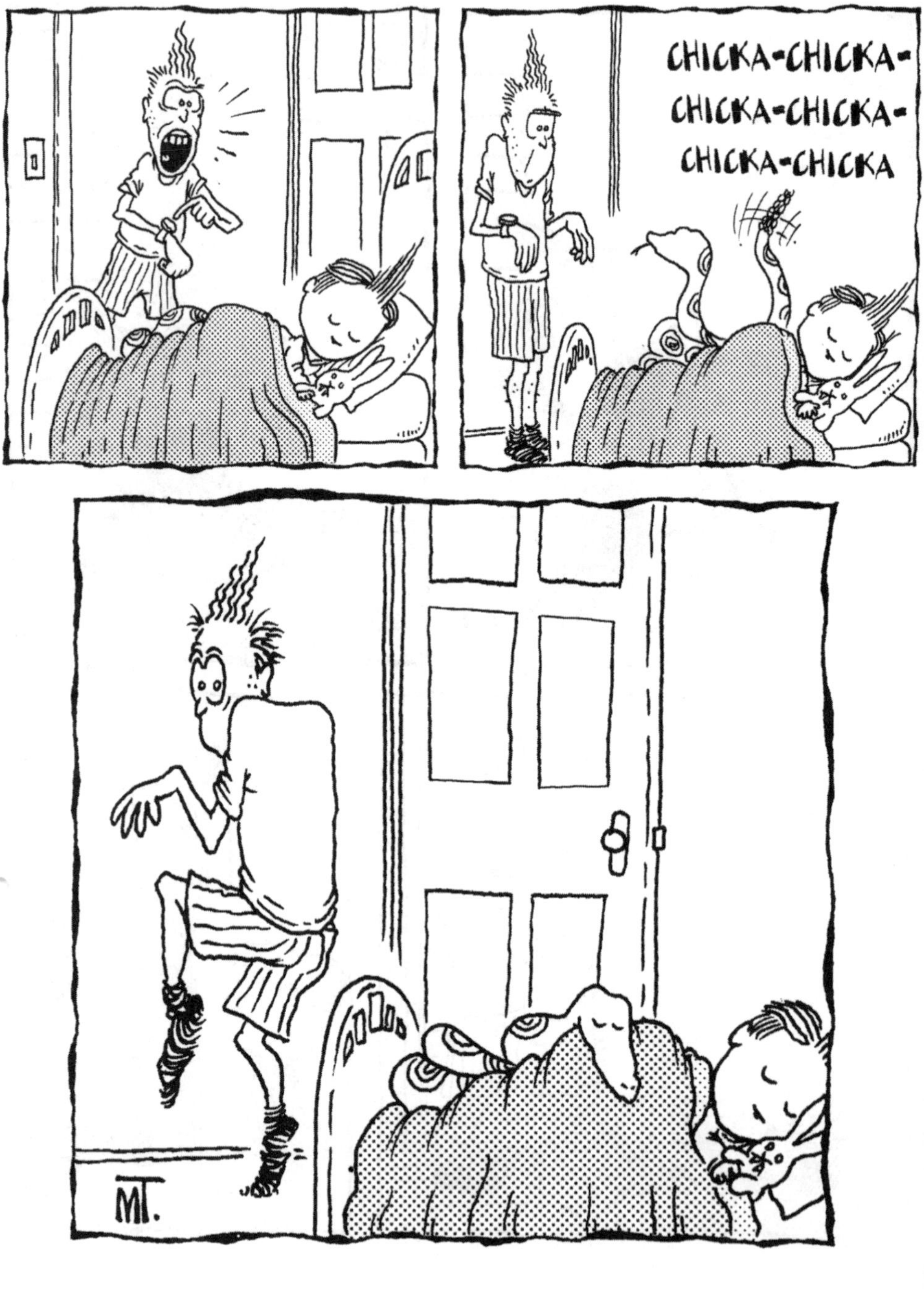
CHICKA-CHICKA-
CHICKA-CHICKA-
CHICKA-CHICKA
MT.

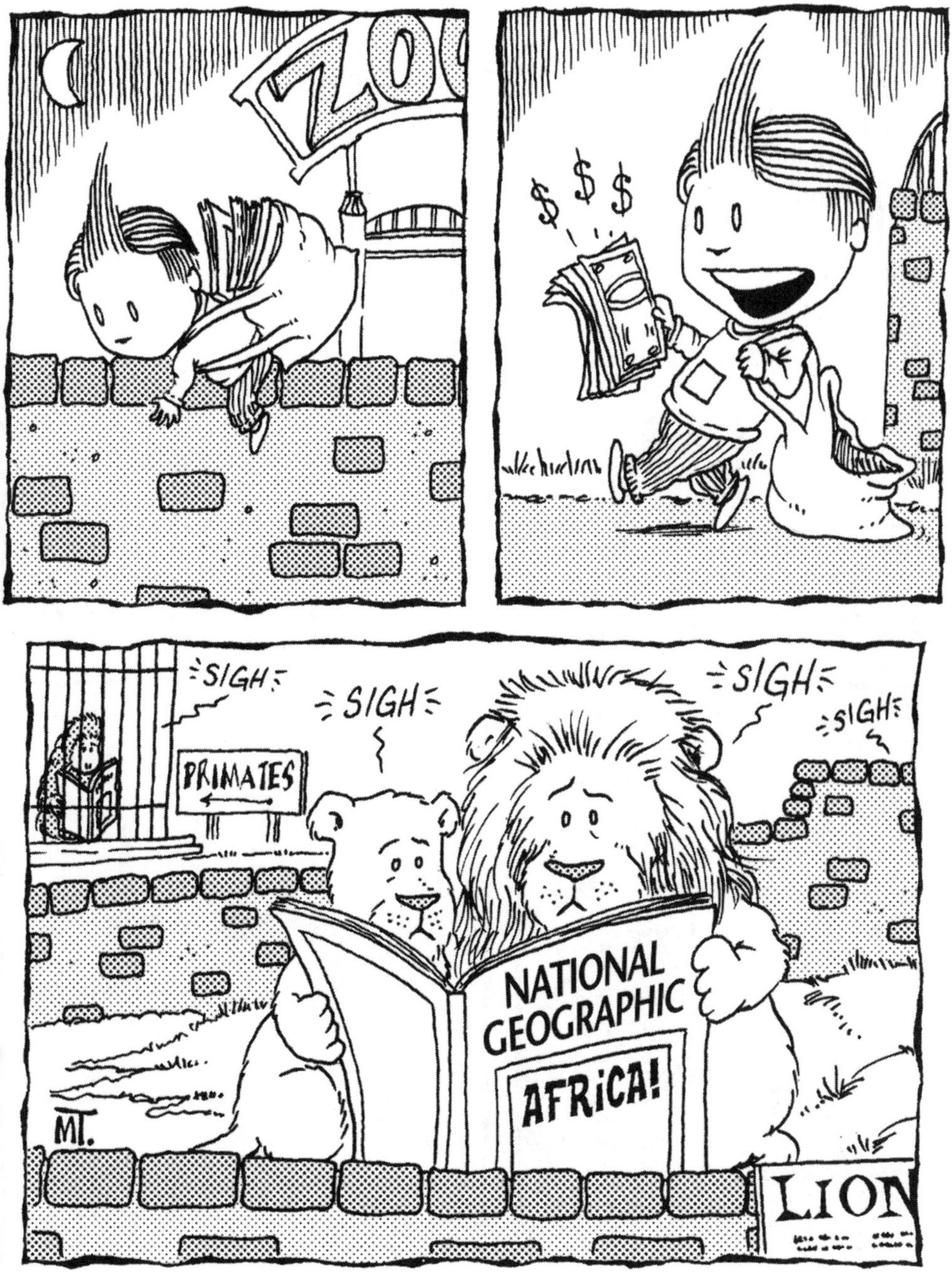
ZOO
$ $ $
SIGH
SIGH
PRIMATES
SIGH
SIGH
NATIONAL GEOGRAPHIC
AFRICA!
LION
MT.

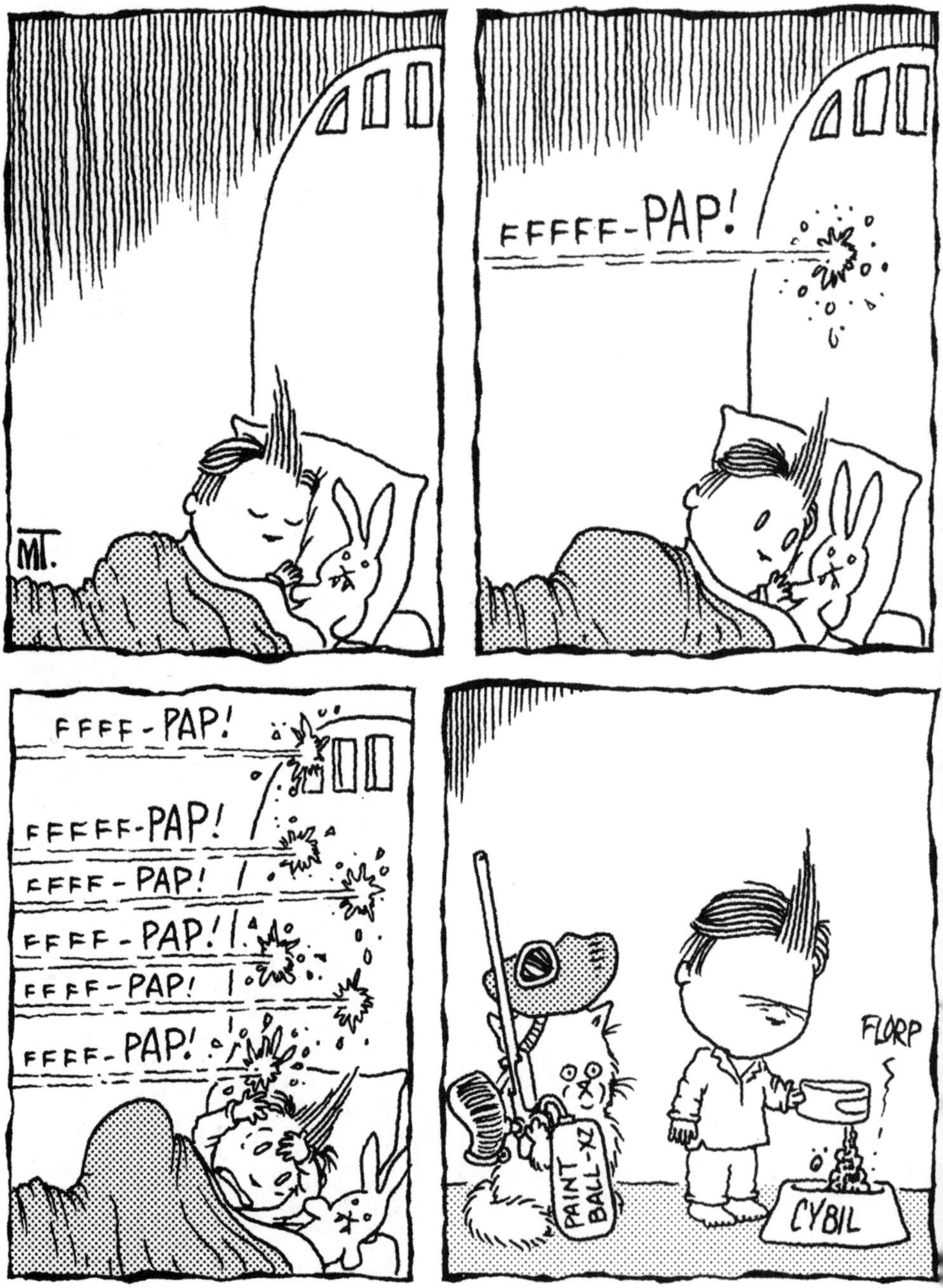

MT.
FFFFF-PAP!
FFFF-PAP!
FFFFF-PAP!
FFFF-PAP!
FFFF-PAP!
FFFF-PAP!
FFFF-PAP!
PAINT BALL-XZ
FLORP
CYBIL

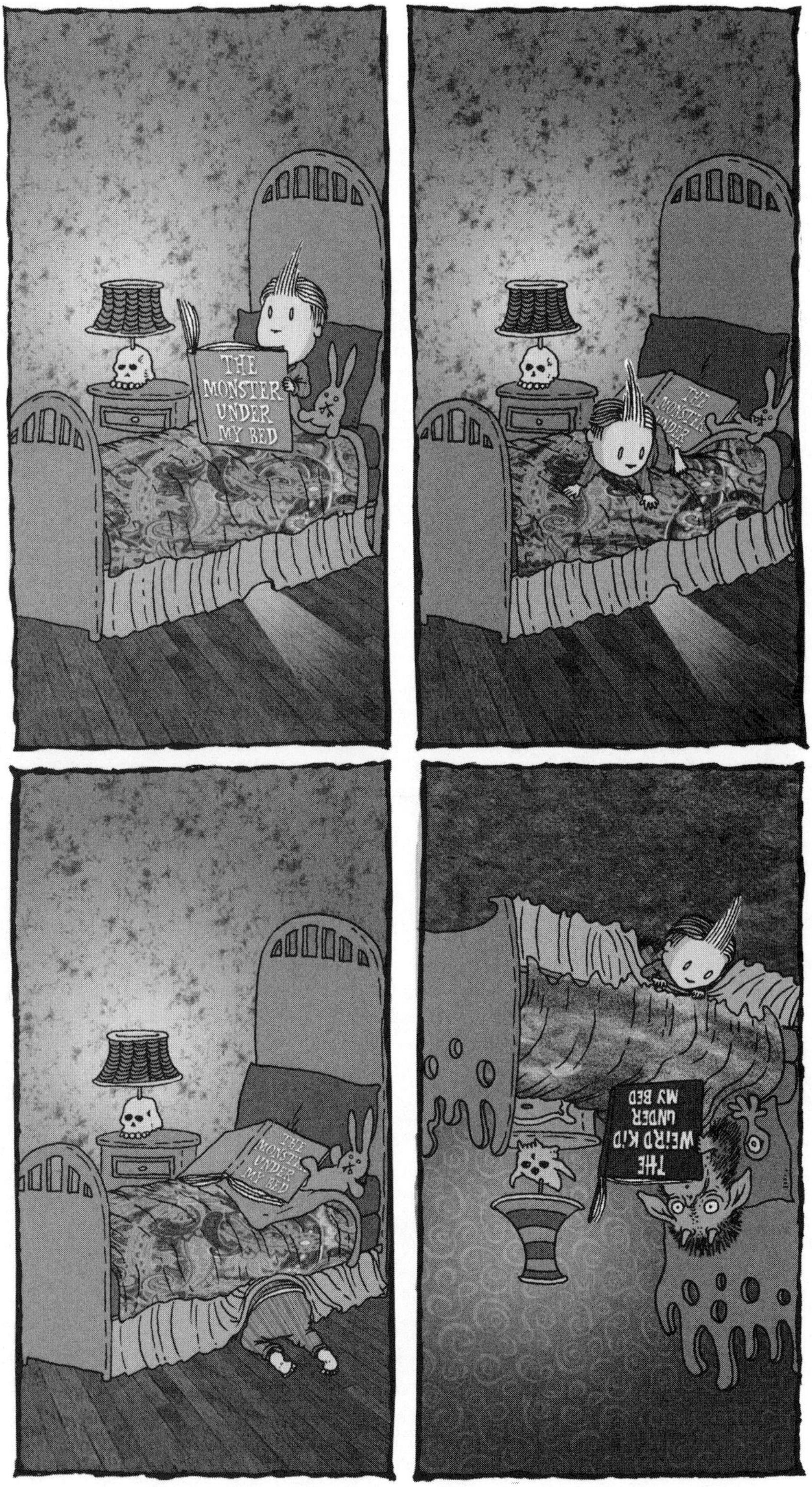

THE MONSTER UNDER MY BED
THE MONSTER UNDER
THE MONSTER UNDER MY BED
THE WEIRD KID UNDER MY BED

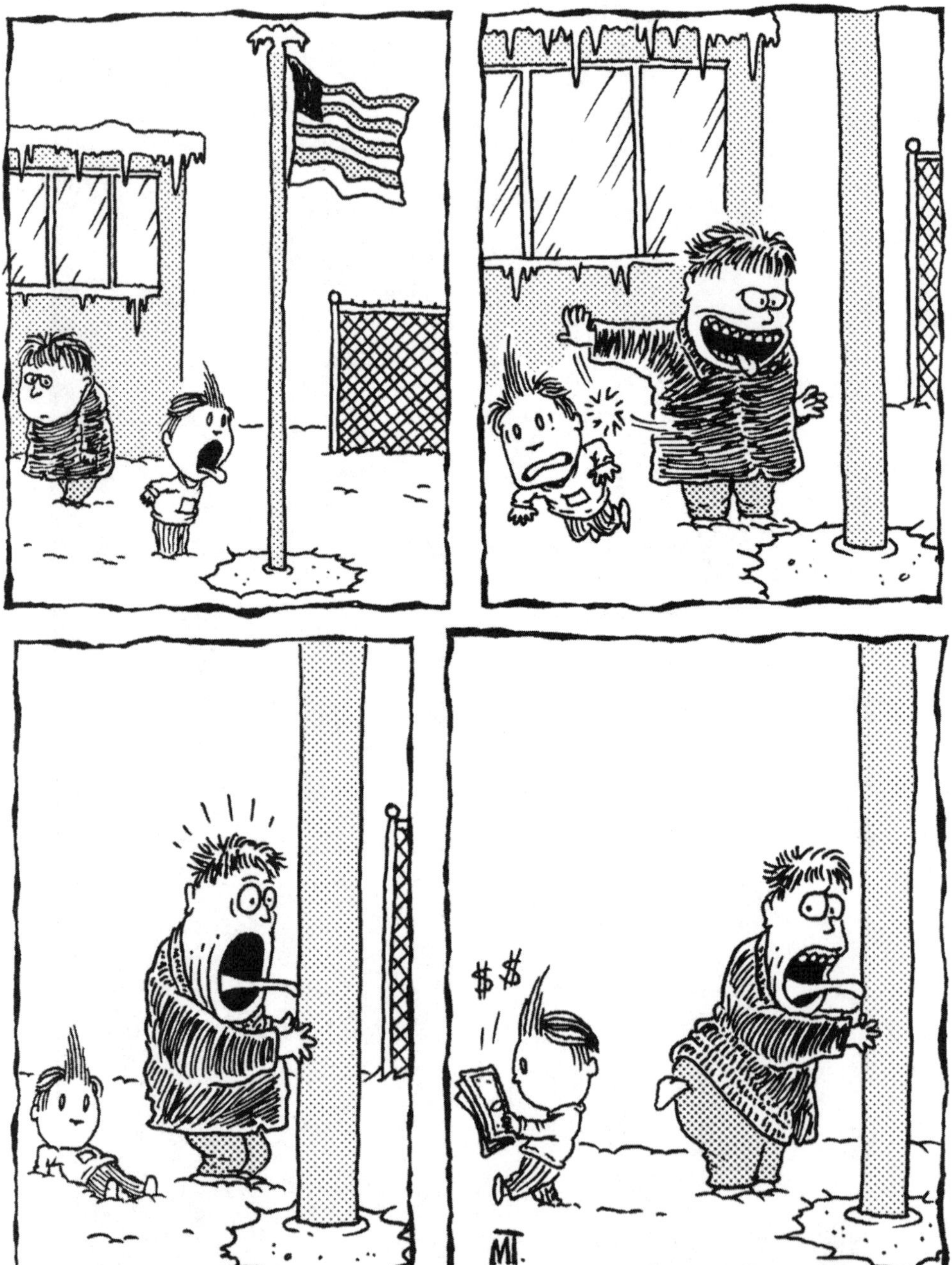
$ $
MT.

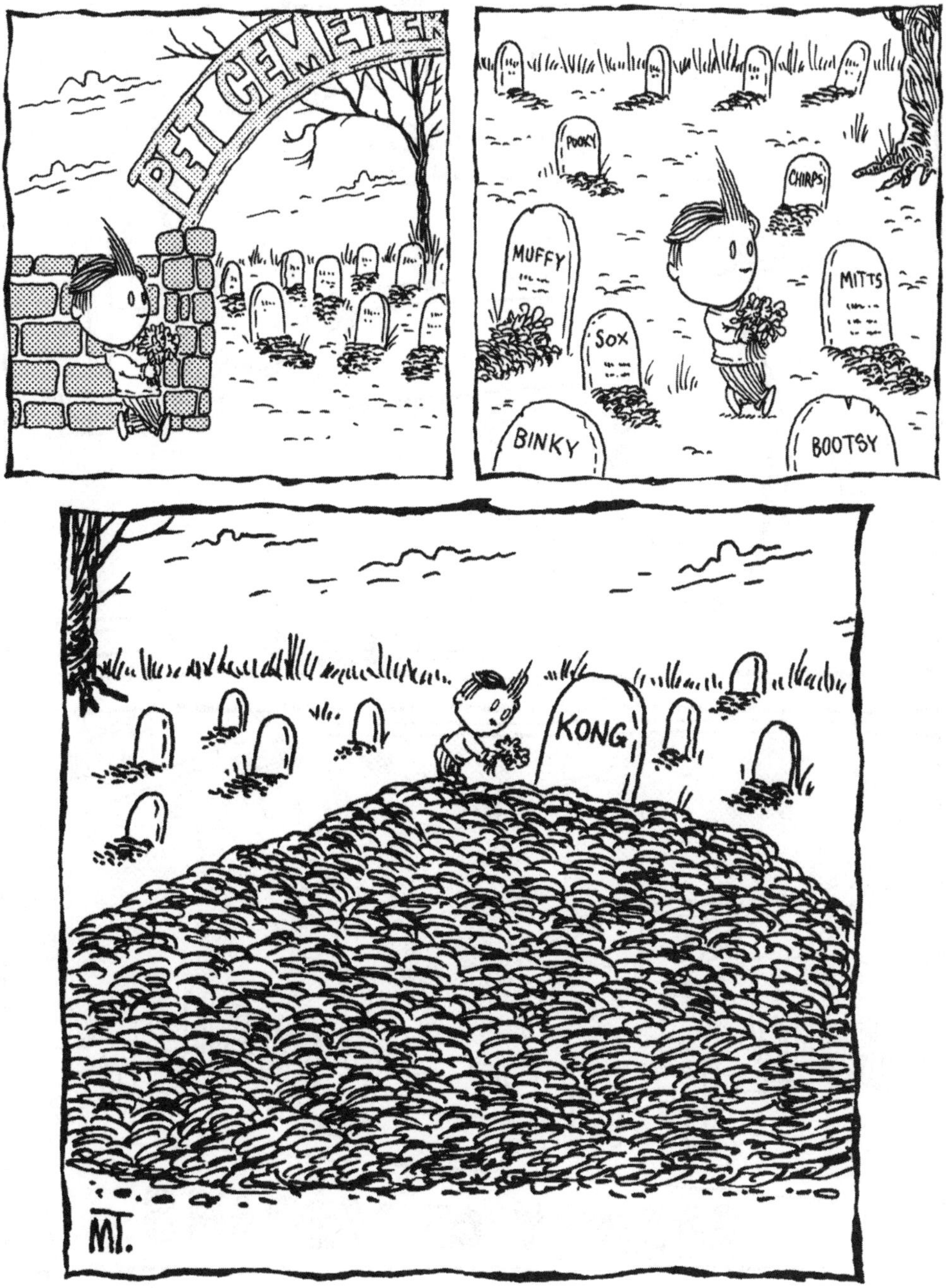
PET CEMETERY
POOKY
CHIRPS
MUFFY
MITTS
SOX
BINKY
BOOTSY
KONG
MT.

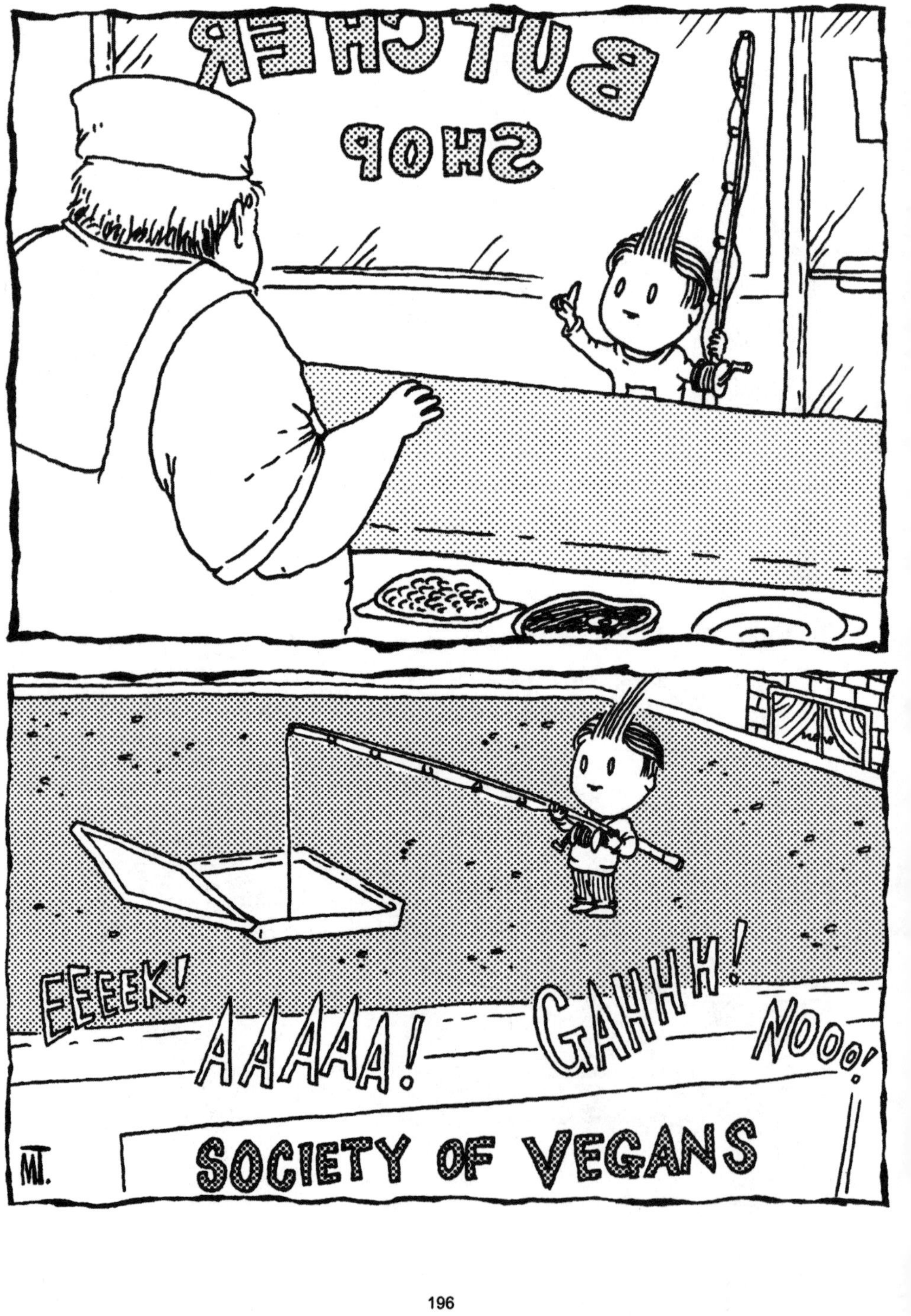
BUTCHER
SHOP
EEEEK!
AAAAA!
GAHHH!
NOOo!
SOCIETY OF VEGANS
MT.

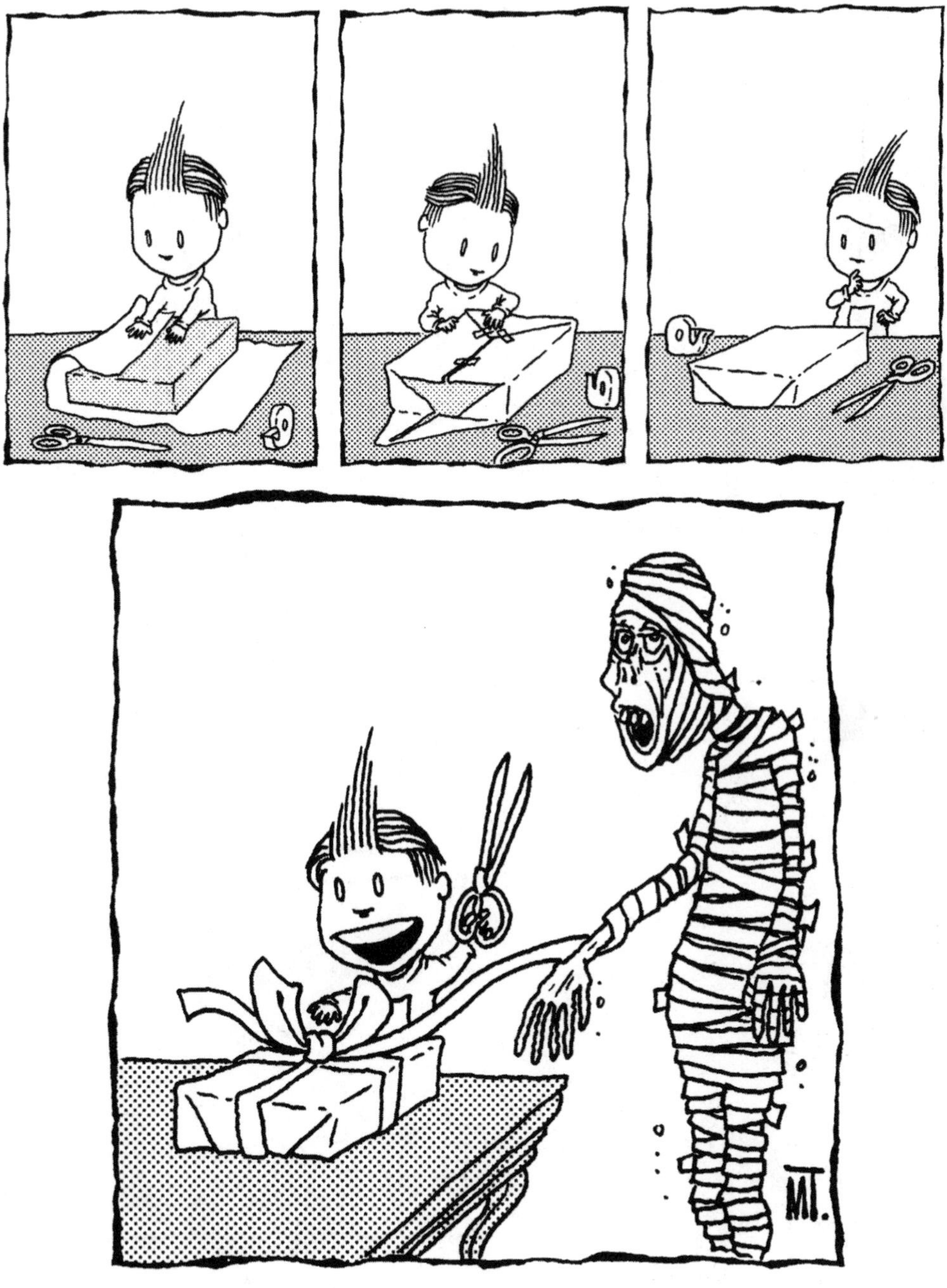
MT.

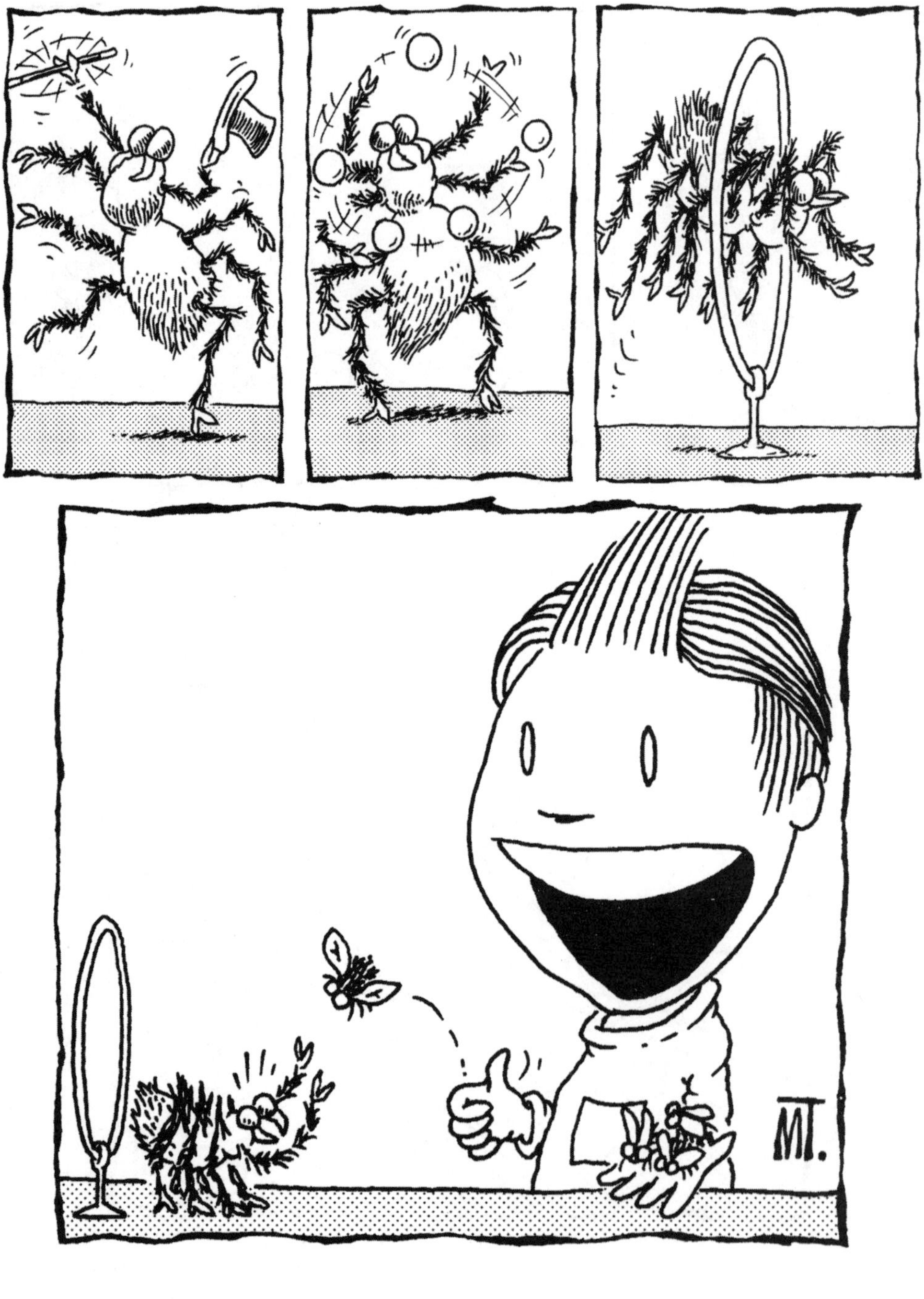
MT.

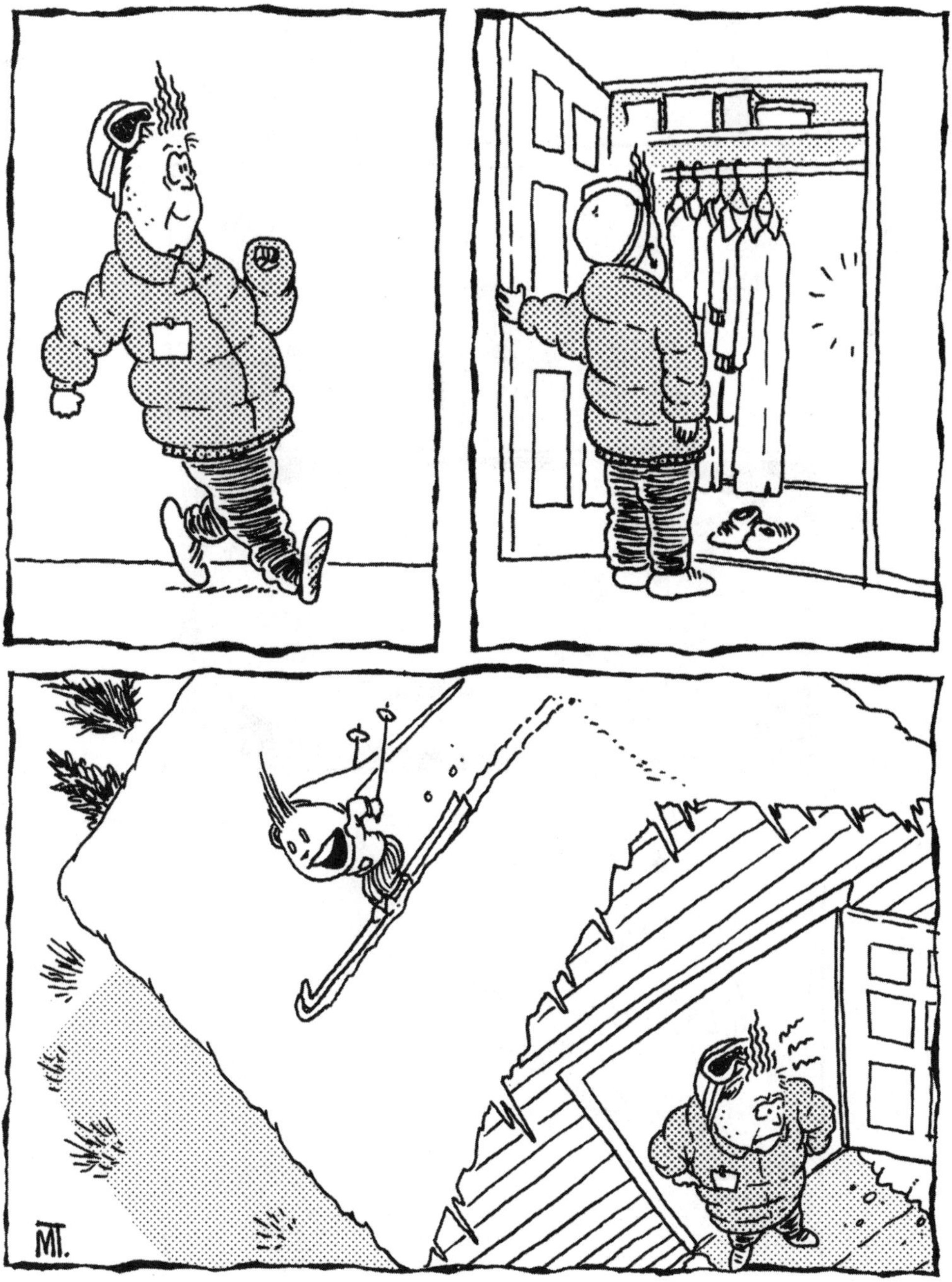
MT.

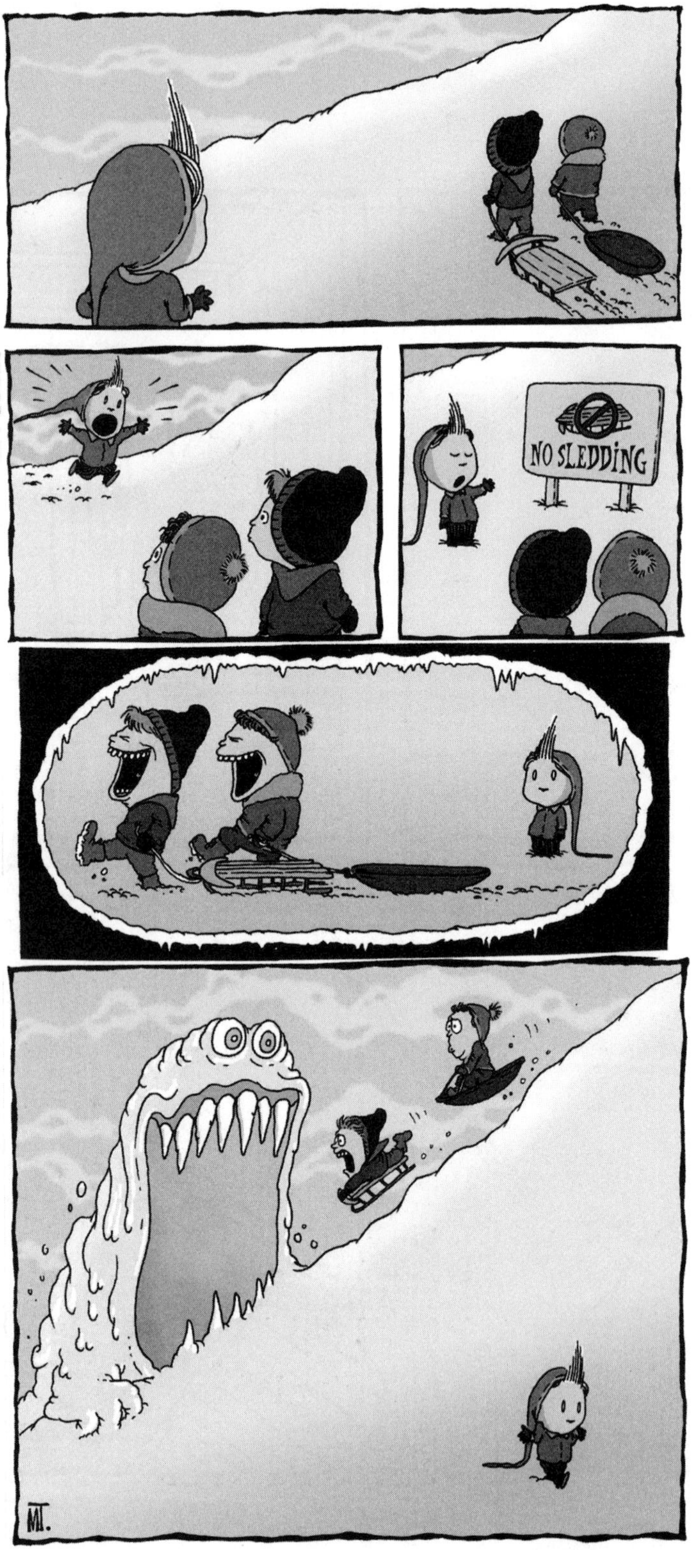
NO SLEDDING
MT.

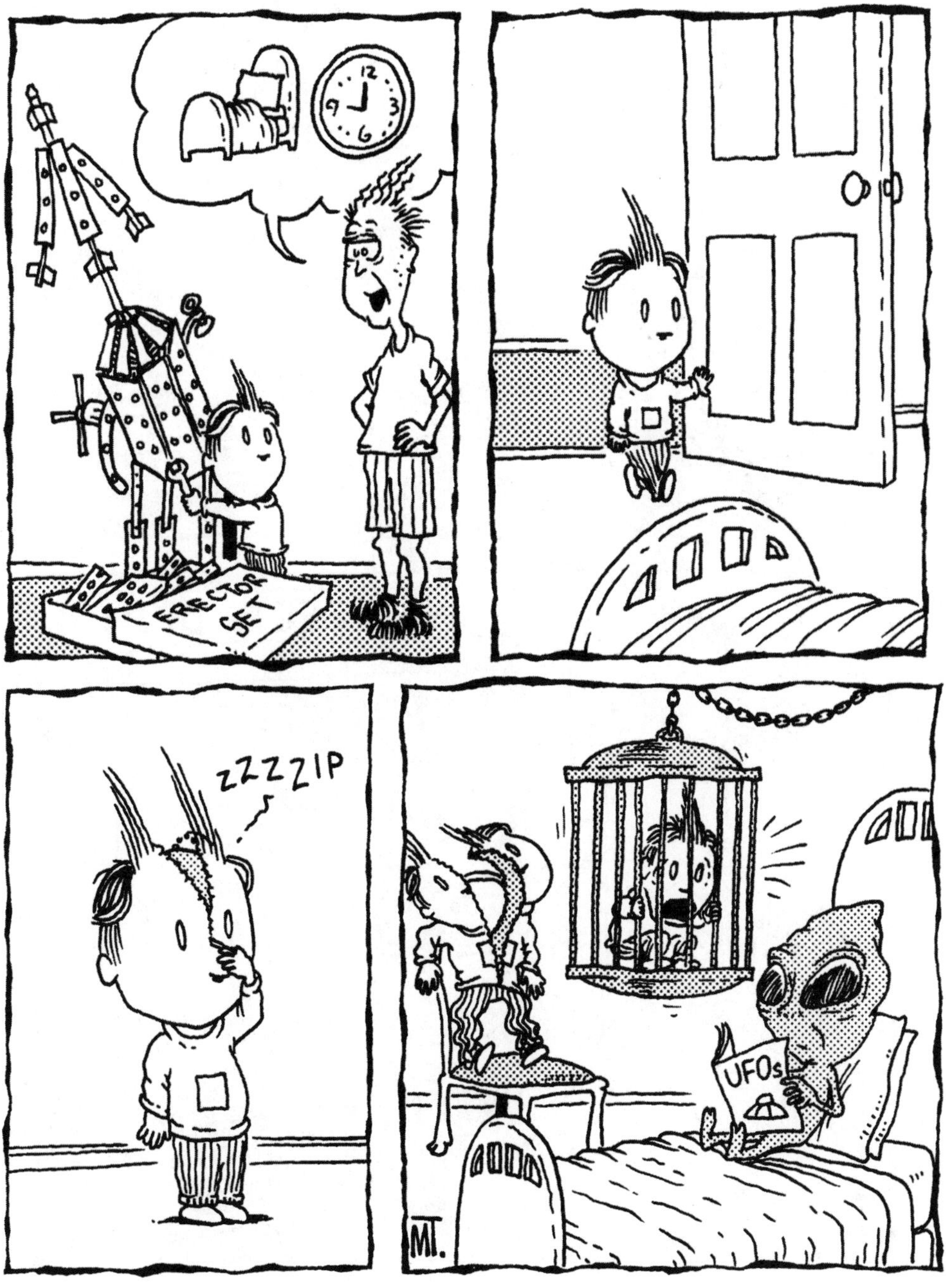
ERECTOR SET
ZZZZIP
UFOs
MT.

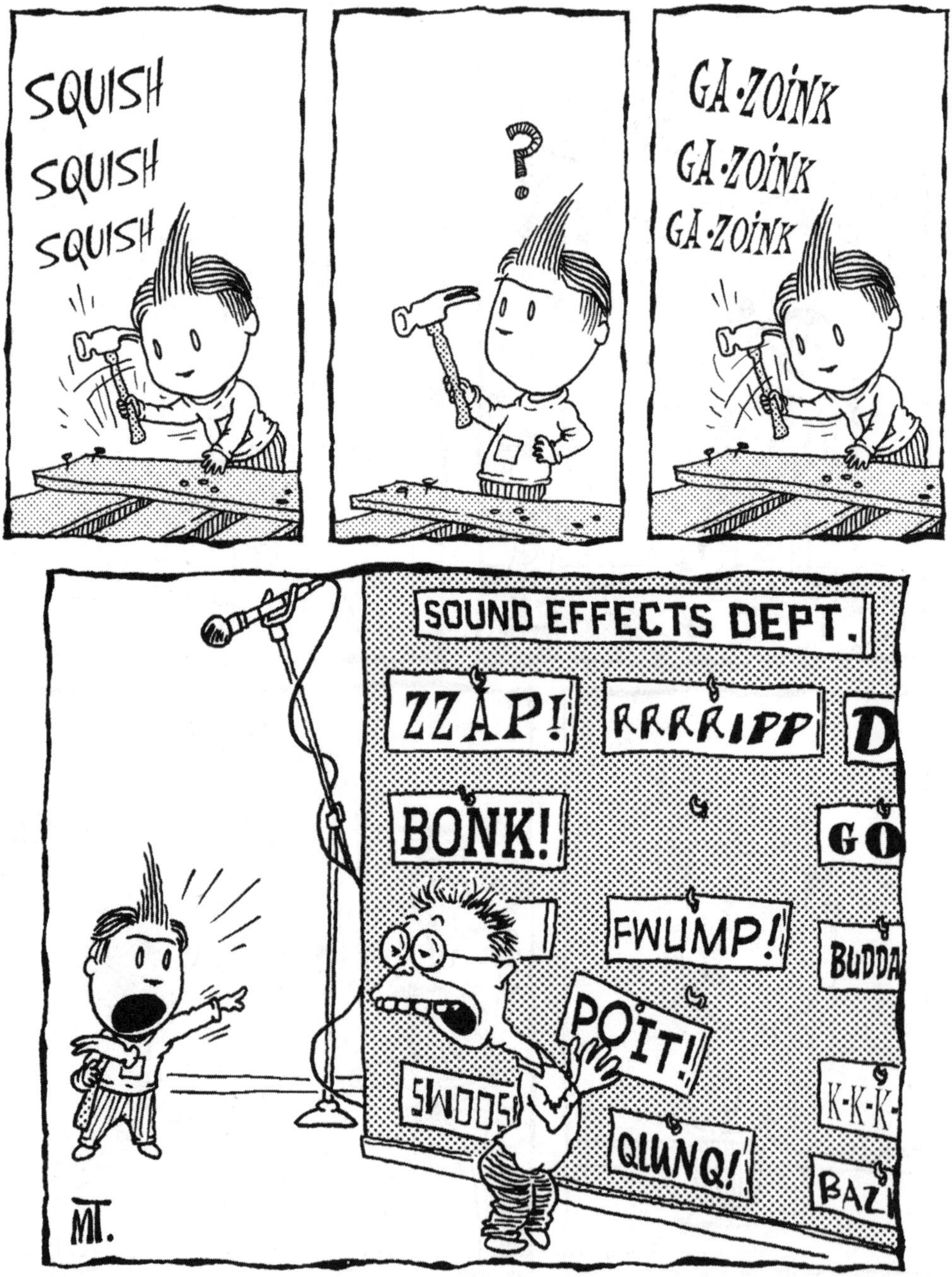

SQUISH
SQUISH
SQUISH
?
GA·ZOINK
GA·ZOINK
GA·ZOINK
SOUND EFFECTS DEPT.
ZZAP!
RRRRIPP
BONK!
FWUMP!
POIT!
QLUNQ!
MT.

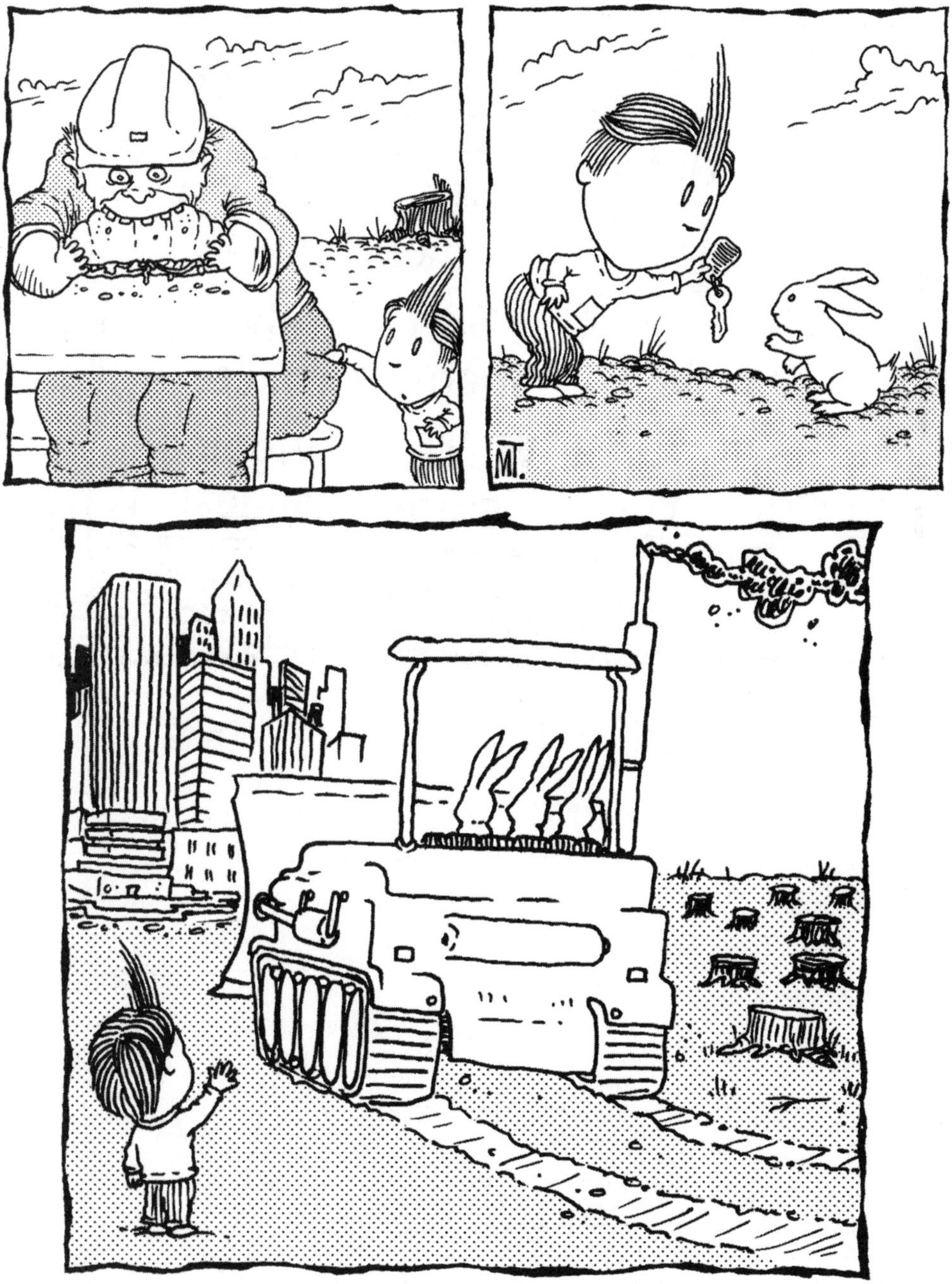
MT.

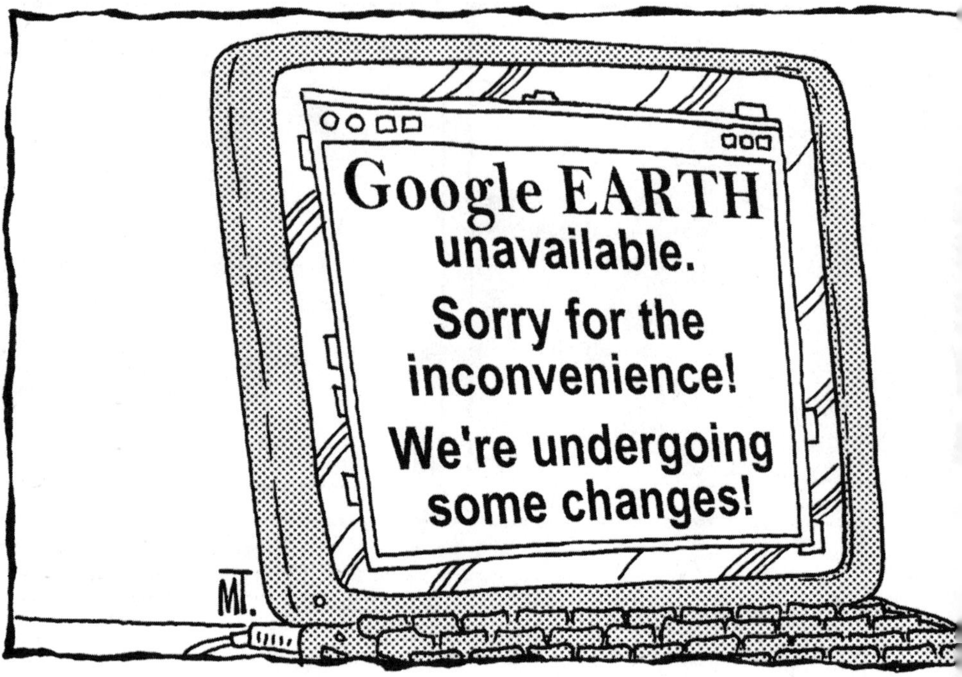
Google EARTH
unavailable.
Sorry for the inconvenience!
We're undergoing some changes!
MT.

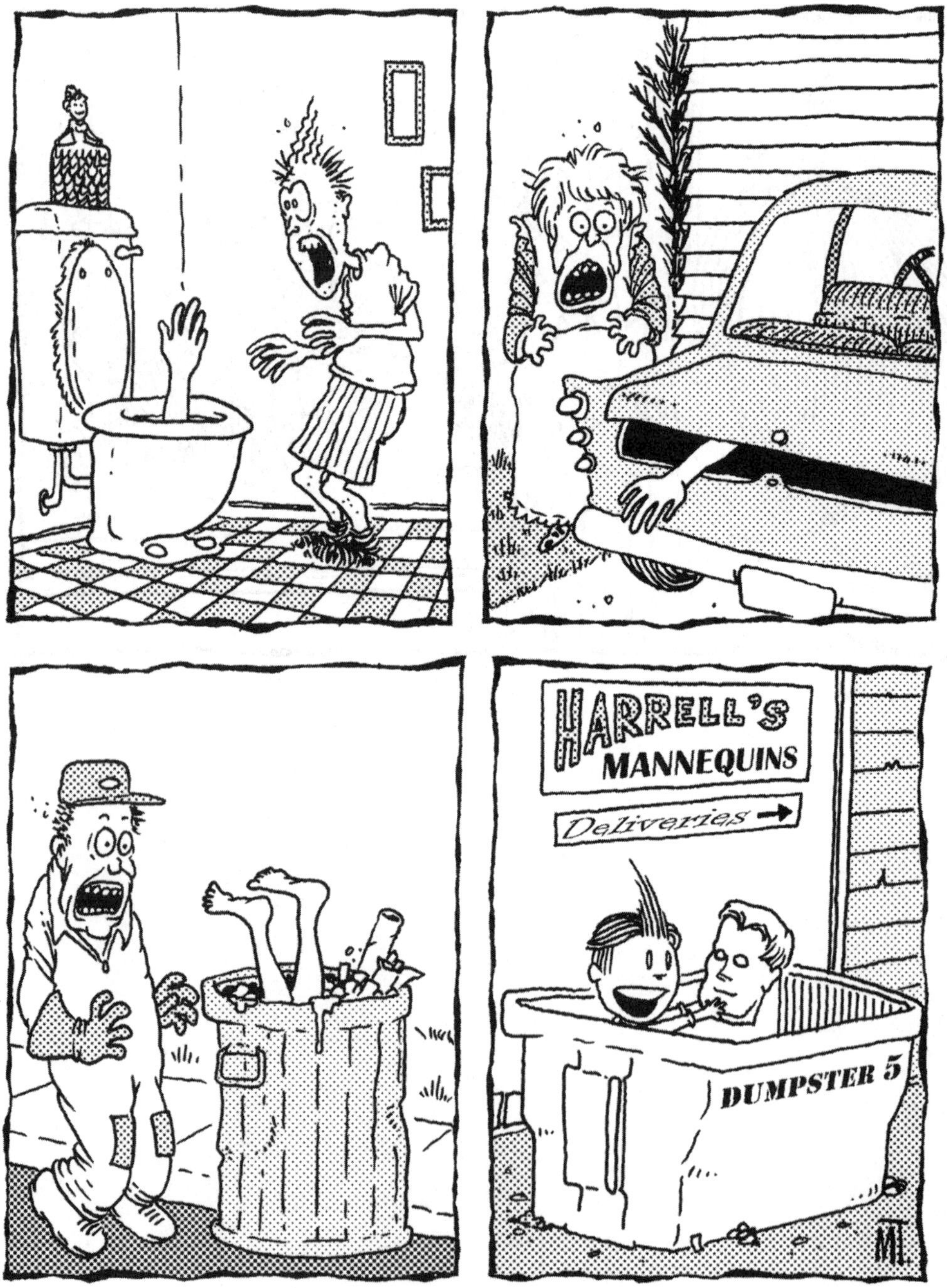
HARRELL'S
MANNEQUINS
Deliveries
DUMPSTER 5
MT.

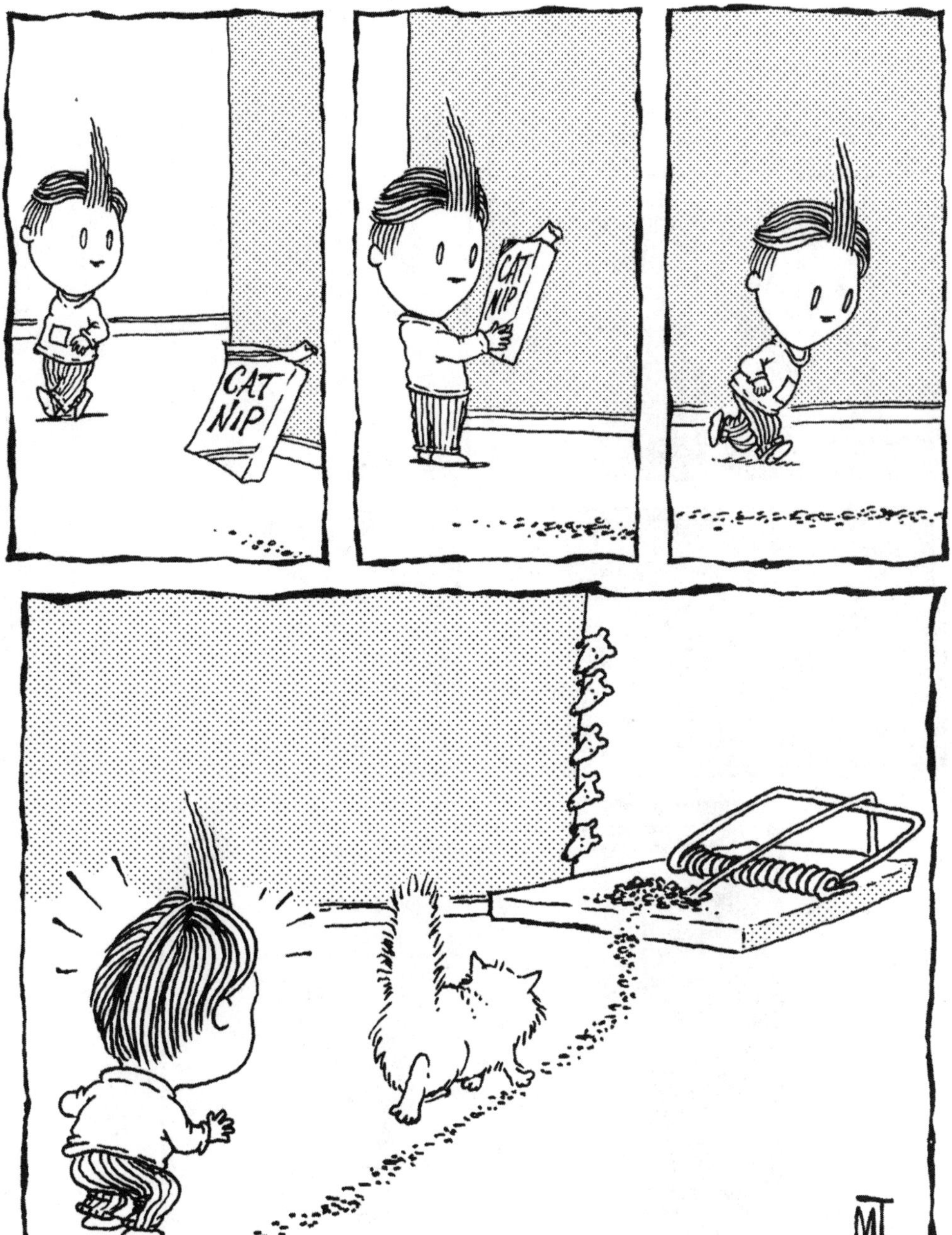
CAT NIP
CAT NIP
MT.

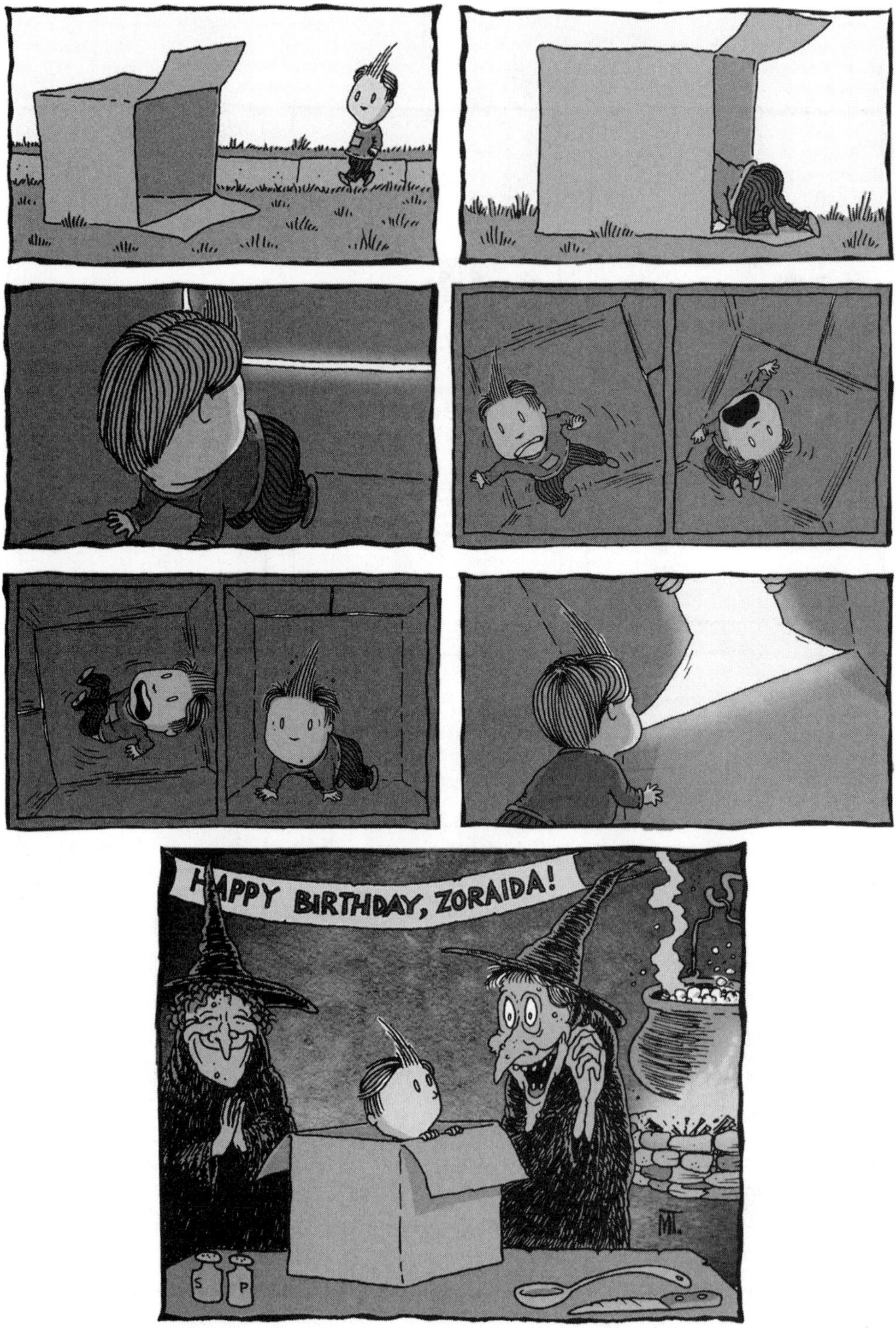
HAPPY BIRTHDAY, ZORAIDA!
S
P
MT.

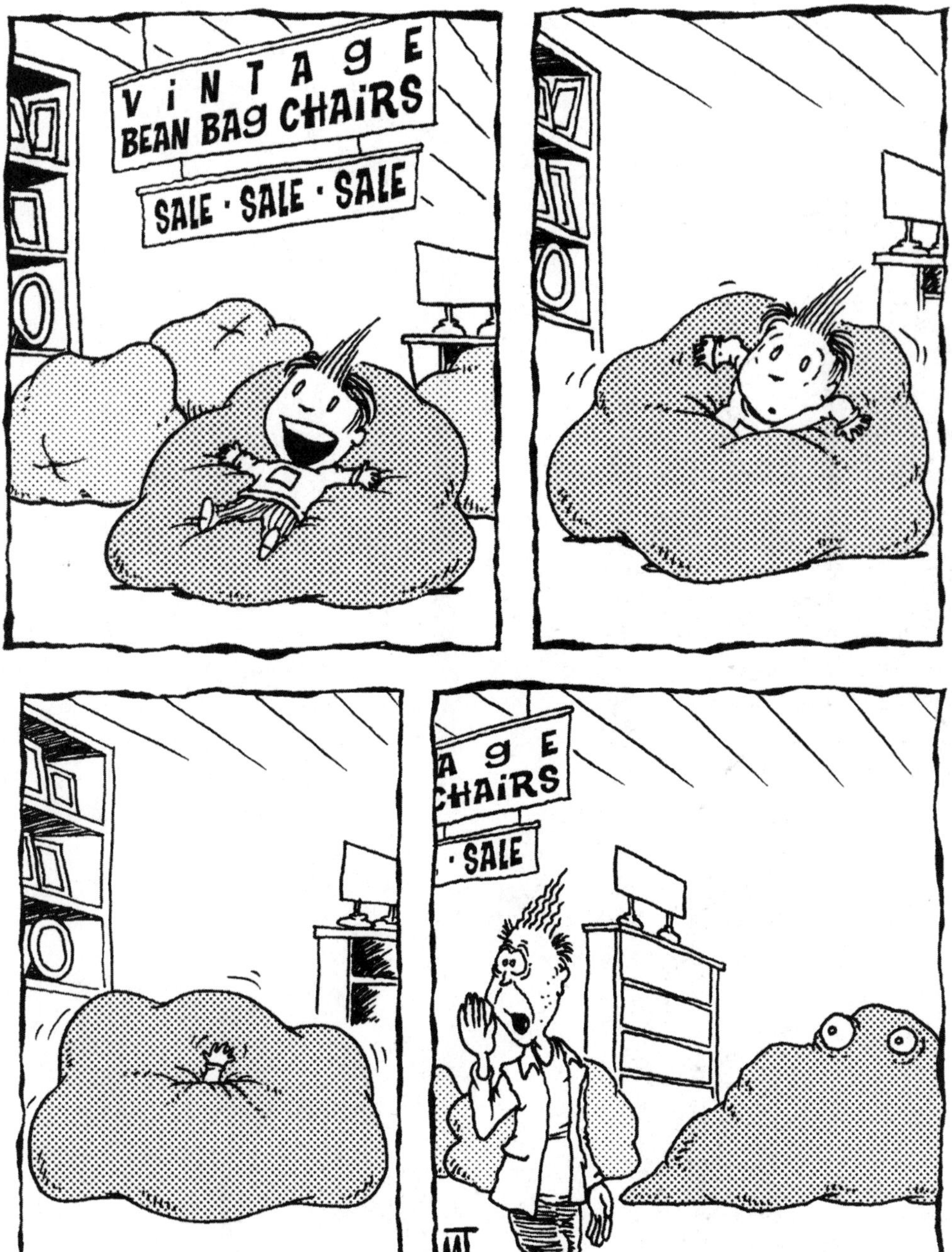
VINTAGE
BEAN BAG CHAIRS
SALE · SALE · SALE
AGE
CHAIRS
· SALE
MT.

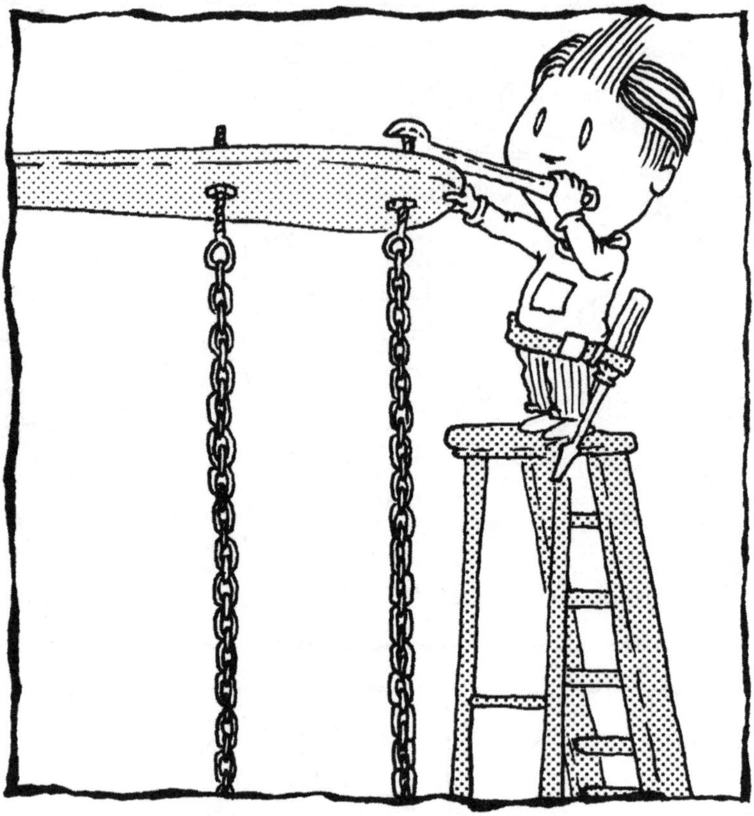

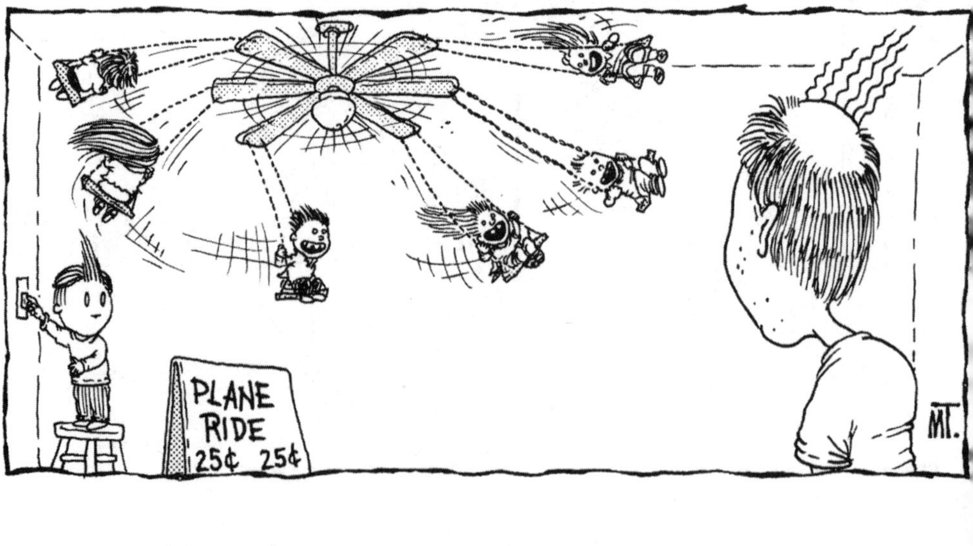
PLANE RIDE
25¢ 25¢
MT.

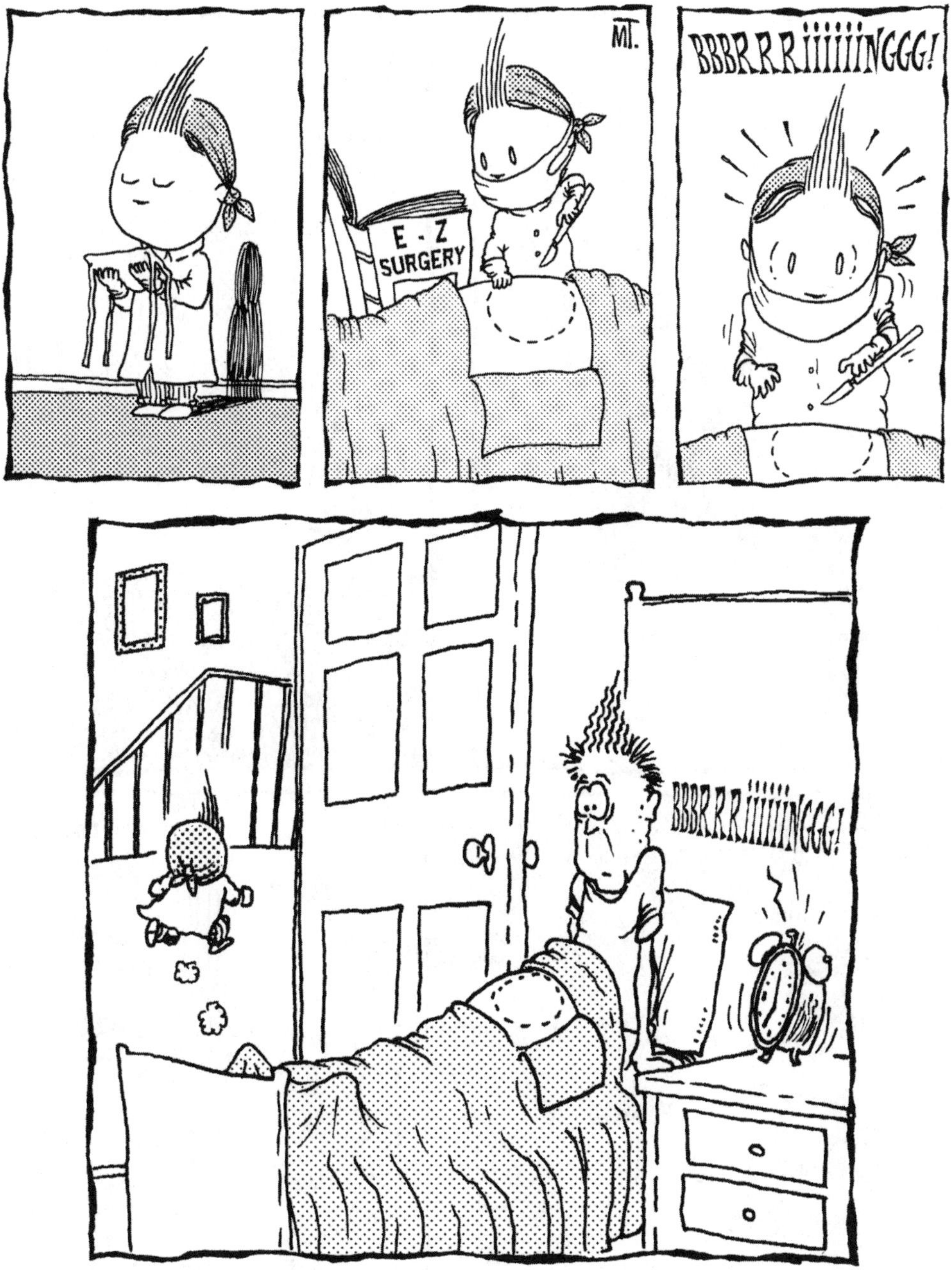
MT.
E-Z SURGERY
BBBRRRiiiiiiNGGG!
BBBRRRiiiiiiNGGG!

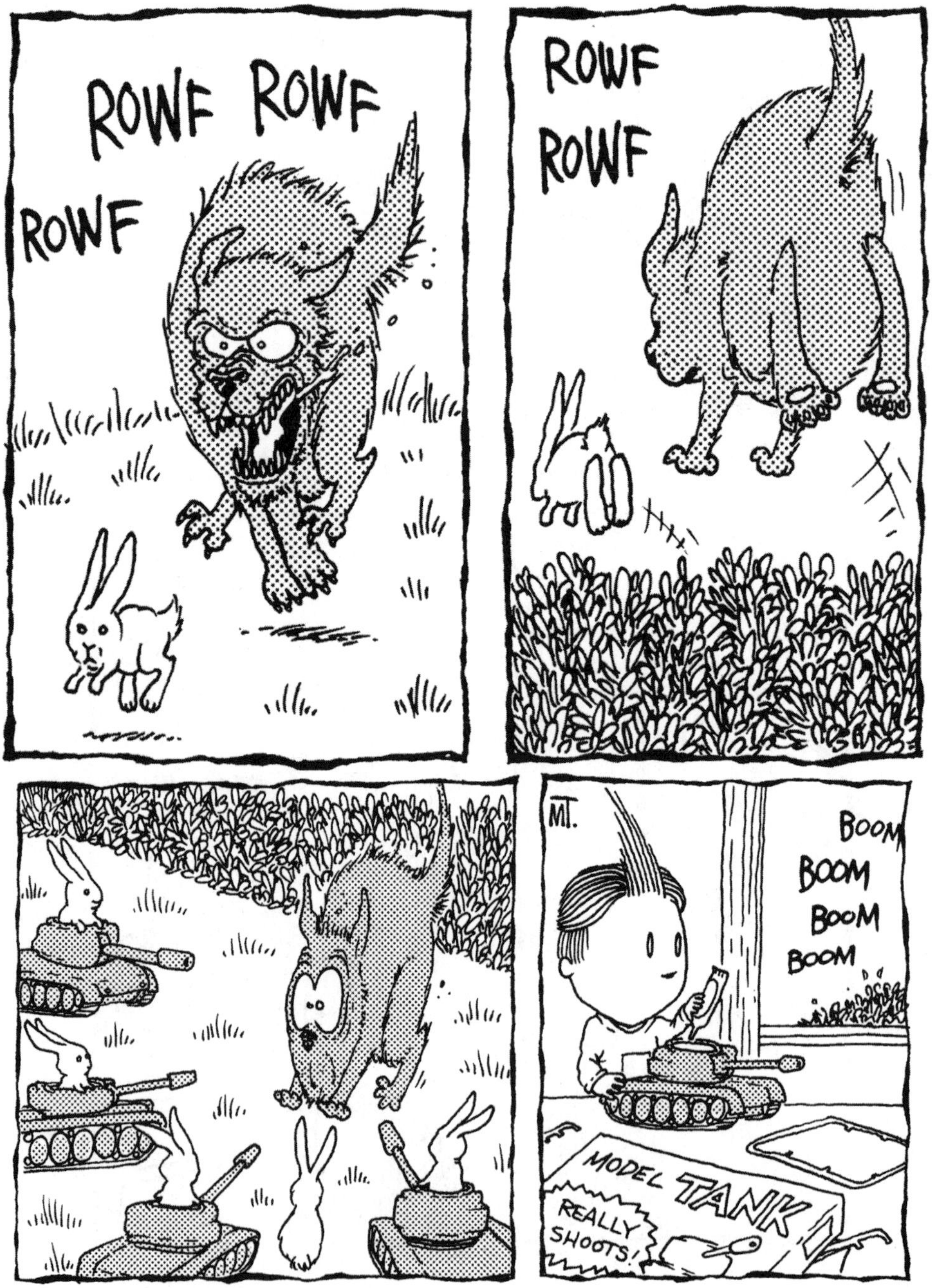
ROWF ROWF
ROWF
ROWF
ROWF
MT.
BOOM
BOOM
BOOM
BOOM
MODEL TANK
REALLY SHOOTS!

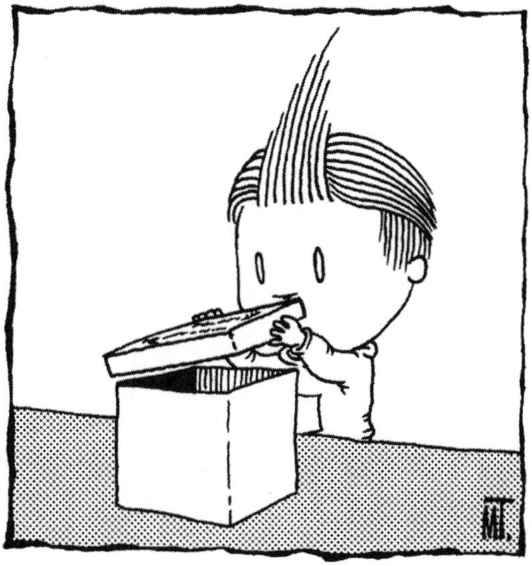

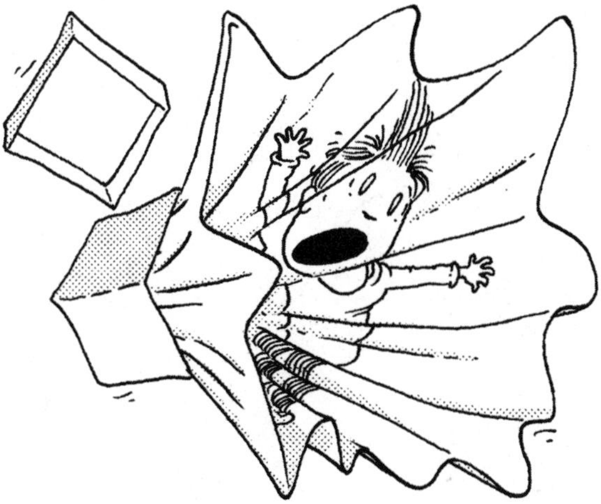

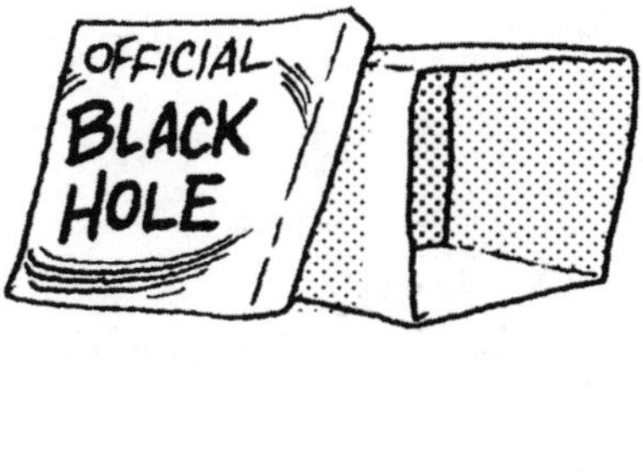
OFFICIAL
BLACK
HOLE

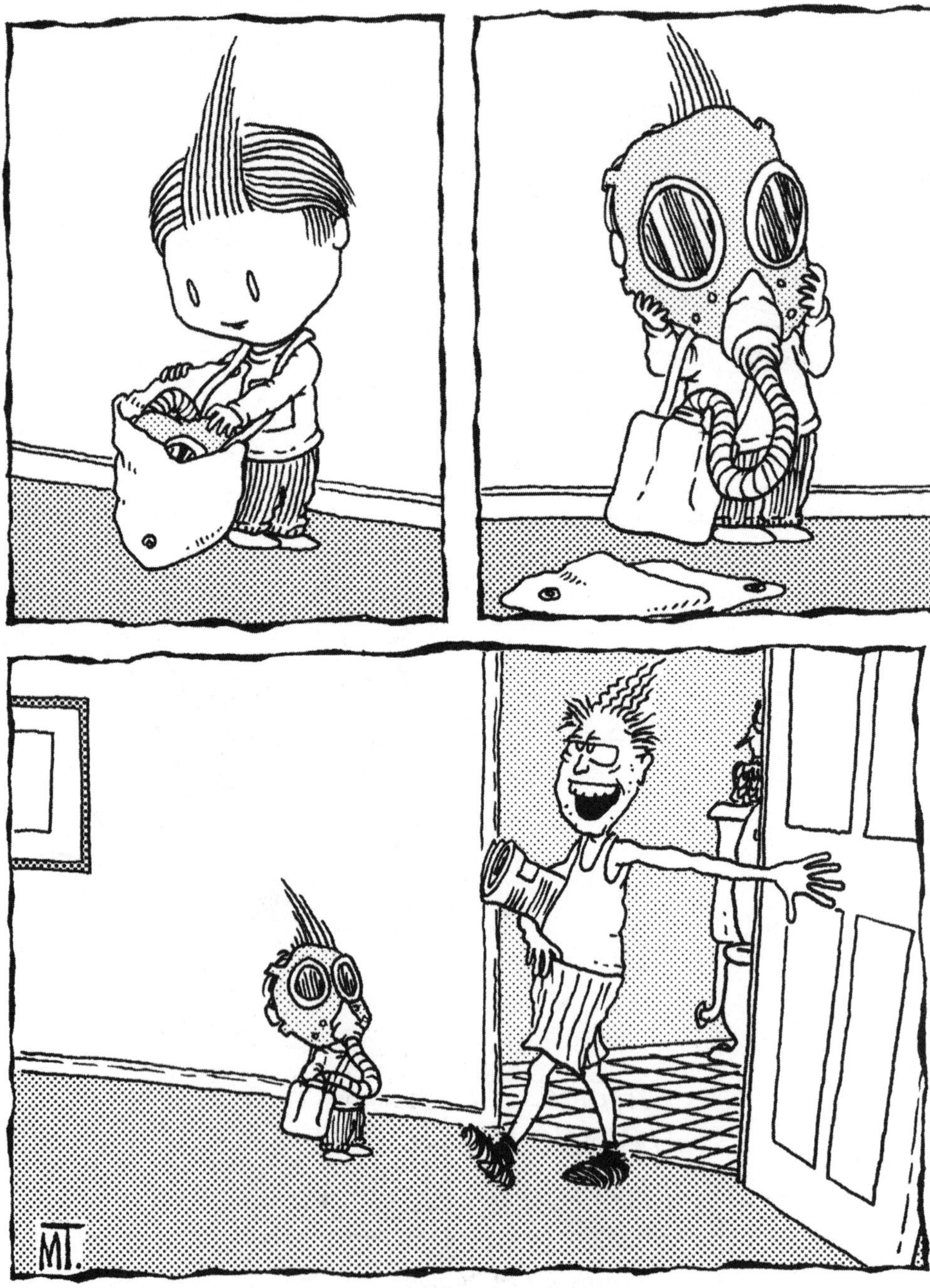
MT.

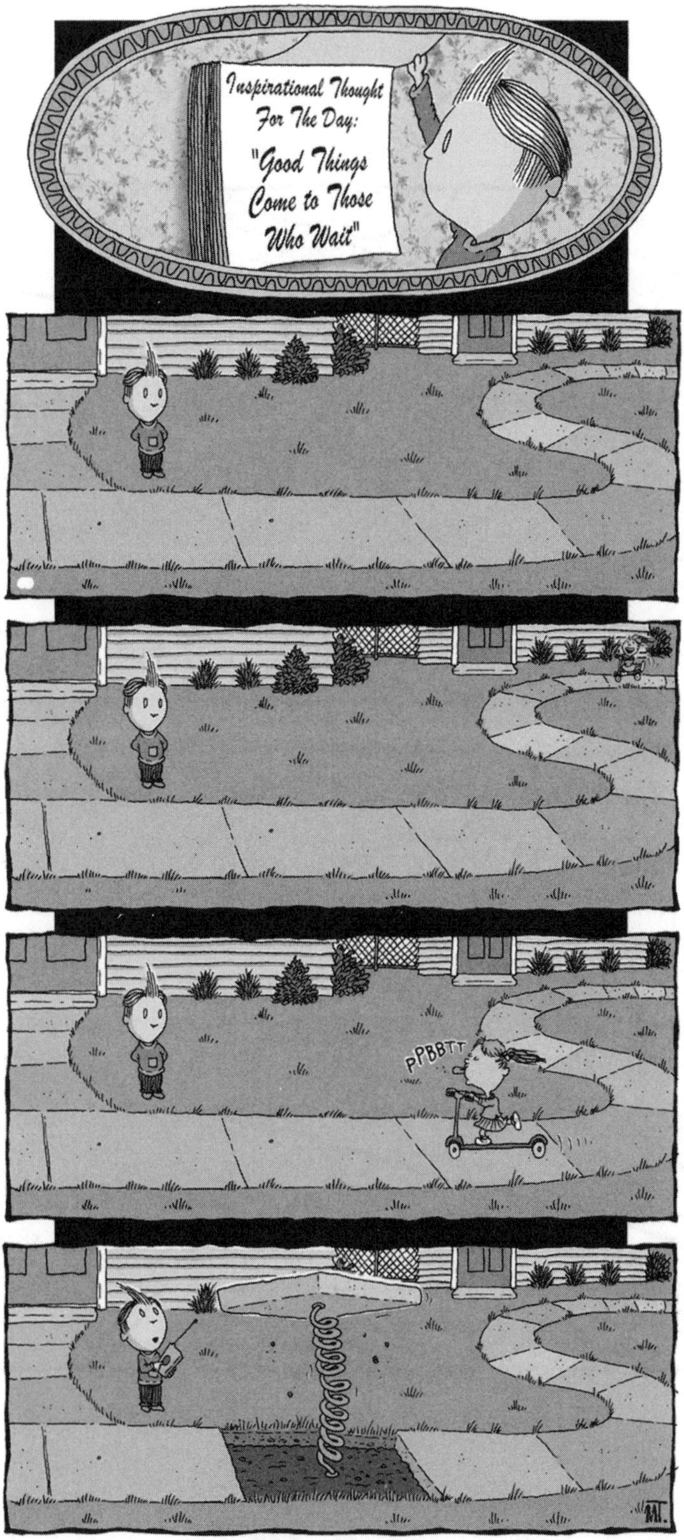
Inspirational Thought For The Day:
"Good Things Come to Those Who Wait"
PPBBTT

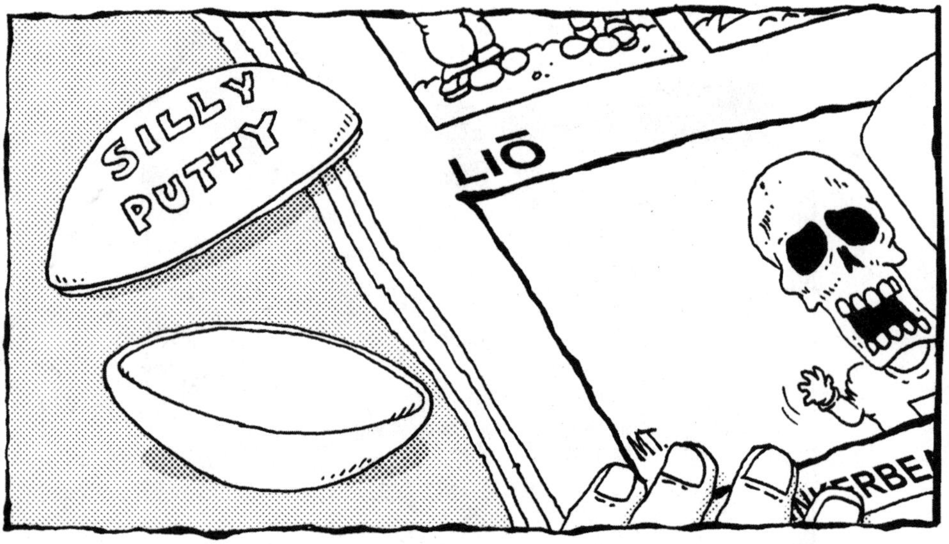
SILLY PUTTY
LIŌ
MT.
ERBEA

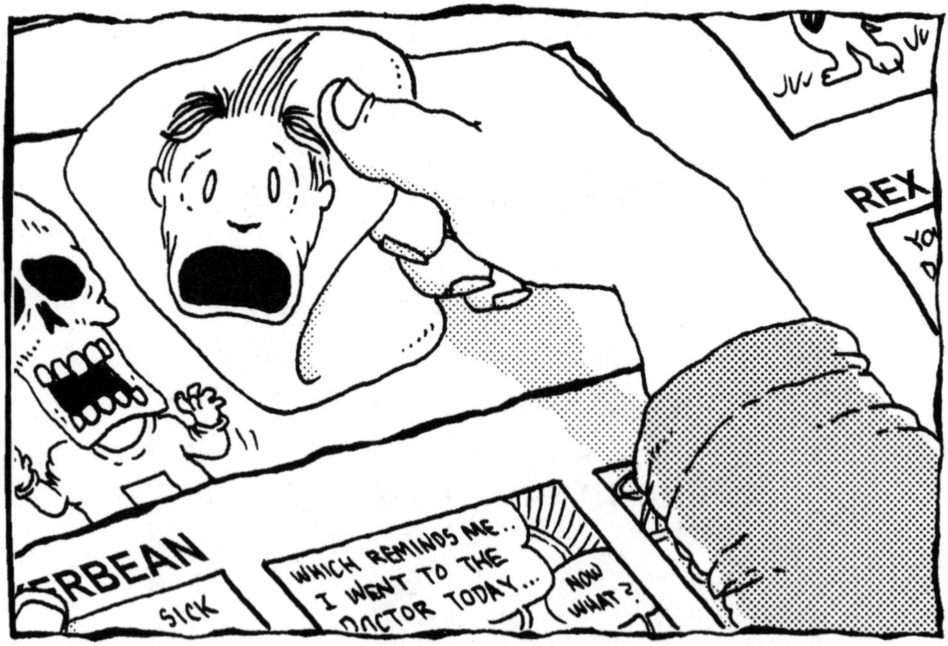
REX
ERBEAN
SICK
WHICH REMINDS ME... I WENT TO THE DOCTOR TODAY...
NOW WHAT?

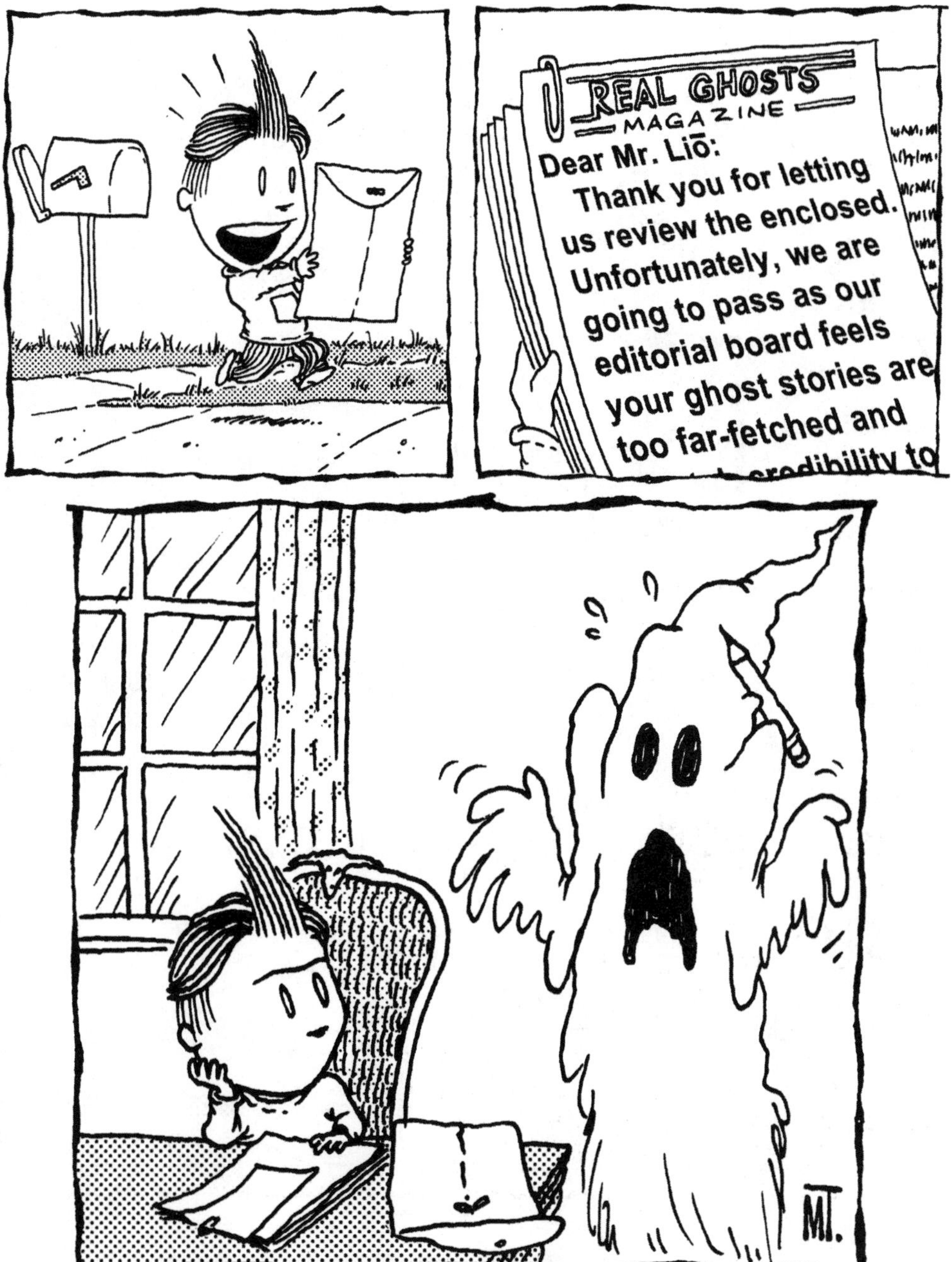
REAL GHOSTS
MAGAZINE
Dear Mr. Liō:
Thank you for letting
us review the enclosed.
Unfortunately, we are
going to pass as our
editorial board feels
your ghost stories are
too far-fetched and
MT.

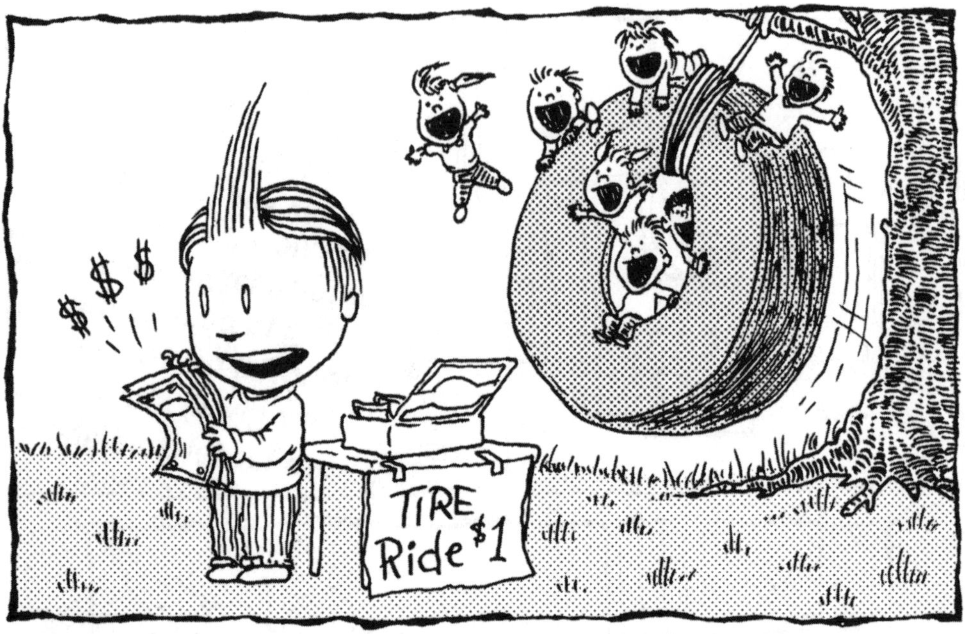
TIRE
Ride $1

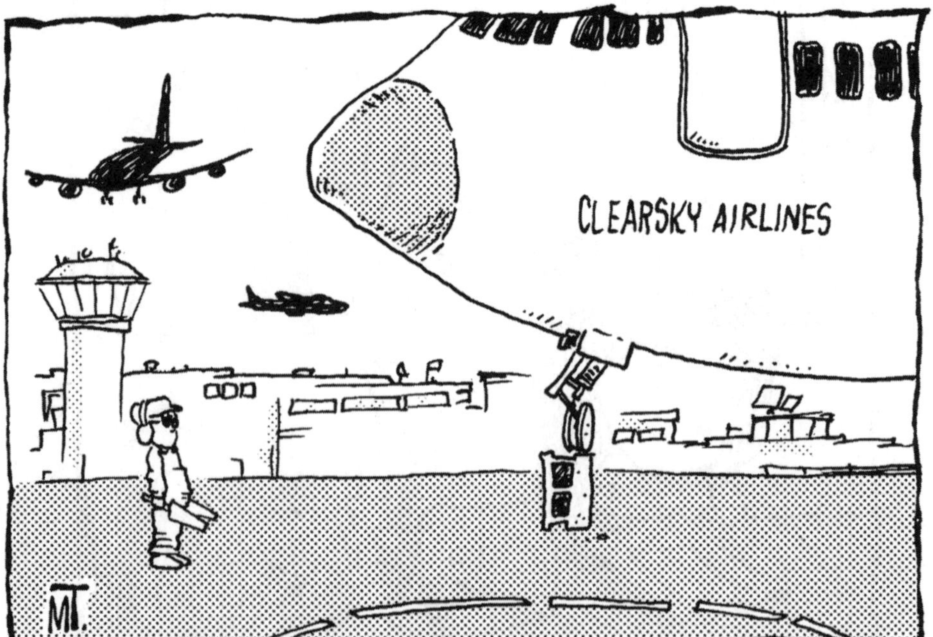
CLEARSKY AIRLINES

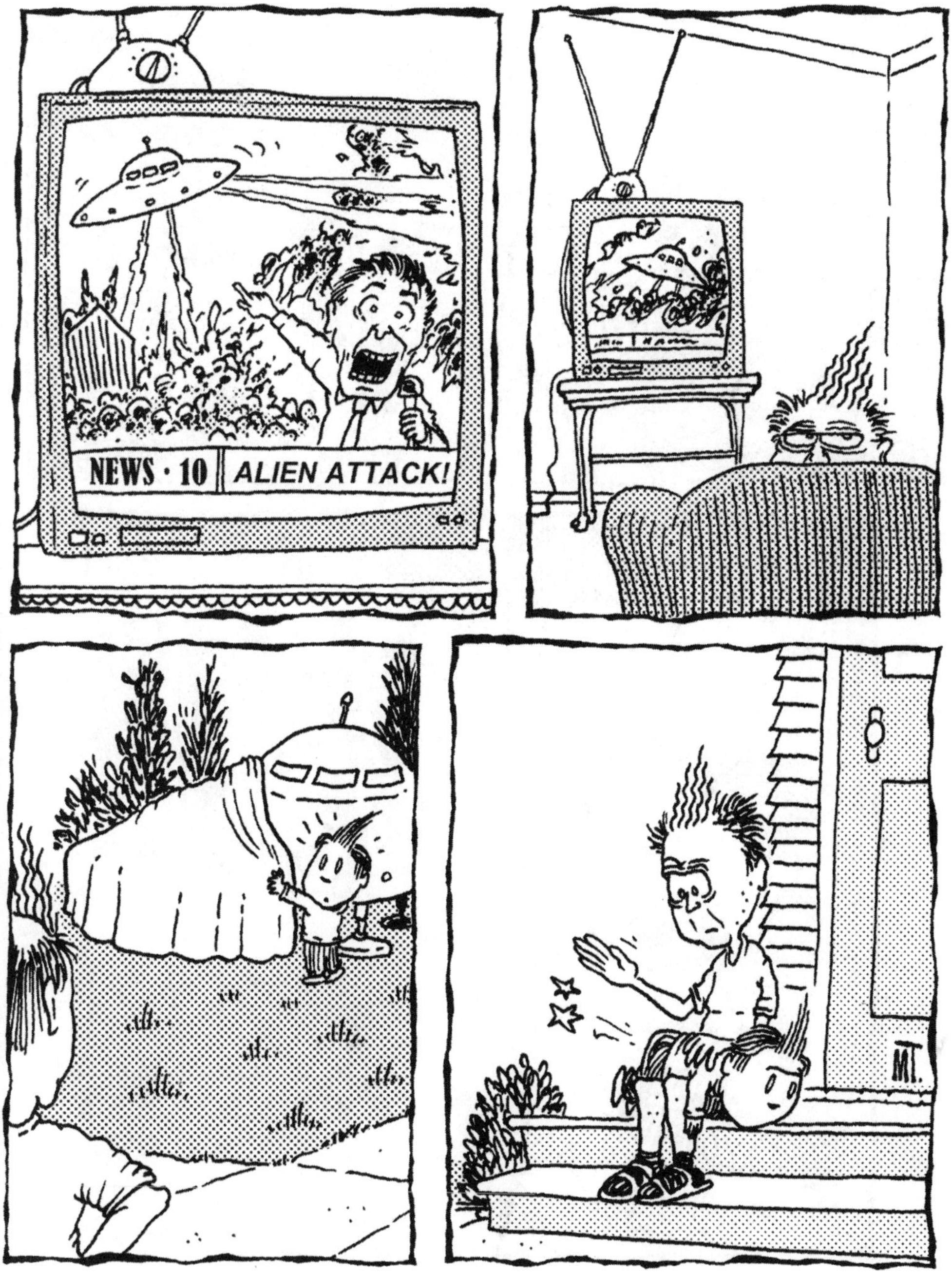
NEWS · 10
ALIEN ATTACK!
MT.

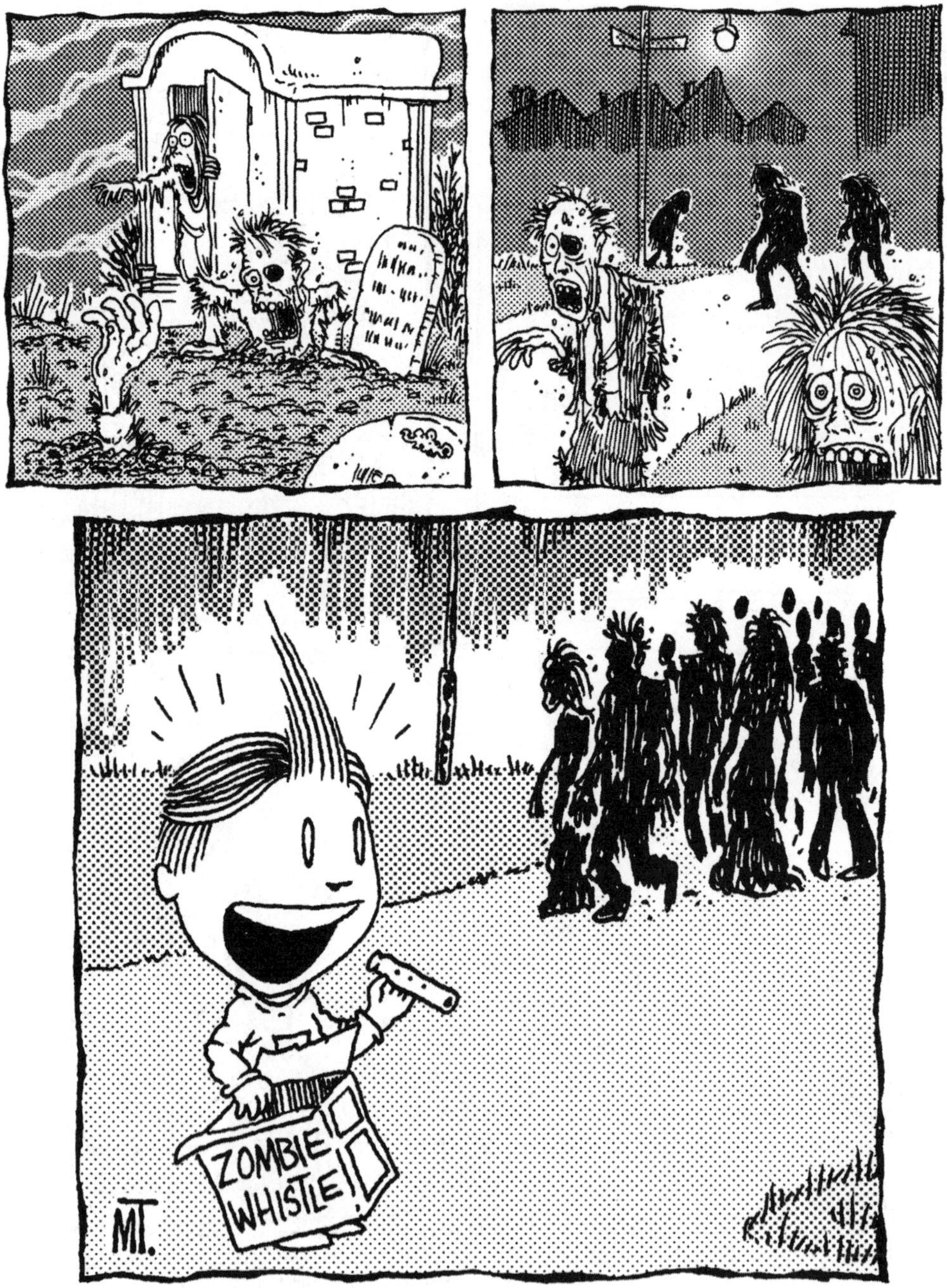
ZOMBIE
WHISTLE
MT.

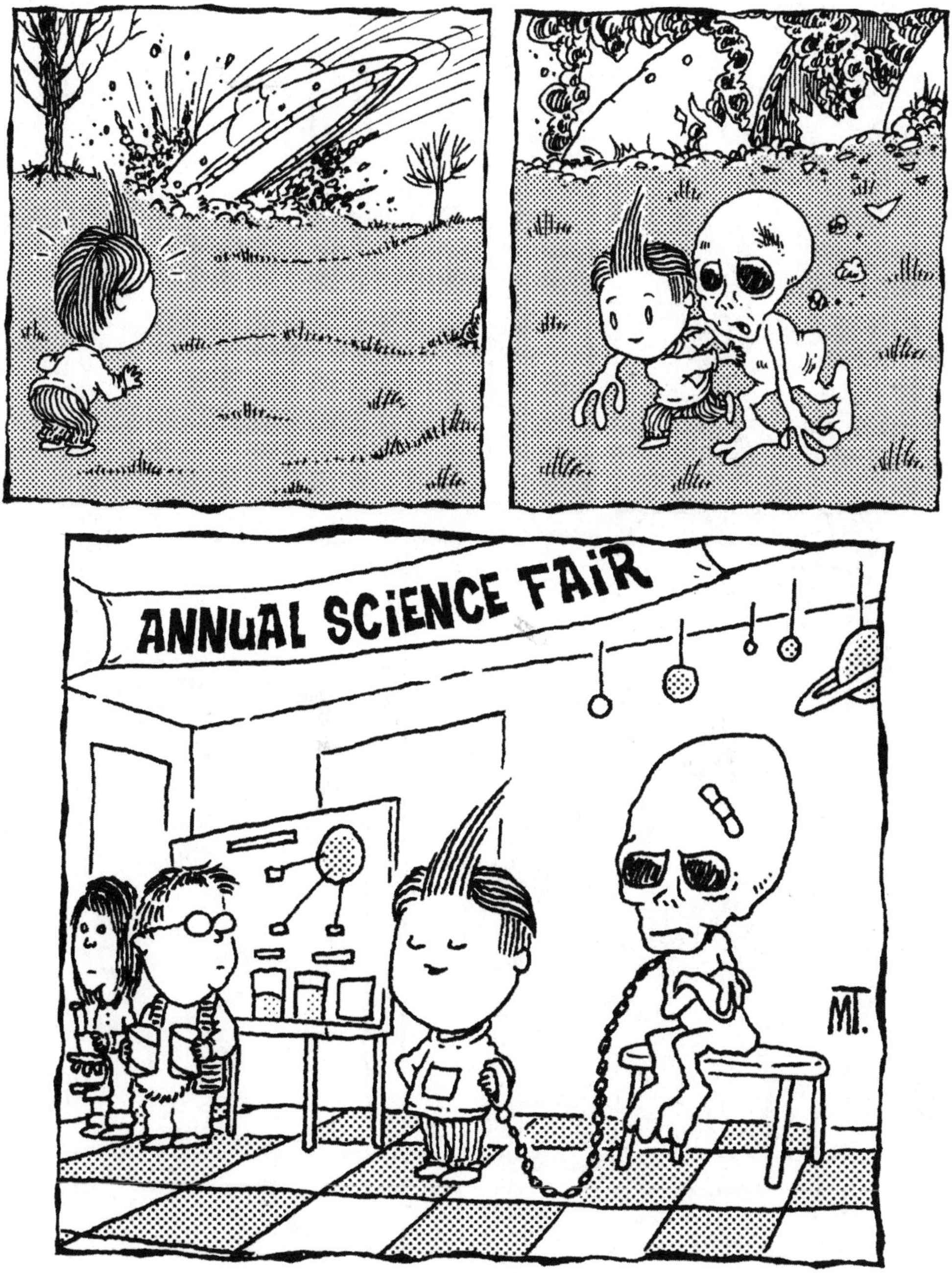
ANNUAL SCIENCE FAIR
MT.

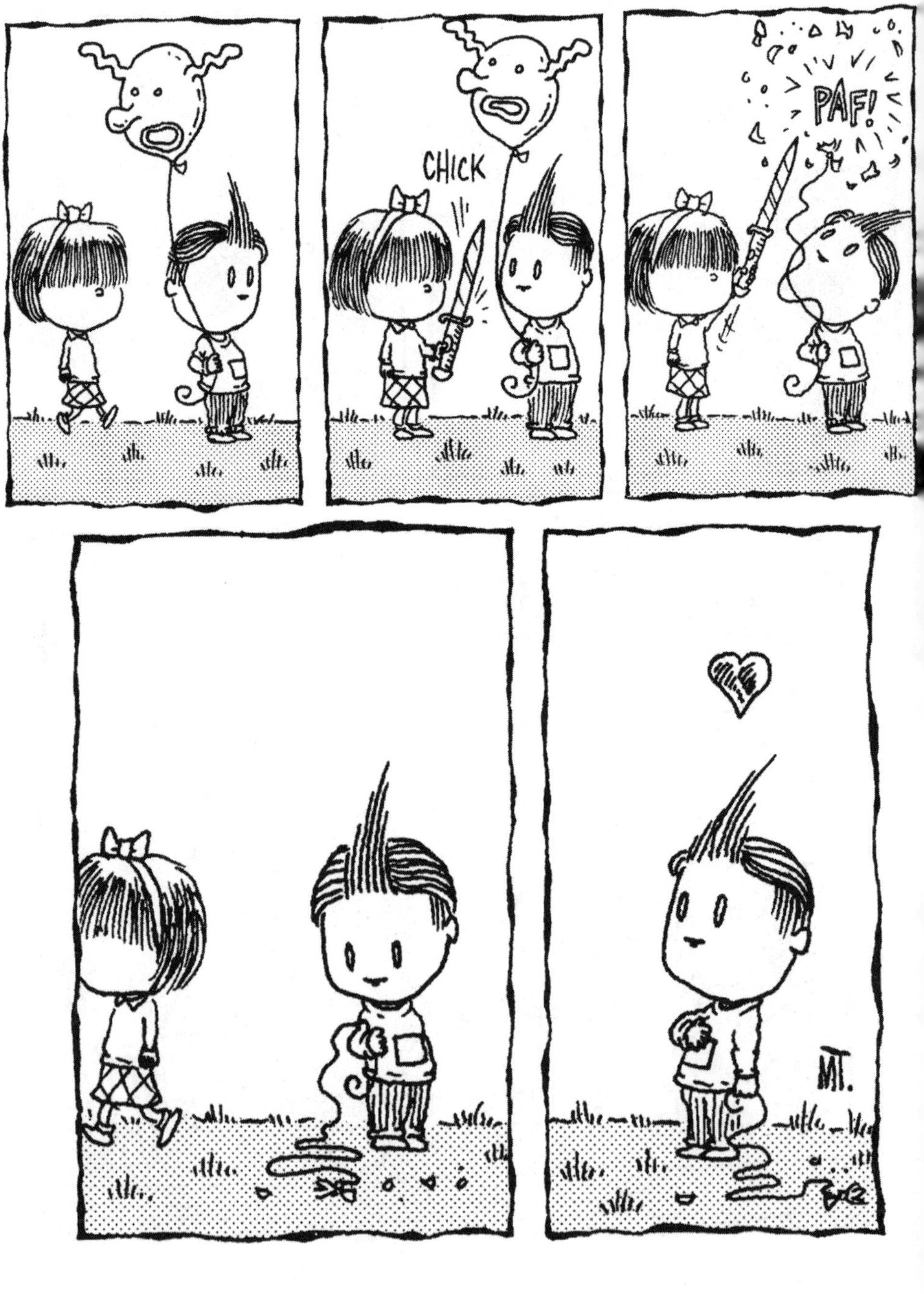
CHICK
PAF!
MT.

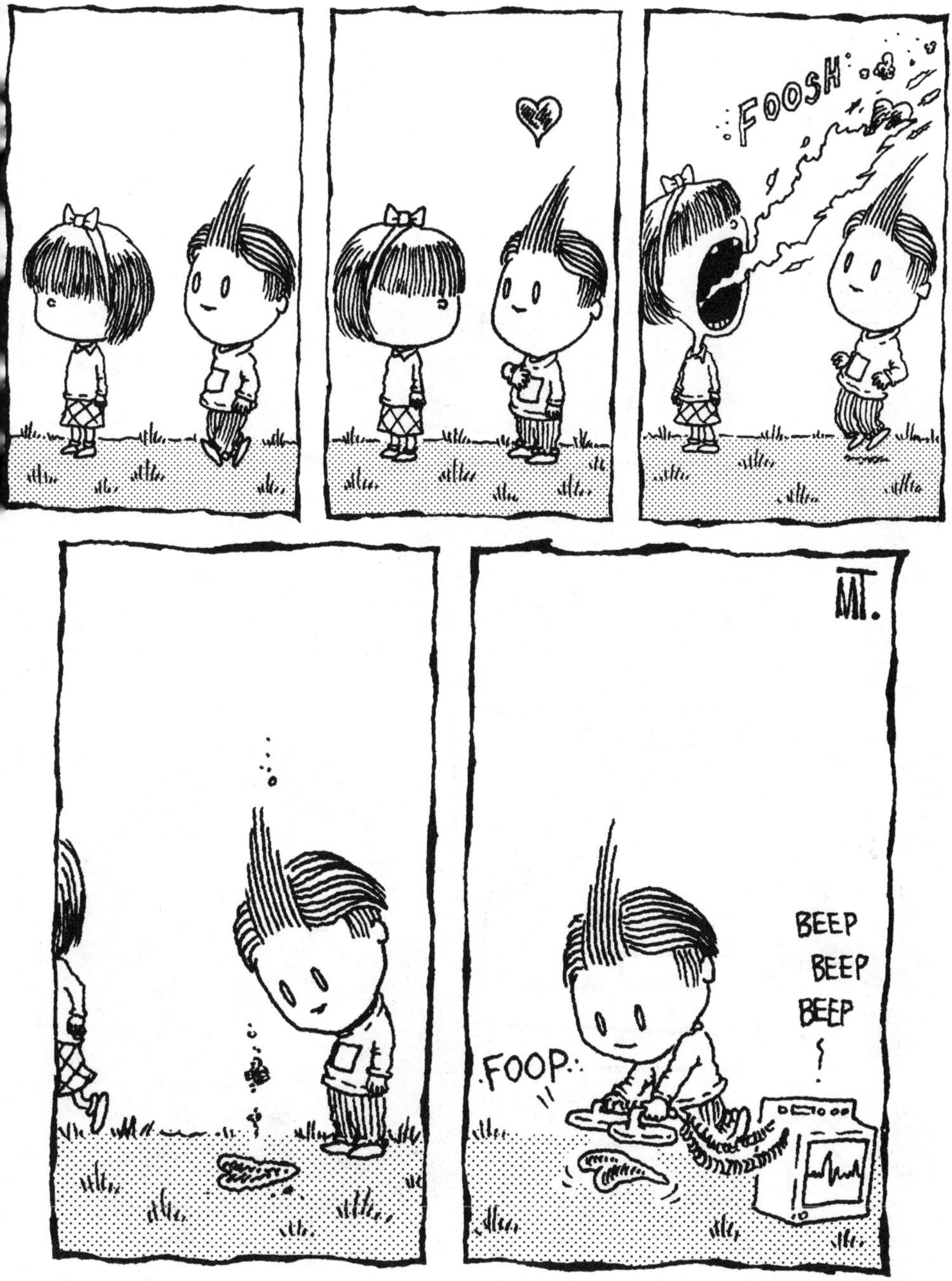
FOOSH
FOOP
BEEP
BEEP
BEEP
MT.

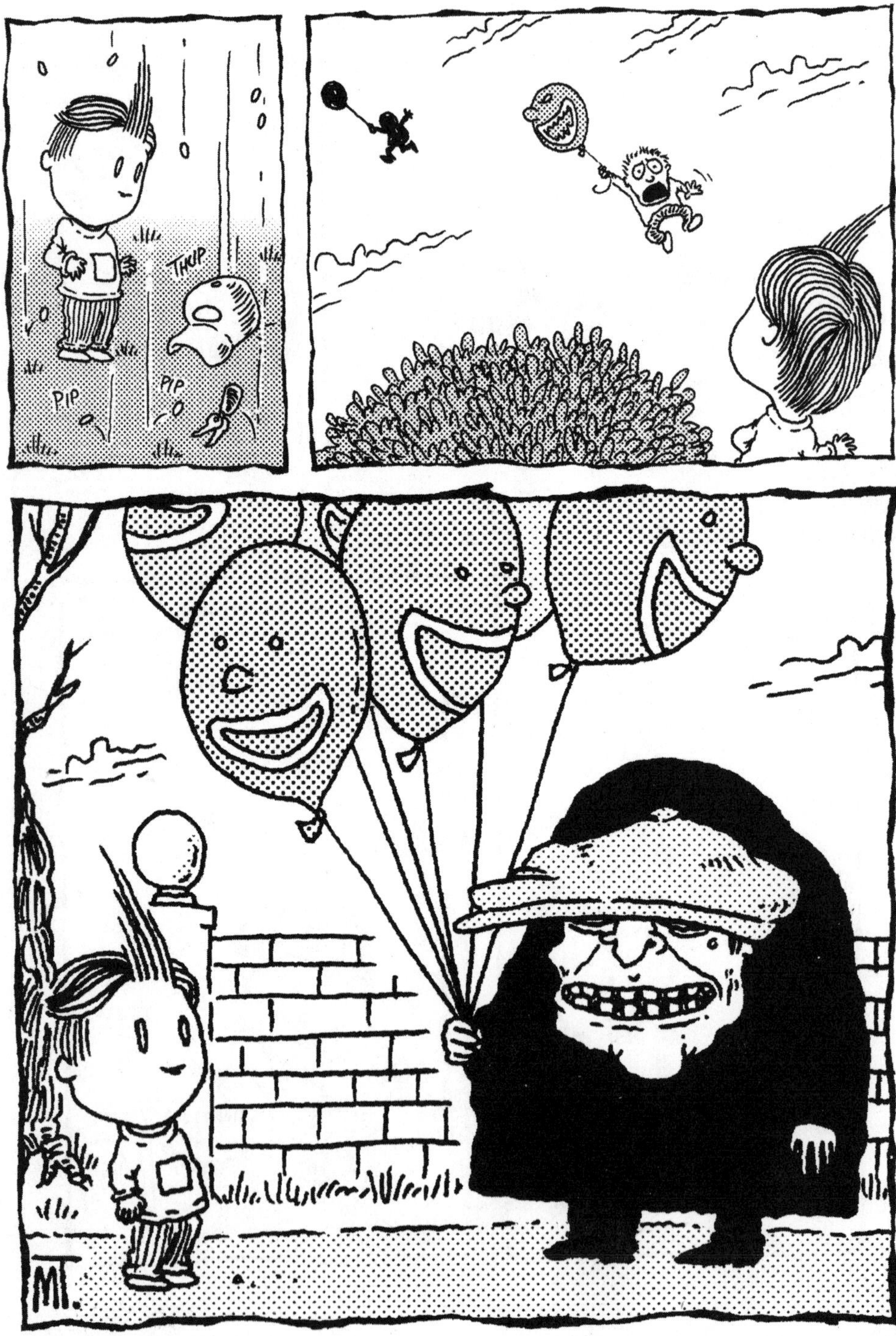
THUP
PIP
PIP
MT.